Hello, I'm James

Emmy's Story, Part 11

By
Kenneth Lee McGee

This is dedicated to the memory of
Grandma and Grandpa Tockstein.
They survived the Eastland tragedy,
moved to southern Illinois and started a farm.
Farms are a great place for kids to grow up.

I would like to thank Denise and Stephanie for their support and for sharing their knowledge and opinions. I will forever be indebted to the people of WriteOn Joliet. It's good to see the group continue to thrive.

I want to thank the people from my church who have graciously allowed me to include fragments of their lives as inspirations.

A special thanks to Sue Midlock for creating the cover.

I want to thank my wife Sheila for everything she does.

Chapter One

"Mommy, is Aunt Kristen having a birthday party for Zachary today?" Isabella Marie asked as she walked up behind Emmy and tugged on her arm.

Emmy Colasanti-Colwell stirred the scrambled eggs while her husband Kenny Colwell flipped the pancakes over. She turned to look at Isabella. "We are going over there after we eat. Aunt Kristen is going to Wisconsin this afternoon."

Heather Rose watched her father turning the pancakes over and asked, "Where's that? Have I ever been there?"

"It's north of here," Kenny answered and then smiled. "The people who live there root for the Green Bay Packers instead of the Bears, and they wear hats made of cheese."

"Oooh! That's gross," Heather said. "I want that pancake. It looks like a bunny rabbit with funny ears."

"Do they really, Mommy?" Isabella asked.

"Some of the football fans wear stupid hats that look like cheese but they're not real cheese," Emmy said and then shook her head at Kenny. "They might be cheeseheads, but you're a dork."

"Breakfast will be ready soon." Kenny pointed to the breakfast nook and told the twins, "You can have a seat with your brother."

The girls joined their younger brother at the table. Emmy and Kenny finished cooking.

"Is today his birthday?" Isabella asked as she colored at the breakfast table.

"His birthday is actually Monday, but we are getting together today. Who is ready for eggs and pancakes?"

"I want ketchup on my eggs," Kevin said.

"Kevin Michael, you can't play with your firetruck at the table," Kenny said.

Kevin pushed his firetruck off the edge and grinned. "It crashed."

"There is one pancake left," Kenny said thirty minutes later. "Who wants it?"

"I do," Heather said.

7

"Me, too," Kevin reached for the pancake.

"You can split it," Emmy suggested. "I'm not making any more batter. You need to finish eating and wash up. Aunt Kristen wants us to come over and watch Zachary open presents. Hustle up so we can go."

"I'm done eating," Isabella said.

"Then go wash your hands and face," Emmy said. She pointed to the powder room.

"Do you need help cleaning up?" Kenny asked a few minutes later.

"I can clean the kitchen if you make sure the kids are clean. See what they're doing in the bathroom. They've been in there long enough to wash up."

"In a minute." Kenny hugged Emmy from behind and tried to nibble on her ear.

She bumped him with her hip and said, "We don't have time for that now."

"Maybe later," he said with a grin.

"Go! Let me finish my job."

Kenny scurried away because he heard the kids splashing water in the powder room.

While rinsing the breakfast dishes, Emmy answered the landline in the kitchen thinking it would be her best friend, Kristen Randolph. Since her hands were wet, she put the phone on speaker mode.

"Hey, Krissy, I'm almost finished with the dishes. We'll be over in ten minutes."

"Uh... is this Emily Colasanti?" A deep male voice asked.

"Oh, sorry. You're not Kristen," Emmy said. "I thought you were my friend, but, yes, I'm Emmy. Who are you?"

"Hello, I'm James." He paused and took a deep breath. "You may not believe this, but I'm your brother."

Emmy stared at the phone for a second. *What did he just say? Is this a crank call? I don't have time for this crap.*

"Are you still there?"

Emmy grabbed the phone. "I don't know who you are, or why you're calling, but I don't have a brother. I'm hanging up now." She stabbed the button to end the call and slammed the phone back in its cradle.

The phone rang again. Emmy shook her head. *If I don't answer you'll probably keep calling.* She picked up the phone. "I'm going to call the police if you keep bothering me."

"Please don't do that and please don't hang up. This isn't a crank call. Let me explain. It's rather important."

Emmy stared at the handset for several seconds. *This isn't possible, but you sound like Daddy.* "You've got ten seconds," Emmy said impatiently.

"My biological father was Raymond Colasanti."

Emmy snorted. "Anyone could call and say that."

"I realize that, but it's true," he said.

"How do I know you're not lying?" Emmy asked.

"I never lie."

Emmy pulled the phone away from her ear and stared at it. *Daddy used to say that and just that way.* She bit her lip, then said, "Daddy passed away over four years ago. He never had a son," Emmy stated emphatically. "I'm hanging up."

"No, please wait. He never knew about me. My biological mother never told him before she gave me up for adoption."

"This is crazy!" Emmy leaned back against the counter.

"I fully understand what a shock this must be, and I'm sorry to spring it on you in this manner."

Emmy shook her head but then chuckled. "I don't think there would be an easy way to tell someone something like this."

"So true. I think I can clear this up fairly easily."

"How?" *I'm not telling you where I live. Of course you probably already know since you have this number.*

"Would you be willing to meet me for lunch? You can choose the place and the time. Anywhere in South Hampshire would work for me."

"Not a chance!" Emmy shouted. "I'm not stupid."

"I don't expect you to meet me alone. I know you are married. I Googled you. Talk to your husband. You can bring him with. You can bring whoever you want."

Emmy thought about it. "Anywhere, huh?"

9

"Somewhere you would feel comfortable and safe."

"Do you know where Darby's is?"

"Not off the top of my head, but I can look it up. What kind of place is it?"

"Darby's Dogs is a locally owned hangout," Emmy said and then gave him directions to the unique restaurant.

"Yes, I remember it now. I drove past it a few weeks ago. Is the food any good?"

"It's the best place in the city for burgers and hot dogs," she said. "They have the best root beer, too."

"I've only lived in South Hampshire for a few months."

"I could tell you're not a local. No one who lives here calls it South Hampshire. Everyone calls it SoHam."

"I have heard that term before," he recalled. "Would you be willing to meet me today? I know this is rather sudden, and if you'd rather think about it for a few days, I understand."

"No, today will be fine. I want to hear what you have to say and clear this up as quickly as possible," she said. "How will I recognize you?"

"I think you might recognize me, but I do have a photograph of you. Actually, I have one of your CDs."

"If you think you're going to get one cent from me..."

"No! No! No!" He shook his head back and forth. "Trust me. I am not calling because I want, or need, money."

"Good, because that's not gonna happen." She bit her lip. "I love the food at Darby's, so I can use this as an excuse to grab a chili dog. I'll be there at noon. If you're not there by twelve fifteen, I'm leaving."

"I'll be there early. I promise."

Chapter Two

Kenny walked into the kitchen just as Emmy hung up. "Hey, Em. Who was on the phone? The kids are in the van, and we're ready to go."

"You're not going to believe it!"

She gathered her thoughts and then explained.

"You're not going to Darby's by yourself! I won't let you." Kenny put his hands on her shoulders. "This guy could be some crazed lunatic."

"I didn't get that impression at all. He claims this is not about money. I want to meet him. He said something along the lines that I would recognize him, and you going to think I'm crazy, but he kinda sounded like Daddy. He even used an expression that Daddy would use. That makes me curious." Emmy put a finger to her mouth. "I'd rather go by myself, but you could drive me there and wait in the car."

"Not a chance, Em. Tell you what. I'll drive you there. Go inside and check it out first. You can follow me after a couple of minutes. That way I'll be inside just in case something happens." Kenny outlined his plan in further detail. "Deal?"

"Deal." She shook his hand. "You're a dork, but I still love you. What will you do if something does happen? Huh? Have you got a plan for that?"

"I'll think of something." He rubbed his jaw.

"Let's hurry over to Krissy's for Zachary's birthday party, so we can be back in time to get to Darby's." She kissed his cheek and ran out of the kitchen. "Come on. Let's go."

Kristen opened the front door to let Emmy and her family inside. "Did you run over here, Em? You're all out of breath."

"We drove, and I have something important to share."

"Hi, Aunt Kristen. Where's Gracie?" Isabella asked.

"She and Zachary are in the family room with everyone else. Hello, Heather," Kristen said to Isabella's older twin. "Did you bring cars with you, Kevin Michael?"

"I brought a police car and an ab-u-lance," he said. He showed Kristen the toys and then scampered away.

"Take off your coats and shoes and do not throw them on the floor," Emmy said. She slipped past Kristen and into the breakfast area where she plopped onto a wooden chair. "You won't believe who I talked to earlier."

Kristen rolled her eyes as she took a seat across the table from Emmy. "Do I have to guess or will you tell me."

"My brother!" Emmy's eyes sparkled.

"What did Tony say to get you so excited? He didn't say anything particularly exciting when they arrived."

"Not Tony." Emmy grinned.

Kristen thought about who Emmy might be talking about. "Craig isn't your brother-in-law anymore. Diane divorced him, remember? Are you talking about Brady? You've never referred to him as your brother before"

"No, not Brady. They're engaged not married."

"Who are you talking..."

"James!"

"... about?" Kristen sighed. "Who? You don't have a brother named James. What have you been drinking?"

Emmy frowned at Kristen. "I haven't been drinking anything stronger than coffee. Will you let me explain..."

Five minutes later Emmy paused.

"Kenny is driving me to Darby's. I will be all right."

"I've known you long enough to know once you make up your mind to do something, nothing on earth will change it. Just be careful."

They spent over an hour at the party before Emmy had to rush back home.

"Call me as soon as you leave Darby's. I want to know you're alive and safe."

"Oh, Krissy! God will protect me."

"You are so trusting. Just call me, or I will hate you forever."

"I will." Emmy helped get the kids into the van and drove down the street to the large home she shared with Kenny and the kids.

"Kenny, I'm ready to go. Who's watching the kids?"

12

Mr. and Mrs. Robertson walked into the kitchen.

"We are!" Mona smiled. "Kenny told us about this man who called. Bill has been on the phone trying to see if he can learn anything. I'm sure he is just trying to exploit you for money, but it pays to be safe."

"You guys arc so sweet." Emmy hugged Mona. "I'll be fine. Even if he's a kook, he won't try anything in a public place like Darby's. Thanks for watching the kids on such short notice."

"Anytime, sweetie." Mr. Robertson smiled.

Kenny pulled into the lot at Darby's and parked on the south side of the building. "Give me two minutes to check out the place before you come in, okay?"

"Got it, 007!" Emmy saluted. *Such a dork! You really look inconspicuous in your long coat, Cardinals baseball cap and goofy sunglasses.*

"Two minutes! Promise?"

"I promise." Emmy immediately spotted two unmarked SoHam squad cars and shook her head. *It's not that big of a deal.*

Kenny walked into Darby's as if he were entering Al Capone's headquarters. He took a step, paused and quickly swiveled his head back and forth. Then he took another step and repeated his actions. Then he dashed to the front counter, leaned against it and surveyed the dining area.

A perky blonde smiled and asked, "Can I take your order, Mr. Colwell?"

Kenny quickly turned to face her, put a finger to his mouth and whispered, "Maybe later. I'm here on an important undercover assignment."

"I see," she said and then giggled. "Good luck."

He turned back around, moved a few feet to his right, scooted around a grandmother with three young kids clamoring for something to drink and spotted Detective Warren Sanders reading a newspaper in one of the booths. He surreptitiously nodded at him, scooted over to the wall of booths along the north side, peeked around the corner for a split-second, drew back, waited for a moment and then looked again.

Oh, my God! He froze in place for several seconds. *This*

13

can't be. My eyes must not be working right. He checked his watch. *I have to get into position.* He moved around the restaurant and found an empty booth where he could observe the man sitting in his and Emmy's favorite spot.

Emmy walked in three minutes later. She smiled at the people working behind the counter and then turned around and instinctively looked toward her favorite booth. She froze in mid-step. A man sitting there stood up. Emmy put a hand to her mouth. The man smiled. Emmy grabbed the wall for support. The man held up a CD.

Oh, my God! Emmy took a step forward.

The man dressed in a dark suit opened his arms in a friendly greeting.

Somehow, Emmy's legs carried her over to the booth. She stood at the end of the stainless steel booth and stared. Neither one spoke for a moment. Kenny smiled from his position. Detective Sanders lowered his newspaper to get a good look.

"You look almost exactly like Daddy did a few years ago," Emmy finally said. Then she bit her lip.

"I believe I do. Please sit down, Emmy."

She slipped onto the bench across from him without taking her eyes off of his face.

"Are you a priest?" She finally asked.

He touched his clerical collar. "Yes, I'm Father James, and I recently moved to SoHam." He smiled. "I'm the pastor at St. John's. Are you familiar with that parish?"

"We went there when I was a kid." She couldn't take her eyes off of him. "You look like Daddy," she whispered slowly. "And you kinda sound like him."

"I bet you must have a thousand questions." His smile exuded friendliness. "Would you like something to drink? I ordered a root beer, but I've been too nervous to take a drink."

Emmy reached out, grasped his drink and took a sip. "How? Why? Who?"

Father James grinned and chuckled. "Where should I start?" He looked up at the photograph above the booth without realizing its significance. "I'm fifty-seven years old. I was born in

14

Topeka, Kansas. My mother's name was Alice Fischer, but she gave me up for adoption."

Emmy took another drink of pop as she continued to stare. *You look so much like Daddy. You have to be his son.*

"My parents are still living. Their names are Josef and Helen Boyanov. My real name is Mickel Boyanov. I chose Father James when I took my vows. Are you all right, Emmy? You look pale."

"I'm okay. You look so much like Daddy."

"I've always known about being adopted. My parents didn't hide that. In fact, they kept in touch with my birth mother through the years. She eventually married and had three other kids. My half-brother and sisters."

"You're really my half-brother," Emmy said rather in disbelief.

"When I was sixteen, I met my birth mother. We didn't have a close relationship, but we did keep in contact over the years. Christmas cards. Birthday cards. That sort of thing. I saw her a few times over the years, but she would never talk about the past. Two years ago she died of cancer. I met her one last time and prayed for her. She told me about my birth father and the circumstances of how they met."

"You said on the phone Daddy never knew. Is that true?" Emmy asked as she spotted Kenny. She waved him over. "My husband is with me. I hope it's all right if he joins us."

"Please! I would like to meet him." Father James stood up as Kenny approached.

Kenny shook his head back and forth. "Unbelievable!"

"Hello, I'm Father James." He offered his hand.

"I'm Kenny Colwell. Em's husband."

"Please have a seat."

Kenny took off his coat and sunglasses, sat down and put an arm around Emmy's shoulders.

"I was just giving Emmy some details about my life."

"Can you believe it, Kenny? I have a brother." Emmy bit her lip as tears escaped. "Daddy never knew."

"I was explaining that my birth mother never told Emmy's

15

father about me." Father James went over the details for Kenny.

"So how long have you been in SoHam?" Kenny asked.

"I was transferred here four months ago. I actually requested the move. Please understand. This is not something I did without a lot of thought and prayer. I would have been content to live out my life without ever revealing myself, but I felt that God had something else in mind. Are you Catholic?"

"We attend Crest Ridge United Nazarene. Emmy is part of the worship team." Kenny tapped the CD. "I guess you know that already."

"I hope this doesn't sound creepy, but I did some research. I know about your careers and even the names of your children. I know about Diane, too."

"Have you talked to Diane?" Emmy asked.

"No. I thought it would be best to approach you first."

"Good idea! Diane wouldn't understand," Emmy said. "So what should I call you? Father James? Michel? What?"

"You can call me James. I don't always wear my collar, but I thought it might be best for today."

"How long have you been a priest?" Emmy asked as she took another drink of his root beer. "Oh, Kenny, would you order root beers for all of us. I'm drinking Father James'."

"Sure, Em. Any fries?"

"Please," Emmy said.

Kenny left to place the order. The same blonde giggled as she took the order.

"For over thirty years," he answered.

"Do your parents know about me?" Emmy wondered.

"I talked to them yesterday, and told them of my plans to call you. They didn't think I should, but I convinced them I needed to. They relented and said to say hi."

"Mom will freak out. She's still alive, but lives in an assisted living place. She has early stages of dementia or Alzheimer's. I don't know the difference."

"My birth mother told me she and Raymond were only together for a weekend. She was visiting friends at a college here and went out to a bar."

16

"Daddy always did like bars."

Detective Sanders joined Kenny at the front counter and set down the newspaper. "Everything all right?"

"Yeah, he seems to be legit."

"I'm going to hang around just in case."

"Thanks, Warren. I appreciate it."

Kenny returned with the drinks and fries.

"How old are your adoptive parents?" Kenny asked.

"Mom is eighty-one and Dad is eighty-three. They were never able to have children, and I'm the only one they adopted."

"Are they in good health?"

"Ha!" Father James laughed. "They are both in great shape. They love to go on those senior tours. They're always on the go."

The questions continued for fifteen minutes. Emmy quickly felt totally comfortable with Father James.

"Kenny, show him some pictures of the kids." Emmy waved a fry around. "I'm assuming you don't have any kids."

Father James chuckled. "That is correct. However, I did recently discover I have several nieces and nephews."

Kenny pulled out his wallet and showed Father James the photographs. "We have tons of them on the computer."

"Have you met your other nieces and nephews?" Emmy asked.

He shook his head, his smile disappeared and he said, "Unfortunately, my half-siblings do not want to acknowledge me. They do not want their children to meet me. I can see their point. Their children are older. I believe the youngest is in high school."

"You can meet our kids!" Emmy said. "I want them to get to know you."

Kenny raised his eyebrows. "Let's slow down a bit."

"I appreciate that, Emmy." He smiled. "You are taking this news much calmer than I anticipated. Why?"

Emmy shrugged. "Well, it seems obvious you are who you claim to be. You look too much like Daddy for it to be otherwise. I mean, who would have plastic surgery to look the way you do." Emmy realized how this might be construed and put a hand to her mouth. "I didn't mean it like that."

Father James laughed. "I understand what you meant."

"So Daddy wasn't perfect. He spent a weekend with a woman and never saw or heard from her again. Is it possible he never knew her name?" Emmy asked.

"My birth mother never mentioned that. I suppose it's possible she didn't tell your father her real name. I guess we'll never know."

"Look at it this way." Emmy grinned. "Because of that weekend of sex, God has a priest."

Father James looked at Kenny, and they both looked at Emmy. No one spoke for a moment. Then Father James began laughing hard enough to shake his plump belly.

"You certainly have a unique way of seeing life, Emmy."

Father James talked about where he had lived and served as a priest. All of it in Kansas. Emmy told him a little about living in SoHam.

"I met Kenny when I was seven and he was ten, so I've always been attracted to older men." Emmy said and then giggled. "But I didn't fall in love with him until I was fourteen. I had a huge crush on him, but he thought I was too young. He started traveling with the band and I missed him. I remember one time he came home from a tour and I offered to let him have me."

"Emmy!" Kenny's eyes opened wide.

"What?" Emmy bit her lip. "Father James is a priest. I can tell him stuff, and he can't tell anyone."

"I believe that pertains to confessions, Em," Kenny said.

"Oh, well, it doesn't matter. He's not just a priest, he's my brother," Emmy said. "Isn't there a song about that?"

"You're a goof." Kenny shook his head.

"We've never used birth control." Emmy blurted out of the blue. "I did have my tubes tied after Kevin Michael was born."

Father James lifted his bushy eyebrows.

"For health reasons. I know the Catholic church doesn't believe in the use of birth control, but I was never supposed to be able to have babies, so it's kinda like a miracle." Emmy finally ran out of breath.

"You are amazing." Father James blinked rapidly.

18

"I am?"

"Absolutely! You are a breath of fresh air in a stale world."

"She is pretty special." Kenny kissed her cheek.

"Will you guys knock it off. You're going to give me a big head. Saying all those nice things about me." Emmy drank the last of her root beer. "When do you want to meet your nieces and nephew? Are you busy this afternoon?"

"I need to be back at St. John's by six, but I have some free time this afternoon."

"You could come home with us and meet everyone. I'll make an early dinner if you tell me what you'd like." Emmy reached across the table to hold her brother's hand.

"My mom used to make a mean meat loaf," he said. "And what she called cheesy potatoes."

Emmy grinned. "I can do that! Daddy used to like that and baked beans along with it." Her grin disappeared instantly as she thought about her father. She bit her lip hard to keep from crying. It didn't work.

"Are you ready to go, Em?" Kenny asked a few minutes later.

She nodded and then looked at Father James. "Would you like a tour of the Raynor Park neighborhood. That's where Kenny and I grew up. It's real close."

"I would like that very much," he answered.

"If you let me ride with you, Kenny can stop at the store for me." Emmy looked at Kenny and added, "You can have Detective Sanders follow us if you want, but I will be safe."

Kenny sighed and said, "Sure, why not? Nothing I'd rather do on a Saturday than stop at the grocery store."

Emmy made a list. "I'll see you at home."

Chapter Three

"Which car is yours?" Emmy asked as she and Father James walked out of Darby's.

He pointed to a green Honda Civic. "It's that one. It's a 1998, but it still runs, and I am just a humble priest." He laughed and added, "I've been meaning to buy something newer, but something more important always comes up."

"It's all right. Kenny drives a Civic, too," Emmy said while noticing the faded paint on the roof.

Emmy rode with Father James on the way home. She didn't say anything about Detective Sanders following in his black Chevy Impala.

"Turn here on Fifth Street." She pointed. "That big, two-story brick house on the corner is where Kenny lived."

He slowed down to take a look. "Looks well maintained."

"It is," she said. "If you stop here for a second, I lived in this house, but it looked different back then. There was a little white fence, and the house was painted gray with different siding. I think it was called clapboard siding, but I'm not positive."

Father James continued west on Fifth Street, and Emmy pointed out where Rory Porter lived.

"Rory is Diane's age. Two, almost three, years older than me and he had an older brother, Owen. He and Diane fooled around some. Owen, I mean." Emmy shrugged and bit her lip at the same time. "Ooops! I probably shouldn't have told you that."

"I will treat it as a sacred confession."

"I hung around with Rory, and we would sneak off to parties, but I was too young to fool around. I did drink beer with him."

"I have an occasional beer, Emmy. I don't see anything wrong with that."

"Daddy was an alcoholic. Sort of. He liked to drink, but he never seemed to get drunk. He was never violent, but he spent a lot of money at Miller's Bar. It's down that street about three blocks." She pointed. "We don't have to go past it."

She continued to point out local landmarks on the way to

20

Bristol Ridge and noticed the black Impala stayed behind her until Father James turned into the Bristol Ridge development. She smiled at the guard at the gate. He recognized her and opened the barrier.

"Up here on the right, on top of the hill is where Tony and Sloane live. You can't just barely see the roofline in summer because of all the trees, but you can see more of it now because it's winter." She paused and looked at Father James. "I'm sorry for rambling on about stuff you probably don't care about."

He chuckled and said, "It's all right. You go ahead and speak your mind. It's rather refreshing."

Emmy bit her lip and then continued, "Tony is Kristen's cousin, and I dated him for a while, but now he's like my big brother. I mean big!" She spread her hands out wide. "He plays for the Chicago Bears. Do you like football?"

"I'm a Chiefs fan," he said.

"If you keep going..."

He drove slowly along the winding road.

"Stop here!"

He did.

"You can see Kristen and John's house through there." She pointed. "Kristen is my best friend, and she's married to John Randolph. He's a tight end."

"I do believe I've heard of those two. I did see the Bears in Chicago once. I was here for a conference, but that was before I knew about you and your father. My father, too."

"Kristen introduced me to Tony, and she wanted us to get married. For a while I couldn't decide whether I was supposed to marry Kenny or Tony. I liked other guys, too. Rory and Christopher. But I never slept with any of them." Emmy realized she had been rambling again and turned bright red. "Please don't hate me. I'm not usually like this. I don't tell everyone I meet my whole life story, and I never talk about my sex life. I'm just kinda nervous and excited."

"I fully understand." Father James smiled and looked around. "Do you live out here somewhere?"

"Oh, yeah. You have to turn around."

21

The road was wide enough for him to easily turn around.

"Kenny used to drive Civics, but he gave one to me and then the newer one to Mary, our nanny. She drove it until she graduated and then she gave it back." Emmy pointed to a driveway with a black wrought iron gate supported by wide brick columns. "That's our driveway. We usually don't close the gates until it gets dark."

Father James turned into the asphalt driveway and wound his way up to the house.

"That's it! We have a guesthouse back that way, and we lived there while this one was being built. I can show it to you later if you want. You can park anywhere."

He parked in front of the garage. "This looks amazing from the outside. You guys must be doing all right with your careers."

"God has blessed up way beyond what we deserve. Grandpa invested money in a company that grew like crazy. Have you ever heard of Robertson Industries?"

"Certainly. They're one of the biggest in their field."

"Grandpa Colasanti... He's your grandpa, too. I just realized that. I'm sorry, but it's going to take a while for all this to sink in. I didn't have a brother for over thirty years and now all of a sudden, I do. It's a bit overwhelming."

"I can understand that, Emmy. You don't mind if I call you Emmy, do you?"

"Everyone does. Daddy and Mom would call me Emily if I was in trouble and Grandma Isabel always called me Emily. She was Mom's mother and she lived to be a hundred, but she passed away."

"I'm sorry to hear that."

"Come on in, and I'll introduce you to the kids. I don't know how they will react to meeting you."

"I will hold back and try not to frighten them." Father James smiled.

Emmy led the way through the garage and mudroom and entered the kitchen. She tossed her purse on the kitchen desk and hollered. "Kenny, we're here. Where are you?"

Father James turned and looked as Kenny answered over

22

the intercom system.

"In the family room. Uncle Tony is here and the girls are climbing all over him."

"Follow me." Emmy motioned while grinning.

She led the way to the family room and snuck up behind Tony as he sat on the couch. "What are you doing to my babies?"

"Mommy! Uncle Tony is tickling us!" Heather squealed and then she spotted Father James. "Are you Mommy's real brother? Daddy told us to be nice to you. He thinks you want money."

Emmy looked at Kenny, who was sitting in his recliner reading a book to Kevin. He shrugged. Isabella snuggled close to Uncle Tony and didn't say anything.

"I'm Heather and that's Isabella. What's your name?"

"My name is James Boyanov." He grinned and noticed her two missing teeth.

"Why are you wearing a funny shirt?" Heather asked.

"I'm wearing it because I'm a priest."

"Like Pastor Tyler?" Isabella turned around, scooted off of the couch and looked at Father James.

"Kind of like Tyler, but at a different church," Emmy explained.

"Hello, Father James. I'm Tony Bertucci." Tony stood up and offered a hand. He stared at Father James. "You look so much like Emmy's father."

Father James shook it firmly. "So I've been told."

Kevin jumped down and ran over to Tony. "Me hold you."

Tony picked up Kevin. "I'm not really related, but all the kids call me Uncle Tony."

"It's a pleasure to meet you even if you play for the wrong team. I'm a Chiefs fan." Father James took in the fireplace and the family pictures on one wall. His eyes settled on a picture of Raymond and Patricia above the fireplace.

"Have a seat, Father James." Emmy took his hand and pulled him around to the front of the couch.

He sat down. "Please call me James. You don't have to be formal with me." He smiled at Heather and Isabella.

23

The girls slowly inched closer to him.

He sat back and smiled without saying anything.

Heather sat on the edge of the couch next to him and stared at his face. "You look like Grandpa."

No one spoke for a few seconds.

Heather pointed to the other side of the room. "That's his picture on top of the fireplace with Grandma. Grandpa died and went to live with Jesus, but Grandma still lives in SoHam."

Isabella gained enough courage to scoot closer and sat on the other side of Father James. "That's our brother." She pointed to Kevin as Tony set him down. "We're five, but he's only two."

Father James smiled, and then Heather and Isabella both scooted up and sat on either side of him.

Emmy bit her lip but that couldn't stem the river of tears flowing down her cheeks.

"How old are you?" Heather looked up at him. "You look older than Mommy. Are you as old as Uncle Andy Walker? He's really old! I think he's over a hundred years old." Heather grinned.

"I'm fifty-seven. I don't know how old Uncle Andy is, but I suspect he's not as old as me."

Isabella looked at Father James as if trying to decide if he was real. "Which half of you is Mommy's brother?"

"Isa!" Emmy tried hard to keep from laughing. "That just means he had a different mommy than I did. We have the same Daddy."

Isabella and Heather looked at Kenny and tilted their heads.

"Not your daddy. My daddy. Your grandpa." Emmy shook her head. "This is too confusing for everyone."

Father James sat still without touching the girls. He didn't want to frighten them, however, he wanted very much to hug them. "What grade are you in?"

Heather answered at once. "We go to pre-school this year. Then we will be in kindergarten."

"We go to Crest Ridge Nazarene School Church," Isabella said mixing up the name.

"I see," Father James said. "Do you like going to school?"

"I like it because we get to see our friends. I don't like story

24

time though." Heather sighed and rolled her eyes. "I like music class. We know how to sing. Do you want to hear us sing?"

"Certainly!" Father James clasped his hands together on his stomach and smiled.

Heather got down and pulled Isabella off of the couch. They stood in front of Father James.

"What song are you going to sing?" Emmy asked.

Heather put her finger on her mouth. She looked at Emmy and then at Father James.

"Let's sing 'I'll Be True To You,' Isa."

Isabella nodded.

"Do you know this song?" Heather asked. "Mommy and Daddy wrote it, but we like to sing it, anyway."

Tony stifled a laugh.

"I'll start and you follow." Heather told Isabella.

They sang the first verse and then the chorus of the song Kenny and Emmy had written over sixteen years before.

"There's more to the song, but I don't remember all the words," Heather explained.

"That was beautiful. You sound like little angels."

"We can sing more songs."

"Why don't we save the other songs for later, girls," Kenny suggested.

"Okay," Heather agreed. "Do you want to see our room? We have a dollhouse that Grandpa built and lots of dolls."

"Maybe later." Father James smiled.

"Maybe you should go upstairs and play in your room. I think we need to talk to Father James for awhile." Kenny pointed to the stairs.

The girls giggled as they ran upstairs. Kevin stared at Father James and then followed the girls up the stairs.

"I'm going to call Diane and tell her to come over for dinner." Emmy jumped up. "Have you seen my cell phone?"

"It's on the island," Kenny said.

Tony sat in a recliner and stared at Father James. "You look like Emmy's father. There's no denying that. How do we know you are who you claim? Mr. Robertson suggested we get a DNA test"

Father James didn't hesitate. "I've thought about how to answer that many times in the last week. The truth is, short of a DNA test, I don't know how to prove anything. By the way, I'm willing to take a DNA test. I'm just as anxious to prove I am who I am as you are to know I'm legit."

Tony nodded and said, "Mr. Robertson can arrange it."

"I don't have a shred of evidence. No paper trail other than a birth certificate that lists Raymond Colasanti as my father. My birth mother gave it to me."

"You have the birth certificate?" Emmy stuck her head around the corner.

"It's a copy, actually. The original is with my parents now," he explained. "I don't want anything from you. I've been a priest all of my adult life. All my material needs are met by the church. It's a calling I take very seriously. The only reason I called you was the possibility of getting to know you. You are the only blood family I have. You and Diane."

Emmy left the room, grabbed her cell phone and hit Diane's speed dial number. She answered after three rings.

"What's up, Em? I was just trying to think of something to make for dinner."

"Don't bother! You have to come over here for dinner tonight," Emmy insisted. "Bring the kids, too."

"Duh! I wouldn't leave them at home." Diane laughed. "What's up? You sound excited."

"You're not going to believe it."

"Believe what?" Diane rolled her eyes. "Are you going to tell me? You always do this to me."

"You have to meet someone."

"Who?"

"Just come over, please!"

"Fine. When?"

"Anytime." Emmy bit her lip. "The sooner the better."

"I can come over with the kids, but Brady is still at his gallery," Diane said.

"What's he doing there?"

"He's helping Jill get ready for an exhibit next week,"

Diane explained. "They're doing a Richard Daye show. Daybreak Photography. Lots of great shots of nature. You should bring the girls. They would like it."

"Just let me know when, but you have to come over now," Emmy insisted. "You're gonna be shocked."

"Fine! I'll be there in a few minutes." Diane sighed.

Thirty minutes later Carson shouted as he and Caden came running into the kitchen. "We're here!"

Emmy turned around and grinned. "I can see that."

"Where's Uncle Kenny? I want to play the drums." Carson hopped around as if he desperately needed to use the bathroom.

"He's in the family room. Go see him." Emmy pointed.

Diane entered the kitchen just as Carson and Caden disappeared. "Don't pester Kenny about the drums." Diane looked toward the oven. "What are you making? It smells like meat loaf."

"It is meat loaf and cheesy potatoes, and I'm going to make some baked beans."

"Why? Daddy isn't here anymore. Who else likes that stuff? I can't stand baked beans anymore." Diane heard Carson yell from the family room. "What did he just yell?" Diane asked as she headed toward the family room.

"Wait a sec, Diane!" Emmy dropped her stirring spoon and ran after Diane. "Let me explain."

Diane rounded the corner, entered the open family room, saw Carson standing absolutely still as he stared at a man sitting on the couch.

"Mom, look!" Carson pointed.

Father James stood, turned and faced Diane. "Hello, I'm..."

"Holy...." Diane swore.

"You shouldn't use that word, Mom," Carson said.

"Who the hell are you, and what are you doing here?" Diane turned to Emmy, who alternately bit her lip and grinned. "What's going on, Emily?"

"Maybe you should sit down and let me explain," Emmy suggested.

"You can explain right here. Who is that?" Diane pointed at Father James. "If this is some kind of joke to get me to come back to church, it's in very poor taste." Diane turned back and stared at Father James. "Who the hell are you?"

Emmy grabbed Diane's hand, and they walked over and stood in front of Father James.

"This is Father James from St. John's." Emmy said with as much calm as she could muster. "He also happens to be our half-brother."

Father James crossed one hand over the other and waited for Diane's reaction without saying anything or even changing his expression.

"What did you say?" Diane whispered without taking her eyes off of the priest.

"He's our half-brother." Emmy said slowly.

"Carson! Caden! Run upstairs and find the girls," Diane shouted orders.

Kenny and Tony heard the commotion from the basement and came back upstairs.

"Who's going to tell me what the hell is going on?" Diane crossed her arms over her chest and stared defiantly at Father James.

Father James smiled and sat down in one of the recliners. "If you would have a seat, I will explain everything," he said in a reassuring voice.

Diane and Emmy sat on the couch and turned to face him.

"Let's go see how the meat loaf is doing," Kenny suggested to Tony.

Tony nodded, and they left the room and headed to the kitchen.

"My name is Father James... " He explained everything to Diane.

"I don't give a damn!" She exclaimed after he finished his story. "What right do you have coming here like this?" Diane squirmed on the couch as Emmy held onto her.

"None at all."

"How do we know you're not trying to scam money from us? I'm not giving you a red cent! Emmy, don't give this guy any money." Diane pushed Emmy away.

"He doesn't want money." Emmy bit her lip and looked at Father James.

"Then what does he want?"

"A family," Emmy said softly.

At that moment Kenny and Tony walked into the room.

"Okay, I can believe Daddy had a fling with some woman." Diane waved her hands dismissively. "It's obvious that you look like him, but that doesn't prove anything. I've heard everyone has a double somewhere in the world. I can't understand how he didn't know. Why did you wait so long to find us? You said you knew your birth mother."

"My birth mother would never tell me about my father. I think she was afraid I would confront him."

"Weren't you curious at all?" Diane asked.

"Certainly. I've wondered about that all my life, but I never obsessed about it. After I became a priest, I had a different father."

Diane laughed.

"Please listen, Diane," Emmy encouraged.

"I'm all ears." Diane sat back and crossed her arms.

"I do not intend to disrupt your life, Diane."

"I won't let you," she spat back.

"I will be in SoHam, and if you want to get to know me, I will be available."

"I want you to be a part of my life," Emmy said. "I know Daddy wanted me to be a boy."

"You acted like a boy, Emmy." Diane laughed. "You were always playing catch with him."

"I was a real tomboy." Emmy smiled at Father James.

"I played football in school," he said.

Diane sighed and looked at Emmy. "I'm not saying I believe your story. I need some physical proof. But just in case this isn't a complete scam, have you given any thought to what we should tell Mom? If you let him be a part of your life, the word will get around eventually. How do you think Mom will react?"

"I don't know. I know we can't keep it a secret. One of the kids is sure to mention Uncle James, and she will want to know who he is."

"We don't have to decide this minute," Diane said. "You better check on dinner. I don't want to eat burnt meat loaf."

"It's done," Kenny said. "We took everything out of the oven."

Two days later Diane and Emmy went to see their mother.

"How are you doing, Mom?" Diane asked.

Mom sat in her chair and watched TV. "I'm doing all right. I haven't been forgetting as much stuff as before."

"That's good." Diane watched as Emmy checked the apartment for anything that might be a clue about Patricia's mental state.

Emmy shrugged. "I don't see anything."

"I'm not totally senile, girls. I might need help remembering what day it is, but I can take care of myself."

"Do you still like the food here, Mom?" Emmy sat down on the couch.

"It's decent, but I like that I don't have to cook or cleanup." She stared at her daughters. "I can tell you have something to ask me. Go ahead."

"It's something to tell you, not something we have to ask."

"Did Betty pass away? Are the kids all right?" Patricia asked. "I still remember my sister even if she doesn't know me."

"Everyone is all right. Kevin Michael scraped his knee, but he's okay. He likes to show everyone his Bandaid."

"Are you going to tell her, or do I need to?" Diane frowned at Emmy.

"You can tell her."

Diane looked at her mother. "It appears that we have a half-brother. He called Emmy out of the blue two days ago, and we met him. Apparently Daddy had a weekend thing with his mother and he claimed Daddy never knew about him. He's a priest, by the way."

Patricia chuckled. "Doesn't surprise me in the least. I'm only surprised that it took so long."

Emmy and Diane stared at each other and then at their mother.

30

"This doesn't bother you?" Emmy asked.

"No, why should it. Raymond isn't here. I can't yell at him for something he did a long time ago."

"How do you know it happened a long time ago?" Diane asked. "We didn't mention Father James' age."

"Give me credit for knowing your father. He might have been a boozer, but he was not a womanizer. He never had to go outside the house for sex."

"Mom!"

"Oh, for crying out loud, Emily. You do realize your father and I had a sex life, right? I know you and Kenny have sex."

"So, it doesn't bother you?" Diane asked.

"Hell, no! You say he's a priest? How old is he? I know your father fooled around with other women, girls, really, during high school."

"He's fifty-seven, so he must have been born in 1955 or late '54. That means Daddy would have been seventeen or eighteen."

"Sounds plausible. How does this priest know it was Raymond?"

Diane chuckled. "He looks almost exactly like Dad. He's a little taller, but his face... You'd have to see him."

"I don't have any desire to see him. He's not my son. I think I would remember that." Mom laughed.

"He's met the kids, and I had him over for dinner. The girls seem to like him, and they're already calling him Uncle James. They don't understand who he is, but they know he looks like Daddy."

"Anything else going on that I need to know about?" Mom looked at her daughters.

Emmy shrugged. Diane shook her head.

"Fine! Then let me get back to my show. I want to know if Dr. Warner is going to murder his wife."

Diane watched the soap opera, but Emmy found a magazine to read.

31

Chapter Four

"I hope you guys like lasagna," Emmy said as she placed the pan on a warming pad on the breakfast nook table. "Do you mind eating in here? It's just the four of us and the dining room is so huge. I feel lost in there."

"This is fine, Emmy," Ethan Hanks said. "The lasagna smells delicious."

"Isn't your nanny going to eat with us?" Fernando Ramos asked as he held a wine glass to his nose.

"I offered to let her, but she didn't want to intrude. You didn't have to bring your own wine, Fernando. We have some in the house... somewhere." Emmy held out a glass and let Fernando pour some for her. She glanced at Fernando's thick hair. *You have to color it. It's as black as when I first met you, and you don't have a single gray hair.* She contrasted Fernando's hair style with what remained of Ethan's close-cropped totally-gray hair. The top of Ethan's head was completely bald.

"I can imagine what kind of wine you have, Emmy." Fernando laughed and then took a sip and let it swirl around in his mouth.

"We're not wine snobs like you and Ethan," Emmy said.

"The salad is ready," Kenny said. He placed a plate of salad at each table setting. "Let's eat."

Kenny offered grace, and Emmy checked to see if Ethan and Fernando closed their eyes. They did.

"Should I dish out the lasagna since it's too hot to pass?"

"Sure, Emmy." Fernando didn't hesitate. He passed his plate to Emmy.

"How much do you want?"

"I suppose I should save some for everyone else."

Kenny laughed and Emmy poked him in the arm.

"What's so funny?" Ethan asked as he spooned some mixed vegetables onto his plate.

"Emmy always makes two pans of lasagna because she is paranoid about burning one. She's never burned anything, but she feels she needs a backup."

"Lots of people say lasagna is better the next day." Fernando waved his hand. "That's plenty. Thank you, Emmy."

""We don't know if that's true because Tony always knows when I make lasagna, and he comes over and steals the extra batch. This is his mother's recipe, by the way." Emmy scooped out some lasagna for Ethan and then Kenny and herself.

"Ummmm! This is an excellent salad, Kenny," Fernando said. "What is your secret?"

Kenny smiled and Emmy rolled her eyes.

"The secret is the order of preparation," Kenny said as he waved his fork.

"God, please help me." Emmy sighed then said, "It's just a salad. Lettuce, tomatoes and stuff."

Fernando grinned and asked, "Do I detect a hint of jealousy?"

Emmy exhaled and let her shoulders sag. "Fine. Be that way."

The guys stopped teasing Emmy and concentrated on eating.

"Oh, I have to tell you about my brother," Emmy said.

Fernando and Ethan stopped eating and stared at her.

"You better explain yourself, Em," Kenny said.

"... and that's the whole story." Emmy finished five minutes later.

"Amazing, but not unique." Fernando finished a second helping and patted his expanding stomach.

"Dinner was delicious, Emmy."

"Thank you, Fernando. I can see you haven't missed any meals lately."

Ethan practically choked as he took a sip of wine. Fernando looked askance at his lifelong friend.

Ethan smiled as he said, "She's got you there."

"I still wear the same size pants as before."

"True. But you have your tailor alter them first," Ethan teased.

"You still look as handsome as ever, Fernando. It's all right if you've put on a couple pounds." Emmy offered him more lasagna. "Ethan, you're too skinny. You could stand to put on a few pounds." Emmy added, "Mama Bertucci used to always say that to me. You look better than when we saw you at Fernando's play. That was two years ago. Have we seen each other since then?"

"We were here for your birthday last summer," Fernando said.

"I feel a lot better, and I know you want to know but are too polite to ask, but the skin cancer is gone, Emmy."

"I'm glad, Ethan. Now I can pray it never returns."

"I can't eat another bite," Ethan said to change the subject.

"Ethan, what are your plans now that Mr. Robertson has sold the company? Does the sale affect you?" Kenny asked.

"Not really. I have started my own consulting company, and had planned to leave in March even before the sale."

"What kind of consulting company?" Emmy asked.

Fernando grinned as he said, "He gets paid big bucks for showing people how to use their new cell phones."

"I'd rather have my own company than be working at a bank. What is your actual title now? Vice-president-in-charge-of-counting-spare-change?" Ethan teased back.

Emmy sat back and listened to her old friends. *You guys have teased each other forever. You must really like each other.*

"I thought I heard you say something about another company at Emmy's birthday party," Kenny mentioned.

"I have a small landscaping company and a crew that does home remodeling, but they're just sidelines. I make some profit but not enough to retire from the bank," Fernando explained as he sat back in his chair with his hands on his stomach.

"Why didn't you guys bring dates? I told you it would be all right," Emmy asked. *And I know what you're going to say, Fernando.*

"I didn't want Ethan to feel bad because he couldn't find a date. I didn't bring anyone because I couldn't make up my mind which lady to bring. So many to choose from."

Ethan chortled and twirled a finger around his ear.

I was right. You are so predictable. Emmy laughed. "You guys are too picky. There must be some women somewhere willing to subject themselves to a night of torture in exchange for a free meal."

"I still see Camille occasionally," Ethan said.

"Once a year is not occasionally." Fernando shook his head. "You should use an online dating service."

"Never happen," Ethan said. "If I can't meet a woman in person, I'm not interested."

"Fernando, how is Mr. Santiago doing?" Emmy asked. "It's been over a year since his wife passed."

"Alejandro is surviving. Liliana made him promise not to grieve for too long."

Ethan looked at Emmy and then Kenny. "Emmy, did you ever tell Kenny about the dinner party?"

Kenny glanced at Emmy and tilted his head.

"I think so. The dinner party where I met Mr. Robertson. Or thought I did. I didn't realize at the time I had known him when I was a little girl."

Kenny nodded. "Did you ever go to another dinner party at the Santiagos?"

"I never did, but these guys would go every year or so."

"I remember the last one before Liliana's health started to fail," Fernando said. "But I think the best one was the time Ethan took you as his guest, Emmy."

"You guys thought I was too young and too much of a tomboy to go to such a formal dinner."

"You surprised us, Emmy. You looked like a beautiful young lady that night," Ethan said.

"Thank you. I remember being so scared to meet Mr. Robertson, and then I almost peed my pants when he sat down next to me for dinner."

"Nice talk, Em." Kenny shook his head.

"Well, I didn't know he was kinda like my godfather at the time. I knew he owned the company and had tons of money."

"Isn't Bennett back in the city?" Ethan asked.

"Yes, he is the administrator for The Barclay Academy now. Have you ever met him?" Emmy asked.

"Once, but it was many years ago."

35

Emmy looked at Fernando. "Is it all right if I talk about Diane and Brady?"

Fernando shrugged. "I consider her a friend, even if she avoids me now."

"She has a problem being friends with old lovers."

"Em, maybe we shouldn't talk about Diane and Brady tonight," Kenny suggested.

"Okay," Emmy agreed. "Have you guys ever thought about moving out of Timberline Ridge?"

"I haven't," Fernando said. "Why should I? I haven't had a mortgage for years. The taxes are reasonable and except for that guy down the street..." He nodded his head toward Ethan. "... the neighborhood is stable."

"What he means is his house is in such poor condition that he can't sell it for more than twenty dollars. I've offered to purchase it for five grand, but he won't sell."

"I saw Diane in the yard last week. I thought she would have moved in with Brady." Fernando emptied the bottle of wine into his glass.

"She's actually waiting until after the wedding," Emmy said.

"Did you have anything to do with that, Emmy?" Fernando asked. "Did you put her on a guilt-trip?"

"I might have suggested it would look better if she waited." Emmy bit her lip. *I didn't threaten her.*

Sofia walked into the kitchen and said, "The kids are asleep."

"Thanks, Sofia. I should introduce my friends. This is Ethan and Fernando. They live in the neighborhood I lived in before I got married."

The guys stood up. Fernando shook her hand and began conversing in Spanish. Sofia smiled at Emmy and laughed.

"What are you saying about me?" Emmy frowned at Fernando. "Tell me, Sofia."

"Certainly, Fernando said you are still a tomboy and a child," Sofia answered. "But a very dear friend as well."

"Yeah, I bet that's what he said." Emmy continued to frown

36

at him. "One of these days I will get back at you."

"I'll be back in the morning, Emmy. Good night. It was a pleasure to meet you." Sofia turned to leave.

"Bye, Sofia. Thanks for coming over tonight."

After Sofia had left, Emmy poked Fernando in the side. "Tell me the truth. What did you really say about me?"

"Exactly what Sofia said." Fernando grinned and carried his plate and the empty wine bottle to the kitchen. "I'll help you with the dishes, and Kenny can show Ethan his studio."

Kenny understood Fernando needed to talk to Emmy in private. "Come on, Ethan, I'll give you the ten cent tour of the basement."

Ethan glanced at Fernando but Fernando didn't change his expression. "I'd love to see the studio. You can explain how to record a CD."

Kenny looked at Emmy. She shrugged to say she didn't have a clue.

Fernando cleared the dishes from the table.

"What's wrong?" Emmy rinsed the plates and placed them in the dishwasher.

"What's up between you and Kenny? I saw you with another man at a Jimmy John's. You were pretty friendly with him." *I think I might have seen him at your party, but I'm not a hundred percent certain.*

"When? I don't remember seeing you." Emmy bit her lip.

"I don't remember the exact day. Do I have to ground you like I would my grandson?"

Emmy thought about it and then said, "That must have been Rory Porter. He lived on Fifth Street when I was a kid."

"It wasn't Rory. I know him, and I know about his relationship with Diane. Who was it, Em?" Fernando put his hands on her shoulders.

"Christopher Braun, and he's just a friend."

He kept his eyes on her eyes. "Can you tell me there's nothing between you and this Christopher fellow?"

"Yes, Grandpa. There is nothing between me and Christopher except friendship."

Fernando kept his attention on Emmy's eyes. Suddenly, he realized the truth. "It's not between you and Christopher. It's someone else."

"I love Kenny, and I've never cheated on him."

"Will you ever?" Fernando asked.

Emmy bit her lip.

Fernando sighed and exhaled deeply. "I never would have expected this from you."

"When I was a kid, I hung out with Rory. We never did anything too bad, but after I saw him again... We hadn't seen each other for ten years or more. I kissed him once."

"Once? One kiss, or one session, or whatever it's called these days?"

"Only one kiss. I swear, Fernando."

"Is there more to the story?"

"Diane accused me of spending too much time with Rory after Daddy passed away."

"Were you?"

"Maybe, but we're just friends."

"So, everything is okay with you and Kenny, right?"

"We disagreed about hiring Sofia. He doesn't want me to go on tour anymore. He wants me to stay at home with the kids while he goes off with his band." Emmy waved her hand like an airplane flying through the sky.

"Did you talk it over? I assume you did because you hired her."

"I think there might still be some hard feelings between us."

"Then you need to talk it out. You have to communicate with each other. You can't hide your feelings inside."

Emmy laughed and said, "Have you ever known me to hide my feelings?"

"Not that I recall. You are almost transparent."

"He hides his feelings better than me."

"Will you promise to talk about this before it becomes more of a problem?"

Emmy nodded.

"Good." Fernando kissed the top of Emmy's head.

"It will have to be tonight because he's leaving for a month in the morning."

"Why?"

"He agreed to be a sideman for this band. The Barefoot Prophets."

"Never heard of them, but that's not unusual. I don't listen to much new music."

"There have been other singers beside Frank Sinatra," Emmy teased.

"I meant what I said to Sofia."

"You think I'm a child?"

"No, I meant you are a very dear friend." He smiled and released her shoulders. "And you still act like a child at times."

"Do not!" Emmy grinned.

"Let's go downstairs. I want to see the recording studio."

"Do you really?"

"Not in the least, but I can fake it."

Despite her promise to Fernando, Emmy didn't talk to Kenny about the issue of touring that night. In fact, she didn't talk to him at all. She went to bed and fell asleep while he worked on a new song in his studio.

"What time did you come to bed last night? I didn't even hear you," Emmy asked after Sofia took the girls to school.

"It was around two. You were zonked."

"Was I on your side of the bed?"

"You were kinda on both sides, Em," he said and then laughed.

"Sorry. Did you move me?"

"Yes, but you didn't wake up."

"What time do you have to leave?"

He checked the time on the microwave. "I need to leave in twenty minutes. Why? Do you want... you know?"

"No, but I need to talk to you about something."

"Does it have to be now? I need to finish packing and the bus will be here soon."

"No, I guess it can wait," she said. "Do you need help?"

"Sure."

She followed him upstairs to their bedroom.

"Are you sure you want to spend a month on a tour bus with these guys?"

He chuckled then said, "I'd rather fly, but they can't afford to, and it wouldn't be fair for me to fly to the gigs while they ride the bus. It won't be forever, and it will be like the old days when we traveled in a bus."

"Will you miss me?" She put a hand on his chest.

"Of course I will, but I need to finish packing, Em."

She stood in the doorway as he threw his clothes in two large suitcases.

"I think I have everything."

"Did you pack any pajamas? You forgot them last time."

"Thanks, Em." He threw some in and then zipped the suitcase closed.

She followed him back downstairs.

"Don't forget your coat. It might be still be cold down south."

He grabbed a coat. "The bus is here, Em. I'll call you everyday. Promise." He kissed her quickly and dragged both suitcases out to the garage.

A week later Kristen came over with Grace for morning coffee. She and Emmy sat at the kitchen island while Kevin and Grace played in the family room.

"Have you talked to Kenny? How is he doing?"

"We talk every day, and we Skype every other day or so." Emmy rested her chin on her hand.

"What's wrong? You seem depressed." Kristen put a hand on Emmy's other hand. "Are you getting any sleep?"

"Not as much as I need."

Kristen shook her head. "Oh, for cripes sake. He's only been gone a week. You can't even make it through a week without sex."

"It's not that!"

40

"What is it? Tell me."

"I think Kenny is taking too much time to get my CD ready because he doesn't want me to go on tour. I think we should release it this summer so I can go on tour, but he says it's not ready. He wants me to keep tweaking the lyrics."

"Why are you so anxious to go on tour. You don't like to travel on a bus."

"I miss singing for people."

"You sing at church."

Emmy rolled her eyes. "Not the same."

"It's your CD. Can't you just tell him it's done?"

"I can't do that. I know it still needs work, but I feel it's taking forever."

"Are you working on it while he's gone?"

"I'm going over to the carriage house, but just to work on lyrics."

Kristen looked at Emmy for a moment without saying anything.

"What? Why are you staring at me like that?"

"You would tell me if there was something else bothering you, right?"

"Yes, Krissy. I would tell you." *Everything except for stuff about Rory.*

"Fine! Now tell me more about Father James," Kristen insisted. "What do the kids think about him?"

"They love him, and don't think anything about how weird it seems to us," Emmy said. "They pester him if he comes over, but he likes the attention."

"Forgive me, but I'm still having difficulty digesting this whole situation. I wouldn't be as accepting if Mom or Dad told me I had another sibling," Kristen said.

Emmy grinned and said, "But it would be a chance to replace Derrick."

"Ha! Ha!" Kristen rolled her eyes.

"Okay, he's a good brother. I was always jealous because you had such a good relationship with him," Emmy admitted. "Oh, Father James and I did the DNA test. We should have results in a few weeks, but I know it's going to show we're related."

Kristen patted Emmy's hand. "I pray you are because you will be devastated otherwise."

The next morning Emmy called her manager at his office.

"Hi, Emmy. What can I do for you this grand morning?"

"Nelson, I want you to book a six week tour for me."

"Really? When would you like to tour?"

"Could you set it up for October and the first part of November?" She looked at the calendar on the fridge.

"I can talk to Prater-Saylor, and we can probably book some dates."

"Not just a few dates. I want it to be a solid six weeks. Not even a night off. I want to work my butt off."

"Okay," he said and then asked, "Do you think the new CD will be released in time?"

"It will have to, won't it?"

"Ah, I get it. You're booking this to force Kenny to finish it." He shook his head.

"He won't let me tour without new material." *And I am going to go on the road.* "Oh, one other thing."

"Yes, Emmy."

"I don't want Kenny to know about the tour."

"All right." *I will try, but it's almost impossible to book a tour and keep it a secret.*

Kenny returned home on the last Sunday of February.

"Emmy! Are you here? I'm back," he shouted as he walked into the kitchen.

"Where should I put the suitcases?" one of the crew asked.

"Over there by the island is fine. Thanks for your help."

"No problem. It was great to have you along. I wish you were a permanent member of the band."

"I did have fun, but I have to do my own music."

"I'll let myself out."

"Emmy! Where are you?" He walked through the kitchen and into the family room. "Where are you? I told you I would be

42

home around one." He checked the living room, the den and even the dining room. He headed upstairs and searched all the bedrooms. No Emmy. No kids. No note. He walked back downstairs and checked the fridge for a note. Nothing.

He called Tony's house and then Kristen's. No one knew where Emmy and the kids might be. He called his parents.

Mom Colwell answered the phone. "She was here yesterday, but she didn't say anything about going anywhere today. Did you try her mother or Diane?"

"Not yet."

"She might have gone over there. I'm sure you don't need to worry."

"Thanks, Mom. That really assures me." He hung up abruptly.

No one answered at Emmy's mother's place or at Diane's house. He dragged his suitcases upstairs, unpacked and checked his phone for the fiftieth time for a message or text.

Where could you be, Em? He booted up the computer and opened the folder with the phone list of all their friends. *What is Rory's number?* He found and dialed it.

"Rory, have you seen Emmy? This is Kenny."

"Hey, Kenny. No, I haven't seen Emmy since last Sunday. I saw her at church, but I didn't go today. Is there anything wrong?"

"I got home from the Barefoot Prophets tour today, and she and the kids aren't here. I've called everyone, but no one has seen or talked to her today. I'm getting worried."

"I'm sure she's all right. Is her car there?"

"Shoot! I didn't think to look. I'll call you back." Kenny sprinted out to the garage and saw all three cars. "Could someone have picked you up? Should I call Chase or Dr. Behren?" He turned to head back in the house when he heard Heather's voice and the service door opened.

"Emmy! Where have you been? I've been worried sick." He rushed over and hugged her tightly.

"We went for a walk since it's such a nice day."

"Didn't you know I was coming home today? Why didn't you leave a note?"

"You said you would be home at one."

"It's after one."

"A.M. You said one A.M. That's after midnight."

Kenny let her go and slapped his forehead. "I'm such an idiot! Did I really? I always get confused about that."

"You're a dork. Not an idiot." Emmy laughed and then kissed him.

"Is idiot a bad word, Mommy?" Isabella asked.

"No, it's not a bad word, but you shouldn't call anyone an idiot."

"Daddy, I got a new fire truck!" Kevin held up his new toy. "Did you have fun playing your guitar?"

"I did, but I missed you guys so much." He put his arms around the kids.

"Why are you crying?" Heather asked. "Did you get fired for making too many mistakes?"

"Yeah, that's it," Kenny said and then chuckled. "Now I can stay home with you guys."

"Maybe if you keep practicing, you will get better," Isabella said as she wiped away his tears.

Chapter Five

"Emmy! Did you check your email this morning?" Kenny hollered from the family room.

"Not yet, I've been rather busy. Why?"

"Andy and Charles are coming home tomorrow, and they want to know if we can pick them up. Can we?"

"What time are are they arriving?" Emmy walked into the family room, stood behind the couch and looked at Kenny's laptop over his shoulder.

"They're getting in at ten."

"A.M. or P.M.?"

"Very funny?"

"If it's in the morning, we can go. Sofia can watch Kevin Michael."

"Should I email him back or will you?"

"You can answer."

"Should we park and go inside?" Emmy asked as she and Kenny fought the traffic on their way to O'Hare.

"No, we'll wait at the Hinsdale Oasis until Andy calls. They don't have to wait for their bags."

"But they're arriving at terminal five. They have to go through customs. Let's park and go inside. No one will recognize you with that scraggly beard, and you need a haircut. You look like a homeless guy."

"Oh, I suppose." Kenny waited for a chance to get the Odyssey around a truck.

"You drive worse than an old lady," Emmy said as she shook her head.

"Do you want to get there in one piece?"

"I'm driving home," Emmy said.

"No way, Jose! I'm making you sit in the back."

Kenny pulled into the hourly parking lot at the International Terminal, and Emmy ran to the glass enclosed walkway.

"They won't be ready yet, Em?"

"I know, but it's cold outside."

45

You should have worn a heavier coat like I am. Kenny shook his head.

Thirty minutes later, she spotted Andy and Charles.

"Over here!" she shouted while waving her arms.

Andy spotted her and laughed. "Do you see Emmy?"

Charles glanced up and smiled. "She looks happy to see us."

"Hi, cuz! Are you glad to see us?" Andy hugged her.

"Oh, I didn't see you guys. I was waving at those people over there. I though they looked familiar."

Kenny looked at Charles and shook his head. "Let me carry that for you."

"Thank you." Charles pushed the small suitcase to Kenny.

"How was the trip? I see you both survived," Kenny asked as they rode the escalator up one floor.

"I was ready to smother him in his sleep a few times," Andy said as he let Emmy put his backpack on her back. "Twice we had to share a hotel room. He snores louder than a jet engine."

"And you snore like an endless freight train."

"Kenny made me promise not to ask you a hundred questions until we got home, but I didn't promise not to ask any at all. So how was the trip? Did you take lots of pictures? Where was your favorite place? Which country has the best food? Does Germany have the best beer? Did you meet any women?"

"Emmy! Stop it!" Kenny warned her.

"I didn't take any pictures," Andy said.

Emmy stepped off of the escalator and faced Andy. She poked him in the chest. "Why didn't you take any pictures? How will you remember what you saw? I can't believe you didn't take any pictures. Are you telling the truth?"

"Sorry." Kenny pulled Emmy out of the way as other people were coming up the escalator.

"I would never lie to you," Andy said.

"Unbelievable!" Emmy shook her head and waved her hands. "You can carry your own backpack."

"You know you're killing me, right?" Andy laughed as he turned Emmy around and put his hands on her shoulders to get her

46

moving. "Charles took all the photographs. He likes doing that crap."

"You're gonna pay for teasing me." Emmy stuck out her lip and didn't say another word until they were back on the tollway heading home.

"Are you guys hungry?" Kenny asked.

"I'm hungry," Emmy said from the backseat.

"Why are you sitting back there, Emmy?" Charles asked. "Sit by me, please."

"Kenny told me I had to sit back here because I complain too much about his driving."

"You can sit with Charles, Em."

"I need a burger," Andy said. "A big fat juicy burger with a load of fries. Is there a place on the way, or do we need to hit Darby's?"

"Yes, Darby's! We can stop at Darby's, can't we, Kenny?"

"If that's what Andy and Charles want," he answered while looking in the rearview mirror.

"Oh, yes. A burger with blue cheese and fries loaded with blue cheese and bacon." Charles nodded with enthusiasm.

Emmy moved next to Charles, and Andy turned and looked at her.

"Are you going to tell me about Father James, or do I have to call Detective Sanders for a report?" Andy asked.

Emmy spent the next ten minutes explaining.

"How soon will the test results take?"

"Not much longer," Emmy said.

"Well, I'm not going to believe a word this guy says until he can prove he's related. I don't care if he's a priest."

They arrived at Darby's. Emmy and Charles claimed a booth while Kenny and Andy placed the order.

"I'm buying," Kenny said.

"No you're not. I am." Andy opened his wallet. "Oh, I guess you will buy after all. All I have are Euros. I forgot to exchange my money."

"I'm glad Darby's has never taken credit cards. Now I get to buy you lunch for a change."

Kenny and Andy brought the food back to the booth. Emmy grabbed one of Andy's fries.

"Hey! Watch it. Those are mine," Andy growled. "They have blue cheese on them."

"I know, but I had to steal one. How can you stand that smelly crap? If I got a sniff of that stuff when I was pregnant, I would gag."

"Are you pregnant now?"

"You know I had my tubes tied. I can't get pregnant again."

"Then leave my fries alone."

"Can I start asking my questions now?"

"You can ask one question, Em," Kenny said.

"Why just one?"

"You just used up your question," Andy said and then laughed so hard he began to cough.

"You guys are dorks! Not you, Charles. Just these two."

"Thank you, Emmy. I love these fries. Bacon and blue cheese. Yum, yum."

Andy took the first bite of his half-pound burger and sighed. "This is awesome. You can't get one like this in Europe."

"What's the difference? Don't they have cows over there?" Emmy asked and then took a drink of her root beer.

"You just don't understand." Andy took another bite. "Heavenly."

"Can I ask about your vacation now?"

"You can talk to Charles, but I'm going to savor this awesome burger."

Emmy shook her head. *You're acting like that burger is better than sex.* "Which country did you like the best?"

"Switzerland," Charles said. "Without question."

"Liechtenstein!" Andy claimed between bites.

"Never heard of it. Where is it? Is he making that up, Charles?"

"No, it's a tiny country next to Switzerland. Smaller than Chicago to give you an idea. Very mountainous and pretty."

"It's about the same size as SoHam, Emmy," Kenny informed her after Googling it on his phone.

48

"That's so good to know. I'll try to remember that if I'm ever on a quiz show."

Charles laughed.

Emmy badgered Andy and Charles about their vacation for thirty minutes.

"I'm finished." Andy patted his stomach while wiping his mouth. "Would you take us home? You can leave her here."

"Don't let him get under your skin, Emmy." Charles patted her shoulder. "I'll make you a disc of all my photos."

"Happy birthday to you! Happy birthday to you..." Kenny sang to help Kevin wake up on Thursday morning.

Kevin opened his eyes and grinned.

"Good morning. How's my big man this morning? Do you know how old you are?" Kenny tried to trap him.

Kevin held up three fingers. "I'm this many now."

"And how many is that?"

"Three! Can I have a new firetruck for my birthday?"

"We'll see. Would you like something special for breakfast?"

"Ice cream!"

"No ice cream for breakfast." Emmy shook her head as she walked into Kevin's room. "I can make you pancakes with blueberries."

"And whipped cream on top?"

"If we have some."

"Thank you, Mommy."

"You're welcome." Emmy picked him up, hugged him and kissed his cheek.

"Mommy, I'm three now. You shouldn't kiss me. I'm not a baby."

"No, but you'll always be my baby."

"Can I have cake today?"

"Would it be all right if we wait until Saturday? Everyone is so busy today. I thought we could have your friends and cousins over Saturday morning for a little party."

"Do I get to open presents today?"

"You can open two presents today." Emmy held up two fingers.

"I hope one of them is a firetruck."

A dozen neighborhood kids helped Kevin celebrate his birthday on Saturday morning. They created enough chaos and noise that Emmy didn't hear the phone ring, but Kenny did.

"Hey, Em, Barry Newton's on the phone. Got a minute to talk to him?" Kenny asked.

"Sure." Emmy took the cordless landline from Kenny. "What's up?" she asked as she walked into the living room and covered one ear. "I'm in the middle of a birthday party."

"Oh, I'm sorry to bother you. Should I call back later?"

"No, it's all right."

"You mentioned coming over sometime to see the house, so I was wondering if you were busy this afternoon?"

"Not that I know."

"Want to stop by and see the place?"

"What about Linda? Is it all right with her?" Emmy asked. *I'm not exactly her favorite person.*

"She's actually working today, and I'm watching the kids. You could bring your kids over. They could play," Barry said.

"Let me ask Kenny. I'll call you back within an hour."

She talked to Kenny. He didn't want to leave the house, but agreed to watch the kids. She called Barry after everyone left.

"Hey, Barry, I talked to Kenny. He's got stuff to do this afternoon, but I could stop by for a little while."

"That's fine. Are you bringing the girls?"

"No, Kenny will watch them. It will just be me."

Emmy arrived at Barry's house at two. She parked in the street and walked up to the sidewalk and stopped.

The trees are bigger than I remember. She glanced toward the front porch. *Tony would never let those bushes grow like that. Maybe you will work on the yard in the spring.* She smiled as Barry opened the front door. She sprinted up the steps.

"Hey, Em. Welcome to my humble abode."

"That's sounds weird."

"Yeah, I bet it does. You are so used to this being Tony's house, huh?"

"Mama's more than Tony's."

"Come on in and tell me what you think."

Emmy walked in and stopped as a young man approached.

"My God! Fender, is that you? You are so big now."

"Hi, Dad said you were coming over."

"How old are you now? You're going to be taller than me if you keep growing."

"I'm eight, and in second grade. I can't wait for school to be over."

Emmy smiled as Hattie walked up and stood next to her brother.

"Hi, Hattie. Do you remember me?"

Hattie looked up at Barry. "No, but Daddy said you are an old friend. You don't look old to me."

"Thank you. Your father and I have been friends since we... Holy cow, Barry. Fender is as old as you when we first met."

"He's actually older, Em. I was still seven when we moved to Fifth Street."

"We are getting old, huh?" Emmy walked into the living room. "You got rid of those heavy drapes."

"Fen, would you and Hattie play while I show Emmy the house?"

"Come on, Hattie. We can watch a show on my computer."

Emmy listened as the kids scrambled up the stairs.

"Linda didn't like them. She thought they made the room too dark."

Emmy glanced over to the fireplace. "There used to be family photos on the mantle."

"Does it feel strange to come back here?"

"It kinda does. I have lots of memories of this house."

"How old were you when you first came here? Do you remember, or was it too long ago?"

She laughed and then poked Barry in the stomach. "I'm not that old. I still remember. It was senior year and I was seventeen. Wow! I thought I was so grown up at seventeen. Now I think of seventeen-year-old kids at church. They are just babies."

Barry gave Emmy a tour of the first floor, and then they walked up the stairs.

"There were photos on this wall, too."

"Linda isn't a big fan of family pictures hanging up all over the place."

Too bad, Barry. I want to put more up at my house.

Barry let Emmy check out the bedrooms. She told him a little about her memories of each one.

"This was Tony's room." She stepped inside. "Whoa! What a difference! Tony used to have huge posters of football players on the walls."

"This is obviously Hattie's room now," Barry explained.

"Duh! I didn't think Fender would have stuffed animals all over his bed and dolls scattered around. Look at those ruffled curtains! Tony would freak if he saw his old room. It's really pink." Emmy touched the wall. "Why isn't this Fender's room?"

"Not sure exactly, but he had first choice and picked that one."

"That was Heather's room." Emmy backed out of Tony's old room, walked a couple of feet, turned and could see into Heather's old room. She bit her lip and sniffled.

"I'm sorry, Em. I totally forgot. I should have known better." Barry put his hands on her shoulders and squeezed tenderly.

"It's all right." She patted his hand.

"Are you going to tell Tony about his room?"

Emmy spun around and looked into Tony's room again. "Maybe. He should really see it for himself though. His bed used to be right there." She pointed.

"Do I want to hear about what happened in this room?" Barry asked as he grinned.

"Hush! Nothing ever happened in here."

"If you say so."

"You are still a dork. You used to ask me about my love life when we were in school."

"And you always told me."

"I didn't have anything to tell." Emmy sat on the edge of Hattie's bed and picked up a panda bear. "Isa has one like this."

"Fender doesn't like sports all that much. He's kinda like his father. He loves computers and electronic games."

"How's he doing in school?"

"Good. He's not as shy as me. You were shy when we first met. What happened?"

"Hey! I'm still quiet around people I don't know." She jumped up. "What's that?"

"You mean that noise." Barry grinned and walked out into the hall.

Emmy followed.

"They like this CD for some reason," he said then shrugged. "Don't ask me why."

"Do they know it's me singing?"

"I told them it was you, but it didn't make a big impression. They kinda accepted that one of my friends would be a rock star."

"Doofus! I'm not a rock star. Kenny is, but not me."

"Want to see the basement?"

"Yeah, will the kids be all right?"

"They're used to entertaining themselves."

"Lucky you. My kids are more high maintenance."

Emmy bounded down the stairs like she did when she first came to visit Tony. She raced down the hall, turned the corner, opened the door and took the stairs to the basement. She turned the corner and flipped on a light. "Wow! You've still got the pool table!"

"Yeah, I had to replace the felt and do some other stuff. It was in pretty sad shape, but I knew it could be fixed."

"Are you aware Tony's father bought this before he died."

Barry chuckled. "That's good."

Emmy rolled her eyes. "I didn't mean it like that. Tony and Marco used to take such good care of it. I used to play."

"Wanna play?" Barry raised his eyebrows up and down.

"Yeah." Emmy grabbed a cue stick from the rack. "Care to make a little wager?"

"Such as?" Barry grinned as he asked.

"Nothing like that. How about a dollar a game."

"Pretty high stakes. Can you cover your losses? Should I ask to see the money up front?"

"Take a check?"

"From you? No way! Cash only."

"That's all right. You won't beat me."

Barry won all five games.

Emmy pulled some cash from her pocket and tossed a five at him. "You cheated!"

"Exactly how did I cheat?" He stuck the five in his pocket.

"You've been practicing. That's not fair."

Later, Emmy said goodbye to the kids and gave Barry a hug. She returned home and immediately called Tony.

"I was at your house today."

"When? I didn't see you."

"No, your old house. I went over to see Barry."

"How's he doing?"

"Fine, but guess what?"

Tony rolled his eyes. "What, brat?"

"Your old room is pink!"

"What do you mean it's pink?"

"It's Hattie's room now, and it's pink. Stuffed animals and dolls everywhere. Lacy, ruffled curtains. You'd love it," she teased.

"You're so funny."

"Guess what else!"

"They probably got rid of the old drapes..."

"Yeah, but Barry fixed the pool table."

Tony didn't say anything.

"Did you hear me?"

"I heard you, Em." Tony blinked a few times. "That's great. Did you beat him? I'm assuming you challenged him to a game. What was the bet?"

"Dollar a game. He won five bucks."

Tony laughed then said, "And I bet you hated to part with the money."

"Hey! Five bucks is five bucks."

54

Chapter Six

In spite of the girls singing at full voice in the back row of the Odyssey, Emmy heard her phone chirp. She checked the text message and then smiled.

"Good news, Em?" Kenny asked as he stopped at a traffic light.

"Digger!" Kevin pointed. "I see digger!"

"Allie and Larry had a baby girl early this morning according to Liz."

"She probably has the correct info." Kenny accelerated smoothly through the intersection after the light changed. "I saw that digger, Kevin."

"What?" Emmy stared at him.

"Never mind."

"Liz says they haven't decided on a name, but everyone is all right. Let's see. Eight pounds on the nose. Big baby."

"That probably means I will play acoustic guitar today. I can't imagine Larry will be there."

"Duh! Ya think?"

Emmy raced ahead of Kenny after they escorted the kids to their Sunday School classrooms. She dodged around people and turned down the hallway toward the music suite.

"Did they decide on a name?" Emmy asked Liz.

"Not yet, Emmy. They promised to text me as soon as they make up their minds. They have time to choose."

Emmy noticed Tyler's cello next to the piano. "Is he playing that today?"

"Only on the response song after the message," Liz explained.

Kenny walked into the rehearsal room with Chase. "I can fill in for Larry. Ross Knapp can play the lead. He likes to say he can't, but if you twist his arm a bit, he can handle it. He's a better player than he realizes."

"I mentioned that to him already," Chase said. "He agreed to play lead but he's nervous."

"I'll talk to him. He knows what to play. He's just afraid of messing up, but he never does."

"Would you like some help?" Emmy saw Heidi Knapp sorting music after the last service.

"I don't mind doing it, but I wouldn't turn down the help." Heidi smiled and reached out to hug Emmy. "How have you been? We haven't had a chance to talk lately."

"I've been so busy. Between the kids and trying to work on my CD, I don't have a lot of spare time." Emmy gathered up the music folders. "Can I ask a silly question?"

"If I can give you a silly answer," Heidi said.

"Why do we bother printing out the music? Everyone is using a laptop or tablet or whatever on the platform. They only use these folders in here for going over the songs on Sundays or when we're first learning new songs. Why don't they just use their laptops in here?"

"My thoughts exactly. There are two filing cabinets in there full of music. We could eliminate most of them because they are online. I've hesitated mentioning it to Chase, but I think it's time to go totally paperless."

"I agree. Let's suggest it to Chase on Thursday, and if he doesn't agree, we will go on strike," Emmy said as she grinned.

"Do all of the musicians have a laptop?" Heidi picked up the folders and carried them to the filing cabinets. *I'm going to leave these here for now. No sense filing them away if we're going to toss them out.*

"The church can afford to buy a couple laptops if some of the guys need one," Emmy said. "The singers aren't allowed to use music stands or anything. We have to memorize the lyrics, or glance up at the screens. We should demand the players do the same."

"I know one player who would never go along with that. Ross has to have his chord sheet in front of him. He knows the songs, but he is so afraid of making a mistake."

"Kenny makes mistakes all the time. No one is perfect." *Well, maybe not all the time, but he played a wrong chord on the second song today.*

"I know there are other talented singers in the church who

56

are better than me," Heidi sighed.

"Don't be so modest. You have a great voice, and you're willing to put in the time and effort. Yeah, there are other good singers, but they aren't willing to spend the time. My friend Kristen is an example. She used to sing with the worship team until the kids came along. Kenny used to say our voices blended perfectly."

"I'm not putting anyone down. I understand how busy people can be. I'm grateful I can work from home most days."

"I've been wanting to ask about work. Have things changed much since Mr. Robertson sold the company?" Emmy heard her phone and opened the text. "Hmmm. That's interesting. Lorraine Allison." Emmy looked at Heidi. "Allie and Larry decided on a name."

"That's pretty. To answer your question, not for me personally. I still work from home four days a week. I can't really comment on other departments."

Emmy grinned and asked, "Why? Is it classified?"

Heidi looked curiously at Emmy. "I really can't say." *I don't have a high enough clearance.*

"The group I worked with would sometimes work on stuff for the Army, and they would tease me about having to kill me if I saw something I shouldn't. They were teasing, I hope."

"I do know there was a certain part of the company that didn't get sold. Not to the German company. I think the Defense Department needed to keep some things top secret," Heidi said.

"Have the new owners ever mentioned changing the name?"

"I doubt it. That would be too complicated."

"I better run. I'm supposed to make lunch, and then I need to work on some lyrics. See you Thursday." Emmy waved as she left.

"Thanks for the help, Emmy." *I wonder how much money you made when the company was sold. I would imagine it was well into seven figures.*

On Friday afternoon Kenny and Emmy were in the basement studio having spent six hours working on a track. Kenny had his elbows on the mixing desk, his chin in his hands and his eyes closed. Emmy leaned back in her chair next to him as they listened to the playback.

"What do you think, Kenny?"

"I hate to even suggest this after all the time we've spent on this track, but..."

"But what? Tell me. You won't hurt my feelings."

"Let's scrap it. It doesn't work."

"What? You don't like my song? What's wrong with it?" Emmy crossed her arms over her chest.

I knew you would take it personally. Kenny sighed. "Sometimes certain songs just don't fit into a certain project. I'm not saying it's a bad song..."

"No, you think it's horrible!"

"Come on, Em. Are you completely satisfied with it?"

"Maybe not, but it's not horrible."

"I know, and I can save it for another day."

"What else? I know that look." She sat up straighter.

"I think the two tracks we've worked on all week should be eliminated from consideration."

"Fine! Just erase them. Delete them from the computer, or whatever. You hate my music, and I never want to work with you again." She started to get up.

"Don't be like that, Em." He grabbed her and pulled her onto his lap. "I love your songs, but some are better than others. I love you, too."

"I should never work with a producer I'm sleeping with." She grinned and then kissed him.

"I would never work with an artist unless we were sleeping together."

Emmy sat up.

"No, I didn't mean it like that."

"Good! Because you've produced other bands besides me."

"I meant... Oh, never mind. Do you trust my judgment?"

"Yes, as far as the music goes. Not with the artwork or anything though."

"Let's call it a week, and start again on Monday."

58

"I like that idea, but what are we going to do with the rest of the afternoon?" She kissed him again as her eyes sparkled.

"Kenny, would you and Sofia watch the kids for me today?" Emmy asked as she came downstairs on Monday morning. She poured a cop of coffee and sat down at the island. "I would like to spend the day at the carriage house."

"I suppose we can. Are you going to tweak the lyrics on those songs we discarded? The backing tracks are still good."

"No. I'm going to come up with completely new lyrics. I woke up in the night and wrote down a few lines. I want to see if I can expand on a couple of ideas."

"Should I bring the kids over after school? Mom and Dad might like to see them."

"I'd rather you didn't. I don't want to be disturbed."

Kenny closed his laptop and stood up. "We could visit my parents without disturbing you."

"Sorry. I didn't mean it like that. Of course you can visit your parents."

"We'll see. I might take the kids to the zoo instead," Kenny said. "Sofia, have you ever been to the zoo?"

"Certainly, but not in the winter. It's kinda cold to be walking around outside."

"Right! I knew that."

Emmy looked at Sofia and shook her head. Sofia grinned as they both whispered, "Dork."

"I heard that! I'm not a dork, and there are some animals who stay outside all year."

Emmy returned home in time for dinner. She checked the stove.

"I made dirty rice and corn," Kenny said. "We didn't know when you'd be home."

"Sorry. I should have called." Emmy kissed him.

"Mommy! We missed you. Daddy and Sofia took us to the zoo. We saw polar bears!" Isabella exclaimed. "What else did we see, Daddy? I forgot."

"We saw penguins, Isa," Heather said. "We didn't stay

long. It was too cold."

Emmy shook her head. "You just had to prove a point, huh?"

"What point might that be, Em?"

Emmy grinned at Sofia. "That you're a dork."

"Kevin Michael and I had a good time at the zoo. Didn't we, buddy?"

Kevin grinned. "We saw bears!"

"What did you do, Mommy?" Isabella asked as she sniffed the plate of rice in front of her.

"I wrote some new songs."

"Can we sing them?" Heather asked.

"They aren't the kind of songs you like to sing, sweetie. They're more for adults."

"Can you write some songs Heather and I can sing?" Isabella asked. "Can you write 'Victory in Jesus' for us?"

"I'll try to write a song for you tomorrow. Let's eat dinner now."

"Mommy, we have to say a prayer first." Heather rolled her eyes.

That night after the kids were asleep, Emmy joined Kenny in the family room.

"Would you like to go downstairs and listen to what I worked on today?"

Kenny looked at Sofia.

"I can listen for Heather. Go ahead with Emmy," Sofia said.

"What's wrong with Heather? Is she sick?" Emmy put her hands on her hips. "She didn't sound sick."

"She complained about her throat hurting, but I think she's okay. I gave her some of that medicine you bought."

"If she wakes up, please let me know, okay?"

"I will if I can't get her back to sleep. You guys should go listen to your songs. I'm going to finish reading."

Emmy held Kenny's hand as they headed downstairs.

"I wrote some new lyrics and managed to record them using the old backing tracks. Here's a copy of the lyrics if you want to follow along. Can you turn on the board and play them."

"Okay, but you know how to turn everything on, Em."

"I probably do, but I'm afraid of doing it wrong and accidentally erasing everything."

"You do know everything is backed up to redundant hard drives, right?"

"Whatever! Could you please play the songs?" She handed him a flash drive.

Kenny read the lyrics while listening to Emmy's rough vocals. He played all three songs twice before stopping.

"These are really personal, Em."

"I know. Does that bother you?"

"I'm not sure."

"Not everyone will know just how personal they are. We aren't the only couple to go through stuff like this. The lyrics could apply to lots of people."

Kenny read through the lyrics again. "They are really good, Em. These songs really show your growth as a writer."

"Good!" Emmy said as she grinned. "Because tomorrow I have to write songs for Heather and Isabella."

Chapter Seven

Annie Mercer O'Dell and Matthew Sullivan chose Hope Lutheran Church in Crest Ridge for their wedding mainly because her father, retired SoHam detective Keith O'Dell, and his second wife, Elisabeth, were married in a private ceremony at the church several years before.

Pastor Jonathan Halverson greeted Annie and Matt on Friday. The day before the wedding. "It's good to see you again. Are you ready for the big day?"

"I'm ready!" Annie grinned. "But I think Matty is getting nervous."

"That's understandable," Jonathan said while looking up at Matt. "While we have a few minutes before the rest of your party arrives, perhaps we could go over the service."

"We could do that."

Pastor Jonathan led them to his office and eased his seventy-five-year-old body into his leather chair. "Please, have a seat." He rubbed his knees to ease his pain.

Annie pulled a piece of paper from her purse. "These are the vows we wrote."

The pastor went over the ceremony with Annie and Matt and then led them to the sanctuary to familiarize them with the layout. Fifteen minutes later members of the wedding party began to arrive. Matt and Annie turned to the rear as they heard voices.

"Liam, get over it. You are not walking Annie down the aisle. Keith is her father and he will manage somehow," Elisabeth Franklin O'Dell stated in no uncertain terms.

Annie hurried to the back. "What's going on? Why would Grandpa need to walk me down the aisle?"

Liam O'Dell, the retired principal of Roosevelt High, rolled his eyes. "Your father sprained his ankle this morning when he fell off a ladder trying to clean the gutters on his house. Dern fool. How are you, Annie? Now don't you fret. I can walk you down the aisle with out tripping and breaking my leg."

Annie watched as her father made his way toward her using crutches.

"Don't listen to your grandfather, Annie. I will walk you down the aisle if I have to crawl on my hands and knees."

"Daddy! Why were you on a ladder?"

"No brains," Liam said.

"The gutters needed to be cleaned, and since it was warm, I decided to start working on them."

Mace and Erin Franklin walked in and Annie introduced them to Pastor Halverson as her matron of honor and Matt's best man.

Pastor Jonathan looked up at Mace. "You're pretty tall. Do you play basketball?"

"Sweet Jesus!" Liam muttered under his breath to Keith and Matt. "Does he assume all tall black men play basketball?"

"Hush, Dad," Keith said.

Mace smiled at Pastor Jonathan. "I did play basketball at North Park College, and now I'm a coach at Roosevelt High."

"You might find it difficult to believe, but I played basketball in college. That was such a long time ago. The game is different now." Pastor Jonathan chuckled and held onto Mace for support. "Are there any other people in the wedding party?"

"No, we wanted to keep it simple," Annie explained.

"But you have someone you want to sing, correct?" Pastor Jonathan asked.

"Yes, she and her husband should be here tonight."

Kenny and Emmy chose that moment to enter the building. Annie spotted them.

"Emmy, we're over here. Come on in."

Emmy held Kenny's hand as they walked toward everyone.

"Emily Colasanti, it's good to see you again." Liam O'Dell walked over and offered his hand to Kenny. "How is your father, Kenny? Your mother doing all right?"

"They are just fine, Principal O'Dell. Thanks for asking."

He turned his attention to Emmy. She didn't look at him and tried to hide behind Kenny.

"I'm sorry about your father."

Emmy bit her lip. "Thank you. I saw you at the wake and funeral, but I didn't get a chance to talk to you."

"You don't look much different than when you were in school."

Emmy blushed.

Annie stood next to her grandfather and put her hand on his arm to steady him.

"Are we expecting anyone else?" Pastor Jonathan asked.

"This is it," Matt said. "We have a couple of guys lined up to help usher people in tomorrow."

"Are there any mothers or grandmothers to be seated?"

"Sweet Mother Mary! Who is this joker? Annie, didn't you tell him about your mother, or Matty's?" Liam muttered as he shook his head.

"Grandpa, be nice. I told him, but he probably forgot."

"My wife and I are the only parents and this old curmudgeon is the only grandparent," Detective O'Dell informed the pastor.

"Well, shall we get started?"

Ten minutes later Annie and Matt were satisfied.

"Should we go over the song?" Pastor Jonathan asked. "Who is singing?"

Annie turned to Emmy. "Would you like to test the sound system? Do a soundcheck. That's what you call it, right?"

Kenny nodded. "Would it be possible?"

Matt looked at the pastor. "Would you mind?"

"Not at all. I can turn on the PA for you. It's rather complicated."

Matt and Annie suppressed a laugh.

"Thank you. I appreciate your help," Kenny said politely.

Liam turned to his son and raised his bushy eyebrows. "How old is this guy? Doesn't he know who he's talking to?"

"Apparently not." Keith hobbled to the front row, sat down, put his crutches next to him and spread his arms along the tops of the wooden pews.

Liam joined him. "Pretty church, but these benches are harder than sitting on rocks."

Pastor Jonathan led Kenny to a booth at the back of the sanctuary and turned on the system.

"I have a backing track." Kenny showed him the CD.

"That would go in here, I think."

"I believe you are right, Pastor. And it appears that the mixing board is labeled. I believe this channel might control the CD player and perhaps this might be the vocal microphone."

"You must be more familiar with this equipment than me."

"I do have some experience with PA gear."

"Who is going to sing?"

"Annie asked my wife if she would sing."

"You mean the young lady with you?"

"Yes."

Kenny stayed in the booth while Pastor Jonathan escorted Emmy to the front.

"Are you nervous about singing in front of people? You don't need to be, my dear. Everyone's attention will be on the bride. You can use this microphone."

Emmy recognized it as a Shure SM58.

"Let me check to see if it's on." He tapped the microphone and then, to Emmy's chagrin, blew into it. "I believe it's on." He waved to Kenny. "Go ahead and play your CD." He turned back to Emmy. "Just relax and pretend no one is here."

"Thank you, sir." Emmy bit her lip and kept a straight face.

Pastor Jonathan sat next to Liam.

Emmy began to sing.

Pastor Jonathan did a double take.

Liam smiled and shook his head. *You old codger, you have no clue.*

Kenny quickly adjusted the monitor level for Emmy using her hand signals as a guide.

Everyone froze and listened as Emmy sang "I Will Be True To You."

Pastor Jonathan's jaw dropped as Emmy sang.

Liam nudged him. "She's rather good, huh?"

"I am blown away. Who is she?"

Emmy finished the song. Kenny turned off the gear and walked up to the front. "Monitors all right, Em?"

"The EQ is terrible, but it's all right."

Pastor Jonathan stood up slowly and approached Emmy and Kenny. "I had no idea, young lady. You have a beautiful voice. I don't know the name of that song, but I'm pretty sure I've heard it before."

Keith got to his feet with help from Elisabeth. "We played the song at our wedding a few years back."

"Did you now?" Pastor Jonathan tilted his head and rubbed his jaw. "I'm sorry, but I don't remember."

"Have you ever heard of Fridays At Five?" Liam asked.

"They are a rock and roll band, right? Local boys."

Annie took over. "May I introduce the lead singer and guitar player of Fridays, Kenny Colwell." Annie put her arm around Emmy's waist. "This young lady is Emmy Colasanti, who happens to be married to him. She also helped write that song."

Pastor Jonathan smiled and said, "It's a pleasure to meet you. I'm sorry for not realizing who you are. Please forgive me."

"Not a problem. Emmy happens to be a singer in her own right."

He shook his head. "I'm getting too old for this. You must think I'm such a dolt."

Annie grinned. *A dolt indeed. I haven't heard that word in like forever.*

Matt helped Pastor Jonathan regain some of his dignity. "Emmy and Kenny like to keep a low profile. There are lots of people in SoHam who don't recognize them. Would you care to join us for the rehearsal dinner? I know you said you needed to be somewhere later, but you are welcome to join us at The Hungry Lion."

"Thank you, Matt, but I promised some of the seniors I would join them for a game of bridge."

"I understand. Thank you for everything."

"We'll see you tomorrow," Annie said. *You might be old and forgetful, but you are so kind.*

They left and Annie put her hand on Emmy's arm as they walked out to the cars. "At least he didn't have a heart attack when you started singing."

"He did turn rather pale." Emmy looked down at Annie's

66

belly. "Does he know you are expecting?"

"Oh, yes, we told him right away."

"What did he say about that?"

"He said so many couples are waiting until after the baby is born to get married, if they even bother at all."

Grandpa Liam overheard the conversation. "Your sainted mother, may she rest in peace, would be very upset if you had the baby without being married."

"Oh, Grandpa," Annie said. "Matty and I have always planned to get married someday."

Keith heard the conversation, too, and hobbled over. "Dad, I'm sure Amy Catherine would be thrilled about having a grandchild no matter the circumstances."

"You are right. You did a great job raising that child on your own. She is just about perfect, other than being pregnant, in every way. Amy Catherine herself, bless her, could not have done a better job. I'm proud of the lot of you."

"That was a beautiful ceremony," Emmy said as she hung onto Kenny while waiting in line with Kristen and John to greet Annie and Matt.

"It was, Em. Short, but perfect. You sounded great, by the way. You should have seen the look on Pastor Jonathan face. He closed his eyes and appeared to be at peace."

"Are you sure he wasn't asleep?" Emmy asked as she laughed.

"Hush, and say hi to Annie's father." Kenny shook hands with Detective O'Dell. "How did you manage to recover from your fall so quickly?"

"I had Elisabeth wrap my ankle and took a handful of pain pills."

Kenny chuckled and said, "You didn't even limp."

"I didn't dare. I was afraid my father would push me aside so he could walk Annie down the aisle. I was not going to let that happen." Detective O'Dell smiled at Emmy. "You have daughters. One day I hope you will have the same privilege. It is an amazing experience."

67

Emmy said to Elisabeth, "Annie looks so beautiful."

"She does. Keith and I are both so proud of her," Elisabeth responded.

"I'm sorry about Keyshon," Emmy whispered.

"We still miss him, but we have tons of great memories."

Emmy felt Kenny's hands on her shoulders as they moved down the line to Mace and Erin with their daughter.

"This must be Kendra," Emmy said.

Mace held his daughter, and she turned to look at Emmy.

"How old is she now?" Emmy asked.

"Nine months. Give or take," Erin answered. "She kept fidgeting during the ceremony, but she sat still and listened when you sang. Thank you."

"Oh, I'm glad you liked my song, Kendra." Emmy smiled at her.

Kendra smiled back, but then clung to her father and hid her face.

Emmy took a couple of steps and smiled at Annie. "You look so beautiful."

Annie held out her arms and Emmy hugged her. "Thank you for singing. We'll talk more at the reception."

Later that night, Emmy paused and gawked at the entrance of the Lincoln Hotel. "I remember when Kristen and I were downtown and she made me come in here."

Kristen and Kenny smiled because they knew this story by heart. John had heard it from Kristen earlier that day.

"You guys had already booked this place for our reception. I thought it was way too expensive, but she talked me into it. She even made me think it was my idea." Emmy poked Kristen in the side.

"Are we going to go inside or stay out here, Em?" Kenny asked. He grabbed her hand and pulled her toward the ornate front doors. Emmy rubbed a hand over the polished wood and gleaming bronze door handles as they walked inside the hotel, which had been renovated and restored to look as good as the day it opened in 1905.

"I love the plaster designs, or whatever you call them,"

Emmy said as she looked up at the ceiling.

"Come on, you guys," Kristen said. "I want to see who is here from North Park."

"Let's find our seats." Kenny led Emmy down the hall to the room for the reception.

"Do you think they will have an open bar?" Emmy asked.

"Probably. Do you plan on drinking tonight?"

"I might have a glass of wine. I wonder if Annie will drink anything."

"Because of the baby?"

"I don't suppose a little wine will hurt the baby."

Kenny asked, "Did she say what they're having?"

"Not to me. Maybe they don't want to know."

They walked into the room and Kenny counted the tables and quickly calculated. "They must be expecting two hundred people."

"Such a dork," Emmy whispered to Kristen.

They found their table and sat down. A moment later they smiled as Randy Braun, his wife Vanessa, his brother Christopher and a petite blonde sat down.

Emmy's eyes sparkled. "Maddy! I haven't seen you since we were in college. How are you? What are you doing now?" Emmy turned to Kenny. "Maddy is Cindy Mackens sister. Do you remember Cindy and Elaine?"

"I do remember them. They were a couple of years younger, I believe."

"How are you guys doing?" Emmy asked.

"Good. I'm glad Annie and Matt have us sitting with people we know." Randy looked around the room. "There are some familiar faces here from both Roosevelt and North Park, but I can't put a name to some of them."

Christopher smiled and then realized John probably didn't know Maddy. "Hi, I should introduce my date. This is Maddy Mackens."

"Where have you been living?" Emmy asked Maddy.

Maddy's steel gray eyes sparkled as she explained. "After North Park, I moved to Pittsburgh for several years. There's a branch of Liberty Manufacturing there. I had a chance to come back to SoHam, so I took it."

"She got a promotion. She's the head of the sales department," Christopher explained. "We met each other and I asked her to lunch, and then dinner, and now here."

Emmy tried to remember Maddy's age and realized she was two years older than Mary Michaelis. *Maddy is still kinda young for you, but she's older than Mary. I guess it's okay for you to date her.* "Have you met Elena?" Emmy asked Maddy.

"Yes, isn't she adorable. Christopher brought her along on our first real date..." Maddy explained more about her job and meeting Christopher.

Good for you, Christopher. Emmy smiled at him.

He grinned back at Emmy.

Kristen asked, "Is Cindy here? I didn't see her at the wedding ceremony."

"She should be here somewhere." Maddy looked around. "She's over there with Elaine and Adrien. Cindy and Raja got a late start."

"Is that her husband next to her?"

"Yes. Raja Dilipa. He's a doctor. Cindy always wanted to marry a doctor, and she got her wish." Maddy waved to her sister.

"Do they have any kids?" Emmy asked.

"Not yet. Would you excuse me for a minute. I need to talk to Cindy."

Christopher stood up and pulled out her chair.

"I'll be right back," Maddy said to Christopher.

Emmy waited until Maddy was across the room. "Way to go, Christopher. Maddy is better looking than Cindy, and Cindy is gorgeous."

"Thank you, Em. Is she old enough for me?"

"Just barely." Emmy made a face at him.

Maddy returned and patted Christopher's arm. "Cindy approves of you."

"Do Elaine and Adrien still live in Colorado?" Kristen asked.

Maddy nodded. "Colorado Springs. Adrien and Lainey are

both on staff at that same church."

"Does she still go by Lainey?"

"Oh, no. Cindy and I are probably the only people she allows to call her that."

"Where does Cindy live?" Emmy asked.

"Rochester, Minnesota. Raja works at the Mayo Clinic and has a private practice. He makes tons of money, so Cindy doesn't have to work. She volunteers at the Clinic."

Emmy squeezed Kenny's hand. *I hope no one mentions our money.*

Annie and Matt arrived with Mace and Erin a few minutes later. The DJ introduced them as they made their way to the head table. The meal was served, the traditional toasts made and the first dances completed. Emmy and Kenny sang their duet and returned to their seats.

"Are you going to dance with me, Kenny?" Emmy asked as she snuggled against him.

"If they DJ plays a slow song, I will dance."

"Kristen, we are going to have to find some men to dance with us. I want to have fun!"

"We can dance together to start."

The ladies danced and were eventually joined by some of the braver men. Annie danced with them, too.

"This is kinda like at your wedding, Emmy. The girls danced together while the men watched," Annie said. "At least Matty can dance with me tonight. He had a sprained ankle at your wedding."

"That's right. He did," Emmy recalled. "Do you mind if I ask him to dance?"

"Go ahead. I have to mingle with the guests."

Emmy saw Matt talking to some friends and walked over. "Annie said I could ask you for a dance. Will you?"

"I'd love to," Matt said.

His friends stood with slack jaws.

"That's Kenny Colwell's wife."

"No kidding," one of Matt's friends said. "She's even hotter than Annie."

71

"Yeah, do you think she would dance with all of us?"

"I'm not going to ask her. That big guy sitting at the table with her husband is probably their bodyguard. He might not like us dancing with her."

"I'm going to ask her to dance. I don't care about her husband or their bodyguard. They won't make a scene at Matt's reception."

Matt held Emmy close at the edge of the dance floor where the music was quieter.

"Thank you for singing today, Emmy."

"You're welcome, Matty. I'm glad you and Annie are finally married."

"You know, I am too. We've been together for so many years. We should have done it years ago, but the time got away from us."

"Are you going to have more kids?"

"Annie wants a son and a daughter."

"Do you know what you're having this time?" Emmy asked. *I shouldn't be so nosy, but I'm dying to know.*

"We just found out two weeks ago."

"Can you tell me, or is it a secret?" Emmy's dark blue eyes sparkled.

"We haven't told too many people yet, but..."

"I won't tell anyone. I promise. Tell me," she pleaded.

"We're having a boy."

"Oh, I'm so happy for you, Matty. Now you have both a daughter and a son." Emmy threw her arms around Matt's neck and hugged him.

Matt put his arms around Emmy and hugged her back.

Matt's friends saw them hugging.

"Oh, man! Look at that. Matt's got his arms around her. What a lucky guy."

"He better hope Annie doesn't see them doing that."

"She will kill him."

"The bodyguard is looking, and he doesn't look pleased," one of the friends pointed.

"Matt can handle himself."

72

"I'm not getting in the middle if there's trouble."

Emmy released Matt. "I won't tell anyone, not even Kristen, until you tell me it's all right."

"I don't think it will be a secret for long. I think Annie is telling people tonight."

"I think everyone can tell she's expecting."

The song ended and Emmy and Matt walked back to his friends.

"Would you dance with me?" one asked.

"Maybe later, but I think in need to take a break."

Emmy walked back to her table, sat down with Kenny and giggled.

Everyone looked at her.

"What's up, Em? We can tell you know something and are dying to tell us," Kristen said.

"I promised not to tell." Emmy grinned.

"If it's about the baby, you're too late. Annie came over and told us they are having a son."

Emmy's smile faded and her lower lip stuck out as she pouted.

"You're such an adorable goof, Emmy." Kristen laughed as she held onto John's arm.

Later as Emmy finished dancing with Kristen, Liam O'Dell approached her. "Would you grant an old man a special request?"

Emmy bit her lip and nodded. "Yes, Mr. O'Dell You aren't going to give me a detention, are you?"

He smiled as he asked, "Did you ever get a detention?"

"Twice, but it wasn't my fault. I swear."

"You used to do that a lot," Liam said and then chuckled. "I always found humor in hearing some creative language from your sweet lips. I asked the DJ to play a slow song. I danced with Annie earlier, and I think I can manage one more."

"I'd be honored to dance with you," Emmy said and then curtsied.

Grandpa Liam nodded to the DJ, and he started the song.

"You are a pretty good dancer, Mr. O'Dell," Emmy said.

"You mean for an old man."

Emmy giggled and then said, "I admit I can't picture you dancing to some of the fast songs, but you move all right."

"My wife Elsie, Annie's grandmother, and I would go ballroom dancing as often as we could. Elsie could have been in the movies. She moved with the grace of Ginger Rogers."

Emmy listened as Grandpa Liam talked about his late wife, his son Keith, Annie, who was his only true grandchild, Keyshon Franklin, Grandpa's best bud and fishing partner, and Amy Catherine, Annie's mother.

"Annie looks a lot like Amy Catherine, bless her soul." He suddenly stopped.

"What is it, Mr. O'Dell? Are you all right?"

"I'm all right, but I need to sit down."

Emmy led him to a nearby chair near the wall out of the way.

"Are you sure you're all right?" Emmy sat beside him. *Oh, God. I hope you're not having another heart attack.*

"I'm fine, child. I was thinking about Annie and Amy Catherine, and I just realized something."

"What was it?"

"Annie will be thirty-one at the end of May. Amy Catherine was only twenty-seven when she passed. I had forgotten how young Amy Catherine was when she got sick."

"You must have loved your daughter-in-law very much?"

"She was a saint just like my Elsie. Keith and Amy Catherine were the perfect couple." He looked around and saw his son and Elisabeth dancing. "I'm glad he and Elisabeth found each other. They were friends for a long time before they fell in love. Did you know that?"

"I think I did."

Liam paused and looked into Emmy's eyes. "I can see your father in you."

"You went to school with Daddy, didn't you?"

"Until he dropped out."

"Was Daddy all that bad?"

"No, child. No!" Liam insisted as he held onto Emmy's shoulders. "Later on after the alcohol took over, he … Well, you

74

know about that."

"What can you tell me about Daddy that I might not know?"

Liam thought for a moment and then chuckled. "We used to go over to North Park College for the dances. Your father loved to dance when he was young. We would dance with as many young ladies as we could. Your father did. I wasn't as successful. Sometimes he would not come home." Liam chuckled as he thought about those days. "He would find a young lady who was willing and spend the night... Shoot! I probably shouldn't have told you that."

"It's all right. I know Daddy wasn't perfect." Emmy thought about telling him about Father James but didn't.

"He might have had his demons, but he loved you girls. You were the light of his life. Even more than Diane."

Emmy waited for him to continue.

"I remember when you got sick. It nearly broke his heart. It would have if you hadn't recovered so quickly." He glanced up at the ceiling. "I remember the priest said a prayer for you, and you recovered just like that." He snapped his fingers. "You were too young to remember."

Emmy wiped away her tears before Liam could see them.

"I should let you get back to your friends." He stood up and let Emmy hug him. "Thank you for indulging this old man."

"Thank you for the dance and the stories." She reached up and kissed his cheek. "Annie is very lucky to have you for a grandpa."

Shortly before eleven Annie came over and sat next to Emmy. "I am exhausted. I'm glad Matty and I are just going home after the reception. I would hate to have to drive somewhere far away." Annie put her feet up on the empty chair in front of her. "Do you mind if I ask where you and Kenny spent your wedding night?"

"Not at all. We spent the night in his parents' carriage house. That's where he first kissed me, and I wanted it to be where we... spent our wedding night."

"That is so adorable. Did I mention the book I'm writing?"

"No, you didn't. Tell me."

"I showed a first draft to Denise Bartell. She works for the *SoHam Herald* and knows Grandpa. She read it and hooked me up with an agent. The agent got me a deal with a publisher in Chicago."

"That sounds great," Emmy said. "Where did you come up with the idea for a book?"

Annie explained how she came to write her novel. "It's fiction, but based on some real people. I use SoHam as the setting, but I call it by another name."

"I would love to read it when it gets published."

"I'll give you a copy. I don't expect it to sell a lot, but I have enjoyed writing it. And re-writing and re-writing. Most of my time has been re-writing it. That can get old. Oh, you probably understand. You write songs."

"I do enjoy writing my songs."

Emmy danced with Kenny again before saying goodbye to Annie and Matt.

"Let's promise not to let too much time go by before we see each other again," Annie said.

"I would like that a lot. I can't wait to read your book." Emmy hugged Annie. *I wonder if any of the characters are based on me.*

Chapter Eight

"I don't want to be disturbed for two hours," Emmy said.

"Why? What's up?" Kenny asked as he looked up from his laptop in the breakfast nook.

She held up a book. "I want to read."

"Is that Annie O'Dell's book?"

"Yes, and I want to see if I can find myself."

"What's the name? I'll look it up online."

"*My Secret Life as a High School Private Eye*," Emmy said.

"Can I read it after you finish?" He opened the Barnes & Nobles website. "Is she using her maiden name?"

"Annie Mercer O'Dell," Emmy said. "Now don't bother me unless the kids are in danger."

Emmy walked into the den, closed the door and flipped on the light switch. *Should I lock it? The girls might get back early with Gra and Me-maw. No, Kenny won't let them interrupt my reading.* She sat down in the recliner in the corner, put her feet up and read the back cover. *This is partly true. You were a type of Veronica Mars or Nancy Drew.* She opened the book and began.

"*My name is Marcella Spencer, and I was a high school private investigator for the C.I.A.*" Emmy laughed. *This should be good.*

Two hours later she marked her place, set the book down and got out of the recliner. She walked out of the den and heard Kenny with the kids.

"How was the book?" He looked up from his position on the floor when he saw her. "Enough, girls, Daddy needs to get up and talk to Mommy."

"It's really good. I'm over halfway through, and I want to read more later."

"Is there a character based on you?" Kenny asked as he rose to his feet.

"Not exactly, but there are things that happen to two of the characters that actually happened to me."

"Like what?"

"One of the characters is named Everly Carmichael, and she has her schoolbooks stolen and nasty notes slipped into her locker."

"Did someone ever steal your books?" Kenny followed Emmy into the kitchen.

"Not all of them, but someone stole my Algebra book my freshman year. Annie found it for me. You know about the notes from Delaney."

"Did the Everly character resemble you physically?" Kenny opened the fridge and grabbed a water.

"Annie described her as petite with short, straight hair."

"What else?"

"Another character, I can't remember the name offhand, but she dated the quarterback of the football team."

"You never dated the quarterback, did you? I thought you only dated Tony, and he played mostly on defense."

"I didn't date anyone else on the team, but the quarterback's name is Tommy Betruschi."

"That sounds a lot like Bertucci. Did anything happen between these characters?"

"He got her pregnant," Emmy said.

"Whoa! Did you really get pregnant in high school and keep it from me?"

"Don't be silly," Emmy said as she blushed.

"Is there a lot of sex in the book?" Kenny picked Emmy up and set her on the island. "Is that why it's so interesting?" Kenny put his hands on the island on either side of her and moved close.

She put her hands on his shoulders and grinned. "There is some, but it's done tastefully. Not like a man would write it."

"So is it a tell-all about who slept with who in high school?"

"No, but I'm pretty sure Annie knows more than she tells about what happened at Roosevelt. In fact, I'm positive."

"She did have her grandfather there."

"I know you were only in high school with me for the first part of my freshman year, but did you know there were rumors about Annie?"

"What kind of rumors?" He leaned closer and kissed Emmy. "Juicy ones like the ones about you?"

"Sorta."

"Do tell," Kenny said.

"Annie and the basketball team," Emmy whispered.

He grinned as he whispered back, "What about her and the basketball team?"

"Are you really that dense?" Emmy rolled her eyes. "Annie and the team... you know." *Such a dork!*

Kenny laughed. "You have got to be kidding! Who on earth would believe that? From what I remember, she was one of the few innocents in school."

"Don't tell her I said this, but I think she started the rumor."

"Why would she do that?"

"So other kids wouldn't think she was Principal O'Dell's informant."

Kenny shook his head.

"She wasn't a bad girl by any stretch, but she wasn't an angel either."

"I don't want to hear anymore about Annie. Finish the book so I can read it."

Later that night after the kids were asleep, Emmy got dressed for bed.

"I'm going downstairs to read," she told Kenny.

"I don't suppose you want to be disturbed, huh?"

"Not unless armed intruders are attacking the house. No, wait. You can deal with intruders. Only disturb me if..."

"You are so funny, Em. I won't disturb you. Do you plan to finish it?"

"I should."

Emmy headed downstairs to the den, made herself comfortable and began to read.

Kenny woke up in the middle of the night and reached out to touch Emmy. He found an empty space. He checked the clock. *Three thirty. Em, where are you?* He sat on the side of the bed, stretched his arms over his head and stood up. He didn't turn on the light in the bedroom and stubbed his toe on the dresser. He hopped up and down on one foot while rubbing his toe.

I better turn on a light on the stairs so I don't fall and break my neck. He flipped the switch and ambled down the stairs. *She's not in the family room, so she's probably in the den.* He turned on the hall light outside the den and slowly opened the door, but it creaked in spite of his precautions. He let his eyes adjust to the dim room and smiled. He saw Emmy curled up in the recliner sound asleep with the book in her hand. He marked the book, closed it and set it on the computer desk. Then he picked her up. She didn't open her eyes, but she put her arms around his neck. He carried her up the stairs and gently set her in bed. She immediately spread out and took up two-thirds of the bed. Kenny shook his head and sighed. *I could have left you downstairs. Then I would have enough room.* He slipped into bed and stayed on the edge.

"You didn't finish the book, Em?" Kenny asked as he cuddled with Emmy in the morning.

She opened one eye at a time and stretched her arms over her head. "I fell asleep. Did you bring me upstairs?"

"No, I had Tony and John come over. They struggled, but they eventually got you up here."

"You're so good to me." She yawned.

"Why didn't you finish the book?"

"I tried, but I kept falling asleep. I'll finish it today." She pulled the covers up to her neck and closed her eyes. "Just a couple more hours, Tommy."

"Tommy! Are you dreaming about the quarterback?"

"Yes, so don't wake me up again. I was having such a romantic dream."

"You're a goof."

Emmy came downstairs at ten.

"Good morning, Emmy. Did you sleep well?" Sofia asked.

"I'm sorry I slept so long. Did you get the girls to school?"

"I got them ready, but Mr. Kenny drove them to school. He said he would be at the office until noon, so he's going to pick them up."

"Is there any coffee ready?"

"I can make you some. Would you like some breakfast?"

"I would love some pancakes, Sofia."

Emmy drank her normal two cups of coffee, ate some pancakes and cleaned up the kitchen by herself to give Sofia a chance to be with Kevin.

"Kevin, what is this in Spanish?" Sofia asked.

He said the correct word.

"Good job." Sofia clapped.

"Sofia, would you watch Kevin Michael while I finish reading a book?"

"Certainly, I'm going to take him to the library. Do you have anything to return?"

"No, I don't think so." Emmy walked over to Kevin. "Be a good little man for Sofia."

"I'm gonna sing songs at the liberry."

"Good for you! Follow instructions, okay?"

"I will, Mommy."

Emmy retired to the den to finish Annie's book.

She read the first page of chapter twenty-eight and sat up straight in the recliner. "This can't be! How could Annie know this?" She closed the book with a snap, jumped out of the recliner and bolted from the den. "Kenny is not going to be pleased if he reads this." She walked into the kitchen and completed three laps around the island before she stopped pacing. *Is it possible that this happened to two different people? Am I reading too much into this?* She paused by the fridge. Opened it out of habit and grabbed a bottle of water. *Maybe I'm overreacting. I need to read it again.*

She returned to the den and reread the chapter. *Okay, it's similar to what happened to me, but the outcome is totally different. I never got caught and certainly didn't get suspended, but only because I was able to flush the drugs down the toilet.* She sat back in the recliner and tried to remember the situation with more clarity. *Who could have slipped that package into my army jacket? It had to be while I was talking to someone and got distracted. I'm pretty certain of that. Maybe if I keep reading, I'll learn who did it. Annie must know or else it wouldn't be in the book. One way or another, I will have to explain this to Kenny.*

She read two more chapters and slapped the arm of the recliner. "Of course! Jayson Mathias! It has to be him, and I was fool enough to go on a blind date with him."

She finished the book and smiled. *That was really good, Annie. I'll have to tell her. Maybe I could write a review and post it on the website.* She heard Kenny get back with the girls and knew Sofia and Kevin must have returned from the library. She set the book down and headed to the kitchen.

"How was school today?" Emmy asked the girls. "Did you stay on green?"

Heather took off her jacket and tossed it on the island.

"That's not where your jacket belongs." Kenny pointed to the mudroom. "Hang it up properly."

Heather grumbled but obeyed.

"We were on green all day, but Zach had to be in timeout."

"What did he do?"

"He kept talking when Miss Liz told him to be quiet."

"Isabella, do you call your teacher Liz, or do you call her Mrs. Hammond?" Emmy asked.

"We call her Miss Liz. She said that's okay. Can we have something special if we eat all our lunch?"

"What would you like?"

"Watermelon or grapes," Heather answered. "I hung up my jacket and put my shoes where they belong."

"Thank you, Heather." Kenny opened the fridge. "We have grapes. No watermelon."

After lunch Emmy and Sofia got the kids down for naps.

"I'll see you in the morning, Sofia," Emmy said. *I have to talk to Kenny about the book.*

"If the weather is nice, I'd like to take the kids to the park. Would that be okay?" Sofia asked.

"They would love it. It's been cold and rainy for so long. I can't remember the last time I saw the sun."

Emmy joined Kenny in the family room.

"Got a minute? I need to talk to you."

"Sure, Em. I was going to head downstairs to work on that track that's been so difficult to finish."

82

Great! Now you want to work on my CD. Emmy sat on the couch with Kenny. "I finished the book."

"Did you like it?"

"I did. I thought it was well written and the story held my attention. There is one thing we need to talk about."

Kenny set down his laptop. "Okay."

Emmy took a deep breath. "When I was a senior at Roosevelt, someone put some drugs in my old army jacket."

Kenny's eyes opened wide.

"They weren't mine, of course. At first I didn't know what they were."

"What kind of drugs, Em? Pills? Pot?"

"Oh, they were pills. Uppers, I think they were called."

"So what happened?"

"It happened one of the days the staff searched the lockers. They did that occasionally. Looking for whatever. Someone put this baggie of pills in my army jacket right before lunch."

Kenny chuckled. "I remember that old jacket. You wore it all the time. Did you think it looked cool?"

"Kinda. The kids I hung around were sorta rebellious and I wore that jacket to try and fit in. Plus, I didn't have a winter coat other than a hand-me-down from Diane that was way too big."

"Em, why didn't you tell me you needed a coat?"

She shrugged. "I didn't want to bother you."

He put an arm around her waist and pulled her close.

"I just happened to feel the baggie and pulled it out. I knew they were pills, but I didn't know what kind. I kept my hands in my pockets, ran to the bathroom and flushed them."

"Did you ever find out who put them there?"

"I didn't but Annie did. Jayson Mathias."

"Who was he?"

"The blind date guy who thought he was so cool because he could play a Tom Petty song."

"Right! I remember you telling me about him. The kid with long stringy hair."

"Everyone thought he was a loser, but Annie discovered he was selling drugs and had a ton of cash hidden in a strong box in

83

one of the maintenance rooms."

Kenny tried to look serious, but then grinned. "You were afraid I would read this and think you were pushing pills, huh?"

Emmy bit her lip. "I didn't want you to think I would do something so stupid."

"I remember kids using drugs in school, and how some of them ruined their life. It can't be any easier for them now."

"Tell me about it. I hope we can teach our kids to make the right choices even if other kids are pressuring them."

"I imagine all kids face peer pressure of some sort. At least we are in a church that helps us parent and teaches our kids how to handle these issues."

"I wasn't brought up in the church," Emmy said.

"True, but God had his eyes on you."

She pressed against him. "Not all of the time, I hope."

"You don't have any secrets from God."

"Maybe not secrets exactly. Anyway, it says that He doesn't remember our sins after we confess them. You know the verse about the East and West, right?"

"I know what you mean, Em." He kissed her and held her close. "So what about the quarterback?"

"My memory is rather fuzzy. Probably because of all the drugs I took," she said and then laughed.

He shook his head. "You shouldn't joke about that. Pastor Tyler mentioned some of the teens from church experimenting with stuff even though they know better."

"Yeah, I could smell pot on a couple guys."

"What did you do? Did you say anything to them?"

"I took them aside and told them I knew what they were smoking. One of them offered to share a joint. I was tempted to take his pot and flush it, but I told them I would pray for them instead."

"We will have to talk to the girls about stuff like that. I don't want them to be ignorant about the temptations of the world."

"Could we wait a while. They are still my babies," Emmy said softly.

Chapter Nine

"Why don't you want a wedding shower?" Emmy asked Diane on the phone.

"Because they are for young women who've never been married. I'm thirty-three and divorced."

"But you never had one when you married Craig," Emmy said. "Don't you want to give your friends the opportunity to buy you gifts?"

"I don't need anything. Maybe we could have a girls night out instead," Diane suggested.

"You mean a bachelor party where everyone gets wasted?"

"Yes, and we go to some bar and watch hunks take off..."

"No way, Diane!"

"That's what my friends did before I married Craig," Diane said and then laughed. "That night was crazy. At least the parts I remember."

"I don't remember it. Was I there?"

"No, you weren't invited."

"Why not? I'm your sister."

"You were too young. You were fifteen."

"Was not! I was twenty-one. Where was the party? In Toledo or here?"

"I came back to SoHam for a weekend."

"You didn't even tell me you were here," Emmy said. "Maybe I would have wanted to be there."

"I thought about telling you, but it was after you got religion. You were trying to save the world. My friends didn't want you around."

"They didn't know me."

"The ones that did, didn't want to be around you."

Emmy bit her lip. "Was I really that much of a nuisance?"

"You were for a while."

"It's because... Never mind."

"Em, if you want to do something, make it a party where my friends can at least have a drink. You don't have to invite dancers..."

"I wouldn't know where to find male dancers," Emmy shouted.

"I'm not saying you do," Diane said. "But I don't want some stuffy party at your house, or, even worse, at the church. My friends don't see anything wrong with drinking... and don't you dare bring up Daddy."

"I wasn't going to. If I decide to have a party for you, what places would be acceptable?" Emmy rolled her eyes.

"Don't bother if you're going to be so sarcastic."

"Sorry. Hey, would it be all right if I have the party here?"

"You mean at your house?"

"Yeah, why not?"

"What about the kids?"

"They could spend the night with Gra and Me-maw."

"Those are ridiculous names for his parents," Diane said.

"No, they're not. Is it all right if I have a small party for you at the house, or not?"

"Fine, but if you mention church, I'm leaving."

"Do I need to hide all of our Bibles?"

"Call me later. I'll think of who I want to invite."

"How many should I plan on having?"

"I might be able to come up with a dozen names. Some of my old friends might want to see your house."

"Is it all right if I invite Mom?"

"You do, and no one else will be there. I can guarantee that."

"Why don't you want Mom to be there?"

"You just answered your own question, Em."

"What," Emmy thought for a minute. "She's our mother, and you need to remember that."

"Trust me. Not a day passes that I don't remember. I'm serious. You invite Mom and it will be a party of two."

"Can I invite Krissy and Sloane?"

"Why?"

"They can help me cook," Emmy said.

Diane rolled her eyes. "Emmy, just call Kerry Lynn's and let them cater it. I'll get back to you in a few days with a number."

"Would it be all right if I ordered pizzas?"

"They have other things. Go online and check out their catering menu. Just keep in mind there won't be a hundred people there."

"Talk to you later. I'll check their prices and order the cheapest thing they have."

"Emily Olivia!" Diane yelled.

"Gotcha!" Emmy said and then giggled.

Emmy was slicing vegetables for dinner when Kenny returned from getting the mail.

He tossed an envelope on the counter and said, "I think you might want to read that. It looks official."

"Is it the results of the DNA test?" Emmy asked. She wiped her hands on a towel and picked up the envelope.

"Only one way to be certain," Kenny said.

She bit her lip while staring at Kenny.

"Go ahead, Em. You know in your heart what it will say."

She sliced open the envelope, pulled out the results and began to read.

"What does it say?"

Emmy set aside the first page and stared at the second and third pages. She smiled and said, "We are definitely related."

Kenny opened his arms, and she rushed forward to be held. "I'm so happy for you, Em. You should invite him over for dinner soon."

"I will." She wiped away a tear and resumed cutting the vegetables.

"I will hate you forever, Emmy." Diane said on the afternoon of the party as she looked at the stack of presents on the dining room table. "I told you no gifts."

Emmy bit her lip and looked up at her sister. "I couldn't tell them not to bring a gift. Please, don't be mad at me."

"I should be furious. I told you not to invite our mother, and you go ahead and do that. Plus! You invite Mona Robertson."

"She's super nice, and she is gonna be your mother-in-law."

"Step-mother-in-law. I get along all right with her, and I'll try to tolerate Mom for today."

"Thank you. I appreciate it." Emmy bit her lip again.

Diane rolled her eyes, but then reached out and hugged Emmy. "You're all right for a little sister. I guess I wouldn't trade you for anyone."

"I can't wait to see what you got." Emmy picked up one of the gifts. "This is heavy."

"Put it down, Emmy. You're worse than the kids."

The party lasted for three hours. Everyone commented positively on the food from Kerry Lynn's Pizza and Pasta. Diane appreciated the gifts, and all her friends liked Mona.

"Everyone is gone now, Emmy," Mom said. "I need to talk to you girls."

They stood by the kitchen island, and Emmy made coffee as she nibbled on the last of the spicy wings.

"What's on your mind, Mom?" Diane asked. "Is there any of that red wine left, Em?"

"In the fridge." Emmy pointed.

Diane found a wine glass and helped herself.

"I hate the food at Sunrise Garden. That's what." Mom sat on one of the barstools. "I'll take a glass of that."

"But you said you liked it last week." Emmy got another wine glass from the cabinet and handed it to Diane. "What's different now?"

"They make the same stuff all the time, and the portions are too small."

"Last week you complained about the portions being too much and you couldn't eat it all." Diane shook her head. "Do you even remember what you ate for dinner yesterday?"

"I had a chicken breast, mashed potatoes and gravy with mixed vegetables. I remember stuff."

"You can't live on your own anymore."

"Yeah! Because you kids sold my house out from under me," Mom complained.

"We couldn't let you live there by yourself. It was the right thing to do," Diane insisted. "I love this wine. Can I take it home?"

"You can keep it," Emmy said. "Mom, do you want us to look for another place?"

"Hell no! I have my bingo friends, and we play cards in our rooms for money. I'm up fifteen dollars for the month."

Diane laughed then said, "One of these days you are going to get busted for gambling, Mom."

"What are they gonna do? Arrest me and throw me in jail?" Mom smiled. "Who's gonna drive me back to prison? I mean Sunrise Garden."

Emmy looked at Diane. "Rock, paper, scissors?"

"I'll take her home. Maybe I'll toss her out when we cross the river."

"Diane!"

"Just kidding, Mom," Diane said. "Maybe."

"Em, I'm going to head up to Midway to pick up Tom and Sherry." Kenny grabbed his keys and wallet on Saturday afternoon.

Emmy walked into the kitchen. "Would you ask them again about staying here tonight?"

"I'll ask them, but I know how they will answer."

Emmy walked over and kissed Kenny. "Yeah, they will stay with Uncle James and Aunt Nora."

"They are his parents."

"I can understand, but we have plenty of room."

"Em!" Kenny laughed. "Uncle James' house has five bedrooms. Tom and Frankie always had their own room."

"I know, but it's old and drafty."

"It's May, Em. It's not winter."

"Fine! But you better make sure they are here for Frankie's party. He turns forty tomorrow, and I want it to be a special day for him."

"You know Frankie doesn't like to be the center of attention. Not even at a party for him."

"Yeah, he wouldn't like the attention if it was his own wedding, or his funeral."

"Em!"

"Sorry, I shouldn't have said that." She kissed Kenny again. "Be careful. See you later."

After church the next afternoon, Emmy hosted a party for Frankie Hanna's fortieth birthday. Nothing too fancy. Frankie requested sloppy joe's and baked beans for lunch. His favorites. Emmy bought a cake and ice cream, and they had plenty of pop and water to drink. Kenny's parents arrived at the house shortly after their service at Faith Bible Church.

"Hello, Emmy, where is my grandson?" Mr. Colwell asked. "I want to spoil him."

"He's upstairs in his room, Dad. You might have to play cars with him."

"He sure loves to play with his cars and trucks." Mr. Colwell left the kitchen heading for the stairs.

"Emmy, is there anything I can do?" Elly Colwell asked.

"Not really, Mom. The sloppy joe stuff just needs to be kept warm. The beans are in the oven, and Aunt Nora is bringing potato salad. I thought we could have everyone fill a plate from in the kitchen and then sit wherever they want."

"Okay, but let me know if you need any help. Right now I will go spoil my grandkids."

"Oh, Mom, you should see the birthday card Isabella made for Frankie. Ask her to show it to you. It's so cute."

"I will. Are they upstairs, too?"

"Yes, but would you bring them downstairs soon?"

"Sure."

Mom Colwell smiled at the family photos on stairway wall and heard Kevin playing with his cars.

"Gra, this one is a police car. I can make it go fast."

Mom Colwell peeked into Kevin's room. *Carter, I'm glad you can still get down on the floor to play with him. My knees hurt too much to play with the girls like that.* She walked into the room Heather and Isabella shared.

Isabella noticed her first. "Me-maw! You're here." Isabella ran over to hug her grandmother.

"How are you girls today? Isa, I heard you made a card for

90

Frankie. Can I see it?'

Isabella picked up the card from the dresser. "I made it by myself, and I helped Heather make one, too." Isabella held up the card for Me-maw.

"This is so beautiful, Isa. Frankie will love it."

"I spelled Uncle Frankie all by myself."

"And you spelled it correctly. Good job."

"Mommy told me what letters to make."

Me-maw sat in the rocker and watched the girls play until Emmy called on the intercom.

"Mom, could you and Gra bring the kids downstairs, please. Everyone is here, and we're going to eat in a couple minutes."

"We'll be right down, Emmy." Me-maw stood up. "Did you hear your mother? It's time to eat."

Heather ran out of the room and dashed down the stairs.

"I'll walk with you," Isabella said.

"Thank you, Isa. Don't forget the cards for Uncle Frankie."

Isabella giggled and then grabbed the cards. "We have to tell Gra and Kevin Michael."

Me-maw stopped outside of Kevin's room and smiled. "Kevin, did Gra fall asleep?"

"We're just pretendin'. He's not really asleep."

"Is it time to eat, Elly?"

"Yes, come downstairs."

"Mom lets me bring three cars when I eat." Kevin picked up four and inspected them for a moment. "I'll leave this one here. It's an ab-u-lance, and I won't need it for now."

Everyone gathered in the kitchen, and Emmy said a prayer.

"Since it's your birthday, you should go first, Frankie," Emmy said.

"The kids can go first."

Heather grabbed a plate and held it up to Emmy. "I want two sloppy joes and beans but no potato salad. I don't like it."

"How do you know? You need to try it."

"I had some before and it made me sick. I threw up," Heather said as she frowned.

91

"This is different. Aunt Nora made it. You need to try some," Emmy insisted.

Heather looked up at Aunt Nora. "Are you Me-maw's mother? You look old."

Kenny regained the use of his voice first. "Heather! That wasn't very nice. You tell Aunt Nora you are sorry."

"Sorry," Heather muttered.

"It's quite all right, child. I do look a lot older than Elly, but I am her sister-in-law, not her mother."

"What does that mean, Daddy?" Kevin asked.

"Well, when Auntie Diane marries Uncle Brady, she will be my sister-in-law, and Brady will be my brother-in-law."

Emmy rolled her eyes.

"Is Uncle Tony your brother-in-law?"

"Well, sorta." Kenny looked at Emmy. "How 'bout a little help, Em?"

"No, you're doing great on your own." Emmy laughed. "You do realize Diane is already your sister-in-law, right?"

"Oh, yeah. I know."

"Is Uncle John your brother-in-law?" Kevin asked.

"He is for the time being. Mommy will explain everything later. Right now we need to eat."

Emmy walked over and kissed Kenny. "You are such a dork, but I still love you."

After lunch everyone gathered in the family room.

"We have presents for you, Uncle Frankie. I made you a special birthday card. Would you like to see it?" Isabella sat on the couch next to Frankie and handed him the card.

"Please," Frankie said.

"Heather made one, too." Isabella motioned for Heather to sit on the other side of Frankie.

Heather stood in front of Frankie, handed him her card and then ran over and sat with Me-maw.

Frankie looked at both cards for a moment without saying anything. Then he hugged Isabella.

"I love you, Uncle Frankie." Isabella snuggled close.

"I love you, too," he said as he sniffled.

Frankie opened the gifts with Isabella's help.

"Thank you for everything," he said. "I appreciate it all."

"Can we have cake and ice cream now, Mommy?" Heather asked.

"And we have to sing happy birthday," Isabella said.

"I promised we would wait until the other kids got here. They want some birthday cake, too."

Kenny called Tony's and Kristen's houses and told them it was time for cake and ice cream. Within five minutes the house was full of kids.

"Okay, let's sing now," Emmy said and started the song

Frankie held Isabella as she sang to him.

"You have to make a wish and blow out all the candles now," Isabella said.

"Will you help me, Isa?"

Isabella helped.

"That was easier than lighting forty candles," Kenny whispered to Emmy. He pointed to the four and zero candles.

"Ya think," she said. "Now all the kids need to sit in the breakfast nook to eat."

The moms helped the kids get situated and passed out slices of cake and scoops of ice cream.

"Is that enough for the kids?" Elly asked.

"I think they each have some. The rest is for the adults."

"Mommy, can we eat or do you have to pray again?" Heather asked.

"You can go ahead and eat. Try not to make a big mess."

A few minutes later Emmy listened to Isabella talking to all the kids.

"Uncle Frankie is Daddy's boss," Isabella said seriously.

"Why do you say that, Isa?" Emmy asked.

"Mommy! He's the boss because he tells Daddy which guitar to play."

Emmy grinned and said, "Oh, I see. He hands Daddy a guitar and tell him which song to sing, huh?"

"You're so smart, Mommy."

Chapter Ten

"We shouldn't be out too late," Emmy said to Sofia. "The rehearsal shouldn't take forever and then we're having dinner at the Barclay Country Club."

"Fancy, huh?" Sofia asked as she grinned. "We will be fine. Stay out as late as you want. I'm going to crash here tonight."

"Thanks," Emmy said. "Your wedding is only a month away. Are you getting anxious?"

"Not anxious, but I am getting excited. We've been planning the wedding for over a year."

A year? Wow! I'm glad I didn't have that long of an engagement. Emmy put a finger to her mouth. "Maybe I can talk Kenny into taking me somewhere so we can have fun."

"I heard that, Em. We're coming straight home."

"Dork," Emmy whispered.

Emmy rushed into the sanctuary at Crest Ridge United Nazarene. "Look, Kenny. They've already moved the chairs to make a center aisle and the platform is ready."

"Did you expect anything less, Em. It looks about the same as when we got married."

"I think we had more flowers." Emmy walked around the platform sniffing the floral arrangements.

"Em, I think those are just for tonight. The flowers for the ceremony won't be delivered until the morning," Kenny explained.

"I knew that." She made a face. "Hi, Dr. Behren, is anyone else here?" Emmy ran to greet him.

"I think you're the first to arrive, Em."

Fifteen minutes later, the entire wedding party lingered on the platform as Paula Kratzsky covered some last minute details with Diane.

"I think we're all set, Dr. Behren," Paula said. "Let's take it from the top."

Dr. Behren led Brady Robertson and his groomsmen onto the platform. They stood on the blue tape Paula had placed on the carpeting.

"All right, ladies. It's your turn." Paula started the

bridesmaids down the aisle. Emmy's turn came last since she was the matron-of-honor, and she practically ran down the aisle.

"Emily Olivia!" Mom hollered from her seat in front. "Will you pretend to be a lady for this occasion."

"Sorry. I'll go slower tomorrow."

"Why don't we try that again, Emmy?" Paula pointed to the back of the sanctuary.

"Fine!" *I know how to walk like a lady.* She skipped toward the back in her shorts and t-shirt.

"Now once more, please."

Emmy slowed down some.

"That was better, but you should go a smidge slower tomorrow, Em." Paula smiled but made sure Emmy knew she meant it.

The rehearsal continued without any mishaps. Emmy and Kenny practiced their song. Carson and Caden's part went without a hitch.

"That should do it," Paula said. "Anyone have any questions?"

Emmy raised her hand.

Diane rolled her eyes. *Why did I let her be a part of this?*

"Yes, Emmy." Paula glared.

"Can I wear my sneakers for the ceremony?" She held out a foot.

"You can wear bedroom slippers if you will walk down the aisle properly." Paula smiled though her voice was deadly serious. "Anyone else?"

No one else dared say a word.

"Diane, can I tell you something?" Emmy asked as they were about to leave the church.

"Give me a second, Brady. This won't take long," Diane said. She let Emmy lead her a few feet away. "What's on your mind?"

Emmy bit her lip for a moment.

"Tell me. We have to get to the country club," Diane said sternly.

"I told Father James about the wedding. I'm not sure he will

95

come, but he might. Will you be upset if he does?"

Diane took a deep breath and looked down at her sister. "It would have been better if you hadn't, but it's too late for that. I don't think it will matter. There will be so many people there that one more won't matter."

"I don't think he would come to the reception, but I thought he might like to be there for the ceremony. Do you hate me?"

"I could never hate you, Em. I might get frustrated with you at times, but that's because you're so... so... you."

Emmy grinned and hugged Diane.

"All right already," Diane said.

Emmy broke off the hug and stepped back. "Tomorrow is going to be an awesome day. You will remember it forever."

"Yeah, I hope so. Come on. We have to go."

Thirty minutes later everyone took their place in the private room at the country club.

"This is different than what I remember," Emmy said as she looked at the gold painted walls and intricate crown molding.

"They remodeled a couple of years ago," Kenny explained. "When were you ever in here?"

"I snuck in with Kristen one time. We got caught and they almost tossed us out. Damon Barclay saw us and saved our butts."

"Nice talk, Em."

"Do you know what we're having for dinner?"

"It's either prime rib or salmon. You had to choose, remember?"

"Right, I forgot. Look at that picture over there. The guy on the left looks like George Washington, but I don't recognize the other man."

"The other man is one of the original Barclays. I think his name was Claymore something Barclay."

"Cool!"

"The legend is that the cherry tree Washington chopped down belonged to Claymore Barclay's father."

"Is that for real?"

"I think it's a myth, Em."

"Why didn't Diane have the reception here?"

"Because there aren't any hotel rooms."

"Duh, I knew that."

Dinner took over an hour, and Emmy began to fidget.

"What's wrong, Em?"

"How much longer will this take? I want to check out the rest of the place. I want to go for a walk on the golf course."

"Be patient. This is Diane and Brady's time to be the center of attention."

"I don't want to be the center of attention," Emmy said. Then she bit her lip. "I really don't."

"I didn't mean it like that. I know you don't."

Her eyes sparkled as she asked, "Can we really go for a walk?"

"Em, what are you planning?"

"I thought we could have some fun."

"I don't think you're allowed to have fun on a golf course."

"Too bad. It would be exciting."

Kenny grinned then said, "We have lots of woods around our house. We could play there."

Not exactly what I imagined, but why not. She shrugged.

"Diane, you look so beautiful," Emmy stared at Diane's V-neck, A-line wedding dress and beamed. "Daddy would be so proud of you."

"Oh, hush. I feel like I'm ready pass out. I don't think I've ever been this nervous in my life." Diane looked in the mirror. "Can we open a window or something? I need some air, or a drink."

"There aren't any windows in here, Diane. This is a room for mothers to bring their children if they get too noisy during church. Don't you remember being in here with me when I got married?" Emmy fixed the bow around Diane's waist for the thousandth time.

"Stop that, Emmy." Diane pushed Emmy's hand away. "Easy for you to say, little sister. You're not the one everyone will be gawking at." *Why did I ever let you and Mom talk me into a big church wedding?* Diane gazed out at the sanctuary of Crest Ridge

97

United Nazarene through the Venetian blinds. "Who are all these people?"

"Who knows?" Emmy asked as she grinned. "All I know is Mr. Robertson rented out almost the entire Lincoln Hotel for guests. Mona told me some of them came from Europe, and one couple flew in from Australia. There are some important and powerful people here. I saw one couple that looked like they might be movie stars, and I saw two men dressed in uniforms. They looked like big shots."

"Brady knows some famous people, and Mr. Robertson is kinda important."

"If I see the movie stars at the reception, I'm gonna get their autographs," Emmy said.

"Whatever. How do I look? Do I look okay?" Diane checked the mirror again.

"You look beautiful," Emmy said. "Mom, doesn't she look beautiful?"

Mom glanced up from her chair. "You look more beautiful than ever. Are you pregnant again? I know you were when you married Craig."

"Mom! Do you have to bring that up today?" Diane shouted. "And I'm not pregnant." Diane turned to Paula. "Isn't it time for her to go sit down?"

Paula Kratzsky, the wedding coordinator, checked her watch. "Five minutes."

"Mom, please. Let Diane relax," Emmy said. "Let me fix your sleeve."

Diane looked at her three bridesmaids. Linda Brasel, Sally Glavine and Francine Dimasio. *I really think those peach colored dresses look perfect on you.* "Have I thanked you for doing this for me today?"

Sally patted her stomach. "It's a good thing you didn't wait until August. I would be too big to even waddle down the aisle."

Francine giggled as she flipped her long blonde hair over her shoulder.

Linda shook her head as she stared down at Francine. "Will you stop laughing like a schoolgirl. You're driving me nuts." Linda

98

checked her lipstick in the mirror and then sat down and sighed.

"I appreciate all of you," Diane said as she took Sally and Francine's hand.

"What about me?" Emmy asked and then giggled.

Diane rolled her eyes. "I never should have listened to you. I should have eloped. We could have been married in the Bahamas or somewhere."

"It's time for you to be seated, Mrs. Colasanti," Paula said. "The men will take their places, and then the bridesmaids will begin their easy stroll down the aisle. Remember, ladies, it's not a race."

"Got that, Emmy?" Linda said as she laughed.

"If you take too long, I will pass you up," Emmy said. *Why did Diane ever pick you? You complain about everything. I know you're Brady's cousin, but she could have picked one of her friends.*

"It's time to take your places, men," Dr. Behren said as he caught the signal from Paula.

Dr. Behren led the way out of the side room and across the platform. Brady smiled as he followed. Bennett Robertson led two of Brady's coworkers, Thomas Hawkins and Vaughn Millican. Mr. Robertson brought up the rear.

"My don't they all look so handsome," Emmy whispered to Diane. "Even the two older guys that worked with Brady."

"Ladies, listen to the music and don't forget to smile," Paula said as she cued Francine.

Francine giggled as she led the bridesmaids out of the room.

"Give me a break." Linda rolled her eyes as she adjusted her sleeveless dress a final time.

"Mom, is it time?" Carson asked. "This tie hurts my neck."

Caden squeezed his mother's hand.

"It's almost time. Let me look at you boys." Diane knelt to check out her two sons.

Emmy bit her lip and closed her eyes, but it didn't help. The tears began to flow.

"Em, why are you crying already?" Paula asked as she

wiped Emmy's tears before they ruined her makeup.

"I was thinking about Daddy. I wish he was here to see this."

"Are you going to cry like Auntie Em?" Carson asked his mother.

"I'm going to try not to, but I just might." Diane straightened Carson's tie. "You look so handsome."

"I'll hold your hand if you start to cry, Mommy," Caden offered.

"Emmy!" Paula jolted Emmy back to reality. "Get your butt moving," Paula ordered.

"Sorry, I'm going now."

Though she tried not to, Emmy walked faster than planned. She was only ten feet behind Sally when Sally climbed the steps to the platform.

Emmy grinned at Brady. "Sorry, I walked too fast."

"It's okay, Em," Brady whispered. "We won't remember fifty years from now."

"Okay, Diane, it's time." Paula started to adjust Diane's hair but stopped. "You look perfect."

"Are you ready, boys?" Diane moved into position with Carson on her right and Caden on her left.

The musicians began to play Mendelssohn's "Wedding March" and the crowd rose.

"Ready, men?" Diane smiled.

"Ready, Mom!" Carson said.

"Ready, too, Mommy." Caden clung to Diane's hand."

"Here we go..."

Carson beamed and Caden trembled as they walked Diane down the aisle and up the steps. She leaned down and kissed them both as they reached Diane's mark.

"Come on, Caden. We have to sit with Grandma." The boys scrambled down the four steps, hurried over to Grandma and sat on either side of her.

Emmy spotted Kenny sitting in the second row on the far left and smiled.

Dr. Behren started the ceremony and soon Emmy joined

Kenny to sing.

"Are you ready, Em?"

"As ready as possible."

Kenny touched his red tie, and Will Consoli cued the backing track.

Emmy looked up at Kenny and grinned. *I would marry you all over if I wasn't already married to you.*

Kenny sang the first verse to "I Will Be True To You," and Emmy joined for the rest of the song.

After the song ended, Tony Bertucci looked at Sloane. "Are we supposed to clap?"

Sloane rolled her eyes. "Go ahead. Just don't whistle."

After the clapping stopped, the ceremony continued and Dr. Behren whispered, "It's time for the rings and the vows."

Diane motioned to Carson.

"Caden, come on. We have to go stand with Mommy and Brady." Carson led his younger brother to the platform.

"Stand in between us, boys," Diane whispered.

Dr. Behren smiled and nodded to Emmy and Bennett.

Bennett handed Brady the ring Grandma Isabel Sandusky wore on her wedding day eighty years before and stepped back. Brady placed the ring on Diane's finger and recited the vows he had written for Diane and her sons. His voice rang out clear and crisp.

Emmy closed her eyes and listened. *Now I understand why Grandma wanted you to have her ring instead of her wearing it after she passed away.*

"Emmy," Dr. Behren whispered.

"Sorry, I was listening to Brady." Emmy handed Diane the ring and stepped back. She bit her lip, but once again, it didn't stop the flood of tears.

Diane's eyes never left Brady's as she recited her vows. She didn't cry nor waver as she held Brady's hand.

Diane, Brady and the boys moved to the candles.

"Is it almost over, Mommy?" Caden asked. "I'm hungry."

"We're almost through," Brady said.

The boys returned to Grandma's side, and Carson pointed at

Emmy. "Grandma, Auntie Em is still crying."

"I know. She's a big baby."

Carson grinned. "I'm going to tell you you called her a baby."

She will always be my baby, Carson. Patricia smiled.

"Bennett, would you switch places with me when we leave?" Mr. Robertson asked.

"Sure, Dad." Bennett looked over at Emmy. "I understand."

Dr. Behren concluded the ceremony by introducing Diane and Brady to the crowd. The music began and Diane and Brady rushed out of the sanctuary.

Emmy moved over and looked up at Mr. Robertson. "Did you pull a fast one? I'm supposed to be with Bennett."

"I promised your grandfather I would always be there for you," Mr. Robertson said. "I don't think anyone will mind if I walk out with my favorite godchild."

Emmy grinned and said, "I always knew I was your favorite."

"Hush, or else I will have to ground you."

Paula organized the reception line. Emmy stood by Bennett and Mr. Robertson and listened as they talked to some of the dignitaries.

"Emmy," someone behind her said.

She turned and grinned at Father James. "You made it. I didn't see you in the crowd."

"It was a beautiful ceremony. I don't want to cause any fuss, so I'm going to sneak out."

"Thanks for coming. I'll talk to you soon," Emmy said.

As the line of guests waiting to see Brady and Diane appeared to be infinite, Emmy kept Carson and Caden amused by singing and dancing with them. Every once in a while, she would also talk to the guests. Usually after receiving a frown from Diane or Paula.

Emmy and the boys stopped for a moment, and Caden looked up at her. "Grandma called you a big baby because you were crying."

"She did? Do you think I'm a big baby, Caden?"

102

"No, but I think you cry because you miss Grandpa."

"I do miss him. I think about him every day, but one day, hopefully a long, long time from now, I will see him again in heaven."

Caden thought about it for a moment. "I will see him, too, because I love Jesus just like you."

"I hope so. I hope so," Emmy said, hugged Caden and then began singing another song.

Later, a white limousine delivered Diane and Brady to the Lincoln Hotel, and they entered the large room right on time. Paula checked her watch and high-fived her assistants, Louise and Thurman.

"You guys are the best," Paula said. "Now let's try to keep to the schedule, so these people can have a good time."

Thirty minutes later, as they sat at the main table, Diane grabbed Brady's arm and pointed.

"What is it, Diane?"

"Look at her. Isn't she just a goof?"

Brady laughed as he watched Emmy leading a group of kids in a line as they circled around the tables as the DJ played "The Pied Piper" song. "She is amazing."

"I'm so glad she is still just a big kid. I love her almost as much as I love you," Diane said and then kissed Brady.

"Hey! Aren't you guys supposed to wait until the guests tap on their glasses?" Bennett put an arm around his older brother.

"We're just getting warmed up." Brady grinned and kissed Diane again.

Emmy joined the rest of the wedding party.

"We're glad you're back. For a moment I thought you were going to sit with all the kids," Diane teased.

"I was doing a good deed for all the parents."

"And what might that be?"

"I've been trying to wear out the kids so they will fall asleep early."

"Hah! The kids have more energy than the rest of us," Diane said. "I hope I can make it to midnight."

"You have to stay awake tonight, Diane." Emmy said and

then giggled. "This is your wedding night."

"I'm gonna smack you when I have the chance."

Paula made sure everything ran according to plan. The meal. The toasts. The first dances. Everything ran with the precision of a Swiss timepiece.

"Are you going to dance with me, Emmy?" Kenny asked after Emmy took a break from dancing with her girlfriends.

"I might as long as you don't try to get too friendly."

"And here I was hoping to sweep you off of your feet and take you home with me tonight," he said. "Do you think I have a chance?"

"Hmmm, I'll see. Are you a good dancer?"

"I'm not Fred Astaire, but I won't trample your feet." He looked down at her feet. "Emmy! When did you change shoes?"

"When I got in the reception line." She lifted a foot and moved it in a circle. "Do you like my new tennies? They match my peach-colored dress."

"You are such a goof, but I still love you."

Mary Michaelis and Sofia Romina corralled Emmy by the open bar just before nine.

"We're going to take the kids home. Do you want to say good night first?"

"Yes, please. I hope they haven't been to fussy."

"They have been darlings. They have been dancing and singing to each other the whole night, but I can tell they are winding down."

"Did Tony and Sloane leave already? I don't see him."

"They gathered up their brood and left twenty minutes ago. We're going to take your kids, Kristen's two and Caden home. Carson wants to stay until the end and Diane agreed. He is staying with you, right?" Mary asked.

"Yes, and I promised him a dance tonight."

Emmy and Kristen said good night to the kids, and John assisted in loading them into the minivans.

"Would you mind dancing with this old man, Emmy?" Mr. Robertson held out a hand.

"I would be honored, sir." Emmy grinned as she curtsied.

They danced as the DJ played the waltz Mr. Robertson requested.

"Do you remember this song, Emmy?"

"It sounds familiar. What is it?"

"It's the 'Blue Danube' by Strauss. It's the song we danced to at the Santiago's party."

"I remember that night like it was yesterday. I didn't know I knew you before, and I was afraid of you. I didn't know you would turn out to be the kindest and most generous man in the world."

Mr. Robertson twirled Emmy around and thought of her grandfather.

"What are you thinking about, Mr. Robertson?"

"Your grandfather. For some reason whenever I share a special moment with you, my thoughts always turn to Joseph." He smiled at Emmy. "He would be so proud of you and Diane."

"He would be grateful to you for all you've done for us," Emmy said.

The "Blue Danube" ended but right away another tune began to quietly fill the air. Emmy stopped. "Can you hear that?" she asked Mr. Robertson.

"Hear what, Emmy?" He tilted his head.

"Nothing." Emmy glanced at Diane, put her hands over her head and began dancing like a ballerina. Diane smiled as they both listened to "Clair de Lune." The song from Emmy's music box.

Later, Diane's bridesmaids cornered Emmy. "Where are they going on their honeymoon? Diane won't tell us. Do you know?" Linda asked for the group.

"They are flying to the Virgin Islands in the morning."

"Are the boys going?" Francine asked while holding a glass of champagne.

Sally poked Francine in the side. "Why would she take the kids on her honeymoon?"

"I didn't think she would, but you never know with Diane." Francine giggled and then spilled her drink.

Linda took a deep breath. *I'll be glad when this night's over. Hopefully, I'll never see you again.*

"Grandpa Bill and Grandma Mona are keeping the boys,"

Emmy said. "The boys don't know it yet, but Grandpa and Grandma are taking them to Disney World the second week. Diane and Brady are going to meet them there for a couple days."

Sally watched Brady with Carson. "The boys really like Brady, and I can tell how much he cares for them."

"I don't think they will have any trouble adjusting to living in Brady's house," Francine mentioned. "Diane gave me a tour the other day. Can you imagine living in a place like that?"

Emmy bit her lip. "There are other kids living in the neighborhood. Carson is good friends with Peter Bertucci, and Caden is the same age as my girls and Zachary Randolph and Noemi Bertucci. They all get along."

"I'm sure there will be some disagreements. It always happens with kids. Sometimes the parents get into it with each other," Sally said.

Emmy grinned. *I don't think the parents are going to fight. We are all close friends.*

Emmy did dance with Carson until Kenny cut in. "Would you mind if I dance with this beautiful young lady, Carson?"

"Aw, Uncle Kenny, I was having fun."

"Tell you what. I'll wait until the next song, but you owe me."

"Deal!"

Diane and Brady disappeared at midnight.

"Where's Diane?" Emmy looked around.

"They slipped out a couple of minutes ago, Em."

"Shoot! I wanted to tell her good night."

"Em!" Kenny dragged out her name. "Promise me you won't call her tonight."

"Why would I do such a despicable thing?"

"Let me see your hands," Kenny frowned. "I knew you had your fingers crossed."

"Party pooper!" Emmy made a face. "She probably wouldn't have answered."

Chapter Eleven

"How has your trip been, Diane? How was the water and your own private beach?" Emmy called after Diane and Brady made it to Disney World.

"Oh, you know. Just another honeymoon in paradise." Diane yawned as she leaned back into Brady's arms as they sat outdoors.

"You're a stinker. How was the sex? Did you guys do it all the time?" Emmy rolled over onto her stomach on her bed.

"Would you like to answer that, Brady?" Diane asked.

Emmy yelled, "Is he right there? Did he hear what I asked?"

"Right here, Emmy, and I can say..."

"I don't want to hear it. Forget I ever existed. I'm going to join a convent and never speak to another soul." Emmy put her head under a pillow. "I can't believe you told Brady."

"How are things back in SoHam, Em? Anything exciting happen while we were away?"

"My friends Cameron and Lindsey Frees had a baby on the twentieth," Emmy said and then paused.

"What did they have, Em?" Diane shook her head. *Such a goof.*

"Oh, they had another daughter and named her Nadine Carol."

"I like that. It's a lovely name."

Emmy giggled and then said, "I like it better than Eloise Mae. Elly Mae. Get it?"

"Em, you do realize your mother-in-law's name is Eloise, right?"

"I know, but it fits her better."

"Anything else you want to share before I hang up?" Diane asked.

"I guess not, but don't hang up yet. I want to talk to you."

"Caden! No running by the pool, please," Brady cautioned.

"Sorry, Brady, I forgot," Caden said.

"How's Mom doing?" Diane asked.

107

"She's doing good. She's complaining about the food, which means she feels good."

"Yeah," Diane scoffed. "If she doesn't feel all right, she's doesn't complain about anything. She just mopes."

"Isa came down with a cold, and she gave it to Kevin Michael. They are better but not totally well. Few more days and they'll be fine."

"Em, is there something important you want to tell me but are afraid to?"

"Kinda," Emmy whispered.

"Tell me before I strangle you through my cell phone."

"Fine. Caden said something at the wedding that surprised me," Emmy said but then waited.

"And you will tell me soon, yes?"

"We were talking about Daddy, and he said I missed him. I told him I do but I will see him again someday. Caden said he would too because he loves Jesus."

"He actually said that?" Diane sat up and put her feet on the warm patio.

"He did. He actually thought about it, and that's what he said."

"He is such a good boy."

"I thought maybe you and Brady might be more open to bringing them to church than before. I'm not trying to shove religion down your throat, but it would..."

Diane interrupted, "We have talked about it, Em."

"Really? You have?"

"Yes. Brady used to go to church when he and Bennett were young."

"I didn't know that. Did his parents take them?"

"Mostly his mother, but Mr. Robertson would go when he could."

"So you guys are really going to bring the boys to church?" Emmy asked as she pumped her fist.

"Yes, but don't get all nuts on me," Diane said. "We aren't going to turn into religious fanatics like you."

"I don't mind being called a fanatic."

"There's just one problem, Em." Diane covered her mouth to suppress a laugh.

"What might that be?" Emmy asked excitedly.

"There is this one singer who tries so hard, but just doesn't float my boat if you know what I mean."

"Oh, I know who you mean. I've been trying to persuade Chase to kick Kenny off of the worship team, but he won't. Maybe if I tell him that Kenny is driving people away, he will get a backbone and do what's right."

"You are such a goof, Em."

"I know. I knew you were trying to tease me, so I turned it on Kenny."

"We are flying home Sunday afternoon, so we won't make it to church this week, but we will try to be there the following Sunday."

"Good! I'll hold you to that."

"Anything else before I hang up?"

"My birthday is coming up pretty soon," Emmy said.

"Yeah, so?"

"Don't you want to buy me a present? Do you want to know what I want?"

"No, I hadn't really given any thought to buying you anything." Diane laughed.

"You're still a stinker. I'm hanging up now."

"Bye, Em. Say hi to Kenny and the kids."

Diane had been back from her honeymoon just shy of two weeks when she called Emmy shortly after nine on Friday morning. "Happy birthday, Emmy. Are you guys doing anything special today, and I don't mean in bed."

"Thank you, Diane, and we are doing something special."

"What?"

"Kenny got the Envoy back from the shop on Tuesday, and the guy there told him we should trade it in because we are going to be pouring money into fixing it. Something about the transmission. It's getting old, I guess. It's a 2003."

"What are you going to do?"

"Kenny talked to a guy at that new BMW dealership..."

"BMW! Are you crazy? They cost a fortune," Diane said and then laughed.

"Ha! Ha! Are you trying to be like me."

"Sorry, but I can't see you guys forking over the money to buy a BMW. Not a new one. What model?"

"It won't be a 5 series whatever like you drive. No way are we spending that much. I want another SUV. Kenny took an X3 out for a drive, and he liked it. We're going to run over there this morning. Could you watch the kids for me? It is my birthday, remember?"

"Yeah, you can bring them over whenever. Maybe I shouldn't have moved so close to you. You're always going to use me as a free babysitter."

"Which reminds me. Sofia's wedding is tomorrow, and they're going on a week-long honeymoon. I might need some help with the kids."

"I suppose, but it will cost you."

"You know I will always watch the boys for you, and if you guys have a baby, I will spoil her."

Diane grinned though Emmy couldn't tell. "I might take you up on that sooner than you think."

"Diane! Are you pregnant already? I thought you guys were gonna wait."

"We did wait until our wedding night. We waited for the prior month."

"Such a sacrifice," Emmy said.

"Okay, so I'm late, and I took one of those home pregnancy tests, and I'm pregnant." Diane snapped her fingers. "Just like that. I think I got pregnant on our wedding night."

"I'm so happy for you. I can't wait to tell everyone."

"Hang on a minute, Em. Let me go to the doctor first before you announce it to the world."

"Fine, but we have to pick out a name soon."

Diane laughed. "You are going to drive me nuts, Em. "Would you mind terribly if me and Brady pick out the name?"

"Oh, I suppose I'll let you."

"Do you have any color in mind, Em?" Kenny asked as they drove the Envoy to the BMW dealership later that morning.

"Not white or black. Maybe gray. Blue would be all right. Bronze."

Kenny laughed. "So pretty much any color other than white or black, huh?"

"Yep!"

"You will have to take it out for a test drive. It handles differently than the Envoy."

"How so? Don't you just step on the gas and make it go?" Emmy asked.

"Very funny." Kenny eased to a stoplight and the Envoy died. "Come on, old girl. Make it to to dealer."

"I'll pray for the transmission," Emmy said and then closed her eyes. "Please, Lord, keep the Envoy running until we can get to the dealer. Then it can fall apart."

Kenny shook his head and sighed.

The Envoy recovered enough to make it to the dealer's lot.

Two hours later, Emmy drove her new BMW X3 home. She settled for gray.

"This is fast, Kenny." Emmy floored it from a traffic light. "Plenty of horsepower. I'm glad I got the turbo."

"You will have to let the police officers know you have a new car. I bet you get pulled over before the end of the week."

"I might get pulled over, but I bet I don't get a ticket." She put a finger to her mouth.

Kenny shook his head. "You won't get away with it forever, Em."

"Oh, come on! You know I drive like a soccer mom if I have the kids in the car. I don't drive as recklessly as before."

"Do you want me to show you how to use the navigation system?"

"Later. For right now I just want to know how to start and stop it."

"Did you pay attention at all when that salesman went over the details?"

"Nope! I figured you would listen. I just care that I can fit the kids in back, and that I can go from zero to sixty in five seconds." She punched it again. "Did I mention Diane is knocked up already?"

"Really? Are you kidding?"

"She peed on a stick."

"You have such a way of putting it so delicately, Em."

"I hope she has a girl."

"Maybe Brady would like a son." Kenny cringed as Emmy blew past a squad car going the opposite way. "Did you happen to notice that squad car?"

"I saw it. They can have more than one baby. Diane is still young enough to have a couple more kids."

"Do you have their names chosen already?" Kenny turned back to face the front. "The squad car kept going."

"Don't be silly! I'll let Diane and Brady pick out the names," she said. "I'll just offer some sisterly advice."

"You do have to let them name their own baby."

"I will... just as long as they choose a name I like." Emmy turned the corner. "Wow! This thing does handle better than the Envoy. Cool!"

"Soccer mom, my butt!"

"Ow! That hurts, Mommy!"

Emmy sat on the edge of Heather's bed while she tried to get the tangles out of her daughter's hair. "Hold still, Heather, and it won't hurt as bad."

"Mommy, is Sofia still going to be our nanny?"

"Yes, Isa. She will be gone for a week, but then she'll be back."

"Where is she going?" Isabella sat next to Emmy. "Is my hair curlier than Heather's?"

"I think it might be, baby." Emmy tugged on a stubborn tangle. "Sorry, Heather, but this... there I got it."

"It didn't hurt too much," Heather said. Then she ran over to the mirror. "I like all my curls."

"Why won't Sofia be here?" Isabella asked.

Emmy started combing Isabella's hair. "She and Niles are

112

going on their... uh... they're going on a vacation together."

"Are they going to Disney World?" Isabella asked. "Can we go with them?"

"I'm sorry, Isa, but they need to go alone. She and Niles are getting married like me and Daddy."

"That's why Sofia likes to kiss him," Isabella said with a grin.

After the ceremony that afternoon, the girls waited in the reception line with Kenny and Emmy while Kevin played in the nursery with other young children.

"Mommy, doesn't Sofia look like a princess?" Isabella held Emmy's hand. "She looks beautiful."

"Yes, she does." *I love the way you have your hair done with those braids wrapped around.*

When Sofia saw the girls, she held out her arms. Heather and Isabella rushed forward.

"Mommy said we can't go on vacation with you because you want to kiss Niles," Heather said.

Sofia looked up at Niles and grinned. "I'm afraid Mommy is right, but I will be back in a week."

"We will miss you, Sofia. You look like a princess." Isabella touched Sofia's gown. "I will get married when I'm older, but I won't let any boys kiss me."

"You might change your mind, Isa." Emmy hugged Sofia and whispered, "You look so beautiful. Have a good time, and we'll see you in a week."

"Congratulations, Niles," Kenny said while shaking his hand. "Come on, girls. We need to let other people talk to Sofia and Niles.

"I'll see you soon." Sofia waved as Heather and Isabella skipped away.

After church Sunday morning Mary Michaelis waved to Emmy and then walked across the sanctuary to talk.

"You look like you are about to burst. What's going on?" Emmy asked.

"You won't believe it, but Jonah asked me out to dinner

113

tonight," Mary said and then clapped her hands.

"Jonah Galves?"

Mary nodded.

"Well, it's about time. Did you say yes?"

"Of course I did." Mary bumped her arm against Emmy.

"I'm teasing. Where are you gonna go? You have to go to The Hungry Lion. I could call Matt Sullivan and let him know you're coming," Emmy said and then waved at Kristen and Sloane.

"Emmy! You don't have to make it into a big deal. We're just having dinner together."

Emmy nodded. "Uh-huh, and the sun will rise in the East again tomorrow."

Mary squinted her eyes as she stared at Emmy. "The sun always... never mind. Let's sit down."

"Do you know what you will order?"

"Not yet. I want to see what he orders. If he orders something inexpensive, I don't want him to spend a lot of money on me." Mary saw Eli looking at her and pointing to his watch. "Give me a minute."

Emmy smiled at Eli and turned her attention back to Mary. "You are worth it, but the burgers at the Lion are reasonable. The steaks are kinda expensive, but they are big. Tony and John can wolf them down, but not me. I love their patty melts."

"I don't often eat steak," Mary said.

"What are you gonna wear? A dress or skirt, or something casual like jeans?"

"What would you wear?"

Emmy put a finger to her lips. "You should wear those black jeans and that new sleeveless top you bought."

"But those jeans are rather tight." Mary twisted her long hair around a finger.

Emmy grinned. "Exactly!"

Jonah picked Mary up at her house at six fifteen. Mary's twenty-one-year-old brother Darian towered over Jonah as he opened the door.

"Hey, Pastor Jonah. How's everything? Come on in. Mary should be ready soon. She's changed clothes twice."

114

"Darian! Don't embarrass your sister." Cora Michaelis pointed to the couch. "Make yourself comfortable. Dahlia, run upstairs and tell Mary Jonah is here."

Dahlia rose from her chair. "Okay, Ma." She walked over to the bottom of the stairs and hollered. "Mary! Your date is here."

"That wasn't what I asked." Cora shook her head.

Dahlia stomped up the stairs as she ran.

Jonah took a seat on the couch and Dylan Michaelis, Mary's father, closed his book and stared at Jonah. "Where are you going? What time do you expect to bring Mary back? She does have a curfew."

Cora rolled her eyes. "Dylan, will you stop that. You know perfectly well they are going to the Lion and Pastor Jonah will have Mary back at a respectable hour."

Jonah gulped and rubbed his hands together. *I'm not sure who I fear the most. I'd hate to have to explain to Mrs. Michaelis if I brought Mary home too late.*

"Say, Pastor Jonah, is the church going to have a basketball league this year?" Eli, the younger brother, asked.

"We have talked about it and it's likely to happen. We have had several planning sessions already."

"Yes!" Eli pumped a fist.

"You guys played ball in high school, right?" Jonah asked.

"Varsity ball for three years at Lincoln High," Eli said. "Darian made the conference first team his last two years."

Jonah relaxed since they were talking about sports. "We are definitely going to have a basketball program for the kids up to junior high. I'm not sure what we will do for high school. The basketball league will be for adults. I suppose high school kids could participate. We're looking at having eight teams from churches in the area. Not necessarily all from SoHam."

"Eight teams would work."

"It would allow for a fourteen game season. Two games going on at once with two time slots. We would have a tournament for the top four teams at the end."

"Sounds like a good plan. Did you play ball in school?" Eli asked.

"Baseball and football. Too short to make the basketball team," Jonah said. "Your sister is almost as tall as me."

"Did I hear something about me?" Mary asked as she walked into the room.

Jonah jumped to his feet and smiled. "Hi, Mary. Are you ready to go?"

"Just need to grab my purse."

"Have a good time, dear," Mrs. Michaelis said. "We'll leave the porch light on for you."

Mary understood that Pastor Jonah would say good night to her on the porch and not come inside. He had to earn her mother's trust just like any other date.

Since Jonah and Mary would see each other at the church almost daily, they knew quite a bit about each other. Mary expected him to be polite and chivalrous. He opened every door for her whenever they were at church, and he followed through on their date. They were seated in a booth by the pretty blonde hostess. They ordered Cokes and tried to avoid getting caught looking at each other. Mary would glance at Jonah, and if he looked at her, she would bury her eyes in the menu.

"Do you see anything that interests you?" Jonah asked.

"What are you having?" *If I know how expensive an entree you plan to order, I will know what I want.*

"I hear the burgers and fries are outstanding."

"I've heard they have the best patty melts in SoHam."

The waitress returned with their drinks and took their order.

Mary smiled shyly at Jonah and after a momentary silence, they both started to speak at once.

"How was your afternoon?"

"Sorry, Mary, you go first."

Nothing remarkable had happened since the morning service, so that conversation thread fizzled out.

"Did I surprise you when I asked you out?" Jonah asked and then sipped his Coke.

"Can I be honest?"

Jonah nodded. *Oh, no, did you only agree out of friendship? That's not why I asked.*

116

Mary wrapped her hair around a finger. "I've been secretly wishing you would ask me for a date."

"You have?" Jonah's eyes widened. "For real?"

"Yes. In fact, if you hadn't asked me today, I might have taken the initiative and mentioned having lunch sometime."

"We can still have lunch," Jonah said. *Shoot! I hope I didn't jinx it by assuming too much.*

"During the school year I have a forty minute lunch break."

"I can pretty much take a lunch whenever. Dr. Behren is rather flexible. He doesn't expect us to report what we do every second of the day."

"I don't have as much freedom. I have to be in my classroom." Mary grinned and swirled the ice in her drink with the straw.

"What are you doing this summer since school is out? Should I know this already?"

"I haven't been doing a lot. I try to help Ma around the house as much as I can. It's not easy to take care of five other people."

"Do you see the twins much?"

"I run over to the house once, sometimes twice, a week. They aren't in school either. Sofia won't be living at the house since she's married."

"How did you like being a nanny?"

Are you really asking how I like children? Do you want to know if I want kids of my own? Mary took a sip of her Dr Pepper. "I thoroughly enjoyed being a nanny. I love Emmy's kids almost as much as I would love my own." *That should answer your question about babies.*

"I grew up in a house with four brothers and three sisters. Obviously, we couldn't afford a nanny, but Mom and Dad managed somehow. I'm in the middle, and all of us have either gotten college degrees, or are in the process."

"That's quite an accomplishment. I earned my degree, and I don't have any students loans hanging over my head."

"I've heard horror stories of students owing over a hundred thousand dollars and aren't able to even find jobs."

117

"I thank God everyday for His blessings." Mary smiled as the waitress brought their dinner.

"Anything else I can get you tonight?" the waitress asked.

"No, thank you," Jonah said.

"Enjoy your meal."

"Should I offer thanks?" Jonah asked.

Mary nodded and closed her eyes as Jonah prayed.

"Could you pass the ketchup, please?" Mary asked. *Maybe I shouldn't have ordered anything with onions.*

Jonah finished his burger and fries and patted his stomach. "That was delicious. Are you going to finish your patty melt? Wasn't it good?"

"Very good, but I want to save the rest. I don't want to stuff myself."

Later, the hostess held out the phone for her boss. "Hey, Matt! There's a call for you."

"Who is it?" he asked while walking toward her.

"Someone named Emmy."

"I'll take it in my office," Matt said with a smile as he turned around and hurried toward the back. "Hello, Emmy, how are you?"

"I'm fine. How's Annie doing?"

Matt caught Emmy up on Annie's condition.

"So another month or so, huh?" Emmy said. "Can I ask you for a favor, Matt?"

"You can ask, and if I can, I will grant it."

"Do you remember my nanny? Mary Michaelis. She's kinda tall compared to me."

"Everyone is tall compared to you... except Annie, but I remember Mary."

"She is having dinner with one of the pastors from church. It's their first date."

Matt stepped out of his office and looked out into the dining area. "I think I see her."

"Would it be too much to ask for you to let them have their dessert on the house? I'll send you a check to cover it."

"I would be happy to do that, Emmy, and you don't need to

118

pay for it."

"Are you sure? I can stop by and pay you."

"I appreciate the offer, but there's no need."

"Thanks, Matt. Please say hi to Annie for me."

"Will do."

"Do you have room for dessert, Mary?" Jonah eyed the picture of apple pie on the front of the dessert menu.

"I could split something with you, but I'm too full to eat one myself."

They ordered apple pie a la mode.

The waitress dropped off the check and a takeaway box for Mary. "No, hurry. I'll take it whenever you're ready."

Matt watched and waited until Jonah picked up the check and had an opportunity to look at the total. He casually walked over.

"Good evening, Mary, do you remember me?"

She looked up and smiled. "Hi, Matt. Of course I remember you. Oh, this is Jonah Galves. Jonah, this is Matt Sullivan. He owns the Lion." She waved a hand to encompass the entire restaurant.

"It's a pleasure to meet you, Jonah. Did you enjoy the meal?"

Jonah nodded. "That's one of the best burgers I've eaten in a long time, and I eat a lot of burgers."

"I'm glad you enjoyed it." He looked at the box on the table. "How was your patty melt?"

"Delicious," Mary said. "Emmy claims they are the best in the city, and I would agree. I'm saving the rest for later."

"Tonight is on the house, but you can leave a tip if you like. I'll tell your waitress." Matt picked up the check. "I hope to see you both again."

Matt walked away before Mary and Jonah could even protest.

"What was that all about?" Jonah stared at Matt as he walked away.

"I'm not sure, but I think I might know." Mary dug her cell phone out of her purse and called Emmy. "I'm going to smack her when I see her next."

Emmy answered after two rings.

"Did you talk to Matt Sullivan and tell him we were coming here tonight?" Mary asked sternly. "And don't you dare lie. No crossing your fingers and pretending that makes it all right. Did you?"

"I might have talked to him, and I probably kinda sorta mentioned this was your first date. Please don't be mad. I asked him if he would let you guys have dessert for free."

"He did more than that, Em. He gave us everything on the house."

"He did!?"

"Yes, he suggested we could leave a tip, but he wouldn't let us pay for our meal."

"Matty surprises me at times. He can be very generous with friends. I guess he figures the best publicity is word-of-mouth, and he will benefit in the long run."

"I thought it was very generous, and we'll leave a bigger tip than normal."

"Okay, but not too much. That would negate Matty's gesture."

"I understand. I know my family eats here once in a while. I'll tell Da to bring them more often."

"Are you mad because I told Matty about your date?"

"No, I'm not mad," Mary whispered.

"So, how's it going? Are you going home, or somewhere else?"

Mary rolled her eyes. "I'm not telling. Good night, Emmy."

Chapter Twelve

Randy Braun spotted Emmy in the hallway outside of the music suite at church. "Hey, Emmy, got a second?"

"Sure, Randy. What's up?"

"Thought I'd let you know that Christopher and Maddy are going to be here today."

"For real?" Emmy grinned.

"He called me last night and told me. He asked if we could join them afterward at The Hungry Lion. I told him Vanni, Stephen and I had a prior engagement. Are you and Kenny doing anything after church? Would you be able to eat at the Lion?"

"We don't have any plans as far as I know. I'd have to see if Mary and Jonah could watch the kids. Sofia isn't working weekends anymore."

"I'd appreciate it if you guys could."

"I'll talk to Kenny and Mary and text you."

"Thanks, Em. See you later."

Emmy walked into the main room of the music suite, saw most of the worship team members but not Kenny.

"Chase, have you seen my husband."

"Which one, Em?" Chase grinned while stroking his beard.

"The dorky one. I need to ask him something, and when are you going to get rid of that ridiculous beard? It has too much gray in it."

"He's in there talking on the phone." Chase jerked her thumb toward his office. "Yvonne likes my beard."

"Thanks and Yvonne is only humoring you."

Emmy walked into Chase's office and sat down while Kenny finished his call. She picked up the photo of Chase, Yvonne and their two daughters. *This is new. The girls are growing so fast, and looking more beautiful all the time.*

Kenny hung up. "What's up, Em?"

"Would we be able to join Christopher and Maddy for lunch at the Lion? Randy asked if we could. He and Vanni are doing something."

"Christopher is bringing Maddy here?"

"Yeah. He must really like her a lot."

"Who will watch the kids? My parents?"

"Only if Mary and Jonah can't. I thought they might be willing. You know how much the kids love her, and they like Pastor Jonah, too."

"I'm willing if you can talk Mary into it."

Emmy saw Mary and Jonah outside the sanctuary in the crowded foyer between services and asked about babysitting.

"Love to, Em. Should we take them to your house?"

"You could take them there. Kevin should go down for a nap this afternoon. I'm not sure how long we'll be gone."

"Don't worry. Jonah and I will make ourselves at home."

"Please don't open the door to our bedroom if you show him the house. It's a total mess, and I didn't make the bed."

Mary laughed. "I don't plan on showing him your room. Who knows what might be laying around."

"You're so funny, but it's probably true." Emmy watched the doors for Christopher and Maddy. Her eyes sparkled as she saw them enter. "Talk to you later. They're here." She hurried over to Christopher without sprinting.

"Hi, Emmy. We made it."

Maddy held onto Christopher's arm as she gazed at the throng of people.

"It's so good to see you here. I hate to leave you, but I have to get back to the music suite. If you save a couple of seats, Kenny and I will sit with you."

Maddy nodded and her lustrous thick blonde hair bounced.

"I suppose you can sit with us, Emmy," Christopher said while grinning wickedly.

"Gee, thanks a lot." Emmy wrinkled her nose at him.

After the service, Emmy walked to the foyer with Christopher and Maddy. "Did you like Dr. Behren's message?"

"He is an amazing speaker," Maddy answered. "I thought he made his points clearly and without repetition. I dislike speakers who reiterate the same idea and lose their focus."

"My thoughts exactly," Emmy said. "Would you guys like to have lunch with us? We're going to The Hungry Lion."

"Emmy, Randy told us he asked you guys about lunch. You don't need to make it seem like your idea." Christopher shook hands with someone he didn't recognize.

"So you don't mind if we horn in on your date?"

Maddy laughed. "I haven't heard that expression since my grandmother passed. And we don't mind one bit."

They were seated in a booth at The Hungry Lion, ordered Cokes and loaded chili fries as an appetizer.

"Emmy, I have three of your CDs at home. The studio ones. When are you going to release a new project?" Christopher asked.

Emmy glanced at Kenny. "We're working on one, but it's taking longer than we expected."

"I'm surprised you guys sing with the band at church. Doesn't that distract people's attention? I'm talking about junior high and high schoolers," Maddy said.

Kenny smiled. "I'll answer that before she calls me a dork. People in SoHam don't see us as anything special like they do in other places. I'm not bragging. It's just the job I do puts me in the spotlight. If I could make music and play for people without the media attention, I would."

"Don't worry, dear. That might happen if you guys don't put out some new material soon." Emmy smiled but she was serious.

"Can we expect a new Fridays At Five CD soon?" Christopher asked.

"It should be out the first week of September. We're finishing up Emmy's project, and it should come out in October," Kenny explained. "What are you going to order, Em."

Way to change the subject, Kenny. "I'm going to order a patty melt."

Christopher sensed some tension between Kenny and Emmy over the CDs. *Don't tell me there is trouble in paradise.*

Everyone concentrated on eating when the food arrived. Emmy only ate half of hers and asked for a takeaway box.

"How does the future look at Liberty Manufacturing?" Kenny asked after everyone declined the waitress' offer of dessert.

"It is becoming more difficult to compete with the foreign labor markets..." Christopher and Maddy talked about the company and their roles for ten minutes.

Emmy listened but soon grew bored and daydreamed about being on stage in front of her fans. *I don't care what you say, Kenny. I'm going on tour when the CD is released. Nelson has me booked for six straight weeks.*

"Do you envision yourself performing twenty years from now?" Maddy asked Kenny.

"Not really. None of us are thinking that far ahead."

"You really should plan for your retirement," Maddy said. "It's never too early to start."

"We are investing our money carefully," Kenny said.

A loud crash drew their attention across the room as a busboy dropped a tray of dishes.

"We really should be getting home. I don't want Mary and Jonah to spend their entire afternoon babysitting," Emmy said.

"Thank you for the dinner." Christopher mentioned after Kenny covered the check and a tip.

"Not a problem. Will we see you guys at church again?"

Christopher and Maddy looked at each other.

"Maybe not every week, but you will see us again." Christopher smiled and put an arm around her waist.

Emmy drove the girls to school on Wednesday and came home to check her email.

"Yes!" He pumped her fist. "Hey, Kenny! Are you up here?" She didn't hear him so she hurried to the basement and found him in the control room. "Annie had the baby last night. Matty sent an email instead of calling in the middle of the night."

"Is Annie okay?"

"She is, and they named him Keyshon Matthew. Matt said Mace gave them his blessing since he and Erin may not have any more kids. Oh, and Mace is the new head basketball coach at Roosevelt High. I saw that on Facebook last week."

"I'm happy for them."

"Me, too. Annie has always been a friend even if we don't

really hang out together."

"They have normal lives, Em."

"Will we ever have a normal life together, Kenny?" She sat in one of the other leather chairs and faced him.

"If you mean normal like living paycheck to paycheck like most people, then no. Even if we never make another dime from music, we will never have to worry about money. Are you concerned because of what Maddy mentioned last Sunday?"

"I trust you to handle our money."

He smiled and then laughed. "You still check the sale papers, Em. At the rate you spend money, we will be broke in ten thousand years."

She thought about mentioning her CD and the tour but got up and went back upstairs instead. She walked into the kitchen, smacked the countertop and walked right back down to the studio. She marched in, placed her hands on her hips and announced, "I'm going on tour in October for six weeks. I just wanted you to know, and I will not cancel it."

"Em, I've known about the tour since April."

"No you haven't! How could you know?" She slumped into the same chair.

"Do you really think you could plan a tour without word getting out?"

"Yes."

"Well, you can't. There are too many logistics to planning a tour. Even one that only lasts six weeks."

"So you will let me go?"

"Yes, Emmy. I won't stop you. I promise the CD will be ready in time."

"Oh, Kenny," she sobbed.

He held out his arms and she climbed onto his lap. He kissed her forehead. "I love you, too."

"Will you help me put a band together?"

"Do you mean a band to do the tour with you, or a more permanent one to record with down the road?"

"Both."

"You're a goof."

She got up and sat on the edge on the mixing desk.

"Is there anyone from The Only Hope you want to keep in the new band? I know most of the guys have other priorities now." He scooted closer and pulled her away from the console.

"Sorry, did I accidentally erase something?"

"No, but you were too close."

She moved back to the chair and put a finger to her mouth. "I know there are probably better drummers out there, but I'd like to keep Bobby O'Connor in the band."

"Why is that?"

"Well, because I know him, and he's fun to have around. I need someone in the band to be kinda like a confidant. You know, someone I can talk to and vent when I need to unwind."

"Kinda like Ryan was originally and then Adam?"

"Yeah, Bobby is still a little young to be in a leadership role, but we get along well."

"He's not that bad of a drummer, Em."

"A touring drummer, right?"

"Yeah, he wouldn't be my first choice for the studio."

"Duh, you didn't use him at all for my CD."

"He needs more experience. Let's talk about this tomorrow. I have a couple of guys in mind who might be interested. They have studio experience and are looking for a new band."

Kenny and Emmy spent the next week jamming with and interviewing several musicians. The two men Kenny wanted Emmy to meet fit perfectly into their idea of her new band. Over the weekend, she and Kenny sat down to make their final decisions.

"Bobby fits in with the other guys, and he's willing to travel."

"You can use Bobby as your drummer."

They discussed the other musicians and made their choices. They called the guys, and they all accepted.

"We can have the legal stuff drawn up this week," Kenny said. "You can keep using the old warehouse to practice if you want. You can borrow the guys from the Friday tech crew. Most of them should be available for the tour."

"I can't wait to start rehearsing," she said while grinning. "How many songs should we have ready?"

"More than you think. I'd plan for getting thirty songs ready. Most of the tracks from the new CD can be played live. You should pick out the best ones from your older studio projects. Don't use any of the cover songs. You should stick to your originals."

They planned to start rehearsals at the warehouse at ten Monday morning. Kenny scheduled the crew.

"I'm so excited and my stomach is full of Monarch butterflies." Emmy said as Kenny drove to the warehouse in the Gordon Hill neighborhood of SoHam.

"You know which specific butterflies are in your stomach, huh?"

"Monarchs are my favorite, so I always choose them."

Kenny shook his head. He pulled into his assigned spot. He keyed in the security code, and they entered the 55,000 thousand square foot building.

"This is one of the best investments we ever made." Kenny waved a hand at the building Fridays At Five began using, and eventually purchased from Jeff Rawlings' father, back in 1995.

"You've certainly got your money's worth out of it," Emmy said as she spotted Nelson Grapella, her manager, and waved. Fridays At Five stored all of their gear in the warehouse when not on the road.

"Is anyone here yet?"

"You're the first to arrive, Emmy." He checked his phone for the time. "You're thirty minutes early."

"I didn't want to be late and have the new guys think I was some kind of diva."

Emmy smiled at Will Consoli and the Belanger brothers; members of the Fridays At Five tech team. She saw a half dozen other crew members.

"Are you really going to let me use all these guys?" She asked as she bit her lip.

"Why not? They're on salary and just sitting around getting

127

fat and lazy." Kenny smiled. "I want this tour to be the best you've ever done."

One by one the new band members drifted in.

Bobby O'Connor arrived with a bag of drumsticks and walked over to Emmy. "Where is everybody?"

"They'll be here soon." Emmy nudged him. "You better make sure that kit is set up the way you like."

"Yes, boss!" he saluted.

Kenny spotted Jared Daniels carrying a guitar case in each hand and walked toward him. "Need a hand?"

"Thanks, but I got it, Mr. Colwell." Jared grinned as his glasses slipped down his nose.

Kenny shook his head. "You are only calling me that because it embarrasses me."

"Plus, Mary calls you that when she wants to tease you."

"I forgot you know her from North Park. Did you have any trouble getting in the building?" Kenny glanced over his shoulder as Bobby pounded on the drums.

"No problem. Does that code have some significance?"

"It's Emmy's birthday."

"Get out! I thought she was still a teenager."

"Please don't tell her that. She gets on my case because I have a few gray hairs."

Jared followed Kenny to the stage and waved at Bobby.

Christian Becton and Micah Hurst chatted about breakfast as they entered together.

"Are you ever going to learn not to burn the pancakes?" Christian smacked his roommate on the arm.

"I like them extra crispy." Micah wore a cloth beret and a long coat even though it was August. "Where are your guitars?"

"I brought them over last week and left them here."

"All of them?"

"Yeah, all six. Did you see how many guitars Kenny used last week?"

"I saw. I'm glad I can use this bass for just about everything." Micah lifted the case with his only bass guitar inside.

"You might want to spring for some new strings."

128

"Hey! These are only a few years old."

"Exactly." Christian waved at the other guys.

"Hey, Mr. Hollywood. You made it," Bobby shouted. "Land any starring roles over the weekend?"

"I had two lines in that movie, Bobby. I'm a musician not an actor."

Everyone turned as Quinten Matthews rushed in with a case in each hand. "Sorry! Am I the last one here? I forgot my flute and had to go back. Then I got mixed up and ended up a mile away. I had to stop and get directions at a gas station. They didn't know anything about this warehouse or Gordon Hill. Who is he?" Quinten only stopped talking because he dropped his car keys.

"Gordon Hill is the name of the neighborhood," Kenny explained. "I don't think he's a real person."

Emmy smiled. *This is going to be a riot. All of these guys are really talented, but they're all low key and not high maintenance.*

Fifteen minutes later, after tuning up, the guys studied their chord charts.

"Is that a B flat?" Micah asked.

Christian checked the chart for the title song from Emmy's *Strength* CD.

"Yeah. I would not have expected that, but it sounds good."

Kenny plugged in and got everyone's attention. "Are you ready, Em?"

Emmy grabbed her wireless Shure microphone from the stand. "Let's get this show started." She wiggled a finger at Bobby, and he counted off the song.

They ran through five songs before stopping.

"Kenny, these guys are really good. We jammed together a little bit last week, but this is their first real rehearsal and they are already tight."

Kenny set his guitar in its stand. "For real, Em. I don't even need to play. I'm just going to hang out and listen."

"Good, because I think you missed a key change in that last song," she teased.

Chapter Thirteen

On Tuesday, September 6 2011, the Steward Music Group released the first new material from Fridays At Five since 2008. *Riders Of The Lonesome Trail* blazed a new sound for the band, according to the full page ad in *Billboard*. While many of the band's fans remained mystified, or at the very least uncertain, by the latest CD, critics lauded the project as an adventurous return to a childhood journey. The band held their usual press conference at the Steward Music complex, but this time Jeremy Lenhart surprised the reporters.

"If there are no more questions," Stephanie glanced around the room. "I will turn this floor over to Jeremy."

The reporters, sensing something different, ceased all conversation and focused their attention on Jeremy.

"I will get straight to the point. It is my intention to leave Fridays At Five at the conclusion of the summer portion of the Riders Tour. I have been extremely blessed to have been a part of the band from the inception. However, the desire to spend more time with my family and to pursue a solo project have prompted this difficult decision."

"How long have you guys known this?" one reporter asked.

"Jeremy informed us several months ago," Jeff said.

"Have you hired a replacement?"

"Adam Vicini formerly of The Only Hope will be touring with us this summer as an extra keyboard player. Unless something drastically changes, he will replace Jeremy in the band," Kenny announced. "We've known Adam for quite a while, and we didn't audition anyone else."

"Isn't that rather risky?"

"We don't think so. Adam is a talented musician and will bring fresh ideas to the band."

One reporter said, "Come on, Dave! That sounded like a canned response from a politician running for office."

The room exploded with laughter.

Dave shrugged. "It happens to be true. Maybe not about us old guys needing fresh ideas, but he is talented."

The reporters fired questions at Jeremy for another ten minutes before Stephanie ended the session.

Kenny shook Jeremy's hand as they left the room. "You will always be a part of this band. If you decide at some point you miss us too much, we can always keep two keyboard players."

"Thanks, Kenny. I don't plan on leaving SoHam in the near future, but we do plan to buy another home somewhere. Probably Arizona or New Mexico. Somewhere warmer than Illinois."

"Are the winters getting to be too much for you to handle, old buddy?" Jeff put an arm around his longtime friend.

"I might miss the snow, but I won't ever miss the extreme cold."

The next morning a caravan of minivans left the Bristol Ridge development and headed west much like the covered wagons of old. Emmy led the way with Heather and Isabella singing "Victory In Jesus" in back. Kristen drove her minivan with Sloane in the front passenger seat. Peter and Dotty sat in the very back on booster seats and tried to spot a red car. Zachary and Noemi squirmed in their car seats and tried to hit each other with any object they could reach as their mothers chatted and ignored the commotion. Diane's new Odyssey played the caboose. Carson and Caden sat quietly.

Several minutes later, Emmy pulled into the parking lot of Crest Ridge United Nazarene. Kristen and Diane parked next to her.

Emmy jumped out, hit the button to open the side doors and smiled. "Everyone who wants to start kindergarten today needs to disembark."

"Oh, Mommy, you're being silly," Heather said.

"I don't want to go to kindergarten." Isabella stayed in her seat.

Sloane shook her head as she opened the door to let Peter, Dotty and Noemi out. "Are you trying to be ridiculous, Emmy?"

Kristen laughed as she unbuckled Zachary's car seat. "She doesn't have to try. It comes naturally."

"Everyone wait right here!" Sloane hollered in her

authoritative teacher's voice.

Carson helped Caden out of his car seat.

"You have to get out, Isa. Mary will be disappointed if you don't come to class."

"Okay, but if I don't like any of the other kids, I'm going to walk home."

"I'm sure you will make new friends, and besides, Heather, Zach, Noemi and Caden will all be in your class."

"What if there are mean boys in my class?" Isabella reached for Emmy's hand.

"I'll keep an eye on you, Isa," Carson said. "I'm in fourth grade, so I can protect you."

"Everyone line up right here, and we will walk together," Sloane ordered as she held out her arm to indicate the place to line up. She waited until all the kids were in a line and said, "Okay, follow me!"

Heather, Zachary and Noemi rushed past Sloane and raced each other to the front doors.

"No running!" Sloane yelled.

Isabella held Emmy's hand. Caden held onto Diane's hand with a death grip. Carson, Peter and Dotty ambled along behind Sloane.

"I spotted a red car before Dotty. I won the game," Peter said as he shifted his backpack.

"I don't care. I wasn't really trying," Dotty replied.

Isabella spotted Mary Michaelis standing outside the front door, let go of Emmy's hand and dashed forward. "Mary! Mary! I'm going to be in your class."

"I'm so glad." Mary held out her arms and hugged Isabella. "I miss you so much."

Tony and John concluded their warm-ups and waited on the sideline for their opening game of the year to begin. The Atlanta Falcons provided the opposition.

Tony looked into the stands and nudged John. "I can see Emmy. She appears to be whistling. Kristen is holding her hands over her ears."

132

"I pity the people sitting in front of her. She may be tiny, but she can whistle louder than any of the guys on the team."

Emmy waved her arms after she stopped whistling. "I can see Tony standing next to John and they're looking this way, Krissy."

"Is it safe to move my hands now?" Kristen asked.

"I stopped whistling." Emmy poked her in the side. "Can you believe how warm it is? It's in the upper seventies. I'm glad I wore shorts."

"You might need your jacket later, Emmy. It can get rather chilly by the lake," Amber reminded her.

"Who needs a tasty beverage?" Derrick asked. "I could go for an ice cold beer."

Kristen eyed him suspiciously. "Are you buying?"

"Yes, dear sister, I'll buy this round."

"I want a beer." Emmy hollered as she swayed in time with the music playing over the PA.

Kristen and Amber ordered Cokes.

"Is anyone coming with me?" Derrick stepped out to the aisle.

"I'll go," Emmy volunteered.

"You better hurry back or you'll miss the kickoff." Amber stood up to let Emmy slip past.

"What is Kenny doing today?" Derrick wondered.

"He's home finishing up my CD."

"Are you getting excited about your tour, Em?" Derrick grabbed her hand as he threaded his way through the crowd.

Emmy slipped through the crowd like a running back making cuts at the line of scrimmage. "I am, but I'm also feeling a bit guilty."

"How so?"

"I feel like I'm escaping in a way. Kenny and the kids won't be with me. I'll be gone for six whole weeks and won't see them except on the computer."

"And you feel guilty."

"Yes, Your Honor, are you going to sentence me to jail for being a bad mommy?" Emmy moved in front of Derrick as they

133

waited in line with hundreds of other people.

"Maybe I will put you on probation for six months." He put his hands on her shoulders. "You are a wonderful mommy, Em."

She leaned back against him. "Do you mean that, or are you just being kind?"

"I've known you for too many years to lie to you."

"I love my family, but I need to sing. Kenny used to say God had a plan for my life. I never believed him at first, but as I've grown older, I'm beginning to understand it more."

"You're trying to tell me I need to obey God, huh?"

"Yes, we all do. If I don't obey, I will be failing Him."

"I've never known you to fail at anything. You can accomplish whatever you decide to try."

"Are you accusing me of stubbornness?"

"What? You stubborn. I would never..."

"Yeah, yeah. I'm still as stubborn as when you first knew me."

They moved ahead in line.

"You were more stubborn than a donkey who refused to move, but at least I could pick you up and carry you if I needed."

"You are such a comedian."

By the time they returned to their seats, the Bears were up by ten points.

"How did they score?" Emmy plopped into her seat next to Kristen.

"John caught a pass up the seam with one hand against a two deep zone. He hurdled one defender. Stiff-armed another and made an awesome spin move around the middle linebacker."

Emmy stared at Kristen.

"What?"

"For someone who never knew a thing about football when we met, you are quite knowledgeable now."

Kristen grinned and flipped her shoulder-length blonde hair over her shoulder with an exaggerated motion. "I know more than you think, but I still don't understand what those posts are that stick up in the air."

Emmy shook her head and rolled her eyes.

Mary brought Jonah back to her parents' house for Sunday dinner. They talked about the church and the school on the way.

"Hey! Where have you guys been?" Eli asked when Mary and Jonah walked into the living room. "We've been back for ten minutes."

"Never you mind, little brother," Mary said. "Who's winning?"

"Bears are up by seventeen already."

"Do you need help, Ma?" Mary left Jonah in the living room with her father and brothers.

"Would you mind peeling some potatoes, dear? I would ask Dahlia, but she is swamped with homework, or so she claims."

"Not at all. The guys are watching the game. Emmy went to Soldier Field today. That's why she missed church."

"I wondered why she didn't sing."

Mary and her mother talked as they prepared the meal.

"It's time to eat," Mary announced later.

Darian turned off the TV and shrugged. "Ma's rule. No TV while we eat."

"Sounds like a reasonable rule." Jonah walked over to Mary and kissed her quickly.

Dahlia grinned.

"Oh, hush." Mary made a face. "It's not like you haven't ever kissed a boy."

That remark drew their father's attention, and he frowned at his fourteen-year-old daughter.

"Don't look at me like that, Da. I haven't let any boys kiss me."

"Maybe not, but I heard you flirting with Kieran Lochlin last week at church," Eli teased.

Dahlia punched Eli's arm. "I did no such thing."

"Now, children, let's not argue at the table. Father, would you offer grace."

The men caught the end of the Bears' game after the meal. The Bears won 30-12.

"They looked pretty strong today," Darian said.

"No doubt. The defense gave up some yards but kept the

135

Falcons out of the end zone," Eli added.

Mary and Dahlia helped Ma in the kitchen.

"I swear I will murder Eli if he says a thing to Kieran," Dahlia warned. "I did not flirt. We discussed a lab project for school."

"Yeah, sure," Mary said with a grin. "I know how it goes."

"Oh, you do, huh?" Dahlia made a kissing motion to tease Mary.

"Enough teasing. Please, help me load the dishwasher so I can take my Sunday afternoon nap." Ma opened the infrequently used machine. "How is your relationship with Jonah going?"

Dahlia snorted and nearly dropped one of the china plates. "Do tell, big sister. Should I start looking for a dress suitable for a wedding?"

"I think it might be getting more serious," Mary replied to the question and then poked Dahlia in the side.

Ma finished filling the dishwasher and closed the door. "He is a lovely man, dear. I only wish he had more Irish blood in him."

"Oh, Ma! I can't help that I've fallen in love with someone who's not Irish."

Ma froze in place. "That sounds very serious."

Mary put a hand to her mouth. "I just realized how I feel about him. I haven't told him yet."

Dahlia made the kissing motion again.

Mary frowned and waved a fist.

"You probably should because I'm absolutely sure he feels the same way about you. Now you run along and watch the second football game with your young man." Ma smiled and pushed Mary out of the kitchen.

Chapter Fourteen

"Before I close the service today, I would like Cathy to join me on the platform." Dr. Behren wiped away a tear as she rose and began walking.

Emmy grabbed Kenny's hand and squeezed it hard. "I have a bad feeling about this. Something's not right. Do you know anything?"

Kenny shook his head. "I don't have a clue, Em."

Dr. Behren put his arm around his wife's waist. "This is not easy for me to tell you, but here goes. I have resigned my position as senior pastor..."

The entire congregation gasped as if they were one.

"What did he say?" Emmy looked up at Kenny and bit her lip."

Kenny patted her hand. "Let's listen, baby."

"... effective as of now. I will be here next Sunday, but..."

"No! This can't be," Emmy sobbed. "He can't leave."

Dr. Behren continued to explain about the university president of his alma mater passing away quite unexpectedly. He explained about a crisis in a building project.

The congregation buzzed as the announcement filtered through their minds.

"What are we going to do, Kenny? Who will replace him?"

Dr. Behren continued to talk.

"I'm not sure, Em, but I believe God knows. This is not a surprise to Him, and I'm sure He has the perfect man for the job."

Although the service was over, no one left. People gathered in small groups to console each other. Grown men wept openly. Women held onto each other to keep from crumbling.

Kenny looked around the sanctuary and spotted Chase and Yvonne near the front talking with Tyler and Liz. "Come on, Em. Let's see if Chase can tells us anything." Emmy let herself be pulled along as she used a tissue to jab at the river of tears flowing down her cheeks.

Chase saw them coming. "I'm so sorry, Emmy. This must be quite a shock for you."

Emmy nodded but couldn't speak. She and Liz held each other.

"Did you know?" Kenny asked.

"Dr. Behren called a special meeting of the ministerial staff and board members on Tuesday and told us. We were as shocked as everyone here." Chase waved a hand to encompass the entire sanctuary.

"Has the board begun to consider a replacement?"

"Ron Smith talked to Dr. Schofield after the meeting. Apparently, we might be on our own for a month or two."

"I want Tyler to take over," Emmy whispered as she looked up at him and hung on even tighter to Liz.

Tyler shook his head. "I'm not ready to take over a church of this size."

"What will happen to the staff?" Kenny asked.

"Normally the staff would resign along with the senior pastor, but Dr. Schofield advised us not to in this situation. He feels that will provide some stability," Chase answered.

"I didn't think Dr. Behren would ever leave. Certainly not like this," Yvonne said. "Of course, this wouldn't have happened if that other man had not passed away."

"Where did Dr. Behren go? He and Cathy left right away."

"They needed to take off for Indiana. He's actually starting his job tomorrow. I guess there is some terrible financial mess, and Dr. Behren is hoping to resolve it."

Kenny, Chase, Yvonne and Tyler talked more about the situation.

Emmy and Liz sat down on the front row of seats, clung to each other and prayed together.

Gradually, people walked out of the sanctuary. Many of them with dazed expressions.

Emmy and Liz stood up and hugged.

"God will provide," Emmy said. "Of that, I am certain." She looked at Pastor Tyler.

Tyler saw the look on Emmy's face, shrugged then said, "You have more faith in me than I do."

Dr. Jaren Schofield flew to SoHam from Denver on Monday morning. He drove to the church to meet with the ministerial staff. The men got on their knees and prayed for nearly an hour about the situation. The Holy Spirit intervened and came down upon them like a mighty rushing wind. By the end, everyone was convinced God would provide for every need and the meeting changed 180 degrees. Now instead of bemoaning their fate, the staff vowed the not let the church stumble or take even one small step backward. Dr. Schofield met privately with Pastor Benson.

After a short discussion, Pastor Benson said, "I appreciate the offer, but a man must know his limitations. I came here because Dr. Behren needed someone to keep the administrative side of things under control. My strength is organizing behind the scenes. I have never been a great speaker. I would drive people away if I had to preach every week. I hope you understand."

"I can certainly understand. You need to take the position in Kansas City." Dr. Schofield patted Russ on the back.

"We have been praying about it for over a month and were fighting against the call. Now I know we are supposed to go back to Kansas. We have been here for four years, but it is time to leave."

"God knows who He wants to lead this church. It is up to us to pray and allow Him to reveal His choice."

Emmy had just returned from taking the girls to school the next morning when her cell phone rang.

"Is this a bad time, or can you talk?" Father James asked.

"I need to check on Kevin Michael. Can I call you back?"

"Certainly. I'm off duty for the rest of the day. Unless the Bishop shows up," he joked.

"You're a real riot. I'll call you back."

Emmy made sure Kevin was fed, dressed and left him in his room playing with his cars and trucks.

"It's me," she said. "Did you have something important to tell me?"

"Not really," Father James said. "I haven't talked to you for a while, so I wanted to make sure you were still alive."

139

"Sorry, but I've been busy, and since you don't have anything important to tell me, I have something to tell you."

"And what might that be?"

Emmy explained about Dr. Behren resigning.

"I see. It was rather sudden and unexpected, correct?"

"Yes, I assumed he would be there for twenty years or more," Emmy replied. "I'm not sure who will replace him. When you left Kansas were your parishioners sad?"

He chuckled and said, "No, they were glad to see me go."

"Come on. Be serious for once."

"Just like in other situations, there were people who didn't want me to leave and others who told me not to let the door hit..."

"Yeah, I know the expression. I doubt if there were more than a handful of people who didn't like Dr. Behren. Mrs. Thompkins complains about everyone and everything."

"We have several of those at St. John's," Father James said. "I try to ignore them, and if they come to confession, I give them a more severe penance than other people."

"You are so bad," Emmy said. "I'm sad because he's leaving, but I have complete faith God will provide the right man for the job."

"Are you sure? That sounded rather like something you say because it's expected."

Emmy bit her lip before answering, "Oh, hush. I worry about stuff sometimes rather than depend on God. I'm human. Will you forgive me?"

"Yes, child, but you need to visit your brother more often as your penance."

The church board met Monday evening and reviewed a short list of candidates for the position. They decided not to waste any time and interviewed three men during the week. On Friday the board met again.

Roger Goldman addressed the group. "Unfortunately, none of the men we interviewed are right for our church. This is too important a decision to make hastily. I suggest we continue the search, and God will provide the right person."

Dr. Behren returned on Saturday afternoon to begin preparation for his final Sunday. Pastor Tyler led the Saturday evening service as he had for the previous year and a half.

"I didn't see Dr. Behren here tonight," Emmy said.

Liz nodded. "Tyler said he didn't want to be a distraction. Like that would be the case."

"In a way I'm glad tomorrow is his final Sunday."

"Why is that, Em?" Liz asked as they walked out of the sanctuary, through the hall and back to the music suite.

"Because I would have been on tour and missed it if he was here one more week. I suppose that's kinda selfish on my part." Emmy sighed as she opened the door for Liz. "In some ways this is easier than when Dr. Ausland left. This is like a quick death."

"Emmy!" Liz made a face. "That's horrible."

Emmy waved her hands. "No, I mean it like this. Dr. Behren won't be here for weeks with us knowing he's leaving. He will just be gone. Poof." Emmy made a motion like a magician. "Would you rather have a family member suffer a long death and the family has to suffer alongside, or would you rather have a loved one pass away in their sleep at night?"

"Are you thinking about your father?"

"Actually, I was thinking about my grandpas. Grandpa Sandusky had cancer for almost two years and Grandpa Colasanti died rather quickly."

"I suppose I would choose the quicker death." Liz thought about Grandpa Lindower.

"Do you realize how much the Saturday night service has increased in size?"

"I don't think about it, I guess." Liz braided her hair. "How long will you be gone?"

"Six weeks without coming home for even a day."

"Maybe by the time you get back, we will have a new pastor."

"That would be great. I hope the church board doesn't take forever to find the right man. It's never good for a church to be without a pastor for long."

"Do we have to go to church today?" Emmy asked. "Can't we just stay home so I won't have to say goodbye and end up bawling like a baby."

Kenny held her shoulders and kissed the top of her head. "Do you really want to?"

"No, of course not, but I hate goodbyes."

"It's not like he's moving to the other side of the world like Dr. Ausland. He will be in Indiana. Maybe you could schedule a concert at the university one of these days."

"Are you still mad because I'm leaving on Wednesday?"

"Let's not talk about that today."

"Let's get ready. Sofia and Niles will bring the kids back after the first service. Three hours is too long for them to be there. I think Pastor Jeremiah teaches the same lesson for both services."

Emmy and Kenny joined the other worship team members in the music suite. Kenny saw Ross Knapp tuning up in the corner and walked over.

"Hey, Ross. How's it going?"

Ross Knapp put his pick in the strings of his guitar and shook hands with Kenny. "Great! It's been a good week at work. You?"

"Busy. The kids are in school so that helps."

Ross nudged Kenny's arm. "Hey, can I talk to you for a second?"

"Sure."

"Let's use the production room."

They walked into the adjoining room Chase used to produce the video announcements.

"What's on your mind?" Kenny closed the door.

"I know Heidi and I haven't been here as long as some people," he paused.

"You guys have been here for what? About five years, right?" Kenny asked.

"Almost to the day. Our first Sunday was October of 2006. Doesn't seem like that long ago."

Kenny waited for Ross to speak.

"Do I play too loud? I heard someone complaining that the

guitars are too loud." He shook his head. "I don't want to play if people are complaining."

"Ross, you don't play too loud, and besides, it is the guys in the booth who really determine how loud the guitars, keyboards, drums, whatever."

"But if people are complaining..."

"I learned a long time ago that some people will complain even if they were born with a golden spoon in their mouth."

"What?" Ross laughed. "I've never heard that expression."

Kenny shrugged. "I know you are a perfectionist and want everything to be done with professionalism, but we can't worry about what one or two people might say."

"So I'm not too loud?"

"Not in the least."

"Thanks." Ross shook Kenny's hand again. "How do you think Emmy will do today? She really likes Dr. Behren."

"Emmy wears her emotions on her sleeve. She never hides them or bottles them up. She will bawl like a baby today, but she'll get over it. She was like that when Dr. Ausland left and when Paul and Lynette Jefferson moved away."

"I heard she has a new CD coming out soon."

"Tuesday. Then she leaves for a six week tour on Wednesday."

"Oh, that's right. Heidi said something about Pastor Chase juggling the lead vocals schedule for a while." Ross opened the door and they rejoined the rest of the team.

"Where have you been? I was looking for you." Emmy approached rapidly with her hands on her hips.

Kenny whispered to Ross, "Something's up. She looks upset."

"I'd say," Ross said. "I'm out of here."

"I need to talk to you." Emmy grabbed Kenny's hand and pulled him back into the production room and slammed the door.

"What did I do now?" Kenny asked with a grin.

Emmy stomped her foot. "This is serious!"

"All right. I'm listening." He put a hand on the wall for support.

"Do you remember when Pastor Ausland left the church bought him a new van?"

"I remember."

"When Paul and Lynette left we bought them a new van."

"Yes," he nodded.

"Why aren't we doing anything for Dr. Behren?" Her voice rose. "And I mean anything! I heard that we're not doing anything special. We're not giving him and Cathy any gift at all."

"Where did you hear this, Em? Who from?"

"I heard some of the older people talking. I'm not sure, but I think they're on the board. I think that sucks big time!"

"I don't know what to say, Em. What can I do about it?"

Emmy plopped down onto a metal chair. "I don't know, but I am so upset." She began to sob.

Kenny knelt in front of her and put his hands on her knees. "We can always buy them a new van ourselves after you get back."

She tilted her head and stared. "For real? Two months down the road we just hand them the keys and say sorry we didn't have a chance earlier."

Kenny dropped his head and stared at the floor.

Emmy leaned forward and rested her head on his shoulder. "I'm sorry, baby. I shouldn't let it bother me. It's out of my hands. I need to trust that God has the situation under control."

They heard a knock on the door.

"Come on in," Kenny said.

Chase entered. "You guys okay?"

"I'm fine now, Chase. Is it true that the board isn't giving Dr. Behren a new van, or anything?"

"It is true that the church isn't buying a van, but I wouldn't go so far as to say they aren't doing anything."

"Can you tell me?"

He sat down next to her. "I really can't, Em. I'm not on the board, remember? I'm one of the staff. I don't make those decisions."

"So, it's possible the board is doing something special?"

"Have you ever known the church to not take care of us. The staff, I mean. I guess it applies to people in general. If the

144

church sees a family in need, they do something to help."

Emmy bit her lip. "I'm sorry for being a big baby. I'm all right now. We should go over the songs."

By the close of the second service, Dr. Behren was drained emotionally. He ended his message and prayed for the church. As Dr. Behren prayed, Ron Smith slowly made his way to the platform with a wireless microphone in his hand. Dr. Behren finished praying and opened his eyes.

"Before we go... is this on?" He tapped the microphone. "Before you all go, the board asked me to make this presentation."

Emmy tapped Kenny's knee. "I knew they wouldn't forget!" She smiled and her eyes sparkled.

"Who is that?" Christopher asked Emmy.

"Mr. Smith. He's the church treasurer. He and Aunt Doris have been members since the very beginning."

"Aunt Doris?" Christopher looked puzzled as he tilted his head.

"I'll explain later."

Ron Smith continued, "We talked about how to honor you for your eight years of service to the church. Jim Rosek wanted to buy you a new motorcycle, but we didn't. You don't need a new van, or other vehicle. We didn't have a lot of time to decide, so we came up with this." He held a card up. "This isn't a going away card. It's a... um... let me take it out and read it to you. Where are my glasses?" He found them in his suit jacket pocket. "I'll skip down to the good part. It says something about a hundred thousand dollar endowment for the church's school in your honor." The congregation gasped. "And the board decided to rename the educational unit... Dr. Dave Behren Hall."

The congregation rose to their feet. Yvonne Hillman presented Cathy Behren with a large bouquet of red roses.

Dr. Behren smiled and shook Mr. Smith's hand. "Behren Hall. I like the sound of that. Wait till I see Jim Rosek. We're supposed to take a trip around Lake Michigan one of these years."

Emmy stood up like everyone else but didn't clap. Didn't cry. Didn't say a word. Simply stood there.

"Em, are you all right?" Christopher asked. "Why aren't

145

you clapping? Everyone else is."

"Huh? Did you say something, Christopher?"

"Are you all right?"

"I'm fine." She smiled. "I just thought of something."

"Thoughts are a wonderful thing, Emmy."

"Will you excuse me? I need to talk to Kenny." She took Kenny's hand and pulled him out a side door and into the hallway.

"What's up, Em?"

"I know you didn't provide all the money for that endowment thing for the school, right?"

"I gave the church the same as I did for the vans," he admitted.

"The church needs money to keep the school going, right?" Emmy started to walk away but stopped suddenly and Kenny bumped into her. "Sorry, I'm just pacing so I can think."

He backed up a step to give her room. "It's not free, Em." Kenny watched as she paced back and forth. "What's going through that pretty head of yours."

She walked up to him, looked into his eyes and said, "I can't tell you right now." *I have to talk to Derrick and maybe Sara would be able to help. Mr. Robertson would know how to do it.* "I have an idea, but I have to talk to some people first. Will you trust me?"

"Of course. I always trust you," he said noticing a sparkle in her eyes.

Chapter Fifteen

"Does the title *The Carriage House Sessions* have any significance?" one of the reporters asked at Emmy's press conference.

Emmy bit her lip. "I suppose I can tell you. I wrote pretty much all of the songs in the old carriage house at my in-law's house. I would take the kids over to see... their grandparents, and I would go out to the carriage house and work. I thought it made a good title."

The next reporter held up a copy of the CD. "Emmy, I've read the lyrics, and I have to admit, I really like them. I'm not a religious person, but these lyrics are deeper and more thought provoking than the typical praise and worships songs which can be so repetitive. Was that intentional? Are you moving away from the type of songs on your earlier projects?"

"When I first became a Christian, I needed to learn... how should I put this? I began to learn much like a child does. Everything was new. Fresh. Now that I'm a little older..."

"You still look like a teenager, Emmy!" someone shouted from the back.

Emmy giggled for a moment. "Thank you, but you need to see an eye doctor. Where was I? Oh, I'm older and hopefully wiser. I'm digging deeper into my Bible and reading devotional books. When the kids let me." She laughed. "I suppose the lyrics are bound to be more thought provoking. At least I hope they are. I'm not saying I won't record another praise and worship CD sometime. I still love to sing those songs, too."

Kenny and Stephanie Grachan listened to Emmy from behind the platform.

"Kenny, it's amazing. She used to be so shy and deathly afraid of these press conferences. Listen to her now. She's like a pro. Have you been teaching her how to handle these events?"

"Not really, but she does have more experience. She realizes she can manipulate these events to a degree."

"I listened to the CD over the weekend. I love it! I think it's the best one yet. The boys liked it, too. They liked track two because you can dance to it."

"What about the tour? You have a new band backing you. How do you think the audience will react to the new guys and songs?" a reporter asked.

"I'll answer the first part of your question..."

"Steph! Did you hear that? She learned that from you. She shut the guy down because of his multi-part question."

"She doesn't need any help from us, Kenny. She can handle this on her own."

"If you check the schedule and venues, you'll learn we are playing in secular venues," Emmy said. "There is only one church on the schedule, and it's in Iowa City. I'm playing for some very dear friends. Next question."

Emmy answered questions for forty minutes. Her longest press conference ever. She thanked everyone for coming and rejoined Kenny, Stephanie and Andy Walker.

"Em, you were awesome!" Andy gushed as he hugged her. "You... you.. just awesome!"

"Thanks. I used that old trick of imagining they were all wearing..."

"Their underwear." Kenny interrupted.

"What? No! That's gross! I pretended they were all wearing Fridays At Five t-shirts. Underwear? Yuck! Can you picture that fat reporter from the Newcastle paper in his underwear?"

Emmy gave the kids a bath later that night and tried to explain the tour.

"I am going to be traveling in a bus and singing in different parts of the country for six whole weeks."

"Why are you singing in a bus, Mommy?" Kevin asked as he poured water over his plastic firetruck.

"I'm not singing in the bus. I'm getting from one town to the next in a big bus."

"Like the one in Daddy's picture?" Heather asked.

"Yes! Like that except a different one."

Isabella washed her dolly's hair. "Why do you need a bus? Can't you use Grandpa Robertson's airplane?"

"Yes! I like airplanes. Can I go with you?" Kevin asked.

"Kevin! Stop it! You splashed water in my eyes."

"Sorry, Heafer."

"I can't use the airplane this time. This isn't Daddy's band."

"Is Daddy going to fly in an airplane soon? Can we go with him?" Heather asked.

Emmy sighed. "Okay, you can play for five more minutes, but then it's time to get ready for bed."

Eventually, Emmy and Sofia got the kids in their pajamas and settled down for the night.

"I'll read one book, but that's all." Emmy sat on the floor in the girls' room.

"Are we going to Skype you?" Heather asked.

"Yes, everyday at three o'clock we will see each other on the computer."

"Mommy, why can't you just send the computer on the bus?" Isabella asked. "Then you could stay home with us."

Emmy thought about it for a few seconds. "Maybe one day I will do that."

"Will you be here in the morning?"

"Yes, but I will have to leave before you get home from school."

Emmy read three books before making the kids turn off the light and get in bed. She carried Kevin to his room.

"Night, night, my little man." She kissed his cheek.

"What should we have for breakfast?" Emmy asked.

"Pancakes!" Heather shouted.

"Hoops and chocolate syrup." Kevin opened the fridge and reached up for the syrup.

"Scrambled eggs, please," Isabella said softly.

"Since today is a special day, I will make everyone a special breakfast, but you have to go to school."

"Do I get anything special for breakfast?" Kenny wrapped his arms around her waist from behind.

"You had a special breakfast in bed."

"I'm still hungry."

"I'll make you some pancakes, or would you prefer eggs?"

149

"Eggs and bacon, please."

Emmy made everyone a special breakfast.

"Sofia, would you help me get the girls ready for school?" Kenny asked.

"Certainly. You do remember that is my job, right?"

"I don't want to be pushy or make you feel like an employee."

Sofia laughed. "You are such a... a.. what is that word Emmy uses?"

"I'm a dork. You can call me that. I won't take offense."

"But you are a very talented dork, Mr. Kenny."

He sighed.

"Let me hug you and give you all one more kiss." Emmy said after the kids were ready for school.

"Mommy!" Heather climbed into the van and rolled her eyes. "You've already kissed us a hundred gazillion times. We have to go see Mary at school."

"Okay, I will let you go, but remember I will Skype every afternoon." Emmy helped Kevin climb into the Odyssey.

Kenny and Sofia helped everyone get buckled in.

"I'll be back as soon as I can, Em." Kenny kissed her cheek and then got in the driver's seat.

"I won't leave before you get back."

Emmy waved as Kenny and Sofia backed out of the garage and drove away. She heard her cell phone.

"Are you finished packing?" Andy Walker asked. "You better shake a leg if you aren't."

"I'm finished except for my backpack."

"Did you clean out your closet?" Andy laughed.

"No! I know how to pack light now. My show wardrobe is already on the truck."

"Did the kids leave for school?"

"Just now."

"Are you crying?"

"No." She sniffled. "A little bit."

"You won't have time to miss them except when you're on the bus." Andy reminded her. "You can always call me if you need, but I have total faith in Nelson. Ty Dalicandro is supervising the crew. I don't remember if I mentioned that before."

"I don't think you did," she said. "I like him. He manages to get the job done without a lot of screaming." She walked toward the back deck.

"I do not scream at anyone," Andy insisted.

"Maybe not now."

"Have a good trip and call if you need anything."

"Thanks, cuz."

Kenny and Sofia returned and ten minutes later, Emmy's leased Prevost tour bus rumbled up the driveway.

"Do you have everything?" Kenny asked for the hundredth time.

"If I have forgotten anything, I will replace it. I have to go. The guys are getting antsy."

He kissed her one more time. She turned and stepped onto the bus. Kenny watched the door close and waited until the bus disappeared from view before going inside. "Sofia, I want to thank you for adjusting your schedule while Emmy's gone."

"Certainly. I don't mind splitting up my day. Niles and I don't live that far away."

"Des Moines, here we come!" Bobby hollered as the bus pulled onto I-80. "Why did you insist on Des Moines being the first stop, Em?"

"Did I ever tell you about the first tour and our disaster in Des Moines. Hey! That sounds like a good title for a movie."

"What happened?"

"We played at a church and didn't realize they had fired their pastor a week before. No one took care of us. We were kinda on our own. The concert was a disaster, and we got out of town as fast as we could. I picked Des Moines for the first stop so I could get that memory out of my head."

"Things are different now," Nelson Grapella said. He sat beside her. "The other buses are almost there. The trucks arrived early this morning. Everything is going according to plan. So far."

"Thanks, Nelson. I've been on enough tours to know that sooner or later something will get screwed up."

It did. Three days later in Dallas. The PA failed in the middle of the show. The crews got it working an hour later.

Emmy Skyped with the kids every afternoon as promised.

"When are you coming home, Mommy?" Isabella asked. "I miss you and Heather is being mean. She hit Kevin yesterday."

"I've only been gone for five days. I won't be home for over a month."

"Don't you miss us, Mommy?"

"Of course I do, Isa, but I'm doing my job. Daddy has to do his job at times. This is my turn."

"I don't like you to have a job."

"I know, sweetie, but I'm doing this job for Jesus."

"Pastor Jeremiah still looks like Jesus. Why can't he do the job?"

Emmy closed her eyes. "We will talk about it later. I have to go to work."

"Bye, Mommy. I love you."

"I love all of you so much." Emmy said as she closed her laptop.

Chapter Sixteen

Emmy opened her email one afternoon while on the way to Sacramento. She deleted the junk but then noticed one from Rory.

What have you been up to, Rory? She read the email and then bit her lip. *You want to spend a week of vacation with me, huh? I know you've talked about that in the past. I never thought you meant it.* She replied back, "I'll put you to work if you want to see how a diva travels." *He probably won't reply.*

The reply arrived within the hour.

Emmy giggled. *It would be fun to have you around for a few days. The guys are great, but they keep their distance. Bobby doesn't, but he is always chasing the cute girls.* She emailed back.

Later that night, she lay on her bed as the bus headed to Portland. She bit her lip. *Are we really going to do this, Rory.* She double checked her schedule and hit send. *That's it. He's going to meet me in Salt Lake City and stay until St. Louis. I should tell Kenny, but after he got on my case for going swimming with the guys, I'm kinda mad at him. We just went swimming because Bobby suggested it. Nothing happened.*

Emmy's bus arrived in Salt Lake City a week later. She emailed Rory the address of her hotel. He caught a shuttle bus at the airport and was waiting in the lobby when she arrived.

"Excuse me, Miss, but could I have an autograph, please?"

"I'll sign something for you. Who should I say..."

"Just make it out to Rory. I'm your biggest fan."

She tried to keep a straight face but ended up giggling. "How was your flight?" She grabbed his hand.

"Not bad. A little bumpy. How was your bus ride?"

"Boring, but that will change now."

Nelson walked over with Emmy's room assignment. "Room 425, Emmy."

"Thanks, Nelson. Oh, this is my old friend Rory Porter. The one I mentioned."

"Right! Nice to meet you, Rory. Em told me you guys grew up together."

"We did, but we lost track of each other for several years."

"Should I get an extra room, Em?"

"No, Rory can hang out with me. He wants to see what I do behind the scenes."

"All right. See you guys later."

Emmy took Rory up to her room. He rolled both small suitcases behind him.

"You can leave those anywhere. I want to check in with the kids, and then I am all yours."

She talked to the kids and Kenny for thirty minutes before shutting down her laptop.

He sat on a chair in the corner. "What now, Em?"

She checked the time. "I have to be at the arena at five for the soundcheck. I usually eat a light supper before the show. You can stuff yourself whenever you want. There will be a ton of food backstage both before and after. Try not to get in the way of the crew when they're eating."

"Why?"

"They eat like a herd of starving elephants. You might get trampled under a stampede," she said.

"I'll try to stay out of the way, Em."

"I usually try to get in a short nap about this time." She kicked off her shoes and stretched out on the king-sized bed.

"Right. I'll hang out in the lobby. There's probably a bar downstairs."

She sat up. "Why? Don't you want to hang out with me?"

"I thought you wanted to take a nap."

"I do, but I'm not going to get undressed. You can watch TV or whatever. You could take a nap if you want."

"No thanks, Em. I don't want to do anything that might appear the least bit inappropriate. I feel kinda guilty just being in your room."

She bit her lip. "But we are going to share the bedroom on the bus, right?"

He froze and his eyes widened.

"I'm yanking your chain. I just wanted to see the expression on your face. There's an empty bunk for you."

"Does Kenny even know I'm here?"

She shook her head. "I haven't told him yet, but I will."

Emmy introduced Rory to the band and some of the crew before the soundcheck. He watched as the crew finished positioning the lights.

"We're ready, Emmy."

"Thanks, Ty." She glanced at Rory. "What do you think?"

"I'm thinking this is like a Fridays At Five show." He pointed to a machine on the stage. "What is that?'

"It's a laser thing. It flashes lasers all over the place."

"Can I ask a dumb question?"

"You just did."

"Huh?"

"You can ask me anything."

"Are the lasers hot?"

She giggled for a few seconds. "They're perfectly safe. This isn't sci-fi."

"I assumed that, but I wanted to ask."

After the thirty minute soundcheck, Emmy took Rory backstage and then downstairs. She met with some fans and a couple of radio people for another thirty minutes.

"Hungry?" She walked over to Rory, who had been trying to fade into the background.

"Starving."

"Let's eat. There's a room down here somewhere with food." She checked to make sure he wore his pass. "This will allow you to roam wherever you want. Make sure you don't lose it."

"Do you have one?"

She pulled it out from under her t-shirt. "I'm supposed to wear it outside of my shirt, but I try to get away without letting it show."

"Hey, Em, are you ready to chow down?" Bobby asked as he talked to one of the college-age female volunteers working the merchandise table.

"We're looking for the dining room. Where is it?"

"Through that door over there." He pointed. "We'll join you if that's all right."

155

After Bobby and his companion left, Rory whispered in Emmy's ear. "Is he like a real rock star with groupies in every town?"

"He's a harmless little flirt who's probably still a virgin," Emmy said. "He loves to flirt, but he has a girlfriend back home."

"Does she know what he does on the road?"

"Do you remember those commercials about what happens in Vegas staying in Vegas?"

"Yeah."

"The same code kinda applies here. We don't talk about everything that goes on behind the scene."

"Are you yanking my chain, Em?"

She grinned. "Maybe. Maybe not. We'll see how it goes."

Rory checked his phone when the bus finally left Salt Lake City. "Em, is it normal for the bus to leave at one thirty in the morning?" He sat next to her in the bus lounge.

"That's pretty much the way it goes. The guys drive us to the next town overnight. We get there. Check in to a hotel. Hang out. Sometimes I go for a run, or do a little sightseeing. Get to the venue... You saw that routine yesterday."

"Don't you get bored?"

"Out of my head bored. That's why you are here. It's your job to keep me entertained, Mr. Porter."

"What time do you usually go to bed?"

Emmy grinned.

"Hey! I asked an innocent question. Don't look at me like that." He poked her in the side. "And do you always wear shorts and a t-shirt on the bus?"

"I don't wear my stage clothes until the show, and I change as soon as I can."

"I asked because the guys in the band don't appear to pay any attention to what you're wearing." *Or not wearing.*

"They're used to me. They think of me as a little sister even though I'm older than most of them. They aren't the least bit interested in me as a... as a ... woman."

"What will they think about us hanging out for a week?"

156

"Depends."

"On what?" Rory sat up straighter and moved to the front edge of the couch.

"On whether or not you stop being so nervous and just be my friend. Rory, I still love Kenny, and I'm not going to jeopardize our relationship by messing around on the road."

"Sorry, Em. I'm being paranoid."

"It's all right. What should we do? I need about an hour to unwind before I even think about going to bed."

"What would you usually do?" He glanced out the window.

"Not much to see on the interstate. They all look the same."

"So true."

"Normally? When the guys from The Only Hope and I were on the road, we goofed around a lot. These guys are more serious."

"Other than Bobby, right?"

"Right. Sometimes I would read or watch TV."

"I actually know how to read now, Em. Surprised?"

"Indeed! When did you learn?"

"Last week," he said.

She put a hand to his chest. "And you learned how to be so funny."

"Wanna watch TV, or play cards? Is that allowed on the bus?"

"As long as we're not gambling or something even naughtier."

"What?"

"Never mind. We can watch TV. Find something boring to help me get sleepy."

An hour later Emmy yawned. "That show did the trick. I can barely keep my eyes open now. I'm going to bed." She rose slowly from the couch and stretched her arms over her head. "Do you know which bunk is yours?"

"Yeah. I checked it out earlier, but my suitcase is in your bedroom."

"Do you need anything from it?"

"My toiletries bag."

"Pajamas?" She looked down at his jeans.

"Boxers, Em," he whispered. "What time does everyone get up?"

"No one will be up before nine. Some of the guys sleep even later." She headed down the hallway, passed the bunks and entered her bedroom at the back of the bus. "Do you want to grab it, or should I?"

Rory waited in the hall and looked over his shoulder. "Maybe you should. I don't want to get caught in your room."

"Stop it! No one will think anything of it if you grab your toiletries."

Rory listened to the rumble of the tires on the highway and the steady drone of the diesel engine as he quickly grabbed what he needed. "How can you sleep with that noise?"

"I'm used to it."

"See you in the morning, Em."

"Night, Rory. I hope you can sleep all right in your bunk. I've done it before, so I know what they're like."

It took Rory most of the next day to relax enough to have fun hanging out with Emmy and the rest of the guys.

"Hey, Rory, can you play a tambourine?" Bobby tossed one to Rory at the soundcheck.

Rory caught it and stared at it. "Don't you just bang it against your hip or something?"

"You can use your hand, too. But what I meant is can you keep time?"

"Don't know. I never tried. Why?"

"I thought since you're going to be hanging around for a week, we might as well make you part of the band." Bobby laughed and did a drum roll.

Rory shook his head and turned to look at Emmy. "Did you put him up to that?"

Emmy put a finger to her heart. "What? Me? Why would I do that?"

"Give it a try, Rory," Micah said.

Rory glanced around the stage at the other guys. "Really?"

158

"Sure, let's have some fun. We could introduce you tonight as one of the leading tambourine players in the world, or something goofy like that."

Christian set his guitar in a stand because he was laughing so hard. "How about this? Every night we find some different percussion instrument for Rory to play and introduce him using some goofy fake name. Like tonight we could introduce him as 'Tam Burine' from Little Rock, Arkansas."

The guys came up with several fake names for Rory and he agreed to give it a try. They played two songs with him on tambourine to end the soundcheck.

"Do you want to do it?" Emmy asked after they finished.

"I don't want to turn your concert into a joke."

"You won't. We try to have fun on stage. Let's see how it goes tonight and play it by ear."

"Like this?" Rory tapped the tambourine against his head.

"Have you been taking dork lessons from Kenny?" Emmy rolled her eyes.

Quinten loaned Rory a sports coat, and Rory appeared on stage that night. Christian introduced him as Tim Burine from Delight, Arkansas. Rory stood next to Micah and played the tambourine as if he were a mechanical man. He stood stiffly erect, barely moved his hand against his leg and kept a serious expression for the entire song. Emmy didn't dare look at him for fear of cracking up.

"Let's hear it for Mr. Tim Burine, ladies and gentlemen." Christian clapped.

The rest of the guys pointed to Rory. He bowed stiffly and then marched off stage. He never broke character later as the band played an encore.

"Rory! You were a riot," Bobby grinned as they entered the green room to unwind for a few minutes before greeting some fans. "I almost lost it during the encore when you added that little wrist flourish. You're a natural entertainer."

Emmy stood in front of Rory with her back to him. He put his hands on her shoulders and smiled. "Who will I be tomorrow?"

"I love the Tim Burine character." Emmy leaned back

against him and he slid his hands to her waist.

"Can I tell you guys a secret?"

"Sure, Rory."

"I wasn't acting out a part. I was scared out of my mind."

The guys laughed as they walked over to a table in the corner to grab a bite to eat.

Emmy turned around and looked up at Rory. "Were you really scared?" She put her hands on his chest.

He stared into her sparkling blue eyes. "I was afraid I was going to pass out."

Emmy bit her lip as she gazed at Rory. They didn't say anything for a moment.

"Hey, Em! Are you guys going to eat anything?" Bobby asked.

"Be right there," Emmy said.

Rory released his grip on her slim waist and took a step back. *Shoot! For a second I thought you were going to kiss me.*

"Mr. Burine, would you like a sandwich or something?" Micah held out a paper plate.

"Sure. What have you got?"

Rory performed as Mr. Tim Burine for the rest of the week much to the amazement of the crowds and the amusement of the band. Nelson Grapella reserved rooms for the band at the St. Louis Carlton Hotel after the St. Louis show because the next night was in Columbia, only a short ride away. Instead of spending the night on their bus, as usual, this night they used the hotel rooms overnight. The crew's buses and the trucks would drive ahead to the campus of the University of Missouri.

"Rory, you stole the show. How did you do that? Have you been practicing?" Bobby asked as the bus made its way to the hotel.

"I am so sorry for that. Please, believe me it was not planned." Rory explained how after taking his bow, he fell forward, did a somersault and rose to his feet without ever changing his expression. "I just didn't want to break my head."

Emmy sat next to Rory on the couch. "I was speechless for

160

a few seconds. I stood there and couldn't move. Then when you walked off without even breaking character, I totally lost it."

"I'm sure the crowd thought you planned it. They went totally nuts," Christian said.

Quinten stood in front of the couch. "I absolutely blanked. I couldn't remember the next song. I didn't know which keyboard to play." He waved his hands around frantically as he spoke. "I watched you march off the platform and then turned back to look at everyone. No one said anything for like an hour. Then Emmy cracked up. Bobby did a drum roll, and I couldn't hold back. I played 'The March of the Wooden Soldiers' and then remembered to check the set list."

"I loved how you segued into 'These Things Take Time' after that. It fit perfectly," Jared said.

"Oh, Rory, I'm so glad you are here." Emmy hugged him even though the guys were watching.

They returned to the hotel, and Emmy and the guys piled out of the bus. Nelson and the guys in the band would return to the rooms they were assigned earlier. Emmy realized Rory didn't have a room.

"Shoot! I'm sorry, Rory. It probably slipped Nelson's mind, since you've been hanging out in my room all week."

"That worked until tonight, Em. We never stayed at the hotel overnight. We only used the hotel for showers and to crash during the day." He waited in the hall outside of her room. "I could always sleep on the bus. The driver is the only one on it."

"Don't be silly. I can get you a room, or you could..."

"Forget it! I'm not sharing a room with you, Em."

"There are two beds, but I was going to suggest you use my bedroom on the bus."

Rory hung his head. "Sorry, Em. I should have known you wouldn't share a hotel room with me."

"Ya think? Which would you prefer? The bus or a room."

"I'll see about getting a room. I don't want to have to lie about sleeping in your bedroom on the bus."

Emmy giggled for a moment. "That might prove awkward even though... Never mind. Come on. Let's ask at the desk for another room. Then you can come back and get your stuff out of mine."

They reserved a room for Rory across the hall from Emmy's. They hit the elevator button to go up. The doors opened a few seconds later and they almost collided with Nelson.

"There you guys are. I'm sorry, Rory. My fault. I totally spaced about making sure you had a room."

"We took care of it, Nelson. No problem." Emmy had one hand on Rory's elbow.

For a split-second Nelson wondered what she meant.

Emmy held up a room key in her other hand. "See! Rory has his own room just across the hall and next to yours."

"Thanks for taking care of that. I promise not to forget again."

They headed back upstairs. Nelson returned to the room he shared with Bobby O'Connor. All the guys shared rooms to cut back on expenses.

Rory needed to get his suitcase and toiletry bag from Emmy's room. He put a hand on the small of her back while she tried to open the door.

"Will you try, Rory? I had trouble with this earlier."

"Sure, Em."

The card worked for him and he opened the door.

"I'll get my stuff and get out of your hair." Rory turned on the light in the bathroom and grabbed his blue toiletry bag.

Emmy sauntered over to the TV and turned it on. She plopped down on the queen-sized bed closest to the bathroom, lay on her side and kicked off her shoes. Rory strode out of the bathroom and started walking over to retrieve his suitcase from the other bed. Emmy stuck out her foot and stopped him. He looked down at her.

"It's too early for me to go to sleep. It's not even midnight. Let's do something."

Rory grabbed her foot and sat down on the front edge of the bed. "Like what?"

"We could go for a walk."

"It's raining, Em."

"We could see if the pool is open."

"Maybe."

"Go down to the bar and get plastered?" She sat up.

Rory frowned.

Emmy threw herself onto her back and stared at the ceiling. "This is the worst part of touring."

"Other than being away from your family, right?"

"Yes. I get bored too easily. I'm not used to sitting in a hotel room and killing time."

"I know what you would do if Kenny was here."

"Rory!"

"What?" He realized what Emmy thought he meant. "Not that. Though it's probably true. I thought you guys would snuggle and watch a movie or something."

"Yeah, uh-huh. Nice try."

Rory rolled his eyes. "Fine. What do you want to do?"

"I'm going to see if we can use the pool."

She called the front desk and flirted until she got her wish. "We can use the pool until two."

"You should be ashamed. You were flirting."

"I know, and I will ask for forgiveness, but for now let's go swimming," she said and then giggled.

"I'm glad I brought trunks."

Emmy grabbed her bikini from her suitcase. I'll change in the bathroom. You can change here, or use your own room. It doesn't matter to me."

"I'm going to get my stuff out of here. I'll change in my room. Knock on my door when you're ready."

"Okay, I'm going to see if Bobby and the guys want to use the pool. They need to chill out, too."

Fifteen minutes later, Emmy and Rory were treading water in the six-foot-deep end of the pool when the rest of the guys barged through the door.

"Your arms are thinner than toothpicks." Micah teased Bobby. "You need to start working out."

"Hey! I don't need to look like The Hulk." Bobby slipped his t-shirt over his head and sprinted for the pool.

163

"No running! Can't you read." Christian pointed to a sign listing pool rules.

Bobby cannonballed into the pool and barely missed landing on Emmy.

"Bobby! Be careful." She slugged his arm when he popped up. "You almost drowned me."

"I did not." He spat out some pool water. "You looked like a drowned rat, Em." He laughed.

"Do not, you little creep." She splashed water at him.

Nelson stood at the edge of the pool and shook his head.

Rory observed Nelson wore regular shorts and a button-down shirt. "Not swimming, Nelson?"

"No, I tend to drown. I'm just here to make sure she behaves. She gets a little wild with the guys."

Emmy stuck out her tongue.

Jared spotted a beach ball and tossed it into the pool.

Bobby hollered, "Let's play keep away from Emmy again."

"I don't think that's a good idea after what happened the last time, Bobby." Micah said.

Rory moved closer behind Emmy. "What happened before, Em?"

She turned to face him and her legs touched his. "If I told you I would have to kill you." She started to smile but then bit her lip. "Nothing too awful, but Kenny found out and was pissed at me."

By one thirty, everyone except Emmy was out of the pool. The guys sat on the edge of the pool and kicked water at her as she kept her head above the water.

"Stop it!" she ordered.

"Aren't you ready to get out?" Bobby asked.

"Yes, but not with you guys staring at me."

"Maybe we should head back upstairs, guys." Nelson stood up from his pool chair. "Don't take too long, Emmy."

The guys got up, dried off their feet and tossed the towels in a laundry bag.

"Will you wait for me, Rory?" Emmy whispered.

"Sure, Em."

164

She watched the guys leave.

"Are you too shy to get out of the pool in front of the guys?"

"Not normally, but I didn't want to tonight. This bikini is new and... you know."

"I get it, Em." He got up and turned around.

"I don't care if you watch. Could you please hand me a towel?"

"Sure." He snatched a clean towel from the stack and, without looking at her, held it out as she climbed out.

"Thanks, Rory."

"No biggie, Em."

She dried off and then slipped on her shorts and t-shirt. "That was fun."

"I hope the guys didn't see when I put my hands on you."

"They won't say anything." She waited for him to open the door for her.

They took the elevator back upstairs and Rory opened her door again.

"Are you tired now, Em?"

"I will be after I shower. I don't want to go to bed smelling like a swimming pool."

He hesitated for a few seconds. "See you in the morning." He turned, crossed the hall and opened the door to his room.

Emmy woke up early, called Rory's room and made arrangements for breakfast. They sat in a booth and Emmy looked out the windows. A few of the trees still had colorful leaves hanging on for dear life. They both ordered blueberry pancakes and coffee.

"Those were good pancakes." Rory said as he slipped out of the booth. "I need to get my stuff, Em. I have to get over to the bus station."

"Do you know where it is? How will you get there?"

"The hotel will shuttle me, and I lived here, remember?"

"I forgot. Who will pick you up in SoHam?"

"I'll either walk or take a cab."

165

They took the elevator back up and saw Nelson in the hallway.

"There you are, Emmy. We're going to leave for Columbus in two hours," Nelson said.

"I'll be ready. Rory's leaving for the bus station soon," Emmy said.

Nelson shook Rory's hand. "It was a blast having you with us, Mr. Burine."

Rory laughed and replied, "I think I'll keep my current job, but if you ever need me for one night, I'll be around."

Nelson walked away and Emmy slipped into Rory's room and sat on the bed as he finished packing.

"That's all of it."

She stood up and hugged him. "Thank you so much for spending your vacation time with me. I had so much fun."

"Me, too, Em. I will never forget being on stage with you guys."

"What about the rest of it?"

"I enjoyed that even more." He put his hands on her lower back and then kissed her cheek.

"Will you text me when you get home?"

He nodded as they left the room.

"I'll be home on the nineteenth."

"Bye, Em." He waited until she was back in her room then headed to the elevator. *Em, I wish you had told Kenny I was here.*

Emmy arrived home Saturday evening to find both Kristen and Kenny upset with her. *They must know Rory spent a week with me, but how did they find out. I should have listened to Rory and told them up front. Now they're gonna think I have something to hide.*

Kenny and Kristen allowed Emmy time to visit with the kids, but after the kids were in their rooms for the night, they both pounced on her.

"Would you care to explain this?" Kristen jabbed her laptop at Emmy's chest.

Emmy bit her lip and took the laptop from Kristen.

166

"That's your band's Facebook page, and if I'm not mistaken, that looks a lot like Rory Porter on stage with you." Kristen glared at Emmy.

"I can explain," Emmy said.

"Please do," Kristen replied.

"Rory wanted to see what it's like to be on tour with a band." Emmy folded her arms across her chest. "He had a week of vacation."

"But it's not just any band, Emmy. It's you and your band." Kristen looked at Kenny and shook her head. "Would you excuse us for now, Kenny."

"Yes, I'll be in the den."

"No, wait. You can stay here, and I'll take her into the den. I can close the door and beat her to death." Kristen grabbed Emmy's hand and dragged her into the den, closed the door and locked it. "Sit!"

Emmy set the laptop on the desk and plopped down onto the computer chair.

"All right. Explain."

"There's nothing to..."

"Don't give me that crap! You were with Rory without Kenny or the kids. How long was he with you? Not that it matters. It would only take a few minutes to..."

"We did nothing to be ashamed of, Kristen!"

"Then why didn't you tell Kenny? Or me?"

"Because I knew you would get mad at me."

Kristen rolled her eyes. "Didn't you think we would find out?"

"I didn't know he would be on stage with us. Rory wanted me to tell Kenny right from the start, so you can't blame him."

"I'm not blaming him for anything. It's you who should have told Kenny." Kristen sighed and closed her eyes. "Where did he stay at night?"

"He slept in a bunk on the bus and the only night we stayed in a hotel, he had his own room. Nothing happened between us. We had fun hanging out. You can ask any of the guys." Emmy jumped up out of the chair. "They can vouch for us."

167

Kristen put her hands on Emmy's shoulders. "Look at me."

Emmy did.

Kristen stared into Emmy's eyes for over thirty seconds. "All right. I believe you, but that doesn't exonerate you. You are going to have to convince Kenny."

"I don't think it will be as difficult to convince him as it was you."

"You're probably right. He knows you the best."

"Will you stay while I talk to him?"

"No way!"

"Please, Krissy. I'd do it for you."

"You would never have to do this for me. I would never hurt John like this."

"I didn't do it to hurt Kenny."

"But it did, and now you have to fix this mess on your own. I'm going home. Give me my laptop."

Emmy handed it to Kristen.

"Talk to him now!" Kristen ordered and then left.

Emmy waited a few minutes and then walked into the family room. "Can I talk to you?"

He patted a spot beside him on the couch.

She sat down.

He turned and looked into her eyes. "Do I have anything to worry about?"

"No. Nothing happened."

"Did you know he would be with you before you went on the tour?"

"No, I didn't. He had mentioned it once, but we had not talked about it before I left. He sent me an email..." Emmy explained everything. She even told him about going swimming. "I'm sorry I didn't tell you right away like Rory suggested. But after you got mad at me for going swimming with the other guys, I wanted to get back at you. I'm sorry."

"I'm sorry for getting upset about the swimming. I overreacted."

An hour later, Emmy sighed and said, "Are we all good?"

Kenny grinned. "You're so good when you're bad."

168

Chapter Seventeen

Kenny heard Emmy return from taking the girls to school and hollered, "Emmy, check your email! Never mind. I'll just tell you."

"What is it, Kenny?" She tossed her keys and purse on the kitchen desk, walked down the hall into the den and stood behind him as he sat at the computer desk.

"You know Tyler has been preaching on Sunday morning, right?"

"Yes. He has been filling in for Dr. Behren."

"You're gonna love this."

"What?"

"The church board has officially hired Tyler to be the senior pastor."

"For real?" Emmy's eyes widened. "Please don't joke about that."

Kenny shook his head. "Not joking. There will be an official election of church members in two weeks, but that's really just a formality. You were right, Em. You suggested Tyler get the position right from the start."

Emmy giggled and then said, "It's about time the church board listened to me."

"I'll let them know."

"What do you think the older people in the church will have to say? I've heard some ladies talk about his age. They don't think he has enough experience to even be a preacher, and now he is the senior pastor."

"Perhaps, but they can't dispute the fact that the Saturday night service had grown because of him. I think his young age is a positive factor." Kenny read the rest of the email. "They hired a new associate pastor, too."

"Does it give his name?" Emmy leaned closer to the computer monitor. "I can't see."

"You could sit on my lap."

She scooted around, plopped down and read the rest of the email. "Darren Eaton. That name rings a bell for some reason."

She tapped her lip with a finger. "Oh my God! I remember Darren now. He's my age, I think. I met him in Ohio on a tour. Columbus, I think. Do you remember him?"

"I remember the name. He invited us to his wedding, but we were in Europe and couldn't go."

"The email says he's coming from Hillsdale. Hillsdale! Can you believe it? That's where Liz and Tyler are from. Do you think they know each other?"

"It's probable. Darren and his wife Jody are coming from the same church Liz and her family attend. Tyler's family, too."

"Wow! We are going to have a senior pastor in his late twenties and an associate who is my age. I think he's a year younger than me. I hope the older people don't have a fit."

"They might be more agreeable once they learn who else is coming back." Kenny smiled.

"Why? Who's coming back?" Emmy tried to read the rest of the email, but Kenny held onto her and spun the chair away from the computer. "Tell me! Who's coming back?"

"Pastor Herb and Carolyn."

"Get out! Are they really?"

"They are returning to the area and he has agreed to serve as... the email says 'the senior associate pastor who will act as an advisor to Pastor Tyler and the staff.' I guess that means he will still be retired but be like a mentor to Tyler and Darren."

"Do you think he will remember me?"

Kenny laughed. "I don't think Pastor Ausland will ever forget you, Em."

"No! I meant Darren Eaton." She jumped off of Kenny's lap and stood facing him while biting her lip. "What if he remembers me?"

"Why would you be worried about that? If I remember correctly, you only saw him a couple of times when you did concerts at his father's church."

"When I first met him, I kinda flirted with him to get him to help me move the merchandise boxes."

"Now why does that not surprise me," Kenny said. "How much flirting?"

170

"Nothing wicked. I smiled a lot and might have tugged on his arm. Little things. Hank got on my case for doing it. I didn't even realize I was flirting. I never kissed him. Oh, that would be so awkward if the church hired a pastor I've kissed."

Kenny looked at her, grinned and asked, "Have you kissed many pastors on your tours?"

She poked his knee. "Of course not. I have hugged some, but I've never kissed one."

"Yeah, sure. You are pretty good at flirting to get your way."

"Can I flirt with you now?"

"Is Kevin Michael asleep?"

"Does it matter?" Emmy asked.

"Mommy! I'm hungry. Can you make me some pancakes?" Kevin hollered from the hallway. "And I can't find my big red firetruck."

Emmy sighed. "Guess not. I'll go check on the crisis."

"Are you going to get up for church today?" Kenny nudged Emmy in the side as he sat on the edge of the bed. "Today is Pastor Benson's final Sunday, and he will be preaching."

Emmy rolled over onto her back, opened her eyes and yawned. "I don't think I've ever heard him preach."

"He did preach the Sunday after Dr. Schofield did. Oh, you were gone. He's... uh... I'll just say I can understand why he declined the chance to be the senior pastor. He is a great guy and makes a great associate, but he's moving to Kansas City to work at the church headquarters."

"Is that like working in Vatican City for the Pope?"

"No, have you been talking to Father James?"

"Should I get up?" She snuggled deeper under the covers.

"I'll leave that up to you. Sofia is helping me get the kids ready, and we'll be leaving in thirty minutes. You could come for the second service if you want."

"I'll be there. It would be disrespectful not to come to church on his final Sunday."

Emmy made it to church in time for the second service. She

walked in a few seconds after Christopher and Maddy and hustled over to talk to them. "Hey, guys. How are things?"

Christopher smiled. "Got a second, Emmy. I really need to talk to you."

"Sure. What's up?"

Christopher held her elbow and escorted her into an empty office. Maddy followed behind.

"This must be serious."

"It is. "Christopher nodded. "I wanted you to hear this from us."

Emmy shifted her attention back and forth between them.

Maddy smiled and held out her hand.

Emmy glanced down and jerked her eyes back up to Christopher.

"I asked Maddy to marry me on Friday, and she said yes."

"Christopher! I'm so happy for you guys." She hugged him for a few seconds and then turned to Maddy. "I'm happy for you, too, Maddy."

"Thank you, Emmy." Maddy smiled up at Christopher as she hugged Emmy. "Christopher didn't want you to hear it from anyone else, or see it on Facebook or Twitter."

"I appreciate it. I'm usually the last person to hear when somebody gets engaged. I think Kristen knew I was engaged to Kenny before I did."

Maddy tilted her head. Christopher shrugged.

"Have you made any plans? Do you have a date in mind?" Emmy reached for Maddy's hand. "I love your ring. I think all wedding rings should be yellow gold." *I can't tell, Kristen probably can, but that looks like a half-carat at least.*

"Let's grab a seat and talk. We have a few minutes before the service starts," Christopher suggested.

They meandered through the crowd and into the sanctuary. Emmy spotted Kristen sitting with Sloane Bertucci and Lindsey Frees.

"Hi, everyone. May we join you?" Emmy smiled at Sloane and Lindsey, but bit her lip when she looked at Kristen.

"Have a seat, Emmy. It's good to see you. You will have to

172

tell us about your trip," Lindsey said.

Emmy nudged Christopher. "Tell them."

Christopher cleared his throat. "Maddy and I are engaged to be married."

Maddy held out her hand. The ladies admired the ring for a moment.

Kristen scrutinized it. *That's close to a full carat and cut perfectly.*

"How long have you guys been dating?" Emmy asked.

Christopher answered, "Eight months, or is it nine?"

That's not very long. Emmy thought. *Kenny and I dated for a hundred years before he proposed.* "Did you set a date, or is it too soon?"

"We talked about it, and we want to get married in early May, so we can take the rest of the month off of work," Maddy answered. "The company shuts down for two weeks."

"That quick, huh?" Emmy narrowed her eyes menacingly and stared at Christopher.

He shook his head almost imperceptibly. *Geez, Em! At least you were a little tactful and didn't come right out and ask if Maddy is expecting.*

"That's not a very long engagement. Some people are engaged for two years."

"Are you forgetting about your engagement?" Kristen asked as she glared at Emmy. "Kenny proposed at the end of October, and you got married in early April. That's about the same length of time."

Emmy bit her lip to keep from replying. *Thanks for mentioning it, Kristen. I wasn't pregnant as everyone knows.*

"We are quite a bit older than you were when you got married," Christopher said to Emmy without stopping to think how she might interpret his remark.

I was old enough to get married. We didn't want a long engagement, and it wasn't because I was pregnant like Diane.

"I'm happy for you both," Sloane said as she looked back and forth at Emmy and Kristen. *What is going on between you two? Did you fight about something?*

173

"Have you been following the Bears this year, Emmy?" Lindsey asked.

"Yes, but not as closely as in the past. I've just been so busy. I know they're tied with the Lions since they beat them last week, but they're three games behind the Packers. They haven't lost a game yet. The Bears started slowly, but they've won four in a row. They should still make the playoffs."

"I hope so," Lindsey said.

Emmy saw Kenny on the platform when the worship band opened the service, but she didn't see him come into the sanctuary later.

"Do you see Kenny anywhere?" she asked Kristen.

Kristen glanced around. "That's weird. He knows where we normally sit, but I don't see him."

Instead of the customary video announcements, Pastor Benson read them.

"In two weeks we will have a vote on Pastor Tyler. All church members above the age of fifteen are eligible to vote. The vote will be a yes or no ballot. I'm sure you understand why we're voting, but I am required to spell it out. If you want Pastor Tyler to be the senior pastor, you vote yes." He paused for a few seconds. "If you do not want him, and please keep in mind the church board has unanimously voted for him, then vote no."

Before he started his message, Pastor Benson thanked the congregation for the opportunity to serve as associate pastor for over four years.

Emmy leaned close to Christopher and whispered, "I didn't realize he has been here that long. Doesn't seem that long."

"He did sorta fade into the background," Christopher acknowledged. "I could tell, and I'm not here every Sunday."

Kristen pinched Emmy's arm and glared at her. "Will you shush and pay attention."

Emmy rubbed her arm, but didn't say a word. She folded her arms over her chest and stared at the platform. *Why are you being so mean to me? If it's still about Rory, get over it. Nothing happened. I don't think I even kissed him.*

At the conclusion of the service, Ron Smith presented

174

Pastor Benson with a parting gift. After Pastor Tyler prayed and dismissed the crowd, Emmy looked around for Kenny. *Where are you? Did you go home early? You could have told me if you were leaving.*

"Congratulations, Christopher. I'm very happy for you, Maddy." Pastor Tyler and Liz greeted them after hearing the news.

"I suppose we should talk to you pretty soon. We would like for you to marry us if we can have the ceremony here," Christopher said.

Maddy chuckled and then explained. "We would like for you to marry us no matter where we hold the ceremony."

"I would be honored. Do you have any idea when you might want the ceremony?"

"Early May."

"You should check with Mrs. Millner in the office. She has a master calendar. Sometimes we are able to have more than one wedding in a day, but that can cause some confusion."

"I will call tomorrow," Maddy said.

Emmy waited until Pastor Tyler was free and dashed over to talk to him. "Pastor, have you seen Kenny or the kids? I've looked all over, but I can't find them."

"I saw Kenny and Sofia leave with the kids about fifteen minutes ago."

"I saw them, too, Em." Liz braided her hair indifferently. "He appeared to be in a hurry to leave, but that's just my opinion."

Great! You must have seen the Facebook page and now you're mad at me, too. Nothing happened. "Thanks, guys. I'll see you later. Oh, I will be voting yes."

"Thank you for your support. I'm a bit nervous."

"You don't need to worry. God has everything under control. I bet Mrs. Thompkins might be the only person to vote no. She always votes no. Doesn't matter." Emmy waved her hands and shook her head. "If Jesus was named senior pastor she would vote against him."

Tyler chuckled. "Thanks for the encouragement, Emmy."

Emmy didn't wait to find Kristen or Sloane. She headed to her BMW and floored it leaving the parking lot. *Since you obviously were upset with me and took off early, I'm going to have lunch at the Lion. Matty might be working, and Annie might even be there.* She whipped the car into the Hungry Lion parking lot, saw an empty space, turned into it and slammed on the brakes. But instead of going in, she sat in the car. She pressed her back into the seat. *Why am I here? I don't want to eat by myself. Shoot! I should go home.* She waited a couple of minutes before zooming out of the lot and back onto Oakland Avenue. *Maybe I should call Rory and see if he's free for lunch.* She used the car's Bluetooth system to call Rory, but before he could answer, she ended the call. *That would make matters worse. I'm going home and confront him about leaving without telling me. I have every much of a right to be pissed at him because of how he reacted.*

Emmy parked in her spot in the garage. Slammed the car door closed and stomped into the house. "Kenny! Are you home? I'm back in case you care."

Sofia hurried into the kitchen. "Please don't yell, Emmy. Kenny is trying to get Kevin to sleep."

"Why? It's too early for his nap." Emmy checked the time on the microwave. "Why did he leave so abruptly?"

"We left because Kevin got sick. He threw up and had some diarrhea. We needed to change him, but we didn't have any other clothes. We cleaned him up as best we could, but he was crying and so upset. Poor baby. Maybe we should always keep extra clothes in the van.

"Oh, crap," Emmy said. "I'm sorry for yelling, Sofia. I didn't know." Emmy sprinted out of the kitchen and dashed up the stairs two at a time. She collided with Kenny upon barging into Kevin's room.

"Sorry, Em."

"I'm sorry, too. How is he?"

"Better now. He's sleeping and hasn't thrown up anymore."

"What about the diarrhea?"

"Nothing after the first two times. I put his clothes in a plastic bag and tossed it in the garbage can. They were a total disaster."

Emmy bit her lip and followed Kenny out of the room after

checking on Kevin. "I owe you an apology."

"Why?"

"Because I thought you were mad at me and left the church early without saying goodbye, so I got in the car and drove like a maniac over to the Lion, but I just sat in the car because I realized I didn't want to eat alone. I floored it out of the Lion and thought about going to Darby's, but it's too far away. Then I almost called Rory to have lunch, but I didn't..."

"Em! Slow down and take a breath." He held her hands.

She stopped talking and took several deep breaths. "I'm sorry." She hugged him close and buried her face in his chest.

"It's okay, baby. I still love you."

"You're not mad at me?" She bit her lip.

"I'm not mad at you," he whispered slowly.

She stopped crying and looked up. "Guess what? Christopher and Maddy are engaged. They want to get married in May, so I told them that wasn't a very long engagement and I asked how long they'd been dating. Christopher said a few months, so I thought they are rushing ..."

Kenny picked her up and kissed her.

"Oh, I like that. I guess I need to shut up, huh?"

Kenny answered with another kiss.

"The Bears better get their act together today," Emmy said as she drained her cup of coffee. "They lost to the Raiders in Oakland last Sunday and their record is 7-4."

"Who are they playing today?" Sofia wiped Kevin's hands and let him down from his seat at the breakfast nook.

Heather and Isabella dashed to the powder room to wash their faces and hands.

"Kansas City Chiefs. They've got a worse record than the Bears, but they have a good defense. I miss going to the games."

"You could have gone to some of them if you were home." Kenny leaned against the kitchen counter and drank his coffee. "You made your choice."

"Are you ever going to forget about the tour? Could you just drop it?"

177

He shrugged. "Just sayin'. You could have gone to the games. You planned your tour for the fall."

Yeah! Just keep poking away at me. You smile and never raise your voice, but you know how to get under my skin. Emmy stared at him for a moment. She checked the calendar on the fridge. "They play Seattle at home next Sunday. Maybe we could go to that game. I'm sure Tony or John could get tickets."

"Better look again, Em." Kenny pointed.

"Why? What?"

"We are both scheduled to play with the worship team."

"Fine!" she shouted. "So we won't ever go to another game. Happy?"

He calmly answered, "You have to choose what is most important to you. The Bears? The worship team? Going on tours?"

"You know where my priorities lie," she snapped.

"Actions speak louder than words."

"I hate you sometimes."

The next Sunday the church members voted for, or against, Tyler before each service. Emmy heard several people talking about the vote between the services.

After the video announcements in the second service, but before Tyler stepped onto the platform, Jim Rosek walked onto the platform and announced, "There have been over six hundred ballots cast. I'll make this simple. Only twelve ballots against. We have a new senior pastor." He shook Pastor Tyler's hand and patted him on the back. "All righty then," he said and then walked back to his seat.

Pastor Tyler paused before praying. "Thank you for that vote of confidence. Liz and I do not take this lightly. We are fully aware of the responsibility you have placed on us the help grow the kingdom."

Emmy grinned and whispered to Kenny, "I wonder if Mrs. Thompkins managed to vote twelve times."

"Regardless of her, I think that's about as close to unanimous as possible."

"Which way did you vote?" she asked.

"Yes, if you must know. How could you doubt me?"

"I didn't."

He held her hand. "I'm sorry about nagging you about the tour. I need to let it go."

"I'm sorry, too. I don't hate you, but sometimes you make me so mad."

"I know, Em." He squeezed her hand.

As in the first service, Pastor Tyler asked Darren and Jody to come up front before he dismissed the congregation.

"Some of you already know Pastor Darren and his wife Jody, but I want to take this opportunity to formally introduce them. Please try to greet them before you leave."

"I'll help Sofia with the kids, Em. Maybe you should see if Darren remembers you," Kenny said while grinning.

"I don't want to embarrass him."

"You mean you don't want him to embarrass you, right?" Kristen picked up her Burberry bag and put on her coat. "You told me how you flirted with him and even let him kiss you."

Emmy froze with a stunned look. "How did you know?"

"You told me, you goof." *You even said you liked it.*

Emmy turned back to Kenny. "I forgot all about the kiss. I'm sure it didn't mean anything."

"Uh-huh," he said.

"It was just one quick little kiss."

"Come on, Emmy. I need to retrieve the kids."

Emmy followed Kristen out of the sanctuary with her head down. She bumped into Kristen when she stopped.

"It's a pleasure to meet you Pastor Darren," Kristen said. "I've heard so much about you from my best friend." *I can see why she wanted to kiss you. I love those dark green eyes.*

Emmy bit her lip as she glanced up. *Crap! I didn't want to run into you today.*

"Emmy! It's so good to see you again." Darren held out his hand. "Jody, do you remember Emmy Colasanti?"

"Hello, Emmy. How are you? You don't look any older than the last time I saw you."

Emmy tried to smile and shook Darren's hand. "I'm fine.

I'm happy you guys are here."

One of the other church ladies twisted Jody around. "You have to meet my children."

"I'll be right back, Darren." Jody followed the lady.

Kristen headed to the educational building to claim Zach and Gracie leaving Emmy alone with Darren. Emmy glanced up at Darren but then looked away.

Darren smiled at Emmy. "I have been listening to your new CD in the car. I think it might be my new favorite."

"Thanks." She rubbed her foot on a small stain in the carpet. Suddenly, she looked up. "Kristen told Kenny that I let you kiss me."

"She did?"

"Kenny knows I flirted with you."

Darren laughed. "You did. You tried to pretend you weren't, but you managed to get me to do your work. I knew you were using me, but I didn't mind in the least. Neither of us has any reason to feel guilty."

"But I did kiss you. More than once if I remember correctly."

"Yes, but it was many years ago before either of us were married. I see no reason why it will affect our relationship now. We will be working together at times."

"Does Jody know?"

He scratched his ear. "I really can't remember if I ever mentioned it to her. I did have another girlfriend before Jody, so I have kissed at least three girls. Not that you were a girlfriend."

Emmy replied, "Good. Please don't mention it to anyone, and I will convince Kristen to keep the information private."

"It will be our secret, Emmy." He turned to shake hands with another member of the church.

Emmy stood behind Darren until he finished talking to the older man.

"You look so serious, Emmy." Darren said as he turned to face her again. "What's on your mind?"

"We've only seen each other a couple of times over the years."

"Yes, you came to Columbus twice for concerts. You never scheduled a concert in Hillsdale."

"Both times I flirted with you, and we used the teen room," Emmy said.

"Yes, we did." Darren smiled and then said, "We played ping pong, and I think I won most of the games. You kept the games close though."

"I won some, but after we played ping pong, we ended up dancing for a while and then kissing each other. We ended up sitting together on that couch. We probably shouldn't have done that."

"We were both single at the time, and I didn't know God would call me to be a pastor at the time. Had I known that, I would have behaved differently."

"I was married the second time I came to Columbus."

Darren took a deep breath before replying, "You were, but I don't think we did anything other than kiss quickly like friends, and it wasn't like the first time."

"I shouldn't have been alone with you at all. I want to make sure it won't be a problem," Emmy whispered.

"I vaguely remember how much I liked kissing you, and you are still very attractive, but we are older and both of us are married. It won't be a problem for me."

"You knew how to kiss, and I did flirt with you. I'll try not to do that again," Emmy said and then smiled. "You still look very sexy though. Jody is lucky to have you."

He adjusted his tie and said, "Thanks, Emmy. I better go. I need to meet more people."

She watched him walk away. *I might challenge you to another game of ping pong one of these days, but only if we aren't alone.*

Chapter Eighteen

Kenny walked into the kitchen, stood with his feet apart and his hands at his hips. "Well, how do I look?"

Emmy stirred the pot of spaghetti one more time, set down the wooden spoon and turned to look at him.

"Well, what do you think?" He pushed his hat up higher on his forehead. "Do I look like a cowboy?"

"I like the long coat. Where did you find it?"

"That used clothes place downtown. How about the hat?"

She took a couple of steps closer and looked up. "It has a rip in the side, but it looks like a real cowboy hat."

"This is my vest. I found it in a box of old clothes I used to wear on stage."

"It feels like real leather." She rubbed a hand over the material. "Why aren't you wearing black jeans?"

"I could, but I thought this fabric looked better. So, do I look like a real cowboy?"

"You smell like a cowboy." She covered her nose and mouth.

"I think it's the coat." He held it open. "I'm only going to wear it to open the show."

"Good idea. Then you can burn it. Take it off and throw it in the garage. I don't want it smelling up my kitchen."

He did as ordered and returned to the kitchen.

"Do you think anyone will show up tonight?" She opened the fridge, grabbed a package of frozen peas and a box of garlic breadsticks. "Whose idea was this?"

"Dave came up with the plan. He thought it might be fun to appear as some unknown band. We've sold some tickets already. The Center draws a decent crowd every weekend no matter who's playing."

She looked at his boots. "Are you going to wear spurs and carry a rope?"

"Do you think I should?"

She rolled her eyes. "You do have to play your guitar, cowboy."

182

"Right." He snapped his fingers. "I'll set the spurs and rope on top of my amp."

"What name did Dave end up using?" She adjusted the oven temperature. "The Dork Band?"

"Ha! Ha! We are The Lonesome Cowboy Band. Catchy, huh?"

"So is the flu," she said. "You need a black belt."

"I've got one upstairs. I need to find a black t-shirt to wear under this shirt. It itches." He scratched his back. "Are you going to come and watch us?"

"Oh, I wouldn't miss this for anything." She laughed as she turned up the heat on the peas. "Do you know what the other guys are wearing?"

"We're supposed to dress in black. Black hats. The whole get-up."

"You could call yourselves Dorks In Black."

"Maybe the next time. I need to change and get ready. We're supposed to be there at six to do a quick soundcheck."

"Should I make some beans, biscuits and burnt coffee for later?"

He stared at her.

"Git! You can eat with all the other cowhands later."

Later that evening, Kenny, Emmy and Dave Persching peeked out from behind the heavy black stage curtain at The Center.

"I would guess there are three hundred. Maybe three fifty. Not too bad for a band no one has ever heard of."

They backed up before anyone noticed them.

Kenny listened to the house music. "Who is that?"

Dave laughed. "It's an old cowboy singer. Wilbur Wilkens, the singing cowpuncher. That's what it said on the record I found."

"They should have recorded the cow instead," Emmy said.

"They've been playing all sorts of country and western music tonight. With the emphasis on western. Gene Autry, Roy Rogers, Sons of the Pioneers. Trying to get the audience in the mood."

"I hope they like the new stuff. We haven't played any of it live before," Kenny said.

"The CD is selling about how we expected," Dave said.

Jeff Rawlings walked up. "Is anyone out there?"

"Six people at last count," Emmy joked.

"How do I look?" Jeff asked.

"Where did you find that belt buckle? Can you even play with that thing on?" Jeremy asked as he adjusted his cowboy hat. "This is never going to stay on right."

"I'm going downstairs to check on the kids," Emmy said. "Don't you dare ask me to sing with you tonight. I am not a cowgirl." Emmy turned and quickly walked away.

Andy Walker strode over. "Howdy, pardners! You got fifteen minutes. Why did I ever agree to this?"

"Come on! It will be fun."

"If you say so. Is the princess coming tonight?"

"She's here. You just missed her."

"Is she going to sing her harmony part, or does she have more sense than to show up on stage with you cowhands?"

"She's not planning to sing," Kenny answered.

"Has anyone seen P.J.?" Jeremy asked. "He said he found a fake beard and was going to wear it. He claimed it made him look like a real gold prospector."

"There he is!" Dave pointed.

The rest of the guys stared at P.J.

"What? Does this beard look real?" he asked as he approached.

Kenny tugged on it. "It does look real. No one in the auditorium will be able to tell it's fake. Nice hat, by the way."

P.J. smiled. "It's my ol' granddad's hat. He actually worked on a ranch in Texas when he were a young one."

"Yeah, don't say anything on stage. That accent is as hokey as when Kenny does his Australian thing."

The guys headed to the green room to wait.

"Who did you get to open the show?" Kenny asked Dave.

"Remember that tape I played about a month ago?"

"The cassette?"

Dave nodded. "Yeah. Guy and an acoustic guitar. His

184

name's Hucky Eichelmann, and he's totally amazing. He's going to do a twenty minute set. If the crowd listens, they'll hear some real talent."

Thirty minutes later the guys took their places onstage.

"Is anyone going to introduce us, or do we just start playing when the curtain opens?" Jeff asked as he sniffed the long coat he wore.

"I think one of the new owners is going to introduce us." Dave pointed and waved.

"Are you guys ready?" the owner asked while perspiring heavily.

"Ready when you are."

The curtain opened, and a lone spotlight highlighted the owner. He shielded his eyes from the light. "Thanks for coming out tonight. Please allow me to introduce from Cody, Wyoming, the Lonesome Cowboy Band!"

The spotlight vanished instantly. A smattering of applause greeted the guys. Kenny hit the opening chord to the title track of *Riders Of The Lonesome Trail* and they started to play. The lights hit the backdrop—a wide scene of cowboys around a campfire. Slowly the lights came up as the band got into the song. Kenny looked out at the crowd. One by one the crowd realized who was on stage. Cell phones began to snap pictures all over the place. By the end of the second song, the frenzied crowd stood and never sat down.

"That tune was called 'Sagebrush.' We are The Lonesome Cowboy Band."

"Yeah, right!" a loud voice hollered from toward the back.

Kenny tried to keep a straight face. "We're going to play the songs off of our new CD, and then we might hang around and play some cover tunes."

By now the crowd realized they were in for a special treat.

Fifty minutes later, the sound of thundering hoofs roared through the PA and then faded as the final track "Posse In The Sky" ended.

Kenny waited for the crowd to stop yelling. He waved his hands to get them to settle down. "We're going to take ten minutes

185

to change out of these duds. We'll come back and play some covers and who knows what. See you in a few."

The owner came back out to make an announcement. "Tickets are on sale now for tomorrow's show. Limit of two per person. The Lonesome Cowboy Band will be back..." He shook his head as practically the entire crowd rushed out of the auditorium and headed to the ticket office. "So much for anonymity."

Kenny and the guys used the dressing rooms to change before gathering in the green room.

"Can I burn this coat now?" Emmy asked.

"We were going to wear them tomorrow night. Does it really smell that bad?"

She grinned and said, "It's a little better than horse manure."

"That went well, I think." Dave opened a bottle of water.

"Ya think!" Jeff laughed. "What'd it take? Ten seconds before they knew who we were."

"At the most. What are we going to play for the next hour?" Kenny checked the time. We could play for two more hours if we wanted."

"Let's do a couple of Eagles covers to start and then play it by ear," Dave suggested.

"Are you going to sing with us, Emmy?" Jeremy asked.

She shook her head. "I'm taking the kids home. They have school in the morning. You cowhands have fun."

The guys returned to the stage in regular clothes. Jeans and shirts. Andy walked up to Kenny.

"You guys can either wait or just start playing. There are still people waiting in line to buy tickets. What do you want to do?"

"Let's start jamming and tell the crowd to be patient. We'll wait until they're all back."

That's what happened. Eventually, the crowd came back to their seats.

"Is it just my imagination, or are there twice as many people in here now?" Kenny whispered to Jeff.

"They must have called friends. Let's have some fun."

186

They played cover songs. Some of their own tunes the crowd requested. A couple of unreleased tunes.

Kenny checked the time. "We've got time for two more. We'd like to close with a couple of old ones. 'Too Bad' and 'Sea Sick.'"

Before the guys hit the last chords of 'Sea Sick' the box office closed. Tomorrow's show was sold out.

"That was fun," Dave said as he toweled off backstage.

"Fun, but we worked our butts off." Jeff sat down.

"I want to check with Will before I leave. He should have a good idea of how the recording sounds."

"Let's try not to repeat any of the encores tomorrow. The cover songs, I mean," Jeremy suggested.

"Then you better come up with a list of suggestions. It's too hard to think of cool tunes while we're playing."

Kenny made it home by one and slipped into bed with Emmy.

"How did it go, cowboy?"

"Great! We had a blast."

"How long did you fool the crowd? You never told me."

"About ten seconds. Maybe."

"That long, huh? Must have been the smelly coats."

The owners of The Center added extra security for the Friday show. Even though the ticket office posted "Sold Out" banners in several places, people tried all day to purchase tickets. Scalpers were encouraged to move along by undercover SoHam officers.

Emmy accompanied Kenny to The Center, and they parked in the lot in back reserved for artists.

"Did you see the crowd outside? The doors don't open for another hour and they're already lined up."

"True, but they looked like they were just hanging out and having fun. Can you imagine if some famous bands were doing this. The crowd would go nuts."

"You are such a dork," Emmy said. "You guys are famous."

"Not like the Stones or The Beatles. Groups like that. We can still live in SoHam without people hassling us. They don't think of us as rock stars."

"I'm grateful for that. I'd hate to not be able to go to church or to the store. Oh, we need milk and bread. Could you stop on the way home. I'm going to catch a ride with Tony."

"Anything else?"

"Grab some cereal, too. The only place open will be the Pantry. I hate to pay their prices, but the kids will want breakfast."

"Do you have any cash?"

"I have a twenty, but I want my change back."

"Could I buy a candy bar if I have enough money?" He grinned and kissed her.

"No, they're too expensive."

The band expected Friday's show to be similar to Thursday's. The difference became apparent as soon as they opened the curtain. Tonight the Lonesome Cowboy Band played to a capacity crowd of over 2,500 people. Many of the people came to the show dressed as cowboys and cowgirls. They only repeated two cover songs, and a few of their own in the encores.

"Should we take the Lonesome Cowboy Band on the road this summer?" Kenny sat in the green room drinking a bottle of water after the show.

"We could start each show by playing the Riders CD," Jeff suggested. "What do you want to do, Jeremy? Since it will be your last tour, we should let you choose the set lists."

"I don't mind playing the Riders material to open, and I like the retrospective aspect of the show. We could come up with fifty songs and rotate them. We are recording everything, right?"

"Yeah, and if they turn out okay, we should offer them as downloads or something. Kids aren't buying as many CDs as in the past."

"Sounds like a plan."

188

Chapter Nineteen

"Should we leave early?" Emmy asked as she lay in bed with Kenny on Christmas morning. "There's only one service today. It might be packed, or there might not be anyone there. Some families will stay home from church because it is Christmas which doesn't make a whole lot of sense because it is Jesus' birthday, and we should go to church to celebrate."

"Are you finished," Kenny said as he grinned.

"Yes." She cuddled up even closer.

"You make perfect sense, Em. We have a half hour before we need to get up. Sofia will take care of Kevin if he wakes up."

"I always make sense, right?"

"Of course you do, Emmy." He nibbled on her ear.

"I'm so glad Sofia agreed to work on Sunday and take Fridays off. It makes getting to church so much easier."

"You should thank Niles for agreeing."

"Did I mention I made my decision about the endowment for the school?"

Kenny stopped and used his elbow to support his head. "What did you decide?"

"I talked to Sara and the guys at Aberdeen Investments. They all agree that we can afford it. Duh! I'd do it anyway. Sara thought we would recover the money in five to seven years as long as the market doesn't crash again. Faster if we wanted to be less conservative."

"I don't want to invest the money in something risky. It doesn't matter if it takes ten years to earn back the money."

"Mr. Robertson and his accountants studied the school's finances. He is of the opinion the church will need to support the school for several years before it will be able to sustain itself. He and Mona agreed to match our contribution."

"That's very generous of them."

"Pffft! It's a drop in the bucket for them."

"Em, a million dollars is more than a drop."

"Okay, it's a few cupfuls for us, but I can earn some money by going on tour every year. Maybe three or four small tours."

189

"You could always see if Darby's needs any part-time help," he teased.

"You're only saying that because you're hoping to get free chili dogs and fries."

"That is one of the perks."

"Mr. Robertson and I are going to meet with Pastor Tyler, Pastor Herb and Mr. Smith tomorrow morning."

"Do they have any idea about what's going on?"

"They might have an idea it's about money, but I haven't mentioned an amount or anything."

"I hope they don't have heart attacks when you guys tell them," Kenny said.

Later, as Emmy led the congregation in singing Christmas songs, she saw Dany Kimmerle sitting next to her sister Liz in the second row. After the service Emmy made her way to the front to hug and talk to Dany.

"Liz told me you graduated."

"I did, and I will be working on my master's. I'm spending the rest of the semester break with Liz and Tyler. I'm taking advantage of the opportunity to spoil Natalie and Grayson. I haven't seen Lorraine as often."

"Cool. We will have to get together while you're here. Have you seen Jason lately?"

"He's home. I think everyone will be here next week."

"Did you guys get together for Christmas?"

"Liz and Tyler made it home for a couple of days, but they needed to get back here for today. Did you ever imagine he would be the senior pastor here?"

"Maybe not this quickly, but I knew he would be leading a church sometime. I'm glad the church board didn't hold his age against him."

"Liz said Dr. Ausland has been a great help."

"Pastor Herb married me and Kenny." Emmy saw Dr. Ausland out of the corner of her eye. "I'll talk to you later. I need to gather the kids and get home. We're celebrating Christmas and my brother is joining us."

"I didn't know you had a brother," Dany said.

"I'll tell you about him later, Dany. I really gotta run," Emmy said. "Or you can ask Liz. She's met him."

"Merry Christmas, Emmy," Dany said as Emmy dashed away.

"Do we have to wait until after lunch to open our presents?" Heather asked as soon as they arrived home.

"Yes," Emmy said. "Be careful up the stairs."

Emmy fixed lunch while Kenny made sure all the gifts were under the tree.

"Can you get the phone, Em? I'm kinda busy," Kenny hollered while carrying an armful of presents.

Heather rushed to the landline in the kitchen, picked it up and said, "Hello, today is Christmas. It's Jesus' birthday."

Father James chuckled and replied, "It's a very special day. Is this Heather or Isabella?"

"I'm Heather. Who are you?"

"This is Father James."

"Who's on the phone Heather?" Emmy asked as she wiped her hands on a towel.

Heather handed the phone to her mother. "It's Father James. Your brother."

"We're home. Are you coming over?" Emmy asked.

"I can be there soon. I do have some gifts. Is that all right?"

"Not toys, I hope."

"I can follow instructions. I bought clothes."

"Good. We're about to eat lunch. Should we wait for you?"

"No, go ahead and eat. I'll grab a sandwich here."

Father James arrived in time to listen to Emmy read the Christmas story from her Bible.

"Now can we open our presents?" Heather asked.

Emmy looked at Kenny.

"Yes, we can open presents as long as you are patient," Kenny said. "Should I play Santa Claus?"

Emmy nodded and sat on the couch.

"Do you always have such a large tree?" Father James asked.

"Daddy chops one down from Uncle Tony's woods. There

191

are lots of them," Isabella answered. She stood next to Father James. "You can sit there if you want."

He sat in one of the recliners. "Do you always rearrange the furniture for Christmas? It wasn't like this before."

"We put the tree in that corner and move stuff around," Emmy explained. "It's a big family room. So we move the couches from the fireplace to face the tree."

Father James glanced over his shoulders at the other side of the room.

"Yeah, we leave that furniture in front of the TV," Kenny said. He picked up a gift and read the tag. "This one is for Kevin Michael. Have you been a good boy this year?"

An hour later Father James helped Emmy stuff all the wrapping paper into garbage bags while Kenny removed some toys from their packaging.

Emmy whispered, "I think we go a little overboard because when Diane and I were kids, sometimes we didn't have a tree. Most years we only got one present from Mom and Dad. When my grandparents were alive, they would bring us gifts."

Father James nodded. "I was more fortunate, Emmy."

"Did I ever tell you about Grandma and Grandpa Colasanti?" Emmy asked.

"You have told me about your music box, and that they passed away when you were quite young."

"Grandma Mary died just before Christmas in 1989, and Grandpa died in February. I was only nine." She looked at the kids and said, "I hope Kenny's parents live a long time."

"I'm sure they will, Emmy."

Chapter Twenty

On Tuesday morning Emmy and Mr. Robertson met with Pastor Tyler, Dr. Ausland and Ron Smith at the church.

"Can I get you something to drink, Mr. Robertson?" Tyler offered as everyone took a seat around the oval conference table.

"Thank you, but I'm good."

"Em?"

"I have some water with me. My throat is dry."

"What can I do for you this morning?" Tyler asked.

"Thank you for meeting with us," Mr. Robertson said and looked at Emmy. "Would you like to inform everyone?"

"You can tell them," Emmy said.

Mr. Robertson cleared his throat. "Emmy talked to me a while back about doing something for the church, but more specifically for the church's school. I asked my finance guy to do the research, and he returned with good news."

"Mr. Robertson." Emmy touched his arm.

"Sorry. I should just get to the point, huh?"

Emmy nodded.

"Emmy and Kenny agreed to provide money for an endowment, and Mona and I are matching it. The money has been transferred into a trust accessible by the church. There are some restrictions to safeguard the funds which I'll explain. We just need some signatures in order to complete the paperwork." Mr. Robertson leaned back in his chair.

Tyler looked at Dr. Ausland and then at Mr. Robertson and Emmy. "Thank you for you generosity."

"Mr. Robertson!" Emmy exclaimed. "You kinda forgot to mention one rather important item. The scholarships."

"Right," Mr. Robertson said and then explained how part of the trust should be used to provide scholarships to needy children.

Mr. Smith had been listening quietly but now said, "Since no one else has mentioned numbers, I will. How much are we talking?"

Emmy looked to Mr. Robertson.

"The initial contribution is for two million."

After a few seconds of silence, Dr. Ausland said, "Praise the Lord!"

Tyler chuckled. "Wow! That is amazing. The school has been a great concern, but we put our faith in God that He would provide the means to complete the vision."

"You won't tell anyone, will you?" Emmy asked.

"We will make every attempt to keep the contributors to the trust anonymous, but it might need to be revealed at some point."

"I just don't want people to get the wrong impression. I'm not doing this out of vanity. God has blessed my family way beyond what we deserve. This is a way for me, and Mr. Robertson, to give back."

"I understand, Emmy. We will keep this quiet for as long as possible."

"You can tell Liz if you want, but tell her not to tell anyone else, please."

"I will tell her, but she might hug you to death the next time she sees you. The school has been at the top of her prayer list. She will be flabbergasted."

No one mentioned the trust money to Emmy at rehearsal on Thursday, but Liz did squeeze Emmy harder than normal.

Emmy rushed home after church on Sunday, sprinted into the house as soon as Kenny turned off the van and hollered over her shoulder. "I'll be back in a minute. I want to check the score."

"That's all right. Sofia and I will get the kids." Kenny shook his head. "Were you ever into sports, Sofia?"

"I played football a bit, but that's all. Not American football. Soccer. Emmy loves football so much because of Tony and John."

Kenny unbuckled Kevin's car seat and helped him down. "Have I ever told you that when I first met her I found out she liked football?"

"Not that I recall." Sofia closed the sliding door after Heather and Isabella escaped from the van.

"I met Emmy and Diane at the same time. Diane tried to impress me by saying she had already kissed a boy. Emmy told me

194

she liked to play catch with her father. That impressed me more so I became close friends with Emmy."

"What would you have done if Diane liked football instead of Emmy?"

Kenny chuckled and watched Kevin scramble up the steps into the house. "I think I still would have liked Emmy better. I thought she was cuter than Diane."

Emmy watched the TV for a moment. She heard the kids talking, so she sat on the couch instead of going back to the garage.

"What's the score, Em?" Kenny sat beside her.

"The Vikings are up by ten. This sucks! If the Bears lose today they will finish under five hundred."

"Should I order something for lunch?"

"No, I'll make lunch. What would you like?"

"Soup and sandwiches for now. Maybe you could cook something else after the game."

While Emmy made lunch, the Bears scored two touchdowns in less than a minute to grab the lead. The only scoring in the second half came on field goals by each team. The Bears held on to win and evened their season record.

"This year has been such a disappointment," Emmy said.

"They aren't going to win the Super Bowl every year, Em." Kenny consoled her by putting an arm around her waist.

"I suppose, but they need to do better. Maybe they need a new coach."

"Emmy, did you see the game yesterday?" Kristen asked over the phone on Monday morning.

"Yeah. At least they beat the Vikings, but it wasn't a very good year."

"Have you heard anything about the team today?"

"No, why? Did they fire the coach? I told Kenny they might need a new coach."

"Not that I know, but John retired. Yesterday was his last game."

"What!? Why?" Emmy yelled into the phone. "He's too young to retire. He's still one of the best tight ends in the league."

195

"His knees are taking a beating. He would need surgery if he wanted to keep playing. He's going to have his knee scoped soon, but he's had enough."

"That sucks," Emmy said. "What's he going to do now?"

"He wants to coach football at some level, but until that happens, he's going to try to build up the Two Bears business. He is going to work for Daddy's company, too. He will keep busy."

"He won't make as much money."

"We aren't going to be filthy rich like you and Kenny, but he will still receive money from the Bears. Part of his salary over the years has been deferred. He will get a salary from the Bears for the next ten years."

"Hey! We are not filthy rich," Emmy protested.

"I didn't mean that in a bad way. You guys make more than the rest of us."

"Maybe so, but we invest the money wisely. Kenny may not always make money from the band."

"Get out! Fridays At Five will always make money. They might not sell millions of CDs, but they will always make money from touring."

Emmy laughed. "Can you picture him at forty or fifty playing his guitar and singing rock songs?"

"Actually, I can."

"Get out! He's not going to be in a band when he's fifty."

Emmy called Andy a week later to check on him.

"What's up, cuz?"

"Just calling to see how you feel today. I didn't see you at church yesterday."

"Awesome!"

"Where are you? I can hear people in the background."

"At the office. Today is my first day back to work," Andy explained. "I thought I told you that the other day."

"You didn't! What are you doing?"

"We have to plan the Riders summer tour, remember?"

"Will you be able to get it organized in time? Those tours aren't as easy to plan as mine." Emmy walked into the family room

196

from the den and plopped onto the couch. "Mine can be planned in a month or so."

"The guys at Prater-Saylor started last fall." Andy laughed and then added. "Today we are throwing darts at a map. We want the guys to fly back and forth across the country as much as possible."

"I'll tell Kenny what you said."

"Go ahead. He's always accused me of doing that. Especially in the early days."

"Are they gonna play in Europe again?"

"The tour will start in Europe in May. Charles has most of that tour already set. The last show will be at Wembley Stadium in London."

"I might go with him to Europe."

"Don't expect to travel for free. I'll put you to work."

"Kenny will take care of me," Emmy said.

"Unless you have something else on your mind, I need to get back to work. Tours like this aren't planned overnight."

Tony came over the next evening after dinner with Peter, Ben and Taylor in tow.

"What are you guys doing here?" Emmy asked as they walked into the kitchen while she loaded the dishwasher. "I don't have any food left from dinner."

"Sloane told me to take some of the kids and get out of her hair. So here we are."

"Oh, Sloane tossed you out for bugging her, and you expect me to entertain you or something, huh?"

Tony nodded.

"Auntie Em, where's Kevin? We want to play. Ben and Taylor brought some cars."

"They're upstairs in the playroom with Kenny. Go on up."

"Thanks! Come on, guys! Let's find Kevin."

Ben grinned and held up a truck. "New dump truck."

"I see. Can I play with it later?"

"Maybe, but you can't keep it."

Peter helped his younger brothers up the stairs.

"Hand me that pot from the stove." Emmy pointed.

"You're welcome, brat."

"You're lucky I can't reach the top of your head. I would brain you if I could."

""I told the boys you might let them have some ice cream later." Tony opened the fridge. "Do you have any coffee flavored ice cream?"

"Yuck! Mama is the only person I know who can eat that."

"Here's some vanilla. Do you have chocolate sauce?"

Emmy rolled her eyes. "If there's none in there, then look in the pantry. You aren't helpless, and I'm not your servant." She added the dishwasher soap, closed the door and pushed the button to start it. "I should start charging you for all the food you eat here."

"Kenny doesn't mind if I come over and eat."

"He likes you for some reason," Emmy teased. "I don't."

"Should I hang you from the ceiling like I used to?"

"You could try, but you're not as young as before. Hey! Are you going to miss having John on the team?" She leaned against the island. "I didn't expect him to retire already. I thought he would play a few more years."

"He didn't let on much, but his knees bothered him all year. He's going to have both of them scoped." Tony picked her up and set her on the island. "Marco emailed me."

"How is he doing? The family all right?"

"Yeah. He wanted me to know Dwight received a scholarship to play at Notre Dame. He won an award as the best lineman in Maryland."

"Good for him. Do you think you can get tickets to the games? I haven't been back since you graduated."

"I might scrape up a couple."

"Could you get me on the field during the game. The sidelines, not the actual playing surface."

"That would cost you."

"I'll let you have an extra scoop of ice cream, and I'll even make my super secret ice cream sauce."

"Deal!" Tony high-fived her.

198

"Thanks for staying at school with us today, Mommy," Isabella said when they got home on Friday.

"I wanted to be there for your birthday. I can't believe you're six already," Emmy said as she pulled her BMW into the garage.

"We're not babies, Mom," Heather said.

Emmy watched the girls run up the stairs and into the house. "I know you're not babies, but you're not grown up either."

Emmy hung up her coat in the mudroom, tossed her keys and purse on the desk and saw Kenny in the kitchen.

"How was it?"

Emmy sat down heavily on a barstool and lowered her head to her hands. "I could never be a teacher. I would go nuts."

"Kinda makes you appreciate those who do teach a little more, huh?"

"Mary is a saint for dealing with all the kids. She has so much more patience than me."

"Would you like some lunch, Em?" Kenny asked. "I can make sandwiches and heat up some of the leftover lasagna."

"I was hoping to save the lasagna for tonight."

"Sandwiches it is," Kenny said with a grin.

Heather and Isabella scampered into the kitchen with Kevin right behind them.

"Whoa! Slow down there," Kenny said. "I'm making sandwiches for lunch."

"We're not hungry," Isabella said. "We just had cake and ice cream."

"Let them play until the sugar wears off," Emmy said. "I should have known better than to let them eat cake and ice cream before lunch."

They heard a crash from the living room.

"Sorry," Heather said. "It was an accident."

The kids raced upstairs while Emmy checked the living room. She came back holding a lamp. "Should I spank her?"

Kenny shook his head. "It was an old lamp, Em."

"Yeah, from Grandma's house."

Chapter Twenty-One

"Girls, come and say goodbye to your mother. She will be gone for six weeks like the last time," Kenny hollered as he held Kevin in the kitchen. "It will feel like an eternity before you see her in person again."

"Do you have to make it sound so terrible?" Emmy frowned. "It's not like I'm leaving for good. I'm doing my job."

Heather rushed into the kitchen from the family room. "Are you going to Skype us everyday after school?" Heather stood back from Emmy.

"Yes, I will try to see you on the computer as often as I can." Emmy held out her hands and Isabella walked up and hugged her.

"I will miss you, Mommy, but you said Jesus wants you to sing for him." Isabella held on to Emmy.

"The bus is here, and I need to go. I'll talk to you tomorrow." She glanced at Kenny but then turned to leave.

"What? No kiss?" Kenny set Kevin on the island and tilted his head.

The kids stared at Emmy.

"Sorry, I forgot." Emmy kissed him quickly. "I gotta go."

Emmy and her band left for another six week tour. This time Prater-Saylor booked them into venues on college campuses. Not a single church could afford the fee the agency charged.

Three weeks into the tour, Emmy and Nelson Grapella returned to the bus after a concert in Oxford, Mississippi.

"Emmy, you were fantastic tonight!" Nelson followed her into the lounge.

She collapsed onto the middle of the leather couch and closed her eyes. "I've never heard a crowd as loud as tonight. I can't believe they wanted three encores."

"I can't believe you guys knew enough songs."

"Barely. I need some tea with honey." Emmy forced herself to get up. "Would you like some, Nelson?"

"Love some." Nelson settled onto the couch.

The guys in the band tramped onto the bus and into the lounge.

"I am beat!" Bobby plopped onto the couch in Emmy's spot. "I've never worked as hard as tonight."

"You've never done a seven minute solo before." Christian sat next to Nelson. "Who agreed to let him have a drum solo?"

"Come on, guys, the girls loved it." Bobby pounded out a rhythm on the couch with his hands.

"And we know how much you like to entertain the girls," Emmy teased. "I'm making tea. Anyone want some?"

The guys declined.

Emmy poured a cup for herself and Nelson. "It's raspberry, and I added the honey already." She motioned for Bobby to scoot over. "You're in my spot."

"Did you like the drum solo, Emmy?" He scooted over enough for her to squeeze in next to him.

"I loved it!"

"Really?" Bobby accidentally bumped her arm.

"Careful! You almost made me spill my tea. I loved the solo because it gave me time to go backstage and change into a fresh dress." She smoothed out the dress she meant. "The other one was soaked. The lights were hot enough to boil water. I'm going to have to buy some new ones."

"Boil water, Em?" Micah laughed.

"You know what I meant. We need to stick to our LEDs."

"We should have made the crew put up our lights instead of using the college's gear."

Quinten dragged himself into the lounge. "Don't ever do that to me again! Three encores! I didn't have those last two songs programmed. I made up the voices on the fly. I hope they sounded all right, Do I smell tea. I could go for a strong cup of tea about now. Did anyone else sweat like a pig? I drank five bottles of water, and I still feel dehydrated."

The guys shook their heads. They were accustomed to Quinten's ramblings by now.

"Do you like touring better now, Em?" Micah sat down with a bottle of water and tossed one to Quinten. "You act like it."

201

"I'm getting used to it, but if we tour in the summer, I want to bring the kids. You guys are great to be around, but I miss the kids so much."

"Did you Skype with them today?" Jared asked. "You didn't have time yesterday."

Emmy leaned against the back of the couch. "Crap! I was supposed to Skype at three, but I was busy doing that interview. I totally forgot about it later. The girls will think I've forgotten them."

"You better make time to Skype tomorrow," Nelson said.

"Don't let me forget, okay?"

Nelson added it to his list of duties.

Kenny let Emmy sleep later than usual on the Sunday she returned from the tour. He sat on the side of their bed and woke her up before he and Sofia left with the kids.

"We're leaving now, Em. You can either sleep in, or come to the second service. I'll let you decide."

She rolled over and stretched her arms above her head. "Thanks, Kenny. I'll get up in a little bit. It feels so good to be back in my own bed."

She made it to church with enough time to stop at the music suite. She checked the schedule on the wall outside of Chase's office.

"Hi, Emmy, it's good to have you back. How was the tour?" Heidi Knapp asked. "We missed you."

"The tour was the best yet! We had a blast." Emmy smiled but then turned her attention back to the schedule just as Chase walked up behind her.

"Look who has returned. Are you ready to sing for us again?" Chase said with an edge to his voice.

"What's going on?" She frowned at Chase and pushed him into his office. She kicked the door closed. "I'm not on the schedule for the next two months. Why? Don't you think I'm good enough to sing at church anymore?"

"It's not a matter of talent, Emily." He stunned her by using her real name. He sat on the front edge of his desk and crossed his arms over his chest. "You have more God-given talent than anyone."

She raised her voice. "Then why did you take me off the schedule?"

"Because I need to make sure you want to sing at church. You've been rather consumed, or maybe obsessed, by your career the last few months."

"I have not! And besides, God wants me to sing for people outside of the church. He gave me this voice, didn't he?"

"Yes, he did," Chase said calmly.

Emmy realized how upset she sounded. She took several deep breaths to slow her racing heart. "I'm sorry for yelling at you, Chase."

"You're forgiven."

She slumped into one of the chairs along the wall stared at the floor for a moment and then looked up at Chase. "I'm a diva, huh?"

"You have adjusted your priorities a bit."

She closed her eyes and leaned back bumping her head on the wall. "Ow! That smarts." She rubbed the back of her head. "What should I do? My career is stronger than ever. I like doing these short tours. I want to tour in the summer so I can bring the kids."

"Do you still want to sing at church?"

"I think so, but right now I'm totally worn out."

"Maybe you should spend some serious time praying and reading the Word this week. You might need to refill your spiritual cup."

"But I read my Bible on the tour. I prayed before every show. Some nights I even had a chance to witness to the crowd instead of just letting the words of the songs speak to them."

Chase listened.

"Why do you say I need to refill my spiritual cup? I'm doing more now to try to reach unchurched people than ever. Some of my songs are even getting played on secular radio stations. Lots of people will hear them."

"You are doing quite a lot, huh?"

203

"I am keeping busy..." She stopped in mid thought. She bit her lip and balled her hands into fists. "You're trying to tell me that I'm trying to do everything, but I need to let God do the work first. Is that right?"

"I believe you know the answer."

She took a deep breath and let it out slowly. "Do you hate me?"

"Not at all, Em." He stood up, put a finger under her chin and lifted her face. "You are still the most talented singer I've ever known."

Emmy spent at least two hours a day for the next week in the den with the door closed. She got on her knees to pray. She read her Bible, and, most importantly, she listened. She allowed God to respond.

"How are you today, Emmy?" Chase asked before the start of the first service the following Sunday.

"I feel so much better. I want to apologize for my horrible behavior last week."

"Accepted."

She explained how much time she spent praying and studying her Bible.

"Did God answer you questions?"

"He didn't message me on Facebook," she answered with a grin. "That would make it so much easier to know His will."

"The Holy Spirit will let you know. Maybe on Twitter," Chase teased while patting her arm.

After the second service Emmy gathered her purse and Bible. She said goodbye to Sloane and Kristen and turned to leave the sanctuary.

"Emmy! Emmy! How are you?"

At first Emmy didn't recognize the Hispanic lady approaching with her family.

"It's so good to see you. We were afraid you wouldn't be here today." The lady smiled and hugged Emmy. "You might not remember me. I'm Juanita Montoya, and this is my family."

Emmy bit her lip and dropped her purse and Bible on the seat. "Juanita? Juanita Garcia?"

Juanita's smile and bright eyes filled the room with the presence of Jesus. "This is my husband Diego Carlos Montoya. He is the pastor of our church in Mexico City."

Diego smiled and offered a hand. "It's a pleasure to finally meet you, Emmy."

"Thank you," Emmy said softly.

"These are our daughters," Juanita said.

Emmy sat on the front edge of the chair to talk to the children. "I'm Emmy. What is your name?"

"I'm Yolanda," the older daughter answered in Spanish.

Emmy bit her lip as her eyes filled with tears. "And what is your name?" She managed to ask after a time.

The younger daughter held her mother's hand as she looked at Emmy and then answered in Spanish, also. "My name is Emmy. Just like yours."

Emmy's tears overflowed as her arms reached out to hug the child. She pulled Emmy onto her lap and smothered her with kisses.

Juanita sat next to Emmy and put an arm around her waist. "Years ago I gave my life to Christ because of Yolanda and your song. We still live in Mexico City. This is our first vacation. Ever. We came to Illinois to see my brother Hector. He lives in Chicago with his family. We are only going to be here for a week and had to stop and see you. I wanted to introduce my girls and Diego."

Emmy wiped her eyes. "They are so beautiful. I am thrilled beyond belief to see you."

Juanita was telling Emmy about living in Mexico City when Kenny and the kids joined them.

"This is my family. This is Kenny."

He shook hands with Diego.

"This is Heather and Isabella. They're my miracle twins."

Heather and Isabella smiled at Yolanda.

"We're six. How old are you?" Heather asked.

"I turned six in January," Yolanda said in English.

Emmy looked at Juanita.

205

"We've spoken both English and Spanish to them."

"And how old are you?" Emmy asked the frail child on her lap.

Emmy Montoya leaned back against her namesake and held up three fingers. "This many," she whispered.

Juanita mentioned, "Emmy was born on March 15, 2008."

Kenny looked at Kevin. "This is Kevin Michael. He was born two days later."

The two families talked for twenty minutes.

"We should go. We are supposed to meet Hector for dinner." Juanita hugged Emmy again. "May God bless you and your family."

"You, too." Emmy bit her lip, but managed to smile as she waved goodbye. "Will you take the kids home, Kenny? I need to see if Chase is still here. I have to talk to him."

"See you at home, Em."

Emmy spotted Chase walking towards the hallway leading to the music suite. "Chase!" she hollered and sprinted after him.

He stopped and turned.

"'I need to talk to you." She caught up to him and almost knocked him over.

"Catch your breath, Emmy, and tell me what's on your mind."

She took several deep breaths. "I have to sing in church. This is where God wants me."

Chapter Twenty-Two

"Mom doesn't feel good so she's not coming to Kevin's birthday party." Carson explained to Emmy on Saturday afternoon. "She told me to make sure I told you. She didn't want you to think she didn't want to come."

"I understand. I'm glad to see you. Did Brady drive you and Caden over here?"

"Yeah, I wanted to walk, but Mom said no. Brady will pick us up later. He doesn't want to be away from Mom for very long."

Kevin and Ben caromed into the kitchen. "Mommy, can me and Ben watch a movie before we have cake and ice cream?"

"I don't think so, Kev. We're ready to have the cake as soon as Aunt Kristen arrives. She's running late for some reason." Emmy heard the mudroom door open. "That might be her now."

Kristen rushed into the kitchen, set two bags on the island, turned on her heals and pointed at Zachary. "I said no! You are still grounded as soon as you get home from the party."

"It's not fair," Zachary said. "He started it."

"That's enough! Go sit at the breakfast table, and I don't want to hear another word." Kristen pointed.

Zachary hung his head but obeyed.

Kevin and Ben dashed out of the kitchen. "Aunt Kristen sounds mad," Ben said.

Emmy looked at Zachary and then back at Kristen.

"Mommy is mad at Zach because he hit a boy at the bouncy house this morning," Grace said.

"Why did he do that?"

Grace shrugged. "I think the other kid pushed him."

"I told Zach it didn't matter who started the fight," Kristen said. "Here is the ice cream. Is everyone here? I'm sorry I'm late."

"It's all right. What happened?"

"I'll tell you later, but it's nothing serious. Just a little altercation between boys."

"Could you get the cake out for me, Krissy. I'll tell everyone to come and sing. There are four candles on the island and some matches." Emmy pointed as she left the room.

Kristen pulled the cake out of the fridge. "I should have guessed there would either be a police car or a firetruck on the cake."

"Can I see, Mommy?" Zachary asked.

"You can look if you put the candles on the cake."

"Can I light them?"

"No! I will take care of that."

Emmy herded everyone into the kitchen.

"Let's sing first and then Kevin Michael can make a wish and blow out the candles."

Kevin grinned while they sang.

"Make a wish, Kevin," Kenny said.

"I already did. Ben, did you see the police car on my cake?"

"Cool!"

"Mom, can you cut my piece from the police car?"

"Okay, but I will have to cut some other pieces first," Emmy said. "What kind of ice cream would you like?" Emmy pulled the two cartons from the plastic bags and looked at Kristen. "Vanilla or vanilla?"

Kristen shrugged. "I thought you might have a different flavor."

"I like vanilla," Kevin said. "With chocolate sauce, please."

An hour later all the kids gathered in the family room and watched Kevin open his presents. Kevin showed Caden his new radio controlled police car.

"That's cool. The lights flash and everything," Caden said.

Zachary pushed Caden and took away the car.

"That's it! We are going home this instant, young man. You will go to your room for the rest of the day," Kristen shouted. "Sloane, would you bring Gracie home?"

"Sure," Sloane agreed.

Kristen dragged Zachary out to the car.

"I know Zach is big for his age, but lately he's been really aggressive with the other kids," Emmy said.

"Maybe I shouldn't say anything, but Kristen took him to the doctor last week. Zach might need some medication," Sloane

208

said. "I hope that's not the case."

"It's probably just a phase," Emmy said.

"Emmy, I'm sorry to call so early in the morning, but Diane insisted."

"Brady, is that you?" Emmy tried to talk without waking up Kenny. "What time is it?"

"It's quarter after four. Diane had the baby about fifteen minutes ago."

Emmy sat up and accidentally nudged Kenny. "Is she okay? Is the baby all right?"

Kenny opened his eyes and listened.

"They are both doing great. Again, I apologize for calling... Hang on a sec. Diane wants to talk to you." Brady handed his cell phone to Diane.

"Emmy, she is absolutely gorgeous! She has lots of dark hair like you did. She is already nursing."

"How much did she weigh?" Emmy put her hand over the phone. "Diane had the baby."

"I kinda figured out that part, Em. If they are all right, I'm going back to sleep. It's the middle of the night." Kenny turned over and closed his eyes.

"Seven pounds and two ounces according to Brady. I don't know how long or anything, but she has some strong lungs."

"Which room are you in? I'm coming up there right away."

"Room 4012. Sound familiar?" Diane laughed. "You can wait until it gets light out, Em."

"I might, but I need to get there soon. I'm singing at church today for the first time since January. Who's watching the boys?"

"Bill and Mona. Actually the boys are spending the night."

"What time did you get to the hospital?"

"I think it might have been around one. I could tell earlier that Lily was not going to wait much longer."

"Duh! I forgot to ask about her name."

"Didn't I already tell you? I thought I did. I know I told Bill and Mona," Diane said.

"You told them before you even told your favorite sister!"

"You're a goof."

"So what's her name? Tell me." Emmy jumped out of bed. "I have to take a shower before I come down to St. Bart's. I can take clothes to change into, but I don't want to shower at the church."

"We named her Lily Patricia..."

"Are you kidding!?"

"You do know Brady's mother's name was Lily, right?"

"I remember that, but Mom will have a cow. She will be mad that you used her name for the middle one." Emmy turned on the shower.

"Am I on speaker? Are you talking to me in the shower?" Diane rolled her eyes.

"Yes, but I can hear you."

"If Mom doesn't like it, we can always call her Lily Petunia or something." Diane laughed and shifted Lily's position.

"Yeah, that would really piss her off."

"Hang up and get ready. I'll see you when you get here. If I'm sleeping, you better not wake me up," Diane warned.

"I don't want to see you. I want to hold Lily," Emmy said and then giggled.

Emmy arrived at St. Bart's just after six. She snuck up to the fourth floor and walked as fast as she could without running from the elevator to the room. She tiptoed into the dark room and spotted Brady sleeping in a chair with his feet up.

"Are you awake, Diane," Emmy whispered.

"I am now. Lily just went to sleep about a half hour ago."

"I won't wake her up, but I have to see her." Emmy leaned over and stared at Lily in her basket. "She does have a lot of hair. Did I have that much?"

"According to Mom, you did. I don't remember, but I do kinda remember when they brought you home. You cried a lot, and I wanted them to take you back to the store."

"The store! I didn't come from the store."

"Ssssh! You'll wake Lily."

"Sorry."

"That's where I thought you came from, I guess."

210

Emmy glanced at Brady. "Does he always snore like that."

"Only when he's asleep," Diane joked.

"You're so funny."

"Will you call Mom for me later? I don't want to have to deal with her today."

Emmy shook her head. "Not a chance. Even if I didn't have church, I would make you call her. She's your mother, too."

"I'll call her. I just wanted to get a reaction from you." Diane pointed. "Could you hand me that water, please?"

Emmy handed it to Diane. "Have you had anything to eat?"

"No, but the nurse said she would try to get me some breakfast as soon as the cafeteria opens."

"I could run out and grab some muffins or something."

"No, thanks. I'll wait. I have a taste for eggs and sausage."

Emmy moved a chair close to the bed and sat down. "I'm kinda nervous about singing today."

"You aren't going to let me go back to sleep, are you?" Diane sighed.

"Don't you want to talk to me? I'm your little sister."

"I wonder if it's too late to take you back to the store."

Emmy stuck out her tongue.

"Go ahead. Why are you nervous?"

"Because I haven't sung at church since January," Emmy explained.

Three minutes later, she glanced at Diane. *Great! I bored you to sleep. I might as well go back to sleep myself.*

Emmy woke up when Diane's breakfast arrived.

"That smells good." Emmy said after yawning.

"I asked them for coffee. I thought you might need some."

"What time is it? Oh, never mind. I remember where the clock is."

"What time do you have to be at church, Emmy?" Brady asked as he held Lily.

"At least by nine, but I wanted to get there by eight thirty."

"You have time. Would you like to hold Lily?"

Emmy sprang from the chair and took Lily from Brady. "She is so tiny. I can't remember when the girls were this small."

"They were only half the size of Lily. Don't you remember?" Diane asked and then took a bite of scrambled eggs. "I know this is hospital food, but it tastes so good this morning."

"Heather and Isa were under four pounds. Heather was a few ounces bigger."

"I remember how long you were in labor. I'm glad it never took me that long."

"I didn't realize the twins were that small at birth," Brady said. "Were they early?"

"Yeah, they stayed in the hospital for two weeks. They were all right. Just small. I spent most of the day and nights with them."

"They are healthy now."

"Yeah. They're still small for their age, but they might never be as big as other kids."

"You aren't exactly a giant, Em." Diane finished the eggs and picked up a piece of toast. "Do you remember this room?"

"I remember everything about it. The closet. The thing with all the wires that always woke me up because it would beep. The TV that never worked right." She pointed. "The view out the window kinda sucks, but it could be worse." Emmy walked over and looked down at the parking lot across the street.

Lily squirmed and made a face.

"Oooh! I think she just pooped. You can have her back." Emmy intended to hand her to Diane.

"I'll take her. It's been a long time since I've changed a messy diaper," Brady said.

"Who's diaper did you ever change?" Emmy asked.

"I changed Spencer's and Abigail's a long time ago."

"Duh! I should have known that."

Emmy stayed until eight.

"I better go. I probably won't see you until you come home. Make sure you call Mom sometime."

"Bye, Emmy. I'll call her, but I might not tell her Lily's name."

"Good luck with that. It will be Mom's first question. See ya. Bye, Brady, congratulations."

212

Emmy walked into the empty music suite, flipped on the lights, sat down and closed her eyes. Liz slipped into the room, saw Emmy and sat beside her without saying anything. Emmy opened her eyes after a moment.

"Hi, Liz."

"Morning, Emmy. I didn't want to bother you because I thought you were praying."

"I was."

"Is everything okay? You look a little pale." Liz touched Emmy's hands. "You're cold."

"I just came from St Bart's. Diane had the baby this morning," Emmy explained.

"Good! For a second I thought maybe someone was sick. How are they doing?" Liz walked over to the table with the coffee pot. "I should get this started."

"Great! Lily is adorable. Diane named her Lily Patricia after both mothers. She's got lots of dark hair like I did. Do you want some help?"

"Where's the decaf?" Liz looked in the cabinet. "I don't see any."

"We might be out. I could run up to the front office. They probably have some."

"Never mind, I found it behind the regular coffee."

"Liz, I'm scared," Emmy admitted. "I haven't sung in church for so long that it feels like the first time." Emmy bit her lip as she looked up at Liz.

"Oh, Emmy, you don't need to be nervous."

"What if the people don't like me anymore. Some of them probably think I'm some kind of diva because I go on tour and stuff."

"Don't be silly! Everyone loves you, and they love to hear you sing. You are so much better than the rest of us. I love watching you dancing and smiling with joy." Liz took Emmy's hands and danced with her for a few seconds. "Since you dance a little, I feel freer to express my joy. You don't hide your emotions at all."

"Gee, thanks. That means today everyone will know I'm

213

scared to death." Emmy grinned as she let go of Liz.

"What's going on in here? Were you two dancing?" Chase made 'dancing' sound like a swear word.

"Emmy is nervous this morning, so I was trying to help her relax."

"Why on earth are you nervous? You are a rock star. You sing in front of huge crowds." Chase ducked into his office and returned with his coffee cup.

Emmy grinned as she saw the caption on his cup. *You might think you're the world's greatest boss, but Mr. Robertson should have a cup like that.*

"Is the coffee ready?"

Liz nodded. "I'm not sure who's bringing the donuts."

"Thanks for making the coffee, Liz. I know it wasn't Emmy because she's such a diva," Chase teased.

"Are you trying to make me so nervous I puke?"

"I've got the donuts," Heidi Knapp announced. "And why would you be sick to your stomach. Are you expecting?"

"Who's expecting?" Cam Frees asked as he took off his coat and hung it up.

Chase opened the box of donuts and took a glazed one. "Emmy's feeling nauseous."

"Congratulations, Emmy," Cam offered.

"Why are we congratulating Emmy?" Regina Collins asked as she and Robby walked in.

"Emmy's expecting again," Heidi said.

Pastor Tyler walked in just in time to hear Heidi's comment.

"Great! Donuts. Are there any strawberry filled." Robby grabbed one he thought might be strawberry.

"When are you due, Emmy? You aren't showing yet." Regina asked.

Emmy looked at Liz and shook her head.

"What isn't Emmy showing?" Kenny asked as he walked in with Ross Knapp.

"Hey! Congratulations, Kenny." Robby high-fived him with one hand while holding his donut in the other and dripping

214

strawberry filling on the carpet. "Number four, huh?"

Kenny looked at Emmy.

She shrugged her shoulders and grinned. "I've been meaning to tell you."

Liz put her arm around Tyler's waist.

"But... but... I thought..." Kenny stammered.

"You guys! Emmy's not expecting! She's nervous about singing today," Liz explained.

"Oh, so you're not?" Heidi poured herself some coffee.

"I am, but not as much now," Emmy said.

Everyone turned to look at her half expecting to see a baby in her arms.

"Not as much pregnant? How can that be?" Regina asked.

Emmy waved her hands. "No! No! I mean I'm not as nervous now. You guys are so amazing."

"Do you know if you're having a boy or a girl yet?" Ross Knapp took a sip of his coffee. "I didn't hear if you said."

Everyone turned to Ross and shouted, "She's not having a baby!"

"Sorry. I thought... never mind."

Emmy walked up to Ross. "It's just a miscommunication. I'm not expecting." She explained what happened.

"I get it, but I can't believe you would be nervous."

"I remember the first time I sang here." She tried to recall the year. "I think it was in 2002."

Liz said, "It was. I remember it because I came to church with Grandma and Grandpa. They wanted me to see the Olivet campus. I don't remember the exact date but it was January of 2002. I can't believe it's been ten years ago."

"That's right," Emmy said. "Holy cow! Ten years ago. I can't believe it's been that long ago. Sure doesn't seem like it."

"I was seventeen when we first met, Em. So much has happened over the years."

"Did you ever think Tyler would be the pastor of such a large church at his age?"

Liz smiled. "Sometimes I still can't believe it. God has blessed us so abundantly."

215

"You have a wonderful family, and you can both walk to work. That's amazing," Emmy said. "Of course that means you can't ever take a day off because you are snowed in and can't get out of the driveway."

Kenny heard Emmy's comment. "You can be a goof at times, Em."

"Are you all right, Emmy? You look a little pale." Liz noticed as they walked onto the platform to start the first service.

"I think I'll be okay as soon as we start singing, but right now I think I'm ready to puke," Emmy admitted.

"Oh, Em, please don't get sick on the new carpet," Liz said.

Emmy laughed in spite of her nervousness. "Thanks, Liz. That made me feel better."

"Glad I could help."

Pastor Tyler opened the service with a prayer. "Would you stand, if able, and join in singing 'Glorious Day' along with the worship team."

The worship band sang four songs and then left the stage. Emmy walked back to the music suite with Liz.

"You made it through without getting sick," Liz said.

"I am so relieved that is over. I'm glad Chase sang the lead on the first two songs. That gave me a chance to relax."

"I'm sorry for making light of the situation, but it is humorous in a way," Liz said. "You don't get this nervous on your tours."

"Thanks for understanding, Liz. I've been worrying about singing ever since I saw Juanita and her family. She helped me to realize I can never get away from singing at church. I had kinda lost sight of the importance of being grounded in the Word and church. I know I should know better, but I messed up."

"We are still imperfect beings. We make mistakes. But Jesus is always there for us."

"It's a good thing!" Emmy hugged Liz.

216

Chapter Twenty-Three

"Hey, Emmy! do you remember what tomorrow is?" Kenny asked as he wiped Kevin's hands after dinner. "Girls, go wash your face and hands."

The girls dashed to the powder room. Kenny lifted Kevin off of his booster chair, set him down and playfully swatted his behind.

"Since today is Wednesday, that makes tomorrow Thursday," Emmy answered. "Anything special about it?" she asked and then giggled.

"No, I guess not." Kenny turned away, but Emmy grabbed his arm.

"Oh, you mean our anniversary, right? How long have we been married? Thirty years?" She asked.

Kenny took a step forward as the phone rang. "It's nine years, not thirty." He checked the caller ID. "It's Diane. Wanna answer it?"

"Yeah, might as well see what she wants." Emmy picked up the phone before it went to the answering machine. "Yes, who is calling, please?"

"You know it's me. You never answer this phone without checking to see who's calling. Are you guys doing anything for your anniversary?"

"Dunno. We really haven't talked about it," Emmy answered as she lifted herself onto the countertop.

"Did you drop the phone? What was that noise?"

"I bumped it."

"If you are interested, but only if you're really interested..."

"In other words, you want us to do something." Emmy rolled her eyes as she kicked her feet against the cabinet door.

"Okay, yes, I would like to have you and Kenny over for dinner on Friday night. Do you have plans?"

"Just us, or are you inviting the kids, too?"

"I'd rather it just be the adults, but, well, I am inviting you..."

"Ha! Ha! Can I talk to Kenny about it and call you back?"

217

Emmy grinned as Kenny touched her knee through a rip in her jeans.

"No! I want an answer right now."

"Are you kidding?" Emmy swatted Kenny's hand away.

"No, I'm serious. I want to know now," Diane insisted.

"Diane wants to have us over for dinner on Friday. No kids. Just adults, and yes I'm an adult." She stuck out her tongue. "Is that all right?"

"We don't have any plans as far as I'm aware," Kenny answered.

Diane heard him. "Good! Then you guys are having dinner here. Sofia can watch your kids, right?"

"Guess so. She is staying overnight all weekend. Niles is away on a business trip. Who's watching your tribe?"

"Bill and Mona are keeping them overnight. This will be Lily's first night away from home. I'll have to make sure... you know."

"I know. Kenny loves those pumps," she teased. "Are you going to invite other people besides us?"

"We do have friends, Emily."

"Friends we know?"

"Does it matter? Bennett and Marissa are coming."

"Oh, so you planned this dinner before you ever asked us, huh?"

"Sorry, Em. I kinda forgot about your anniversary until I talked to Mom. How can she remember dates but can't remember where to put the milk?"

"Beats me." Emmy shrugged. "Who is this anyway?"

"I'm hanging up now. I'll talk to you later about dinner. Who can I invite that will understand your childish sense of humor?"

"I heard that!" Emmy frowned as she jumped down and placed the phone back in the base.

In the morning while everyone ate breakfast, Kenny kissed Emmy.

"Daddy, why are you kissing Mommy at the table?"

Heather asked as her eyes sparkled.

"Because I love her, and this is a very special day," he answered. "Do you know why?"

"It's not Christmas. There's no tree," Kevin said. "Do I have to go to school today?"

"Yes, but why is this day special?"

Isabella put a finger to her mouth and looked up at the ceiling. "It's not summer, so it's not Mommy's birthday."

"It's not my birthday." Emmy gazed at Kenny.

"Do you give up?" Kenny asked.

"Yes, tell us." Heather sighed as she spread more butter on her toast.   .

"Nine years ago today I married your mother." Kenny kissed her again.

"Oh," Heather said and took another bite of toast.

"Don't you think that's special?" Kenny held out his hands palms up.

"I think it's very special," Emmy said. "Maybe after you get back from school today, Daddy can show you some pictures of the day we were married."

"Did they take pictures back then, Mommy?" Kevin asked.

"Did you wear a princess dress like Sofia?" Isabella asked.

Emmy nodded. "I wore my wedding dress, and it's in a box in my closet."

"Are you saving it so you can wear it again?" Heather asked.

"No! I'm never going to get married again. I'm married to your father forever."

"Then why did you put the dress in a box? Why don't you wear it?"

"Kevin Michael!" Isabella rolled her eyes. "Don't you know princess dresses can only be worn one time." She sighed and said, "Boys don't know anything."

The girls rushed into the house after being picked up at school. Heather dropped her backpack on the floor and threw her jacket at the hook on the wall.

"Heather! You're supposed to hang them up." Isabella

219

scolded while she reached up and placed her backpack in its proper place.

"I'll hang up your coat, Isa." Sofia said while picking up Heather's jacket and book bag. "Thank you for trying, Isabella."

"Daddy! Where are you? I want to see the pictures."

"I'm in the family room. Did you hang up your jacket?" Kenny closed his book and got up from his recliner. "I'll show you the pictures if you hang up your stuff."

"Fine!" Heather turned, stuck out her lower lip and stomped toward the mudroom.

"Sofia hung up your stuff, Heather," Isabella said.

"Daddy!" Heather hollered as she ran back to the family room. "My stuff is where it belongs. Can we see the pictures now?"

"Not so fast. Did you hang up your jacket, or did Sofia have to do it for you?" Kenny frowned as he pointed at Heather.

"I tried."

"If you want to see the pictures, you have to do your homework first."

"We don't have any," Isabella said.

"Is your room clean? Is it ready for inspection?"

"Give us two minutes!" Heather hollered as she and Isabella raced each other up the stairs.

"Where is Emmy?" Sofia asked.

"She ran to the store for a few items. She wants to make something special for dinner."

"She shouldn't have to cook today. I could make dinner."

"Thanks, Sofia. She might let you help," Kenny said.

"Do you know what she's..."

"Heather! That's my Doll Kitty!" Isabella shouted.

"No, it's mine! Let go!" Heather tugged on the fragile doll.

"I better run. Doll Kitty is getting too old to repair." Kenny sprinted up the stairs and into the girls' room. "What's going on?"

"Heather wants to put Doll Kitty on her bed. It's my turn," Isabella explained.

"You can have the new Doll Kitty, Isa." Heather pulled hard enough that when Isabella let go, Heather lost her balance, tumbled against the wall and began to cry.

"Heather, are you okay?" Isabella rushed over and knelt beside her sister. "You can have Doll Kitty."

"I bumped my head, but I'm all right." She handed old Doll Kitty to Isabella. "I think it's your turn to have Doll Kitty."

"Maybe we should put Doll Kitty back on the top shelf where she will be safer," Kenny suggested.

The original Doll Kitty belonged to Emmy as a little girl. She found a new Doll Kitty for the twins to share shortly after their birth.

Kenny explained, "You need to treat Doll Kitty with care. You are only supposed to let her sleep on your bed if you do something extra special for Mommy or me."

"You can put her back. We can share new Doll Kitty," Isabella said.

Kenny inspected the room. "Looks pretty good. Just put those books away and come downstairs. I'll show you pictures of Mommy in her princess dress."

The girls finished straightening their room and scurried down the stairs.

"We're ready. Our room is extra clean," Isabella said and Heather nodded.

Kenny hooked his laptop to the large TV and used it to show the pictures.

"Okay, these are pictures of Mommy before she had her wedding dress on," He explained.

"We want to see the princess dress." The girls sat on their knees close together on the floor facing the TV.

Kenny skipped forward until Emmy was in her dress. "Here's one."

"Oooh! She's a beautiful princess," the girls agreed.

"I think so, too," Kenny said.

"That's Grandpa and Mommy!" Isabella pointed. "I miss Grandpa."

"Is Grandpa in heaven with Jesus?" Heather turned to Kenny and asked. "Will we get to see him again?"

Kenny clenched his jaw for a moment. "Yes, Grandpa is

with Jesus, and if you love Him, you will get to see Grandpa in heaven."

"Can we see more pictures?"

Kenny restarted the slideshow.

"There's one of you and Mommy kissing!" Heather squealed.

"Daddy?"

"Yes, Isa."

"Have you always kissed Mommy? Did you kiss her when she was little?"

"I don't think I kissed her until later, but we were best friends."

"There's Gra and Me-maw." Isabella pointed. "They're holding hands."

The girls sat through fifteen minutes of pictures.

"That's all." Kenny closed the folder on the laptop.

"Do you have any pictures of you and Mommy when you were little?" Isabella got up and sat next to Kenny.

"I might have some."

"I wanna see!"

Kenny opened a folder and found one of his favorites. "How about this one?"

"Is that you, Daddy?" Heather grinned. "You had funny ears."

"I did not! You're only saying that because you've heard Mommy say it."

"Is that Mommy?" Isabella jumped down, moved close to the TV and pointed.

"That's Mommy," Kenny said.

"But she looks like us." Isabella stared at Heather.

"You do look a lot like Emmy."

"Who looks a lot like me?" Emmy walked up behind the couch and kissed Kenny's cheek. "You need to shave." Then she looked at the TV. "Why are you looking at those old pictures?"

"Mommy, we saw pictures of you in your princess dress. You were beautiful!"

"Thank you, Isa." Emmy looked more closely at the photo

222

on the TV. "I did look a lot like the girls, huh?"

"Daddy has funny ears." Heather pointed and then giggled.

"He did, but I loved him anyway."

Kevin walked into the family room with a cookie in each hand. He sat down in front of the TV. "Who's that?"

"That's Mommy and me. You need to scoot back, and why are you eating in here?"

"I won't drop any crumbs." He continued to stare at the TV as Kenny advanced the photos. "You have funny ears, Daddy." Kevin laughed.

Kenny reached back and pulled Emmy over the couch and onto his lap. "Did you tell him to say that?"

"Nope! He figured it out on his own. He's a smart kid." Kenny kissed her.

"Daddy!" Heather rolled her eyes. "More kissing?"

"Should I tickle her instead?"

"Yes, let's tickle Mommy."

Kenny held onto Emmy as the kids tickled her.

"Stop it! I'm going to have an accident." Emmy squirmed to get away from Kenny.

Kenny let go and Emmy fell on the floor. Kevin and Heather climbed on top of her.

"Are you all right, Mommy?" Isabella asked.

Emmy put her arms around all three kids. "I couldn't be better."

"What are you going to wear tonight, Em? Does Diane expect us to dress formally?" Kenny checked his closet for a sport coat.

"I'm not dressing up just because she's inviting some of her society friends." Emmy made 'society friends' sound like swearing. "I'll wear newer jeans and a nice top instead of an old sweatshirt."

"Diane will be so pleased. Not! Couldn't you wear a skirt?"

"I'd rather not. You can dress up if you want. This jacket looks great with tight black jeans." She grinned and patted his bottom.

"I'll wear that if you..."

"Fine! Resort to blackmail if you must."

"Come on, Em. I bet the other wives will be wearing skirts or dresses."

She poked him in the side. "What kind of bet?"

"I didn't mean it literally."

"What time is Sofia coming?" Emmy asked as she searched for a skirt.

"She should be here shortly. I like that skirt." He grabbed one from the rack."

"No way, Jose! That one's too short. You know what. Forget it. I'm wearing jeans. I don't care if all the other wives are in ten thousand dollar designer gowns. This party is for our anniversary. I'm going to dress comfortably."

Kenny and Emmy arrived at Brady and Diane's at six thirty.

"'Bout time you guys got here." Diane opened the front door."

"Why? Are we late? I thought you said six thirty." Emmy checked Diane's slacks as she scooted past. *Skirts and dresses, huh?*

"You're not late, but I need to ask you something."

Emmy turned around in the hall to face Diane. "What?"

"Did you mention anything about tonight to Kristen or Sloane?"

"I might have mentioned it to Kristen, but I haven't talked to Sloane."

"Tony?" Diane asked as she walked through the entryway into the living room.

"I talked to him, and he teased me about my anniversary, but I don't remember if I mentioned tonight. Why?"

"I don't want them to be mad at me for not inviting them," Diane said.

Emmy smiled at Marissa Robertson and walked toward her. "Then why didn't you invite them? You have plenty of room," Emmy said over her shoulder. "It's good to see you again, Marissa. How are Spencer and Abby doing?"

"Spencer is enjoying his time at North Park. Unfortunately, Abigail is not appreciating the opportunity of receiving her

224

education at The Barclay Academy." Marissa sat on the couch and fanned herself with a colorful paper fan.

"Oh," Emmy said. *You should be wearing a dress like the women in Gone With The Wind. You would fit in perfectly with that era.*

"It appears she feels some resentment from the other students because her father is the headmaster." Marissa rolled her eyes. "As if that should make a difference."

"I remember at Roosevelt High when my friend Annie's grandfather was the principal. She used it to her advantage."

"How so?" Marissa patted the couch beside her.

Emmy sat next to Marissa. "Annie is the daughter of a SoHam police detective. She would investigate things at school."

"Did she report to her grandfather?" Marissa asked.

Emmy shook her head. "Oh, no! That would have made her like a snitch. She solved a couple of petty crimes and gave Vice-Principal Kemmerick the credit."

"Abigail would never involve herself in such tomfoolery." Marissa sighed as she fanned herself faster.

Kenny walked up to Brady and Bennett as they stood in front of the stone fireplace.

Bennett offered a hand. "Congratulations on your anniversary, Kenny. How many years?"

"Nine." He shook hands with Brady. "Are you keeping busy with the gallery now that you're sort of retired?"

"Not really. I thought it might occupy more of my time, but it hasn't. I love photography as a hobby, but, frankly, I'm bored. I need a challenge."

"Are you thinking of returning to work?" Kenny asked.

Bennett lifted his brow. "Really, Brady? In business or another field?"

"I'm hesitant to become involved in an existing business. The thought of starting one from scratch would certainly be challenging, but I have given some thought to teaching. I might try to finish my doctorate in computer science."

"Really? A doctorate, huh? I never knew," Kenny said. "Are you sure you could deal with today's generation?"

225

Brady chuckled. "No, I might not have the patience. For the time being, Lily keeps me busy. Diane feeds her, and I change all the diapers."

"Kenny, Spencer informed me your band performed under an assumed name back in December. He went to both shows with some friends from North Park."

"Did he enjoy the music?"

"He did remark quite positively about the new music. Why did you perform anonymously?" Bennett asked.

"We wanted to be able to perform the new music in an intimate setting. The Center offered that opportunity."

"Please excuse me for a moment. I see our other guests have arrived." Brady waved as Diane led two couples into the room.

Kenny turned to Bennett. "Is the Academy enduring the criticism from the alumni about accepting males into the school?"

"There was quite a storm of pushback at first, but most of the feedback lately has been positive. Mr. Barclay mentioned at our last meeting that he wished it happened years ago. He admitted his mother forbade it happening in her lifetime, but now that she has passed he decided to forge a new future for the school."

"It's a number of years in the future, but Emmy and I will have to decide where the kids will go to high school. Our church has an elementary school, but I'm not sure if there are plans to expand it to a full twelve years. Right now it's kindergarten through sixth grade."

"It's not easy to start a private high school in this day and age. There is St. Raymond's as an alternative to the public schools."

"True. Perhaps things will change before the girls are that old."

They paused their conversation and turned toward Brady and Diane.

"May I have your attention," Brady said. "I'd like to introduce Dr. Edgar Manning and his lovely wife, Catarina. Edgar enjoyed the privilege of being my roommate for three years at Purdue."

226

Emmy whispered to Kenny, "His wife reminds me of Grandma Colasanti. She about as wide as she is tall."

Kenny looked up at Dr. Manning. "He's tall and skinny. They remind me of you and Tony."

"Get out! Tony and I don't look anything like them."

"I meant he's tall and his wife is short like you and Tony. I know you don't look like her."

"Such a dork."

Brady turned to his right. "Some of you might already know Dr. Thomas Walski and his wife, Ann." Brady glanced at Emmy. Brady made sure he introduced everyone to his friends.

"Hello, Dr. Walski, do you remember me?" Emmy stood with her hands behind her back and grinned as she looked up at him.

He peered through his wire-rimmed glasses. "My, my! Emmy Colasanti! You don't look a day older than when you took my accounting classes. How many years ago would that have been?"

"Too many, but I still remember some of the principles you taught us. How is Kimberly? We were in the same class at Roosevelt."

"She is married and living in England at the moment. She and her husband are teachers, and they have two daughters."

"Kenny and I have three kids. Two girls and a son. The girls are twins. Do you have other grandkids?"

"Cate and Devon each have three children. Thankfully, they live in the area so we get to see them more often," Dr. Walski explained. "I do believe Randy Braun told me about your family. Although we aren't in the same department, North Park is still small enough for the faculty to know one another."

Kenny put his hands on Emmy's shoulders. "I remember Devon from Roosevelt High. We graduated together. Did she pester you in class, Dr. Walski?"

Emmy stuck her elbow in Kenny's stomach.

He laughed. "If I remember correctly, she probably never said a word. She caught on to accounting quicker than any of the other students."

Emmy turned to Kenny. "See? I was a good student."

Diane talked to the caterers and then announced, "Dinner is ready. If we could make our way to the dining room." She led the way. "Please sit wherever you want. Emmy, you and Kenny should sit next to each other over here since this is kinda for your anniversary."

Everyone found a seat at the elegant mahogany table.

"Dinner is family style, so please take some of whatever might be in front of you and pass it along. Left or right?" Brady looked at Diane at the opposite end of the table.

"Left, I think."

Marissa will let us know if we aren't following the proper etiquette. Emmy smiled as she spooned some mashed potatoes onto her plate.

Kenny listened to the conversation as everyone ate. *Wow! Diane and I are the only people here without college educations. I hope I don't ever regret not going to college for more than a year.* He learned that Dr. Manning taught in the science department at Purdue University. *You look like a typical college professor with your ponytail and that sport coat with the patches on the elbows.*

Dr. Manning talked about his research in genetics with Brady and Dr. Walski.

"Emmy, do you understand what they're saying?" Kenny asked. "All these guys are like super intelligent."

Emmy giggled and then whispered, "Then how would I understand? I worked my butt off just to get a degree."

Kenny smiled. *That settles it! One of these days I'm going back to college. I'll earn a degree in the media department. Maybe I can teach after the band decides to retire.*

"Are you all right, Kenny?" Emmy asked. "You look like you're a thousand miles away."

"I'm all right. I thought of something I'd like to achieve, but it might be too much of a challenge."

"You like challenges. I'm sure you can accomplish whatever it is."

"Thank you for your faith in me, Em."

"How old is Grandma?" Isabella asked as the family waited for the elevator at Sunrise Garden.

The doors opened and Emmy grabbed Heather and Isabella. "You need to wait until the people get out of the elevator, and your grandmother turned seventy today."

Can we get in the elevator now, Mommy?" Heather asked. "All the old people are gone,"

Kenny kept the door stayed open. "We can get in now."

As soon as the elevator doors opened, Heather and Isabella stepped out and raced down the hall.

"Which one is it? I forgot," Heather said.

"Wait for us," Kenny said. He paused by the door.

"Can we knock?" Isabella asked.

"You can go on in," Emmy said. She helped Kevin pick up two cars. "She knows we're coming."

Heather and Isabella opened the door, walked in and hollered, "Happy birthday, Grandma!"

They stopped, looked around and turned back to Emmy and Kenny. "She's not here. Is she lost?"

"Check the bedroom," Emmy said.

"Nope! She's lost," Heather said.

"I talked to her this morning," Emmy said as she checked the bathroom.

"Let's check where they play bingo," Kenny suggested.

They did, and found Grandma Patricia playing bingo.

"Happy birthday!" the kids shouted.

"Mom, did you forget we were coming?" Emmy asked.

"I guess I did. Is it really my birthday?"

"Yes, you are seventy today," Isabella said.

"That's really old, Grandma," Kevin said.

"Be nice," Kenny said.

"Are you ready to come back to your apartment?" Emmy asked.

"Not yet. I need to make some money," Patricia said.

"Oh, Mom, you don't need any money," Emmy said with a sigh.

Chapter Twenty-Four

"Em, I talked to Dr. Shea from North Park again. Want to know what he said?" Kenny asked while driving to the church for Christopher and Maddy's wedding Saturday afternoon.

"Are you still determined to go back to school? You haven't said much about it the last month. I thought you had given up on that."

"Not at all, but he suggested I take some online courses."

"Ow! Stop that!" Isabella shouted from the back of the van.

"Are you going to follow his suggestions?" Emmy turned to frown at Heather. "Do not try to hit your sister."

"What grade will you be in if you go to school, Daddy?" Isabella asked.

"Remember when Mary went to college?"

"I remember," Isabella said. "Will you live at the college? Can we come and visit you?"

"No, I won't move to the college. I will live at home."

"Will you ride a school bus?" Kevin asked.

"No, I will drive my Civic to school."

Emmy laughed.

"What is so funny?" Kenny stopped at a yellow light.

"You could have gone through the light, you know."

"There was no one behind us. Why did you laugh?"

"The other students will know who you are eventually. You will lose all your rock star mystique once they learn you drive an old Civic."

"I'm not going to buy a new car just to impress people. The Civic runs great and it still looks mint," Kenny reminded her.

"Do you realize that newer cars have improved technology? They have better electronics. They don't have eight track players anymore."

"So funny, Em."

"They have better safety features. The kids would be safer."

"I don't use the Civic if I'm taking the kids somewhere," Kenny protested.

"You took Kevin to the store the other day." Emmy pointed to Kevin, whose attention was riveted on a SoHam police car with its lights flashing.

"That was an exception."

"Look!" Kevin shouted. "That police man is arresting someone. Probably a bank robber."

"Where?" Heather asked as she looked out the wrong side of the van.

"Over here! See?" Kevin pointed. "Look! Look!"

"How do you know it's a bank robber?" Emmy asked.

"Because that's what police do. They help good people and arrest bad guys and bank robbers. Can we watch?"

"Sorry, Kev, but we have to get to the church," Kenny said.

"Will Maddy be wearing a princess dress?" Isabella asked.

"Probably. Most brides wear fancy wedding gowns," Emmy explained. "So, are you going to take online classes or not?"

"I will, but I want to take some classes on campus. I want it to feel like I've earned my college degree the old-fashioned way. I want to sit in a classroom with other students and listen to professors."

Emmy grinned and poked Kenny's arm. "You want to check out the young college girls."

"Get out! I'm thirty-five. Old enough to be be their... much older brother."

"You're a goof. The girls will be all over you. Do you think you will have the strength to resist?"

"I believe once the other students, male and female, realize I'm serious about getting an education, they will treat me like any other student. There must be a few adults taking classes on campus."

Yeah, but how many of them are rock stars? Emmy thought but then giggled. *Dorky rock stars who drive old cars.*

"Mommy, where is Maddy? I want to see her dress." Isabella stood up in the sanctuary to look around. "Oh! There's Miss Liz talking to those old people." Isabella and Heather waved. "Liz! Liz! Can we go see her, please?"

"Please stay here. I think she might come over and talk to you."

Liz walked over. "My but you both look so beautiful this afternoon. Are those new dresses?"

"Mommy let us pick out new dresses." Isabella pirouetted for Liz. "But we can only wear them to church."

"Your dresses are gorgeous and your hair looks adorable with those purple ribbons. I better go sit down. The ceremony is about to start. Talk to you later." Liz returned to her seat near the front as Pastor Tyler led the men into position.

A few minutes later, Heather and Isabella stood in front of Emmy as Maddy's father walked her down the aisle. Maddy's eyes twinkled as she spotted Heather and Isabella. She waved at the girls and smiled.

"Mommy! Did you see that?" Isabella whispered. "Maddy waved at us. Doesn't she look like a beautiful princess?"

"Yes, she certainly does, Isa," Emmy said.

The white canopy and the floral arrangements fascinated the girls as they glanced around the church during the ceremony.

Isabella looked up at Emmy as Christopher and Maddy exchanged rings and spoke their vows. "Mommy, should I wipe your eyes because you are crying?"

"I'll be okay in a minute, Isa. I'm crying because I'm happy for them."

The reception started an hour after the ceremony ended; right there at the church. Emmy found Liz and they walked into the large gym together.

"Holy moly!" Emmy gasped as she entered. "They really fixed this up nice. When did it happen?"

"Yesterday," Liz answered. "Maddy's parents hired a company to decorate and set everything up. They will return the room to its original state after the reception."

"Too bad. We should leave it like this." Emmy touched some of the streamers and flowers. "These are real. That must have cost a bundle."

"Perhaps her parents decided since they weren't paying for alcohol, they could afford to pay more for decorations." Liz braided her hair as she regarded the multipurpose area.

"I'll have to ask Christopher later about that," Emmy said. "It really surprised me that they are having the reception here. I would have assumed they would have it somewhere people could drink and dance and go nuts."

"I believe the parents might have requested it. Both families are members of other conservative SoHam churches." Liz waved at Tyler as he mingled with the guests. "Tyler mentioned that Christopher and Maddy have taken a membership class and are going to join the church."

"That is great news. I told him they should join the church after he told me he accepted Jesus. He felt that maybe God wouldn't accept him because of his past, but I explained how all our sins are forgotten."

"There are lots of other people who have been married more than once."

Emmy hugged Liz. "I'm so glad we aren't in that group."

A few days later Kenny approached Emmy as she checked her email. "Have you decided yet? Are you coming to Europe with the band? Andy needs to know so they can make hotel arrangements."

Emmy spun her chair around to face Kenny. "Both Sofia and Mary have agreed to help with the kids. Mary will still have a week of school left after we leave, but she has agreed to meet us somewhere in Europe. She's going to fly to Dublin first. That will give her a chance to see some family for a couple days."

"So, I can tell Andy that you, the kids and Sofia and Mary are officially going with us, right?"

"Yes. You may tell him officially. Should I put it in writing?" Emmy grinned.

"No, I don't think he needs that. Do you know where everyone's passport is?"

"Yes, all the kids' passports are in the desk in this drawer. Sofia and Mary have their passports with them. Did you thank Mr. Robertson for allowing the band to use his plane?" Emmy double checked to make sure all three passports were in the drawer.

"Numerous times. He must be able to write the plane off on his taxes or something."

On May twenty-first, the Fridays At Five entourage flew into Frankfurt, Germany, to begin the three-week-long European tour. Mary Michaelis flew to Dublin a week later and after spending two days with family, joined Emmy and the kids in Madrid, Spain.

"Thank you for spending part of your summer vacation with us." Emmy said as she met Mary in the hotel lobby. "Were you afraid flying into Spain by yourself?"

"Don't be silly, Em. I'm not afraid to fly by myself."

"I would be," Emmy admitted. *I would be scared to death.*

"I only have my backpack, since most of my luggage flew over with you guys. I walked through the terminal and spotted Ty Dalicandro holding a sign with my name. We got in a limo and the driver dropped us off here at the hotel. Piece of cake!"

"The kids have been asking everyday how soon you would get here. They have been behaving for Sofia, but they still miss you."

"I won't interfere with Sofia. She is their nanny now."

They waited for the elevator.

"How have you handled traveling to different countries?" Mary asked. "Any trouble with a language barrier?"

"Oh, yeah, but I hang out with Charles. He speaks just about everything, and a lot of people speak English. It hasn't been that big a concern."

Mary chuckled. "I sometimes have trouble understanding some of my Irish family. They laugh at me when I look confused. They tried to teach me a few Gaelic words, but I'm not very good at learning new languages."

"Charles has a knack for it. I bet if he tried, he could learn Russian or Chinese or whatever."

The elevator stopped, the doors opened and Emmy and Mary stepped into the hall

"Mary! Mary! You're finally here!" Heather and Isabella shrieked. "We missed you."

Mary squatted and hugged both girls. "Have you been behaving for Sofia?"

They nodded. "She is our nanny now, but you're still our nanny, too."

Mary looked up and noticed Sofia and Kevin approaching.

"Hello, Mary. It's good to see you again. The kids have been a handful. I could use a long siesta."

"I'm help out in any way you need. Have they been learning Spanish?"

"Oh, yes. They are all learning. Kevin can count to ten in Spanish."

Kevin rattled off the numbers without missing a single one.

"Mary, we took a train ride. It was so awesome," Heather shouted.

"Where did you go on the train?" Mary asked.

"I don't know, but we got to eat on a train," Isabella added.

Mary looked at Emmy.

"The girls wanted to ride a train, so Charles and Andy took us from Hamburg to Berlin. Taking the train in Europe is so much nicer than back home. The girls had a blast. Kevin didn't like it as much. He loves the thrill of flying," Emmy explained, "The pilots even let him sit in the cockpit and touch knobs and turn the wheel thing."

"While you were flying!?" Mary put a hand to her mouth.

"No, no! We were on the ground," Emmy said.

"I'm going to be a fireman when I grow up and fly airplanes, too," Kevin insisted.

"I hope you don't mind sharing a room with me," Sofia said. "There are two beds."

"Not a problem. I had to share a bed with one of my distant cousins in Dublin."

"Come on, kids. Let's give Mary and Sofia some time to relax." Emmy took the kids back to their suite.

"Can we eat dinner with Sofia and Mary later?" Heather asked.

"Yes, but try not to pester them too much."

235

The tour continued with stops in Rome, Vienna, Zurich and Paris before arriving in Dublin. Kenny provided fifty tickets for Mary's family and their friends to attend the concert in Croke Park. After a show in Glasgow, Scotland, the band arrived in London for the final night of the tour.

"One of these days we will have to bring the kids over here for a real vacation," Emmy said as she rushed the kids into the elevator and then to a waiting limo for the trip to Wembley Stadium. "We did get to see some sites in a few cities. I loved Prague and Rome, but we've never had a chance to really see Great Britain as tourists."

"Em, you did spend your honeymoon over here, remember?" Mary grinned.

Emmy bit her lip. "Yeah, but we were kinda busy."

"Didn't you ever leave your room?" Sofia asked. *Niles and I did.*

"We didn't spend all our time in our room. We saw some stuff and took walks together," Emmy insisted.

"Uh-huh, sure," Mary teased.

"Just wait, Mary. One of these days you will get married, and I will ask you all about your honeymoon."

The band played to a crowd of ninety thousand people in Wembley Stadium that night. Kenny didn't make it back to the hotel until after Emmy was asleep. He slipped into bed next to her and kissed her ear, then her neck and finally her lips.

"Are you awake?"

"I am now. What time is it?" Emmy opened her eyes.

He kissed her again. "It's a bit past two. We won't see each other for three weeks."

"Then you better kiss me again."

The next morning Emmy, Sofia, Mary and the kids were flying home from Heathrow on a commercial flight.

"Em, you can upgrade to first class. You don't have to fly on the cheap." Kenny helped her pack.

"That's too expensive. We will be fine."

"How are you getting home from O'Hare?" He lifted one of

236

the large suitcases. *What's in here? Bricks?*

"Tony and John are meeting us at the airport."

"Why both of them? That won't leave much room for everyone." Kenny shrugged.

"They are each driving a minivan," Emmy said. "I told Tony how much luggage we had. He wanted to rent a truck, but I convinced him the luggage would fit in his van."

"What about on the plane?"

"We already know how much it will cost for the extra bags. You don't need to worry. We will be all right."

"Sorry, but it's my job to worry about you." He kissed her on the mouth and pulled her close.

Mary cleared her throat. "We need to get downstairs. We are supposed to be at the airport in an hour."

Kenny kissed Emmy again, and then kissed and hugged each of the kids. "I will see you in three weeks or so."

"Have a good time at work, Daddy." Isabella waved and then stepped into the elevator. "We will take care of Mommy for you."

Kenny and the guys flew back to the States on Mr. Robertson's plane later that day. They landed in Boston where on Saturday they would play the first of three nights in the city. The east coast portion of the tour would last for twenty-two nights without a break.

On June thirtieth the band ended the show in Montreal and headed backstage.

"Thanks, Frankie," Kenny said as Frankie handed him a dry towel. "I'll be glad to sleep in my own bed tonight."

Jana Cordell handed Kenny his Gatorade and grinned. "Emmy texted me earlier. She says she will wait up as long as she can, but you are supposed to wake her up if she falls asleep."

"She really texted that?"

Jana nodded. "I guess she missed you."

Kenny took a long drink before adding. "This is the first time since we've been married that she hasn't made an appearance onstage to sing with me. She sang in Europe, but decided to stay

237

home for this part of the tour. She promised to do a set in SoHam, but I don't think she will appear anywhere else with us."

"She needs to take care of the kids," Jana said. "Plus, she has her own career."

"Thanks for reminding me, Jana," Kenny said sarcastically.

Garrett Hainsey from The Barefoot Prophets spotted Kenny and hustled over. "I want to express our gratitude for allowing us to open your shows. I'm pretty sure we made some new fans."

Kenny shook his hand. "You guys are playing SoHam with us, right?"

"Yes, but then we are off on our own again. No more flying to the gigs. It will be back to the bus for us."

"Fridays At Five spent a lot of time traveling on buses," Kenny said. "In some ways I miss those days, but I do like to sleep in hotels instead of a bus rolling down the road."

"I don't know if you saw, but our CD is climbing up the *Billboard* chart again. It's taken over a year but it's finally sold enough for a gold record. Three of the tracks have received heavy radio airplay."

"Are you guys ready for the next project? If I you want, I might find some time to help."

"Are you kidding? Without your help *Resurrection Ghost* wouldn't have made a dent in the charts. Thank you for your input and for offering to keep working with us."

"I'll see you on Wednesday, Garrett. Good luck on your tour."

Chapter Twenty-Five

"How many times have you guys played at the SoHam Stadium?" a fan asked backstage before the band's Fourth of July show.

"Kenny, do you know?" Jeff asked. "I don't remember."

"I'm not sure, but I know who would know," Kenny said. "My father keeps a record of each place we play. Dates, set lists, attendance, where known. All sorts of facts. I think he wants to write a book someday. He would be able to answer your question. I'm sorry we can't."

"It's all right," the fan said. "I'm simply glad you guys still play here, and the tickets don't cost a small fortune."

Kenny and the guys laughed because the tickets for today's show could only be purchased at the stadium in the prior weeks with a valid SoHam proof of address. Once a person provided the proof, they received two tickets for twenty dollars. The ticket money was donated to local food banks and shelters for the homeless.

"Emmy, who are you calling? You need to do your soundcheck." Kenny caught her talking on her cell phone backstage.

"Sorry, but I had to talk to the kids. I'll be right there."

"The kids are with Sofia and Niles. They are okay." Kenny took her hand. "Are you all right? Is there something bothering you?"

She bit her lip for a moment. "I yelled at Heather before I left the house. She hit Kevin, and I raised my voice and swatted her. I needed to make sure she knew I still loved her."

"Does she know?"

"She had forgotten about me swatting her, and she said she loved me. She said to do a good job singing and to make sure I kiss her good night when I got home."

Kenny hugged Emmy. "It's not easy to discipline the kids, but it is necessary."

"I know, but you know that old saying about this hurting me more..."

239

"I remember it." Kenny laughed.

"I never believed it when I was a kid, but I understand it now."

Kenny wiped her eyes. "You need to do your job now. The kids are all right with Sofia and Niles."

Twenty minutes later the soundcheck was completed.

"We're good to go," Emmy told Will Consoli and handed her wireless microphone to Noah Belanger.

The Katie Hollins Band opened the show at six. The Barefoot Prophets followed and played for forty-five minutes.

Emmy approached Garrett Hainsey as he walked backstage. "You guys sounded awesome."

"Did you say awful, Emmy?" Garrett wiped his glasses with a tissue.

Emmy laughed and then said. "Not awful. Awesome! You guys are going to blow people away on your tour."

"Thanks for the encouragement. You might be seeing more of us when we get back. Kenny offered to let us use the studio."

"Did he promise to feed you guys?" Emmy looked up at him with hands on her hips.

"No, he didn't mention food." Garrett shrugged.

"Good, because I'm not feeding you guys. I've seen how much you all can eat. I couldn't afford to buy enough groceries."

She talked to Garrett and the other guys in the band for fifteen minutes until Nelson Grapella tapped her on the shoulder.

"Emmy, I think everyone is waiting for you," Nelson said. "The stage is ready. Frankie will lead you out there. He's got your mic."

"I'm sorry, Nelson. I lost track of time. Am I really late?"

"No, Ty just called me a minute ago."

Frankie approached. "Ready, Emmy?"

"Yes, Frankie. Thank you." Emmy walked beside Kenny's cousin and the original member of the Friday's crew. "Can you ever see yourself doing anything else?"

He shook his head. "Now why would I ever do anything else, Em. Like Isabella said. I get to tell Kenny what songs to sing." He grinned. "Watch out for that cable."

"Frankie Hanna! I think you just tried to make me laugh. Are you finally loosening up?"

"Aw, Emmy. You know how much I care for you and Kenny and the kids."

"I know, Frankie. Thank you." She took the microphone and ran out to center stage just as Andy Walker finished introducing her.

"Good timing, princess." Andy smiled.

Emmy kept the crowd on their feet for the first five songs.

"Thank you for the encouragement," she said. "We're going to slow things down and do a couple songs from the new CD."

The crowd settled down as Emmy sang three new songs. She ramped up the energy with three uptempo songs and then ended her set with "Yolanda's Song."

"Thank you for making me feel appreciated. We'll see you again soon." She left the stage and handed her microphone to Frankie.

"Great job, Emmy." He handed her a towel and a bottle of water.

"Thanks, Frankie. Have you seen Kenny?"

"He's with the guys in their dressing room."

"I won't bother him. I'll hang out with my guys."

Emmy waited backstage until Fridays At Five finished their last encore. Kenny spotted her and walked in her direction.

"Are you ready to go home?" Emmy asked. "You guys sounded pretty good tonight. One of your best shows."

"I'm ready. What makes you think we sounded better than usual?"

Emmy grinned. "Because I was back here and couldn't hear you."

Kenny picked her up and put her on his shoulder as she giggled. "I should swat you like you did Heather."

"Don't you dare. I'm kidding. You guys really did sound amazing. Have you finally learned how to play your guitar in the right key?" she asked and then giggled again.

Kenny set her down and put his hands on her shoulders. "Are you finished making fun of me? Can I take you home now?"

241

"That depends."

"On what?" he asked.

She stood on her toes and whispered to him.

He cleared his throat. "I might, but only if the kids are asleep."

Andy Walker had been watching and listening to everything. He stared sternly at Emmy. "What did you ask Kenny to do? Or should I not ask?"

Emmy grinned. "I asked him to make me a chocolate shake and put whipped cream and a cherry on top."

Andy turned his gaze to Kenny. "Did she?"

Kenny nodded.

Andy stared at them both for a few seconds. "Go on. Get out of here." Andy pointed. *Why is it I don't believe either of you?*

"How soon do you have to leave, Daddy?" Isabella asked the next morning. She looked at the counter by the sink. "Did you and Mommy have milkshakes last night?" She glared at Kenny.

"Mommy wanted a milkshake before she went to bed. I forgot to wash the blender thing," Kenny admitted.

"I want a milkshake when you get back."

"I will make everyone super thick milkshakes when I return."

"Promise?"

"Yes, Isa, I promise." Kenny raised his right hand.

He made breakfast for everyone before he caught a ride to the airport.

"I'll be back on Sunday morning. Everyone be good for Mommy and Sofia."

Emmy kissed him. "I'm glad the band has resumed the Wednesday through Saturday schedule. I didn't like it when you were gone for three straight weeks."

"Em, remember you survived when I was gone for eighteen months back in the early days." Kenny kissed her again. "We only saw each other once in a year and a half."

"Are you forgetting we weren't married then?" She poked him in the belly. "If you're ever gone for even three months now,

242

you will have to find another wife and kids."

"You don't really mean that, do you?"

"Are you sure you want to find out?"

He peered intently into her eyes. "No, I don't want to ever be gone that long."

Kenny returned home around three in the morning on Sunday. He didn't wake up Emmy as he slept on the edge of the bed while she sprawled across it nearly sideways.

"Kenny, are you going to church this morning?" Emmy asked around eight thirty.

"Yes! I'm awake." He jumped out of bed and landed on a firetruck.

"Sorry, I let Kevin sleep with me for a couple of hours. Are you hurt?"

"No." He sat on the bed and rubbed his big toe. "I don't think it's broken."

"Anything you want to tell me?" Emmy asked and then bit her lip.

He glanced at her as she stood on the other side of the bed in a sexy nightgown. "Uh... How soon do we need to be at church?"

"Too soon for that!"

"Oh, shoot. I almost forgot. Happy birthday, Em. How old are you now? Nineteen?"

She grinned. "Maybe we could go to the second service."

"Happy birthday, Mommy!" All three kids ran into the bedroom.

"I brought you some donuts. Can we have breakfast in your bed?" Heather asked.

"So much for that," Emmy said with a sigh. "And I'm thirty-two today for your information. Are you looking for someone who's nineteen?"

"Not a chance." Kenny grabbed a donut.

"You guys are going to get crumbs all over the bed," Emmy whined.

"Let them have fun. I'll strip the bed and remake it this

243

afternoon," Kenny promised.

"Okay, but I'm not changing the sheets. Are there any chocolate glazed donuts? I like those the best."

Everyone sat on the bed to eat a donut.

"I like donuts with filling," Kevin said.

"Try to get more of the filling inside your mouth, Kev."

He wiped his chin with his hand and then wiped that hand on his pajamas.

"Put those pajamas in the dirty clothes when you get dressed for church," Kenny said while shaking his head.

"Thank you for breakfast in bed, but now we've got to hurry. Kenny, you take Kevin and give him a quick shower. I'll help the girls get ready. We've got thirty minutes to get ready to leave," Emmy instructed.

"We made it, Mommy! We're on time." Isabella shouted as she and Heather dashed off to their church service with Pastor Jeremiah.

"Kevin, will you stay with your sisters?" Emmy asked.

"I'll sit with Gracie. She's already here." He pointed.

"Okay, we'll see you after church."

"Emmy, do you have a minute?" Kristen walked up to Emmy.

"Sure, what's up?"

"Let's talk on the way to the sanctuary," Kristen suggested.

They walked with other parents who had dropped off their children.

"I've been thinking of going back to work."

"Why? Is this because of John retiring?"

"If you're wondering about the change in our income level, no. Part of John's salary has been deferred, and we've lived on a strict budget. We won't have to make any drastic changes."

Emmy grinned. "Actually, I meant since he's retired from the Bears, he will be around all the time. I thought you were looking for a job so you wouldn't be together 24/7."

"That's not it. He's gone just as much as ever. He's busy with Two Bears. Don't even make fun of that name." Kristen frowned.

244

"I'm used to it now, but I still think it's goofy."

"John is helping with Daddy's company. He is even busier now than before."

"Is your father ever going to retire completely?"

"I don't think so. He feels so much better since he had hip replacement surgery. Even when they're in Florida, he keeps checking on projects, but Derrick did tell me the company will be sold to the employees when Daddy passes away."

"Why? All of the employees?" Emmy asked.

"Not all. A group of the executives."

"Even Mama Bertucci's half?"

"She gave her share to Tony and Marco. Derrick said they agreed to sell. I guess no one wants to take over the business."

"You could run it." Emmy pulled Kristen into an empty room.

"Me! Are you crazy? I don't know enough about the construction business."

"You could learn."

"Not interested. John suggested I take over the office management of Two Bears. I could do that from home."

"I didn't know they had an office," Emmy said.

"They don't. Unless you call a website and a telephone an office. Come on. We need to get to the sanctuary before the service starts."

That afternoon after lunch Emmy looked through her *Style* magazine as she and Kenny relaxed in the family room. She held it up to show Kenny a page.

"I need to get my hair styled again. Do you like this?"

"What's wrong with your hair now? I like it," Kenny answered.

"It's getting too long again. In fact, the girls need to get their hair trimmed. How about tomorrow we all get our hair done? You can take Kevin with you to that real barber shop while I take the girls with me. Deal?"

"I need a cut, and Kevin likes to watch those guys."

"He needs a haircut, too."

"Okay with me."

Emmy called the next morning and scheduled an appointment in the afternoon. Kenny took Kevin to the barber shop after lunch. No appointment necessary.

Later, Emmy ran her hand through Kenny's hair. "It's still long. Did they cut it at all?"

"They trimmed it all over."

"It's still thick, and it hides your funny ears," she teased.

"What about me, Mommy?" Kevin asked.

"Your hair is straight like your father's. You look very handsome with your hair combed."

"Do we look like princesses, Daddy?" Heather asked.

She and Isabella pirouetted for him.

"Isabella's hair looks curlier than Heather's now. Why is that?"

Emmy checked the girls out from the back. "It is. I don't know why. How do you like my new style?"

"Isn't it the same style as before?"

"It's layered differently, and I don't think it's as curly. Now it's more wavy, and it will be easy to maintain."

"Are you trying to look grown up, Em?" Kenny grinned.

"I won't be nineteen forever."

Chapter Twenty-Six

Father James parked his car and walked around the side of the house. He heard a commotion from the pool area and headed that way.

"Mommy, watch me swim underwater," Heather said. "I can go back and forth like a fish."

"I'm watching, Heather, but I have to keep an eye out for Father James," Emmy said. Her eyes darted back and forth.

"I'm here," Father James said. He opened the wrought iron gate and walked to the lounge chair where Emmy was working on her tan. "It's a beautiful day for a swim, huh?"

Emmy put a hand to her eyes to shield the sun and smiled. "It is, and the kids would spend all afternoon in the pool if I let them."

Father James heard the kids splashing, glanced in that direction, waved and then looked down at Emmy. He turned away.

Emmy sat up on the edge of the lounge chair. "Are you embarrassed because I'm in a bikini?"

He walked over to a plastic pool chair and sat down. He looked out at the pool and said, "I've never seen you in one before."

"Sorry, I forgot priests are different than other clergy. The pastors at our church are married, so they can have sex."

"You have such a tactful way of putting it, Emmy," he replied.

"I'll put my t-shirt on if that will make you more comfortable." She grabbed her t-shirt, which was really Kenny's, and put it on. "I'm decent now."

Father James turned to look. "That's better."

Kevin climbed out of the pool at the far end and ran all the way around it to Father James. "Are you going to swim with us?"

"Kevin Michael, you know better than to run by the pool," Emmy scolded.

"Sorry, Mommy. I forgot." He moved closer to Father James. "I can swim real good."

"I saw you swimming. You and your sisters should be in

the Olympics," Father James said as he dried his arms.

"Kevin Michael, you are dripping all over Father James," Emmy said.

"Sorry," Kevin said and then backed up a step. "What are Olympics?"

Father James explained.

"I'm going to be a police man and a fireman when I grow up. I'm going to drive an ab-u-lance, too," Kevin said, turned around, ran back to the pool and jumped in.

"Be careful not to land on your sisters," Emmy said. She walked up to her brother, pulled one of the other chairs closer and sat down. "Did you bring trunks? It's probably pretty hot in black jeans and a polo shirt."

He shook his head. "Priests aren't allowed to wear swim trunks in mixed company. Where is Kenny?"

Emmy laughed. "I'm not mixed company. I'm your little sister, and Kenny is supervising a work crew from Two Bears landscaping. They're clearing out some of the dead trees and brush since it's been rather dry." She pointed behind her. "Somewhere on that side of the property."

"I see," Father James said.

"Did you bring trunks or not?"

"No, I did not."

Emmy tilted her head. "I don't buy that bit about mixed company. What gives?"

Father James shrugged. "I need to keep covered, or else I will get a sunburn."

"I have sunscreen. It's this marvelous new invention that can prevent sunburns. You should try it."

"I'll pass."

Emmy stared at him for a moment and then chuckled. "You don't know how to swim, do you?"

"Is that a crime? I never had much of a chance to learn where we lived. There wasn't a community pool within fifty miles, and I wasn't about to go swimming in some farmer's scummy pond."

"I learned how to swim when I was real young. Mr.

Robertson had a pool at his house, and that's where I learned. I don't really remember it, but that's what I've been told."

"I'm glad the kids know how," he said as a beach ball came sailing out of the pool. He grabbed it and tossed it back.

"All the kids in the neighborhood come over here to swim. Tony and Kristen plan to put in their own pool soon."

Father James looked at Emmy and asked, "How is it that Mr. Robertson taught you to swim, but you told me how you first met him at that dinner?"

"Brady helped teach me to swim, too. Anyway, Mr. Robertson promised Grandpa he would kinda watch over me and Diane. We didn't realize it when we were kids. He started his company and that took up most of his time. Brady and Bennett went off to college, and we didn't see them for years. We didn't see Mr. Robertson either."

Emmy explained more as they watched and listened to the kids playing in the water.

"I wish I could have been there when you met again," Father James said.

"Oh, hush. You just want to see me embarrass myself," Emmy said as she poked his arm.

"Do you still have your music box?"

Emmy nodded. "I'll show it to you sometime, and I'll show you the book our great-great grandfather wrote. Do you know any Italian?"

"I know enough to order something to eat, but I can't read it. I'm better at Spanish. I can understand some of what Sofia is saying if she doesn't talk super fast."

"I love how the kids are picking up the language. It will help when they get older," Emmy said. "Are you thirsty? Hungry?"

"I ate lunch, but I could use a cold beverage."

Emmy grinned and pointed at the garage. "You know where the fridge is. You can have a beer and I'll take a Dr Pepper."

Father James returned with the beverages and water for the kids.

"Thank you," Emmy said. "Would you mind if I use the pool?"

"Go ahead," he answered while sipping on his Sam Adams. "I'll play lifeguard."

"Some lifeguard you'll be. I'd have to rescue you," Emmy teased.

"The pool isn't that deep. I can keep my head above water if I walk on the bottom."

Emmy shook her head. "It gets too deep for that in parts." She removed her t-shirt and dove into the pool.

"Mommy, isn't Father James going to swim with us?" Isabella asked.

"Not today," Emmy answered.

Father James moved his chair under one of the umbrellas that covered the tables to watch.

Kenny walked up to the fence and hollered, "Father James, I didn't know you were here. Where's Emmy?"

Father James pointed and said, "In the pool." He explained why he wasn't swimming after Kenny asked.

"I'm done with the crew. I'll go downstairs and shower and be right back."

Kenny showered in the basement and returned wearing swim trunks.

"Daddy! Come and swim with us," Heather hollered.

"Don't mind if I do," Kenny said and then jumped it splashing Emmy.

"Thanks for almost drowning me," Emmy said as she spat some water at him.

"Should we chase Mommy?" Kenny asked with a gleam in his eyes.

"Yes! Let's chase Mommy," Kevin said.

Kenny helped the kids surround Emmy.

"You better be careful," she warned. "Father James is here and this bikini doesn't cover much."

"At least you're wearing it," Kenny whispered.

"Shush! I always wear a suit during the day."

Twenty minutes later everyone got out of the pool.

"Grab a towel and dry off. Then I want you to run inside and change clothes," Emmy said.

The kids obeyed with some help from Kenny.

Emmy walked up to Father James as she dried off with a large beach towel.

"It sounded like everyone had fun," he said.

"I used to worry about having a pool, but now that the kids are older, I don't. I still worry, but at least now they know they can't swim unless an adult is here. Do you get my meaning?"

Father James chuckled and his belly jiggled. "You're meaning is as clear as Irish whiskey."

Emmy stuck out her tongue at him. "I will assume whiskey isn't clear like some other libations."

"Are you pulling my leg?" he asked. "You told me about drinking beer when you were nine."

"Daddy never drank anything stronger than beer or wine. He never had any in the house at least."

"It's an acquired taste."

"Are you staying for dinner? I'd rather not have to use the oven, but I could make a meat loaf if you want."

"It's too hot for that. I'll stay and you can make whatever you guys want. I am a man of simple tastes and habits."

"Yeah, you're that all right," Emmy said. She shook her head to let the water spray onto her brother.

"Hey!" he shouted and moved to the side. "I would let the girls get away with that, but you're older and should know better."

Emmy grinned and whispered, "True, but I'm making up for all the time I lost when I didn't know I had a real big brother."

Chapter Twenty-Seven

"Sloane, now that the kids are asleep, we need to talk." Tony sat beside his wife on the family room couch.

"What about? It must be serious from the look on your face." Sloane marked her place and set down her book.

"Now that training camp is over, and I've made the final roster..."

Sloane rolled her eyes. "Did you think they might cut you?"

"Not really, I guess. Anyway, I've given this a lot of thought." He took a deep breath. "This is going to be my last season with the Bears."

"Are you going to be a free agent? Is your contract up? Do you want to play somewhere else?" She picked up her book.

"No! This is my last season period. I'm calling it a career after this year. This will be my eleventh season. If you add up college, high school and junior high, I've been playing for twenty years. It would be great if we win the Super Bowl, and I can retire like Elway did."

"Are you sure?" Sloane tilted her head and stared at him. "Does this have anything to do with John not playing?"

Tony put his arm around Sloane's shoulders. "Maybe a little. This is the first time since my freshman year at Notre Dame that we won't be teammates. It's kinda strange not having him in the locker room."

"Have you talked to anyone else?"

"Not yet. I wanted to know how you felt first."

Sloane grinned. "Emmy will be devastated."

"She knows I can't play forever."

"True, but she won't expect this to be your final year," Sloane said. "The kids will love it. You will be home more. I'm assuming you won't take a coaching job somewhere on the other side of the country."

"Right now I don't have any interest in coaching. That might change down the road, but as of now... no way. It's not for me."

"When are you going to tell the team?"

"I'll talk to Coach Smith tomorrow."

"Do you think he'll be surprised?"

Tony gazed at the ceiling and crossed his arms over his chest. "Maybe, maybe not."

"Duh! What kind of an answer is that?" Sloane poked him in the side. "Have you thought about how you will occupy your time after this season?"

"John and I have Two Bears to keep us busy."

"You do realize that unless you guys actively seek more clients who need landscaping design work, it will never be more than mowing yards, right?"

"I suppose so. I know John is getting more and more involved with the construction company."

"That might be a better alternative than Two Bears. Bertucci and Keasling Construction has been around a long time. It's huge and has survived through some serious depressions in the construction business."

"Okay, I can see your point. I like doing landscaping around the house, but I'm not all that great at designing stuff. John isn't either. I want to keep Two Bears going even if it's just mowing yards. We've got three crews, and they depend on that job."

"I'm not saying you need to close up shop."

"The house will be paid off in three years, or sooner. We've got that covered."

"One of these days all your deferred salary from the Bears will end," Sloane pointed out.

"Yes, but we've invested our money wisely. I've heard about some players who end up bankrupt a couple of years after they stop playing. That won't happen to us, Sloane."

"I'm not worried about that. I can always teach. Once the house is paid off, we won't need to earn as high of an income."

"Are you forgetting we have six kids who will need to go to college."

"I haven't forgotten. We have trust funds started for each of them. Peter and Dotty have the life insurance money."

253

"That will cover college for them unless tuition costs skyrocket in twenty years."

Sloane laughed. "Tony, you do realize Peter turned nine last month. He will be ready for college in just ten years. Dotty a year later."

"I can't believe our little Dotty is eight already. Holy cow!"

"What?"

"In a few years she's going to start all that female stuff. I'll have to worry about boys being interested in her."

"And Noemi..."

"Noemi's a baby."

Sloane shook her head. "She's six, you goof. It's a good thing we have more boys than girls. You would be a total wreck if we had six girls."

"So it's all right with you if this is my last year, right?" Tony asked.

"Yes. You have my permission to retire. You need to tell your mother."

"She won't mind. She's always worried about me getting hurt."

"There is one more person you might want to talk to and get her permission." Sloane grinned.

"Yeah. I don't know what I fear more. Telling Coach Smith or telling the brat."

"I know who I'd fear more." Sloane got up.

Tony leaned back against the couch and closed his eyes. "Emmy will be so pissed."

"Make sure you tell her before you have a press conference."

Tony checked the time. "Do you think it's too late to tell her now?"

"They're probably still up. Go ahead." Sloane turned to face him. "If you have the nerve."

"I'm not afraid of her," Tony insisted.

Yeah, right. Sloane smiled. "You should be very afraid."

Tony jogged over to Kenny and Emmy's and rang the back door bell.

Kenny walked out to the garage to see who was there. "Tony! Come on in."

"I'm sorry to bother you, but I need to talk to Emmy for a second. Is she still up?"

"Yeah, she's in the family room."

Tony followed Kenny into the family room.

"Em, Tony needs to talk to you."

She removed the headphones and paused the CD. "What are you doing here, creep? You better start playing better than you did in the preseason. The team, I mean. You did all right for an old guy who can't cover the running backs."

"I need to tell you something, Em." He hung his head for a moment.

"Are the kids all right? Is Mama okay? Sloane? What is it?" she asked. "Don't keep me in suspense."

Tony lifted his head and looked into her eyes. "This is going to be my last year with the Bears. I'm retiring after this season."

"So everyone is okay, right?"

"Yes, no one is sick or anything."

"Good." Emmy threw a pillow at him. "What do you mean you're retiring? You can't leave the Bears. I know you've lost a step, but you're still the best middle linebacker in the league."

"Em, I'm not even sure I'm the best linebacker on the Bears anymore. The younger guys are so quick and they're getting bigger every year. There are running backs in the league bigger than me."

"So what. You are smarter than them. You aren't hurt, are you?"

"No. I'm in good shape. I actually feel better than the last couple of years, but I'm still going to retire."

"So it's official, huh?" Emmy sighed.

"Yes, I told Sloane already."

"Did you tell the team?"

"Not yet. I wanted to talk to you first."

Emmy grinned. "You didn't want me to hear it on ESPN or *Sports Center*, huh?"

"I thought you would get pissed."

"I would have. Thank you for telling me beforehand."

"So, it's all right with you?"

"I know you can't play forever. It won't be the same without you though. I've always loved watching football. How many years has it been that I've watched you play?"

"Well, I guess since 1996. I played varsity ball as a sophomore."

"Holy crap! That's like sixteen years. That's half of my life. Kenny, what do you think?"

"I'm envious. Tony gets to retire, and I have to keep working."

"You don't have to keep working," Emmy said. "Oh, did you tell Tony about your plans?"

"I haven't told anyone."

"What plans?" Tony asked.

"Can I tell him?" Emmy bit her lip.

"Go ahead, Em," Kenny said.

"Kenny is going back to college. Remember, he went one year to Paul Frank? It was a long time ago so I don't know if it would even count."

"I remember."

"He's going to take some courses online, but then finish at North Park."

"For real?" Tony asked.

Kenny nodded.

"Good for you."

"I know it really won't amount to anything, but I'd like to say I earned a degree."

"How hard can it be?" Tony shrugged. "She did it." He pointed at Emmy and then ducked.

"Creep!" She threw another small pillow.

"I was more worried about telling you than telling Coach Smith," Tony admitted.

"When are you telling him?"

"In the morning." Tony stood up and tossed the pillows back to Emmy.

She caught the pillows, set them on the couch and then

256

stood up. She hugged Tony. "Thank you for considering my feelings."

"No problem, brat. Thanks for understanding. I better go. I have to think about what I'm going to say tomorrow."

Emmy walked Tony out. They paused outside the garage service door.

"It's a gorgeous night. Not too hot or humid." Emmy looked up at the stars. "A good night for a run. Did you talk to Sloane about how you're going to earn money in the future? You don't have many brain cells left after all these years of getting hit in the head."

"You're a riot, brat. We talked. I have some plans."

She put a finger to her mouth, tapped her chin and then said, "I'll pay you twenty bucks for mowing the yard."

"Wow! Twenty? I would do it for ten." He picked her up and held her in the air.

"Put me down!" She insisted.

"I bet I can still pick you up by your ankles."

"So what? Put me down."

He set her down. "Did you get your hair cut?"

"Styled. And thanks for noticing. Do you like?" She twirled in a circle.

"Yeah, looks good, I guess."

"Creep! Men don't notice anything."

"I'd notice if you shaved it," he said.

"Never happen."

"See ya later, Em. Make sure you watch *Sports Center* tomorrow." Tony waved and jogged home.

He told his mother before she went to bed.

"Are you sure about this? You will miss the competition and being with your teammates."

"I realize that, but I've given it a lot of thought. The time is right."

"Football has enabled you to get an education and pay for this house." She hugged him. "But I'll be glad when you stop playing."

257

Tony called John Randolph in the morning and told him the news.

"Are you sure? You could play a few more years if you want."

"I don't want to play until I embarrass myself. This is it for me. I'll give everything I've got this year. I think we might make it back to the Super Bowl. I really do. But when the season ends, I'm done. No regrets."

"Can I tell Kristen?" John asked. "Oh, did you tell Emmy?"

"I told her last night after I talked to Sloane. She gave me her blessing." Tony laughed.

"Yeah, I bet. She probably pounded on you." John laughed. "How did Mama react?"

"She hugged me and said she was glad."

"I was going to wait until later, but I might as well tell you now. North Park offered me a position as a part-time receivers coach."

"Did you accept?"

"Yeah, I start Wednesday. It won't pay for groceries, but it's a start. I can see myself as a college coach one day. Not sure about coaching in the NFL."

"I can see you as a head coach for some college, but I don't have any interest in coaching. I might coach the kids if they want to get into sports."

Tony told Coach Smith of his decision as soon as he arrived at Halas Hall and then talked to the players. At a news conference that afternoon, he told his plans to everyone else. He thanked the Bears for their support over the years and left before anyone could see his eyes filling with tears.

Chapter Twenty-Eight

Tuesday evening Sloane, Kristen, Diane and Emmy sat in the breakfast nook at Emmy's house to discuss the school situation.

"Wouldn't it be nice if the school had bus service," Emmy said. "I have coffee and some brownies. They're from a box. Not homemade, sorry."

Emmy poured coffee for everyone and let them take a brownie if they desired.

Sloane nodded. "It would make getting the kids to school a whole lot simpler."

"How many kids are going to Crest Ridge?" Diane asked.

Emmy quickly figured it out. "Eleven counting the ones in pre-school. Kevin, Ben and Grace only go a half day. Everyone else is is there all day."

"Maybe we should buy a school bus," Kristen said. "Just kidding."

"Wait! That might not be a bad idea." Emmy's eyes sparkled. "Maybe not a real school bus, but a large van."

"Who would drive it?" Diane asked.

"We could take turns," Emmy suggested.

Sloane finished a brownie and wondered, "Where would we keep it? Who would pay for maintenance. What about insurance?"

"All that stuff could be figured out later," Emmy said. "It's not going to happen tonight, and, since school starts tomorrow, we should figure out how to get all the kids to school using the minimum number of vehicles."

"Do they all need to be there at the same time?" Kristen asked.

"Yes, the only difference is when we pick up the younger ones," Emmy said. "But tomorrow is a short day. I'm staying to help Liz Hammond. The school expects parents to volunteer twenty hours a year."

"Do the twins know Liz is going to be their teacher again?" Diane asked.

"Yes, and they are so excited."

"Emmy, each one of us has a minivan," Sloane said. "We don't need to buy something specifically to haul kids to school. Let's use what we have and figure out the most effective way."

After a short discussion, the ladies agreed on a plan.

"Diane and I will take our kids to school, and Sloane and Kristen will drive their tribes. We can alternate weeks, or however you want to do it. Should we buy more car seats, or switch them back and forth?" Emmy asked.

"I don't know about you guys, but I don't want to be switching car seats in and out," Diane said and then got up to pour herself another cup of coffee. "That's a pain in the butt. Anyone else need more?"

"I'll take just enough to warm up my cup," Kristen said. "Thanks, Diane."

"We need four car seats in each van unless we change them around," Emmy said.

"I've got a booster seat for Dotty. It's easy to switch around." Sloane finished her coffee. "I don't mind having four car seats in our van. I need them if we take the whole family anywhere. That's why we bought a new minivan with bench seats in both rows. Even with that, we can't take Mama with us if we're all going somewhere."

"You need a small bus," Emmy said with a grin.

"The only time I use our van is if I'm taking Zach and Gracie somewhere. I use my Acura if it's just me, or if I'm taking Mom and Dad."

"Your van only seats seven, Krissy." Emmy reminded her as she took another brownie. "Will that work if you take Sloane's kids to school?"

"Peter will have to sit in the front seat and Dotty's booster can go in the back. It will work," Sloane explained.

"Taking two vans to school is better than all of us driving," Emmy said. "Who wants to take the rest of the brownies home?"

"I'll take them if no one else wants them. Tony will eat them," Sloane said.

Kristen hesitated when everyone stood.

"What's wrong, Krissy?" Emmy asked.

"I want to take my kids to school tomorrow. It's the first day, and I want to make sure they know where to go."

"You can do that," Sloane assured her. "We can start carpooling next week if you want."

Kristen's face lit up. "I'd like that better. I can't believe Gracie is going to school already. She's my baby."

Emmy looked at Diane.

"You can take the boys tomorrow, Emmy. They know the routine."

Three minivans left Bristol Ridge the next morning. Emmy dropped off her kids and then parked. She found Liz Hammond's classroom and stepped inside.

"I'm here, Liz. How can I help?"

"Right now I'm trying to get all the kids seated so I can take attendance. There are names on each desk." Liz pointed.

"I can do that."

Thirty minutes later Emmy sat in the back to observe. *I'm so glad all the kids from Bristol Ridge are in Liz's class together.* She watched Heather, Isabella, Caden, Zachary and Noemi sitting quietly as Liz read a story.

Time flew and soon the school day ended.

"Mommy, are you going to come to school every day?" Heather asked.

"Not every day, but I will sometimes. Why?"

"I don't want you to treat us like babies. Isa and I are first graders now. We're big." Heather raised her hands above her head.

"Yes, you are. Are you pleased that Miss Liz is going to be your teacher?" Emmy asked Heather and Isabella.

"It will be so awesome!" Isabella shouted. "Noemi and Zachary and Caden are in our class. It's like the most awesomest thing ever!"

Emmy laughed because the girls were so excited about school.

"Let's round up Carson and Kevin so we can head home."

The girls gathered their book bags as Emmy paused to talk to Liz. "Was it a coincidence that all the Bristol Ridge kids are in

261

your class?" Emmy asked.

Liz gathered her students. "Everyone follow Miss Emmy and me. We're going to march quietly down the hall to where you will be picked up."

The kids followed obediently.

"It was not a coincidence. There are two classes for kindergarten up through third grade this year. I don't know exactly how many students we have enrolled. More than last year I know. There are even more churches represented then before. I have sixteen in my class and Mrs. Ferguson has fifteen. I made sure all the Bristol Ridge kids were in my class. I taught them two years ago, except for Caden, and when I had the opportunity to switch to first grade, I jumped on it. I think this is where I'll stay for the next forty years."

Emmy gathered Carson and Kevin. "Carson, will you watch everyone while I help Liz?"

"Sure, Aunt Emmy. We will wait right here until you come back. I know the routine."

"Thank you Carson." *I can't believe how grown up you are. You're the same age as Kenny when I first met him. The twins are a year younger than I was, but it's hard to believe how fast the years have passed.*

The next two days passed quickly. On Saturday morning Carson finished his breakfast and put his dirty plate on the countertop. "Mom, can I run over and play with Peter now? You said we could play today."

"Yes, I remember. I called Sloane and told her you would be over. Do you want me to drive you?" Diane asked.

"Mom! It's just past Andy Walker's house and Zachary's. I won't get lost."

"I know. I need to stop treating you like a baby."

Carson smiled. "I'll take my cell phone with me."

"Good idea. What are you and Peter going to do?"

"We're going to play in the woods in back of his house. Peter wants to build a fort."

"Just be careful."

"I will. See you later."

Carson grabbed his phone, stuffed it in a pocket, put on a SoHam Hammers baseball cap and slung his gray plastic toy machine gun over his shoulder. He sprinted out the door, through the narrow strip of woods that separated Brady's property from Andy's, across Andy's manicured yard and into the trees that belonged to John and Kristen. He stopped for a moment and watched two squirrels chasing each other up and down a tree. He continued across Zachary's yard and into the thicker woods where he and Peter liked to play. He jumped over a fallen tree and climbed a hill. He broke out of the woods, dashed up another hill and raced along Tony's driveway. He ran around to the back of the house, flew up the steps to the deck and knocked on the sliding glass door.

"Peter! Carson is here," Sloane hollered as she opened the door.

"Hi, Mrs. Bertucci. Is Peter ready to play?" Carson asked after catching his breath.

"He should be right here. I made him wash his face and hands."

Peter appeared a second later. He held up his hands and let Sloane inspect his face. "I don't understand why I have to wash up to go play outside. We're going to play in the woods and build a fort. We're gonna get all dirty." He looked at Tony for support. "You understand right, Papa?"

"We men understand the need to get our hands dirty, but moms just don't get it. Have fun and you can show me the fort later."

"Come on, Carson. I know the perfect place to build a fort. Come on, Scout. You can play with us."

Scout, Peter and Carson dashed through the yard and entered the woods to the east of the house. Soon Scout disappeared to hunt for rabbits, and the boys couldn't see anything other than the thick woods that surrounded them.

"Do you ever get lost back here, Peter?" Carson stopped to look around. "I can't even tell which direction the house is."

Peter pointed to the south. "I'm pretty sure it's that way.

263

Come on. Over that hill is a creek and across that is a great spot to play Cowboys and Indians. We can build our fort there. Scout! Stay with us, girl."

Peter led the way up the hill and down to the nearly dry stream. Only a trickle of water flowed in the bottom of the three foot deep stream bed. The boys jumped into the creek, walked across and scrambled up the other side. Scout reappeared and leaped across the creek.

"Sometimes that creek is full of water. Mostly in the Spring," Peter said. "It's too dangerous to cross it then."

"It's so hot. That's why there isn't much water in it now," Carson said.

"Papa is going to build me a bridge someday."

"Why do you call him Papa and not Dad?" Carson asked as he followed Peter up yet another hill.

"Don't know. I guess 'cause I always have. Did you know Dotty and I are adopted?" Peter pointed to a depression in the ground behind a fallen tree. "We can build a fort right there."

"I didn't know you were adopted."

"Yeah. Our first mother died a long time ago. Her name was Heather." Peter picked up a branch and leaned it against the fallen tree. "If we find enough branches, we can pretend it's the wall of our fort."

"My cousin is named Heather just like your other mom."

"Yeah, according to Mama, Aunt Emmy named her for our mother." Peter sat down on the three-foot thick tree trunk and watched a small snake slither away. "What do you call Brady?"

"He let's us call him Brady. Was that a snake?" Carson pointed.

"It's only a garter snake. They're harmless. You'll get used to snakes living out here," Peter said.

"We've always lived in the city. This is like a wilderness out here."

"Yeah. Cool, huh?"

Carson nodded. "My real father is a jerk according to Mom."

"I don't remember my other father at all. He died a long

264

time ago. Do you have to spend weekends with yours very often?"

"We used to, but not as much now. He moved back to Ohio. He calls on our birthdays, but that's about it now."

"Do you think your mom and Brady will have more kids? There are six of us, but Mom isn't going to have any more."

"I heard Brady say he wants one more baby. I like Lily. She likes it when I hold her. She smiles at me."

"Yeah, little brothers and sisters are like that, but then they get bigger."

"Do you and Dotty ever play together?" Carson found two more branches to add to their collection. "I don't play with Caden because he's too little."

"Dotty's all right for a girl. She plays with her dolls and stuff, but we get along all right."

The boys spent the next hour working on their fort. Once it was finished, they played Cowboys and Indians for close to another hour.

"Let's take a break, Peter. I'm hot and thirsty. We should have brought water bottles with us."

"Sorry, I didn't think about that."

The boys sat in their fort. Scout fell asleep in the shade under a large maple tree.

"At least it's out of the sun in the woods," Peter said.

"How come Aunt Emmy calls your papa a creep all the time?" Carson asked.

Peter shrugged. "Dunno. He calls her brat."

"I've heard them call each other brother and sister before, but they're not really. Mom and Emmy are real sisters."

"Yeah, I've heard that, too. I think they just like to be weird."

"Grown-ups sure can be strange at times."

After resting for a while, Peter stood up and pointed to a nearby tree. "I've climbed that before. I almost made it to the top," Peter bragged. "Let's see how high we can get."

Carson shielded his eyes from the overhead sun and stared at the twenty foot tall tree. "I've never climbed a tree before."

"It's easy. I'll show you how. We have to start on this

265

branch and pull up like this." Peter made it onto the lowest branch, moved up to the next one and waited for Carson.

"I'll try," Carson said. He struggled but made it onto the branch.

Peter climbed higher and Carson followed. Scout barked as she ran around the tree.

"We need to stay close to the trunk because some of the branches up here aren't big enough to hold us," Peter said.

Carson reached up to the next branch, but his hand slipped, and he moved his foot to regain his balance. He scratched his hand and elbow on the bark.

"Are you all right, Carson?"

"I hurt my hand and my elbow is bleeding. I can't move my foot. It's stuck!"

Peter scrambled around Carson. "I'll see if I can free your foot."

Peter tried but Carson's foot wedged even deeper into the place between the trunk and a branch.

"I can't move it, Carson. You're elbow is really bleeding."

"It hurts." Carson sniffled but didn't cry. "Take my cell phone and call for help. It's in my pocket."

Peter reached into the pocket but dropped the phone. "Shoot! I'll climb down and call home. I know my number."

Peter cautiously climbed down as Scout barked at the cell phone. Peter picked up the phone and punched in his number. Nothing happened. He looked at the screen.

"Carson, the battery won't work. I can't call. I'll run home and bring Papa back with me."

"No! Carson, don't leave me out here. My foot is starting to hurt."

"What should I do?"

"I don't know but don't leave me," Carson whimpered.

"I know. I'll send Scout." Peter knelt in front of Scout. "Scout! Run home and bring Papa. Bring help, girl. Home!" Peter pointed.

Scout looked up into the tree as Carson hollered, "Hurry, Peter. My foot hurts a lot. I think it's broken."

266

"Scout, go get Papa."

Scout barked and ran down the hill, across the creek and soon disappeared from sight.

"I'll stay with you, Carson. Scout will bring help. She's the smartest dog in the world."

Tony set down his glass of lemonade as Scout appeared at the edge of the woods. Quick as a flash, Scout sprinted across the yard and leaped onto the deck. She stopped at Tony's side and gently tugged on his shorts.

"What is it, girl?"

Scout let go and barked. She moved toward the steps but then stopped and came back to Tony. Once again she tugged on Tony's shorts.

"I think she wants you to follow her, Tony." Sloane said. "Is that it, Scout? Do you want Tony to follow you?"

Scout barked and ran back and forth across the deck.

"Where's Peter?" Tony asked.

Scout barked even louder.

"Maybe I should go with her. Something might have happened to the boys." Tony drained his lemonade and stood up.

"Take your cell phone with you. Call me when you find the boys."

"I'm sure they're all right. Scout has probably been chasing rabbits."

Tony followed Scout toward the woods. Scout ran back and forth to make sure Tony followed. About ten minutes later, Tony arrived at the creek and heard Peter talking to Carson. Scout leaped across the creek and barked furiously

"Carson! Scout's back with Papa Tony."

"What seems to be the matter?" Tony looked up into the tree. "How did you get up so high, Carson?

"Papa, we were climbing and Carson hurt his elbow and now his foot is stuck and I couldn't move it. He needs your help." Peter rambled while pointing up at Carson.

Scout sat next to Tony.

"Good girl, Scout!" Tony patted her head as he gauged the strength of the branches. He grabbed one and pulled on it. He and

Peter heard a loud snap. "That's not good. There's no way I can climb up there." He reached into his pocket for his cell phone. *I could see if Sloane could bring a ladder.*

"Hang on, Carson," Peter hollered. "Papa will get you down. He will call your mom and tell her where we are."

"I'll call her, Carson, hang on and... Shoot! Why didn't I think of this sooner?"

"Rory, I have a new firetruck. Want to see it?" Kevin's eyes shone.

"Yes, I want to see it, buddy. Can you bring it here?" Rory held up his wet and dirty hands.

Kevin nodded. "It's in my room. I'll get it. Don't go away." Kevin dashed out of the kitchen.

"Thanks for coming over, Rory. I panicked when my ring went down the drain. I don't know what I would have done if I lost it." She hugged him even thought his hands were still dirty from taking apart the trap in the powder room.

"No problem, Em. PVC pipes are easy to loosen. I'm glad I found your ring."

"Oh, use this towel." She handed him a dish towel. "I'm so glad you were home."

"I wasn't home. I was heading to the store to pick up a few groceries."

"Right! I forgot you don't have a landline. If you don't have plans, you could stay for dinner. I was going to make spaghetti, but I could make something else."

"You could make the spaghetti for the kids, and we could order a pizza for us."

"I want pizza, too!" Kevin held up a red firetruck. "Pizza, not pasghetti."

"Pizza it is, but later." Emmy smiled as she took the dish towel from Rory.

Instead of dialing Diane's number, Tony called Emmy.

"Hey, creep! What's up?"

"Emmy, I need your help."

Tony explained the situation.

Emmy told Rory what had happened.

"Go! Find Carson." Rory waved. "I'll bring the kids over to Tony's. Maybe Sloane and Mama can watch them."

"Thanks, Rory," She bit her lip. *What will they think about Rory dropping off the kids? Too bad! It's an emergency.* "I'll be there as fast as I can, Tony. How will I find you though?"

"There's that opening in the back yard by the gazebo thing."

"Yeah, I know it."

"Try to go straight east from there. Remember the creek?"

"I remember."

Rory nodded. "I think I know where the creek is. I'll drop off the kids and try to find you guys. Hurry! I'll catch up."

Emmy didn't bother with her car. She hopped on her mountain bike and raced down the driveway.

"Come on girls," Rory said. "I need to take you and Kevin over to Tony's house."

"Why? We want to play," Heather said.

"Carson is stuck in a tree, and your mother is going to rescue him."

"I can help, Rory. I'm going to be a fireman when I get big." Kevin ran for the mudroom.

Rory spotted the keys to the Odyssey hanging up by the door. Heather and Isabella followed Kevin out to the garage.

"Will Carson be all right?" Isabella asked.

"I'm sure he will." Rory guessed the middle switch on the wall would open the garage door behind the Odyssey. He punched it and the right door opened. "Come on, kids. Let's have an adventure."

Emmy had slowed only enough at the gate to make sure there was no traffic coming. *Good thing not many people use this road.* She crossed the street, pedaled up Tony's driveway and rode around the house. She slid to a stop and hopped off the bike.

"Tony called me."

Sloane pointed to the gazebo. "I just talked to him."

Emmy ran through the yard. She entered the woods and zigzagged back and forth through the woods while trying to keep her eyes to the east. Up and down the hills she scrambled ignoring a couple of scratches on her legs. She reached the top of one hill and spied the creek at the bottom. She heard Scout bark.

There you are! She waved and hollered, "I'm here!"

"Papa! Look! There's Auntie Em." Peter pointed and then frantically waved both arms. "We're over here!"

Rory stopped in front of one of the garage doors at Tony's house. He helped the kids get out and they ran to the front door.

"Who is here to see me?" Mama smiled as she saw the kids.

"Mama! Carson is lost in the woods, and Mommy is going to find him," Heather squealed.

"My goodness." Mama put a hand to her mouth. "You come with me, so Rory can help find Carson and Peter." Mama gathered the girls and Kevin into the house. "I'll watch them."

"Thanks, Mrs. Bertucci... I mean Mama," Rory said and then rushed around the house.

Sloane saw him and gave him some quick directions.

Emmy scrambled down the hill, across the creek, past the fort and stopped next to Scout. "Good job, Scout. You're a real hero." Emmy scratched Scout's ears. "Nice fort."

"Do you think you can climb this tree. I'm too heavy."

"No sweat! Boost me up."

Tony boosted Emmy up as easily as lifting a child. She reached Carson in less than a minute and found a branch strong enough to hold her weight as she sat down.

"Hey, Carson. I didn't know you could climb trees. Good job."

"My foot's stuck and my elbow was bleeding but it stopped. My foot doesn't hurt as much now, but I can't move it, and I can't reach down to untie my shoe."

"Let me see if I can fix that."

Within a minute Emmy freed Carson's foot, and he climbed down. He looked back up at Emmy.

"Thanks, Auntie Em. I saw a snake earlier."

Emmy climbed back down but stopped and waited on a branch above Tony.

"Are you going to stay there, brat?" Tony asked.

"Will you make sure there are no snakes around?"

Tony stomped his foot in a couple of spots of brush. "There! No more snakes."

"Like that really scared them away." Emmy rolled her eyes. "You better catch me." Emmy jumped into Tony's arms just as Rory crossed the creek.

"Is Carson okay?" Rory asked and then saw Tony holding Emmy. "Em, are you all right?"

"I'm fine, but Carson saw a snake earlier." Emmy looked around the area. "Put me down, creep."

"With pleasure, brat!" Tony laughed as he let go of her.

She landed on her feet but lost her balance and ended up on her bottom. She jumped up immediately. "There better not be any snakes around here."

"Since when are you afraid of snakes, Em?" Rory grinned. "We used to catch them when we were kids."

"I wasn't old enough to be scared of them back then."

"Aunt Emmy rescued me, Uncle Rory. My foot was stuck, and she climbed way up there." Carson pointed to the top of the tree.

"Let me see your elbow."

Carson allowed Rory to wipe the died blood away. Tony looked at Rory and then at Emmy.

"I'll explain later," Emmy whispered.

"Whatever, Em." Tony put his hands on Peter's shoulders.

"Just a scratch. A Bandaid will fix you right up," Rory said. "Does your foot hurt? Can you walk?"

Carson took a few steps. "I can walk."

"Maybe from now on, you boys should stick to climbing trees closer to the house," Tony said.

Scout barked.

"I agree with you, Scout." Emmy let Scout lick her face.

Chapter Twenty-Nine

"Sounds like you had quite a day, Em." Kenny called a few minutes before he and the guys needed to take the stage in Portland, Oregon. "I'm glad Carson is all right, and Rory found your ring."

"I promise not to lose my ring. I was taking it off, and it slipped out of my hands."

"It's okay, Em. It's just a ring. I can always buy a new one."

"Do you remember where you bought that one?"

Kenny chuckled. "Of course. I bought it from Tony."

"Are you upset that I called Rory to recover the ring?"

"Not upset, but surprised," Kenny said and then sighed. "Tony and John are much closer. Brady could have tried to take the plumbing apart."

"I didn't think they would know how, and I was afraid Tony would yell at me for being such a klutz."

I can understand that. "How are the kids? What did you guys have for dinner?"

"They're asleep. It's almost ten o'clock here. I was planning to make spaghetti before Rory suggested pizza. We ordered from Kerry Lynn's and had it delivered."

"How late did Rory stay?"

Emmy looked at Rory, who sat in one of the recliners. "Uh... He's still here. We watched *Winnie the Pooh*, and he helped get the kids to bed. Then we started watching Netflix."

"I see," Kenny said.

"Don't be like that."

"I gotta run, Em. I'll be home sometime this morning."

"I love you, Kenny," she whispered.

"I know you do, and I love you, too." He ended the call and then stared at the phone. *I love you, Em, but everything is changing and not for the better.*

"Are you ready, Kenny?" Jeff asked. "Was that Emmy?"

Kenny forced a smile. "Yeah, she had a crazy day and had to climb a tree."

"Would you mind driving, Em. I'm wiped out. I caught a couple hours of sleep on the plane, but I don't think I should drive. Especially not your car," Kenny said as they walked out of the church.

"Are you afraid you will get a speeding ticket? It's got a bit more pep than your Civic." Emmy held Kevin's hand as they walked to her BMW.

"I've driven it a few times." Kenny yawned.

"Daddy, are you ready for a nap?" Heather grabbed his hand. "You should probably take a nap after you eat lunch."

That sounds like a good idea. Emmy grinned. "Would you kids like to go see Gra and Me-maw?"

"Yes!" Heather shouted and bounced on her toes. "We haven't see them in like forever."

"I'll call and see if they're home from church. If they're not busy, we can have lunch with them. Maybe Daddy will run over to Darby's for me. What do you say?" Emmy squeezed Kenny's hand. "Would you do that for me? I'll make it worth your while later."

"Darby's is all right for us, but the kids should eat something healthier," he responded ignoring Emmy's proposition.

"Let me call and see if Mom has anything for the kids."

Kenny's mom answered the landline on the third ring.

"Mom, would you mind if Kenny and I come over for lunch? We are still at the church, but will be leaving in a minute."

"I'd love to see you. Should I make something for lunch? Carter and I were going to have soup and sandwiches."

"Do you have enough for the kids?"

"Of course. I could make them something different if they don't want soup. It's homemade potato and leek, and I have chicken salad for sandwiches."

"They might not like the soup, but they can try it. They will like the chicken salad. If you wait, I will help you get lunch ready."

"Nonsense! I will have lunch ready when you arrive."

"Uh, Mom, Kenny is going to Darby's. I wanted a chili dog and fries, but he insists the kids eat healthy." Emmy rolled her eyes. "As if Darby's isn't good for you."

"Would you pick up one of their chocolate cakes for

273

dessert, please? Carter and I love those."

"Should I order a whole cake?" Emmy unlocked the car and helped Kevin climb up to his car seat while the girls scrambled into theirs.

"We will need several pieces, and it's cheaper to buy a whole cake."

"Okay, should I have Kenny order anything else for you and Dad?"

"No, the last time he ate one of their dogs, he suffered later. It's better if he doesn't know you are going there."

"I'll have Kenny drop me and the kids off, and he can run to Darby's. See you in a half hour, or so."

Kenny pulled into the driveway and stopped at the back of the house. Emmy helped the kids exit the van, and then Kenny drove past the carriage house to the alley and on to Darby's.

Carter Colwell walked out onto the back porch. "How are my angels and my big man today?"

"Gra!" Heather shouted as she and Isabella ran up the steps and threw their arms around his legs. "We miss you."

"I miss you, too." He smiled at Kevin and Emmy. "I'm glad you decided to stop by. Do you remember Pastor Rojas?"

"Girls! Be careful you don't knock Gra over," Emmy ordered. "Do you mean the former youth leader?"

"Yes."

"I remember him, but haven't thought about him for a long time." Emmy walked behind Kevin as he scrambled up the steps.

Dad Colwell held the door open. "Today was his first Sunday as the associate pastor."

"Did you have a chance to talk to him? Where's he been the last few years?" Emmy asked as she caught the aroma of homemade soup. "That smells good, Mom."

Heather and Isabella stood on either side of their grandmother as she stirred the soup. "Can we help, Me-maw?"

"You can put those plates around the table and get out some silverware."

Dad Colwell took a seat at the breakfast nook table as Emmy sat on one of the barstools at the counter and spun it around to face him. "I didn't have an opportunity to talk to him, but Pastor Johnston mentioned Pastor Rojas spent the last three years working in East Los Angeles. He's married and has five kids now."

"Five! Was he married when I knew him? I don't think I ever met his wife if he was."

"You might not have met her, Emmy. Florentina didn't come to church. She didn't become a believer until after they moved to California."

"I think I would have remembered that name. Wow! Five kids."

"And one grandson," Mom Colwell added.

"He's a grandpa? How old is he?"

"I think he's in his early or mid-forties, but he looks older because of his gray hair."

Kenny walked into the kitchen a few minutes later carrying the bags from Darby's. "I'm back. Are we ready to eat?"

"Did you know Pastor Rojas is back?"

"No, when did he come back?"

Emmy explained.

"I knew he moved to LA, and he's in his early fifties."

"Everything is ready," Me-maw said. "Carter, will you pray, please?"

Everyone sat at the breakfast table and Gra prayed.

"Mommy, I don't like the soup," Heather said.

"Have you tried it?"

"No, but it looks funny."

"You know the rules, Heather," Emmy said.

Isabella dipped her spoon into the thick soup and took a bite. She hesitated but then took another bite. "I like it. It's yummy."

Heather watched Isabella and decided to try it. "It's okay. I guess I'll eat a little bit."

"Can we watch a movie, Mommy?" Heather asked later after the lunch dishes were placed in the dishwasher. "I cleaned up my plate and helped do dishes."

"It's up to Me-maw," Emmy said. "Daddy and I need to take a nap in the carriage house."

"I'll watch a movie with them." Me-maw grinned and turned on the dishwasher. "You can pick out one of your movies," she told the girls who immediately dashed into the living room.

"Let's watch *Tangled*." Heather grabbed the DVD from under the TV.

"That's my favorite movie of all time," Isabella gushed.

Emmy heard Isabella's comment. "You say that about every movie. Come on, Kenny. We need to check the carriage house."

"We do? Why?"

Because I want to take you to bed. Emmy pulled him up from the couch with both hands. "I want to work on a song."

"Okay, be right there." *Are you still embarrassed about letting Dad know what you really want?*

"Let's go now. I have an idea."

I bet you do, Em. "Girls, be good. Kevin, you obey Gra."

"They will be fine," Gra said.

Emmy led Kenny by the hand out to the carriage house. She stood on the first step, faced him, pulled his face down to hers, kissed him deeply and pressed against him.

"What was that for?" He rubbed his mouth after breaking off the kiss.

"What do you think? Come on." She teased him by unzipping her dress as she climbed the stairs.

He followed her up the stairs and into the apartment.

"Do you want to undress me like you did on our wedding night?" She bit her lip and led him toward the bedroom.

"You aren't wearing a wedding dress, Em, and the apartment isn't exactly the same after the fire."

"I know, but it's still the same building in a way, and I am wearing a dress."

Kenny grabbed the doorjamb as Emmy pulled on his arm.

She let go and placed her hands on her hips. "What's wrong? Don't you want to fool around?"

"No! I'm not in the mood," he said.

"I can put you in the mood."

He walked back to the couch in the middle of the great room and plopped down. Emmy rolled her eyes and then followed.

276

"Will you at least look at me?" She stood in front of him as he stared at the floor.

He raised his eyes to hers. "I just don't feel like it, Em."

"You haven't felt like it the last three weekends. We've never gone this long before."

"We have so."

"I mean when I wasn't pregnant." She sat sideways on the couch facing him with her feet tucked under her. "We went for two months then because you were afraid you would hurt the baby."

Kenny leaned back against the couch and looked away.

"You're not gonna make this easy, are you?"

"We need to talk."

"We could talk afterward while we're in bed."

"We should talk first. We can always..."

"Apparently not."

"Come on, Em. Can't you be serious for one second?"

"Fine! I'll be as serious as a heart attack."

Kenny shook his head and started to get up.

She grabbed his arm. "Okay, let's talk." *Are you still upset that Rory came over?*

"Why did Rory stay so long yesterday?"

"I knew it! You're pissed because I called Rory instead of Tony or an actual plumber, huh?"

"Tony could have figured out to take apart the thing under the sink. I could do it myself, so I know he could."

"I explained why." Her voice rose in pitch.

"But why was he still there when I called? That was ten o'clock your time."

"After we watched *Winnie the Pooh*, he helped get the kids to bed."

"Did he help with baths?"

"He helped with Kevin's bath." She punched his arm. "We put the kids to bed, and he offered to leave, but I asked him to hang around. We watched one of those BBC detective shows on Netflix. I don't remember the name. He sat in my recliner, and I sat on the couch, FYI."

"I'm not accusing you of doing anything."

277

"You better not be. He's not Becky." Emmy spat out the name as if it were vulgar.

"Hey! That's a low blow." He scooted to the far end of the couch. "We weren't married, or even together then."

"Sorry. I apologize."

"Apology accepted."

"Rory is a friend."

"Oh, come on! You had a thing for him when we were in school. Don't say you didn't."

"That was a long time ago, and nothing ever happened between us."

Kenny tilted his head and stared at her.

"Nothing too serious." She bit her lip.

"What about now? What about on your tour bus?"

She rose to her knees on the couch. "Screw you, Kenneth Travis Robert Colwell! How can you even think that?" She attempted to punch his arm, but Kenny grabbed her fist.

"Even if nothing happened..."

"Nothing did! Not even a little kiss." She squirmed. "Let go of my hand, you creep!"

He let go.

"Even so, he shouldn't have been traveling with you when the kids and I weren't along. How do you think that looked to the guys in the band or the crew?"

"I don't care what the crew thinks."

"Perhaps you should."

"Shut up!"

"Great attitude, Em."

"You don't need to be so sarcastic. None of the guys in the band complained about Rory being around."

"Of course not. They see you as their boss."

"Bobby doesn't."

"Okay, I'll give you that, but have you talked to the rest of the guys since the tour?"

"They've been busy."

"Yeah, right."

She frowned and stuck out her tongue. "They're friends."

278

"Absolutely."

"What about Jana? Is she your friend?"

"No, she's not. She's an employee. Sure, we are both kinda friends with her because of church, but have you ever heard her call? Have you ever seen her at the house? Other than for business?"

"You spend time at the guesthouse with her."

"Yes, I do. I spend time there with Jana and the other staff. It is the band's business office."

"What about the pictures of you and Jana at the press conference? How do you explain them?"

"We sat next to each other in front of a room full of people. What's to explain?"

"You were smiling at each other."

"You got me there. I confess." He raised his hands in surrender. "I've committed a horrible transgression. I smiled at another woman. It obviously makes me a terrible husband and father. I'll pack my stuff and leave tonight."

"If you smile at her like that in a room full of people, how do you act when you're alone? And don't try to tell me you're never alone with her."

"We are alone at times. Like in the dressing room or wherever, but if at all possible, I leave the door open."

"Have you ever kissed her?"

The question stunned Kenny for a few seconds.

"No! Never! I don't think I've ever hugged her."

Shoot! I shouldn't have asked that because now you might ask if I've ever kissed Rory. I won't lie, but I hope you don't ask. "Good! How many more shows are left?" *That should make you think of something besides Jana or Rory.*

"Two weeks worth." *I know you changed the subject so I wouldn't ask if you've ever kissed Rory.*

"How many shows in all?"

"Ask Dad if you really want to know, Em." He shrugged. "Can we go back to the house now?"

"Might as well since you aren't interested in me anymore."

279

Chapter Thirty

Kenny exchanged his Gibson ES-5 Switchmaster guitar for a dry towel from Frankie Hanna and headed off the stage and toward the steps in Little Rock, Arkansas.

"Thanks, Frankie."

"You're welcome." Frankie placed the guitar in the travel case and walked with Kenny.

"Any calls or texts from Emmy tonight?" Kenny wiped his face and then wrapped the towel around his neck. "She didn't communicate during the day."

Frankie shook his head and handed Kenny his cell phone. "Sorry, boss."

"It's all right." Kenny patted Frankie on the back. "Well, another tour in the books. God only knows when we might go back on the road. When we do, it will be different because Jeremy won't be there."

"He will still be a part of the team in my mind." Frankie watched as Jeff and Dave escorted Jeremy backstage.

"Absolutely! He needs to be able to spend his time with his family now. They need him more than we do."

Jeff saw Jeremy's family waiting for him. "Hey, Amanda, did you hear that keyboard solo in 'Common Experience?'"

She nodded and held out her arms for her husband.

"I heard it! You nailed it, Dad." Joshua Lenhart rushed over and high-fived his father.

"Thank you for letting us come to the show, Daddy." Jennifer hugged him.

Jeremy hugged his wife and kids and fought back tears. "I wanted my family here tonight. Although this might not be the last time I play with the band, it was the final show as a member of Fridays At Five."

"Technically, you are still an equal member in the company," Dave said. "You just don't have to go on tour. I don't know whether I'm happy for you, or sad because you won't be there when I look at the keyboards."

"Adam did a great job. He will bring new ideas to the

band." Paul Joseph felt comfortable enough to voice his opinion after seven years as the second guitarist in the band.

Kenny waited until Jeff finished hugging his family. "Jeremy, you know you will always be one of the guys."

"I want to thank you guys for supporting my decision." He smiled at the guys who stood around him and then chuckled. "We know so many other bands where the egos and stuff create friction and animosity. Everyone sues everyone." He shook hands with every member of the band. "I'm glad we can still call each other a good friend."

"Hey! What's going on?" Andy Walker bellowed. "You guys need to get downstairs. It appears someone has planned some kind of a end-of-the-tour party or something. There's this big banner and balloons and crap all over. We've never done that before. I don't see what the big deal is. You guys have to get back to work on Tuesday. For some reason the record company thinks they might want to release another CD one of these years."

Seven-year-old Jennifer Lenhart walked up to Andy, put her hands on her hips and frowned. "Mr. Walker! You might try to sound mean, but I know better. You are a big teddy bear. You always send me a card and a present for my birthday. I'm not afraid of you."

Andy tried to scowl and look intimidating, but it didn't work on Jennifer. After a few seconds he reached down and lifted her off of her feet. He hugged her close and whispered. "You are a very brave princess, and I love you so much." He set her down and glanced away so no one could see the tears filling his eyes. No one outside of the tight group of friends knew Jennifer suffered from acute lymphoblastic leukemia.

After landing at O'Hare, Kenny shared a ride to SoHam with Frankie.

"Thanks for letting me fly home," Frankie said.

"You can always fly home when you need, Frankie. I know you'd rather be on the bus, but your mom will appreciate you getting home early. Say hi to her for me, and I hope your father feels better soon."

Even though Frankie was forty-one years old, he still lived at home with his parents James and Nora.

"Mom said he ignores his doctor. He won't stay in bed."

"He needs to let his hip heal before he goes traipsing off around the city. They have other city inspectors. He should retire and take his pension. I know he's stubborn." Kenny laughed. "He's kinda like someone else I know."

"You mean Andy?"

"Him too, but I was thinking about Emmy," Kenny said.

The van driver dropped Frankie off at home, helped unload Frankie's luggage, got back in the van and looked at Kenny. "Bristol Ridge?"

"Not tonight. Take me to my parents' house, please."

Kenny yawned and stretched his arms over his head. *No one would mind if I stayed home from church this morning. I'm not scheduled to play.* He turned onto his side and smacked the snooze button again. *Shoot! The kids will wonder why I'm not there. Better get my lazy butt up.* He lingered in the shower and then had to hurry to get out the door. He pulled into the rear parking lot and slipped in the back door at church. He walked around a corner and nearly collided with Robby Collins.

"Hey, Kenny. Didn't know you were back. Tour over?" Robby asked.

"Yes, last night was it."

"Are you playing for the second service today?"

"Not this Sunday, but I wanted to let Chase know I can resume my regular schedule." Kenny glanced over Robby's shoulder and noticed Emmy and Liz walking toward the music suite. "Talk to you later, Robby."

"There he is," Emmy said to Liz. "He made it in time. I'll meet up with you in a few."

"Okay, I'm sure the band must have been delayed getting home," Liz said. She walked past Kenny without saying anything.

"Hey, Em."

"Morning. I'm sorry I didn't talk to you yesterday. How did it go? Jeremy's last show, huh?"

282

"It didn't really hit any of us until after the show. There was a big party and Amanda and the kids were there. Jennifer got after Andy for trying to be a bully. He picked her up and had to turn away."

"Was he crying?"

"He started to."

"Jennifer is doing better according to Amanda."

"Yes, but only time will tell if she can kick it."

"Is that why you guys were late getting home?"

Kenny turned his head and stared at the opposite wall.

"You guys weren't late, were you?"

He shook his head. "Not real late."

"Did you stay at the carriage house?"

"I thought it would be best."

"Are you coming home after church?"

"Unless you don't want me to."

"I want you to, and the kids want to see you. They will think something's wrong if you aren't home."

There is something wrong, but the kids don't need to know. "Should I stop and pick up something for lunch?"

"No need. I made a taco salad this morning. Most of it. I will need to add the chips, romaine and dressing."

"Did you use the slotted spoon?" Kenny asked with a big grin.

"Yes, and I tried to remember the correct order to add the ingredients." *Like it matters.*

"I'm going to grab a couple of seats. See you after you finish." Kenny thought about kissing Emmy but didn't because of other people walking past.

Emmy spotted Kenny from the platform and after the worship band finished, she joined him.

He patted her hand. "You sounded great, Em."

She smiled at him but then turned her attention to the platform.

"Who are the Bears playing today?"

"Indianapolis at home," Emmy answered but didn't elaborate.

283

Fine! Don't talk to me. He sighed.

"I'll find the kids," Kenny said at the end of the service. "Meet you at home?"

"How did you get here this morning? Your car is at home."

"I borrowed Dad's Odyssey. There are car seats in it."

"Do you have to take it back today?"

"Probably not, but I thought I would later."

"Okay, grab the kids. I'll meet you at home."

Kenny put the rest of the taco salad together after waiting for nearly an hour for Emmy to get home.

"Are we going to eat before Mommy gets home?" Kevin asked.

"Yes." Kenny filled bowls for Kevin and the girls. "Everyone is hungry, and I'm not sure where Mommy is. I'll say a prayer and we can eat."

Emmy made it home two hours later. She checked the fridge and saw the large Tupperware bowl of taco salad. She fixed herself a bowl and then walked into the family room. She saw Kenny sleeping in his recliner, so she sat on the couch to eat.

"Where have you been?" Kenny asked a couple of minutes later. "I see you found the leftover salad."

"Sorry, I didn't call. Mom wanted me to come over. I ate lunch with her and then ran to the store to buy some supplies. She needed water and stuff."

"You could have called. I was worried."

"Phones work both ways." *Shoot! Why did I say that?*

Kenny frowned at her.

"I talked to Father James on the way home."

"What did he have to say?"

"He called to see how I was doing. He asked if he could come over this afternoon, but I told him it might not be a good time. We agreed to get together later in the week."

"Now that you're home, I'm going downstairs. I want to work on a guitar part."

"I won't bother you. Are you staying for dinner?"

"Do you want me to?"

"Do you want to stay?"

284

"Can't you just answer instead of answering my question with a question?"

She rolled her eyes. "Yes, I would like for you to have dinner with me and the kids. Any special request?" *Sorry, I know that's a question.*

"What are my options?"

"Nothing too complicated. I don't feel like cooking all afternoon."

"Sandwiches are fine with me."

"I could make BLTs. The kids like them. Maybe some soup."

Sounds good. Call me later."

"What time?"

Kenny shrugged. "Whenever the kids get hungry. I'll take a break."

Emmy came downstairs to the studio control room at six and found Kenny listening to a guitar track.

"If you have time for a break, I made the sandwiches and some tomato soup."

"Be there in a minute."

Emmy turned to leave.

"Before you go, how does this sound? I'll play just the guitar track first, and then add everything else."

Emmy listened to the guitar. "Can I hear the rest?"

He added the other instruments.

"I like it. Does it have a name yet? Have you written any lyrics?"

"I've got most of it written. I'm calling it 'Circumstances of Life' for the time being."

"I like. Come upstairs if you want to eat with the kids."

He saved everything, shut down the system and followed her up the stairs and into the kitchen.

"Daddy, I'm eating soup and a bread and lettuce sandwich." Kevin held up his half-eaten sandwich and the tomato fell out. "I can still eat it."

Heather rolled her eyes. "It's a BLT."

"Not anymore! His tomato fell out." Isabella pointed. "Will

you sit by me, Daddy?"

"The soup's on the stove, and I'll make you a sandwich if you want one," Emmy said.

"Thanks. Was there any taco salad left?"

"In the fridge if you'd rather have that." Emmy pointed.

"Maybe later. I'd like a BLT."

Kenny and Emmy listened to the kids as they jabbered about school and their favorite movie. They glanced at each other but didn't talk.

"We're done, Mommy. Can we go play?" Heather asked.

"You may be excused. You can play for an hour, but you need baths tonight. You have school tomorrow."

Kenny helped clear the dishes and wiped off the table.

"Do you need help with baths?" He tossed the wet paper towel in the trash.

"I can handle bath time if you want to do something."

"I'll check emails and Facebook. I'll help tuck them in bed when you're ready."

Later, Emmy walked into the den.

"The kids are ready for bed. They want you to read them a story."

"I can do that."

"No more than two books."

Kenny closed his laptop, stood up and grinned. "Trust me. I know how they are."

"One more, Daddy. Please!" Heather insisted later.

"No more. It's time for lights out." Kenny closed the fourth book. "Kevin, scoot along to your own room. I'll be there in a minute."

"We need kisses," Isabella said.

"One kiss." Kenny kissed the girls, tucked them in and turned off the light. "No talking. It's time to go to sleep."

He did the same for Kevin and then headed downstairs.

"How many?" Emmy asked without looking away from the TV.

"Four," he admitted.

"They know better with me."

Kenny plopped down on the couch beside her.

"Are you going to take the Odyssey back tonight?"

"I should."

"That means you are spending the night at the carriage house again."

"I guess so. Would you pick me up after you take the kids to school? Is it your week or Diane's? I forgot."

"My week. Yeah, I can pick you up. Do your parents know you spent the night there?"

"Yeah. Mom made breakfast."

"Did they wonder why?"

Kenny shrugged. "Probably, but they didn't ask."

"There's taco salad left if you're hungry."

"Would you mind if I ate it?"

"Go ahead. You can finish it."

Kenny brought the large Tupperware bowl into the family room, sat in his recliner and began eating.

Emmy frowned at him.

"What?"

"You couldn't use a smaller bowl?"

"There's just a little left. I didn't want to dirty up more dishes. I was thinking of you."

"Yeah, sure."

Kenny finished the taco salad and stood up. "I'm going to run the van back now."

"Fine. Have a good night."

"I could wait until tomorrow."

Emmy waved. "No, go ahead. I might get used to having the bed to myself every night instead of four nights a week."

"Hey! It's not always easy, and it's certainly not cheap to fly back and forth across the country. The tour is over now."

"Sorry." Emmy bit her lip. "You can stay."

"Are you sure?"

"Yes, I'm sure. Please stay. You can run the van back in the morning, and I'll pick you up. You guys aren't working tomorrow, are you?"

"No, we are starting on Tuesday."

"I'm going to bed," Emmy said around eleven. "Are you coming up?"

"I'll be up soon. I want to read a couple more chapters."

Kenny came upstairs at midnight, got undressed and looked at the bed. *Thanks for leaving me a couple of inches, Em.* He moved her feet over to her side without waking her.

"Come on, girls! It's time to go." Emmy hollered and then looked at Kenny. "Could you please make sure Kevin has washed his face and hands?"

Kenny drained his coffee cup and set in in the sink. "Kev! Let me check you out."

Kevin rushed into the kitchen from the family room and held up his hands. "I'm clean, Daddy."

Kenny wiped some dried oatmeal from Kevin's chin. "Now you're clean. I'll see you after school, okay?"

"Bye, Daddy!" Heather and Isabella grabbed their book bags and dashed toward the mudroom.

"Lunches!" Emmy hollered and pointed at the fridge. "Are you going to run the van back this morning? Should I go to your parents or come home?"

"Do good at school, girls. I'll see you this afternoon." He tried to give them hugs, but they scooted past. "I'm leaving right after you. I'll wait in the apartment."

"See you when I get there." Emmy waited for a kiss, but Kenny turned away without realizing what she wanted.

An hour later Emmy pulled into the Colwell's driveway, drove past the house and parked in front of the carriage house. She dodged the raindrops, entered through the service door and dashed up the stairs. She tried the door. *At least you didn't lock me out.* She walked in and tossed her keys and purse on the counter. "Where are you?" When he didn't answer, she checked the bedroom and bathroom. *You did say you would wait out here.* She went back to the kitchen, dug her phone out of her purse and dialed Kenny's cell. She ended the call when she heard it ringing in the bedroom. *Where are you? Should I wait here, or go talk to your parents?*

288

She set her phone on the counter and looked at an old couch against the wall in the great room. *I know it's not the same one. It's not really where you first kissed me, but close.* She bit her lip and tried to stop the tears from overflowing. *Oh, Kenny, what's happened to us? Have we lost our focus on what's really important?* She walked over to the couch and sat down. She closed her eyes and pictured the way the place looked the first time she braved climbing the stairs. She pictured the cobwebs, dust and the accumulation of fifty years of junk. She pictured the place as it looked when Kenny first kissed her. Amplifiers, guitars, keyboards, a drum kit and PA gear scattered about the room. She opened her eyes and looked into the bedroom. *I remember how tired I was on our wedding night. I'm sorry I fell asleep right after you... we... We have made up for it through the years.*

Kenny increased his pace as his legs warmed up. *I haven't run through Raynor Park since high school and probably never in the rain. So much of it has changed, but I bet there are some families still living here that I would remember.* He turned the corner onto Fourth Street and ducked under a tree branch. *I guess not too many people go for morning runs along here.* He slowed his speed as he passed the old playground. *We used to play football here. How did we manage? There isn't much room.* He continued and made his way to Robert T. Colwell Elementary School. *Geez! How many years ago did I start kindergarten here?* He stopped quickly, lost his footing as he slid and nearly tripped on the sidewalk. *Holy cow! It's been thirty years ago. Almost exactly thirty years ago. How is that possible?* He stared into the building and could see students at their desks. He waited until his breathing returned to normal, moved his feet one after the other and began to jog instead of run as the rain intensified. *I wonder if I would know any of the teachers. Is it possible that Mrs. Prater or Mrs. Saylor might still be teaching? Oh, well.* He glanced at his wristwatch. *I should get back. Emmy is probably there and wondering where I am. What will I say to her? How can I explain?* He jogged to the corner and stopped. He inhaled deeply, held his breath as long as he could and then exhaled sharply. *We have to face the facts. Things have changed. Does she even still love me?*

We have to figure it out.

He closed his eyes. "Lord, please give me the wisdom to know what to say. I put my life in Your hands. Everything! My life. The kids lives. Emmy's life if I could do that. I know we can do nothing on our own. We need your strength. I remember reading about when Jesus went for forty days without eating. The devil offered all kinds of temptations. Jesus resisted all of them. He turned the temptations into triumphs. Help me to turn my temptations into triumphs." He opened his eyes and began to jog again. Faster and faster until he was sprinting through the pouring rain.

Emmy closed her eyes again as she listened to the rain drops on the roof. She moved to her knees and let her head fall onto the couch as she wept. After a time, she clasped her hands together and lifted her head. "Jesus, I know there are things in my life I need to change. You know what they are. You know everything about us. We can't hide things from you the way we do people on earth. If there is anything else I need to change, please tell me. Am I holding something back? If so, please show me. I want to surrender everything to you. I will give up my career if I need to. I will sell the house, the cars, everything. It all belongs to You anyway." She paused and allowed God to speak to her.

She opened her eyes and jerked her head to her left as she heard someone pounding up the stairs. She rose to her feet as the door banged open and Kenny slid into the room. Water dripped from every part of him. He wiped his face and shook his head and hands spraying water everywhere.

"Emmy, I need to tell you something. I need to confess," he said as a bolt of lightning flashed and thunder boomed. "We have to talk about our future." He held out his arms.

Emmy bit her lip. She took a step forward but then stopped. "Oh, Kenny." She closed her eyes. "I don't know if we have a future," she whispered as she turned away.

Check out these other titles by the author. Visit the website:
kennethleemcgee.com

The Emmy's Story Series

1. We We're 'posed to Get Married
2. One Of The Guys
3. A New Friend
4. Did You Like the Ravioli Tonight?
5. Completely and Forever: A Wedding
6. It's Time To Go!
7. How Difficult Can It Be?
8. Forever... Isabella... Forever
9. The Forgettable Year
10. Turning Thirty

The Annie Mercer O'Dell Series

1. Roosevelt High
2. North Park College

Stand Alone Books

1. Growing Up In Kinmundy Junction
2. Grandpa, Lions and Kitty Cats: A Collection Of Short Stories For Children Of All Ages